Brian Stc

Brian Stoddart is a m...
of dialogue, in particular; he uses setting superbly, captures the political absurdities of the place and time, and subtly foreshadows the loss of a colonial grip on the region. First class crime writing.

Ngaio Marsh Award judges, 2017. (*A Straits Settlement* was in 2017 longlisted for the Ngaio Marsh Award for best New Zealand crime novel.)

A ripper of a tale.
Susan Kurosawa in *The Australian.*

This series has been a joy to read.
Amazon reviewer.

One of the strengths of the novel is the author's rich feel for life on the streets.
Bernard Whimpress in the *Newtown Review of Books.*

The author, who has set himself the difficult task of capturing Madras of the 1920s, has excelled himself.
Sriram V, *The Hindu.*

Each one is better than the last.
Amazon reviewer.

Brian Stoddart's writing is excellent.
Crime Pieces.

Stoddart has created a character with huge potential for development, both as a person and as a witness to momentous historical events … the plotting of the book is as impressive as the narrative style, and the description of the bloody end to the industrial protest is as gripping as anything I have read in a long while.
David Prestidge, *Crime Fiction Lover.*

Great writing, a poetic and deep-feeling hero, terrific story with a wonderful feel of India.
Amazon reviewer.

Other books by Brian Stoddart

Superintendent Le Fanu Mystery series

A Madras Miasma

The Pallampur Predicament

A Straits Settlement

A GREATER GOD

A Superintendent LE FANU Mystery

Brian Stoddart

Selkirk Books

A GREATER GOD

ISBN 978-0-6483938-0-1

Available from www.amazon.com and all good online book retailers.

Also available as ebooks:
Kindle ebook ISBN 978-0-6483938-1-8
ePub ebook ISBN 978-0-6483938-2-5

First produced in 2018 for Brian Stoddart by
AM Publishing New Zealand www.ampublishingnz.com

Published by Selkirk Books
brianstoddartwriter.com

Printed by IngramSpark

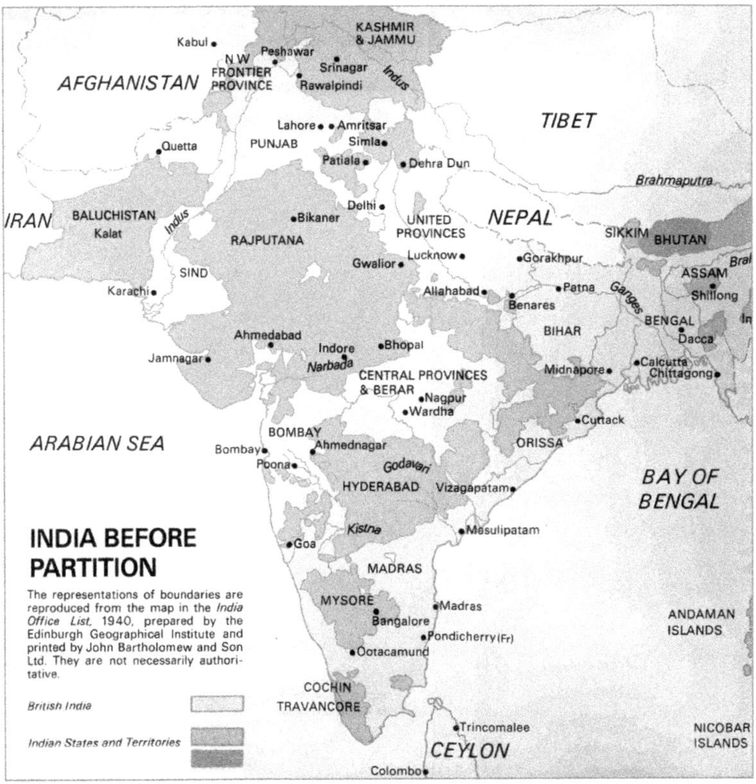

India before Partition

British India and the Bay of Bengal

One

As the shimmer on the horizon resolved into Madras city's coastline, Le Fanu wondered yet again if his return was wise, having left Penang reluctantly with only unpleasant prospects awaiting here. And this voyage back across the Bay of Bengal to India on the SS *Ekma* was joyless, unlike the one out to the Straits Settlements on which he met Jenlin Koh. The following weeks had passed in a blur, but now here he was while she remained in Penang – 'The Pearl of the Orient' – expecting to visit Madras sometime but with no date fixed. Would his life ever be straightforward?

Oddly, though, leaning on the rail and watching the city loom up was still somehow like coming home. He should have expected that. Madras had been his home for twenty years, since 1905, apart from the five away at what he could never call the 'Great' War. He was comfortable here. His British memories involved family strains, unhappy experiences and a failed marriage. India had certainly changed since his arrival but, despite rising calls for political independence, Gandhi's mass civil disobedience campaigns, British India's obdurate response and his own allegiances being challenged by a growing sympathy for India's cause, the place still mesmerised him.

He picked out the wharves and buildings in what was now one of India's largest ports. That was a big British achievement in the south. In earlier days, ships were serviced by small lighters that pitched up directly onto the sands. The nineteenth-century Charles Hunt prints gracing most Madras mansions depicted boats, crew and luggage tossed by the waves, passengers struggling to reach land both dry and in style. Madras had no natural harbour. Storms smashed piers and enclosures, tides and currents silted entrances in the first attempts to create one. However, Sir Francis Spring's rule at the turn-of-the-century Madras Port Trust transformed everything.

In true British style, he also established the elitist Royal Madras Yacht Club in the harbour precinct, an incongruous Cowes on the Bay. Another attempt to make India something it was not.

The city's smells and sounds increasingly filtered across on the breeze as the *Ekma* eased closer. Ahead, Le Fanu glimpsed the upper levels of Fort St George, Britain's south Indian power base ever since Sir Eyre Coote saw off the French in 1761. These days it housed the Secretariat for the Madras Presidency whose forty-three million inhabitants matched the United Kingdom's entire population. He would visit there later today and confront the Indian Civil Service mandarins.

Away on the left stood the Chepauk Palace, built by the Muslim Princes of Arcot but stolen mid-nineteenth century by the British. The Board of Revenue skulked there now, tax gatherers who fancied themselves above the Secretariat bosses. The mutual disdain between these two forces was legendary. Le Fanu hoped not to appear at Chepauk anytime soon, or before First Member Arthur Jamieson.

To the right, First Line Beach and the great trading firms that flourished on the ocean trade spurred by Spring's harbour. Behind those imposing buildings lay George Town proper. Until 1911 it was called Black

Town, as in 'home of the blacks' even though Indians were not black. The British Empire's ruling classes applied that term automatically to all non-whites everywhere. Le Fanu knew too many police and civil service officers who held that view – recusants all, irked, outraged and challenged by rising demands that Indians receive more political power and by London's reluctant, cautious agreement. Madras Europeans were among India's most vociferously conservative, a further source of his rising discomfort.

More cheerfully, he would soon visit Acharappan Street and his chef friend Krishna Rao who ran the city's best Udipi restaurant. Penang's south Indian food was excellent. So were its Chinese and Malay counterparts and all the hybrids. But he had missed his friend's fare.

Tenders nudged the ship towards a berth.

Le Fanu watched the swarm of labourers with their trolleys waiting to board in search of luggage and cargo but corralled by harassed European port officials dressed in white suits and carrying pieces of paper. Off in another huddle, immigration bosses wore dark blue uniforms, straining unsuccessfully to look like naval officers. Real military officers lolled about feigning both importance and diffidence.

Two figures on the wharf stood out. One short, squat and crammed into a deep-blue suit. He was dark complexioned with a face framed by a luxurious but more or less tamed beard. The other was taller, slimmer, whiter, a clothes horse draped in a pale-lemon linen suit and a matching silk shirt, offset by a neatly knotted pale-green tie contrasting with the polished tan shoes.

Le Fanu waved to Assistant Superintendent Mohammad Habibullah, head of the Madras Police Crime Unit, and Assistant Superintendent Jackson Caldicott, former businessman and wartime spy now heading Special Branch. Excellent officers, they were also among his now increasingly few friends. They waved back, pointing to the waiting police porters. There was little for them to carry. He was travelling light, not intending to stay. Habi and Caldicott steered the porters closer as the ship butted up against the wharf to be festooned in ropes then coupled with a gangway. Police passes spirited the pair on board immediately.

"Sir," said Habi, "wonderful to see you because it seems far longer than four months since you left."

"Wonderful to see you, too, Habi." He wondered if his friend would ever call him by name rather than 'sir'. British India's stiff hierarchy was hard to break. "Jackson, great to see you, too, of course. Thank you both for rescuing me."

He directed the porters to his cabin and its miserable offerings.

"Doubt you ever need rescuing, LF," Caldicott replied, shaking Le Fanu's hand. "Several people here did while you were away, including us, but you've charged on as ever. Great result in Penang."

Chief Secretary Sir Charles Whitney had sent Le Fanu after an absconding Indian Civil Service officer who tried to fund a new life by selling temple artefacts stolen from the district where he was Collector, the senior European officer. While catching him in Penang, Le Fanu also solved a murder case in which the victim's father, a prominent Madras textile mill and palm plantation owner, had recruited labourers illegally in the missing Collector's district.

Whitney's real purpose, though, had been to distance Le Fanu from the unexpectedly returned Inspector-General of Police, Arthur Jepson who hated Le Fanu following innumerable clashes. More significantly, Jepson's hard-line approach to change was gaining support among an aggrieved Indian Police Service senior echelon and the wider European population. More reasons Le Fanu might not stay long.

"We were lucky, Jackson, but the Straits police and your intelligence counterparts there were excellent. Not as good as you, of course, but still excellent."

Carrying as he was an open job offer from the Governor of the Straits Settlements and his chief intelligence officer, Le Fanu felt like a hypocrite. It was a close-to-irresistible offer. For starters, the post was in Penang, Jenlin Koh's home town. He might as well resign from the Indian police and begin a new life across the Bay. Ironic, perhaps, that in some ways he differed little from his ICS quarry in Penang.

"Even so, sir, it reminded people how good you are, and we really need you back here. Especially with all that's going on inside and outside the force. You can fix all that." Habi was beaming, as he did mostly.

"Habi, no one's that good." Le Fanu felt worse.

"Habi's right," Caldicott chipped in. "Things haven't fallen apart totally in your absence, but they are chaotic. Even your enemies concede you were way better than Jepson."

They remained at the rail, watching the gangway confusion as disembarking passengers jostled ahead of each other while simultaneously trying to track the porters carrying their luggage. Agents, touts, messengers, snack sellers and a myriad of others pressed in from the wharf. None were supposed to be there, but all somehow found a way through, as ever. The roar welled up and over the trio. They had to raise their voices.

"Put simply," Caldicott continued, "Jepson's return has been catastrophic."

That strengthened Le Fanu's intention to resign. The volcanic-tempered, blame-shifting, bombastic Jepson had tyrannised him. Just after Le Fanu's own appointment as inaugural head of the Crime Unit, Jepson was compromise choice for Commissioner of Police in Madras. Already dismissive of Le Fanu, Jepson automatically derided the unit. By extension, that included its use of the Austrian Hans Gross's criminal investigation methods. Jepson began an elimination campaign.

Le Fanu and the unit survived by saving the Government of Madras from embarrassment and winning respect from the Governor and Chief Secretary. Even they, however, could not prevent Jepson from later becoming Inspector-General of Police for the Presidency, again a compromise despite his copybook blots that included ordering a fatal firing on a peaceful political demonstration.

Then Jepson's wife fell ill and returned to England. Jepson himself followed amidst the assumption he would never return. Le Fanu became Acting Inspector-General and resented his case work being replaced by a paper chase. When Jepson's wife died, the man unexpectedly returned to Madras and reassumed his position. Le Fanu was shipped off to Penang.

"Has it been that bad?" Le Fanu failed to sound neutral.

"Worse," Habi responded. "He was always a poor policeman and a worse leader, but now he's impossible. The riding crop's so worn out the rumour is he's looking for a replacement."

The other two laughed. Upon becoming Commissioner Jepson took to carrying a crop even though he had visited few horses, especially in these later years. Barrel-like, he would now need a ladder to mount anything bar a Shetland pony. Whenever he was agitated, which was most of the time, everyone knew Jepson was nearby as crop thwacked against polished riding boots worn specifically for the purpose.

That idiosyncrasy sparked one of the great nicknames, Jepson known now as "The Jockey" to all and sundry right up to the Governor.

"Your Muslim leather merchant friends will get some new trade then, Habi". Le Fanu placed a hand on the man's shoulder. "It *is* good to see you," he said.

"Of course, sir." Habi's grin widened. "We knew you couldn't stay away."

Jackson Caldicott seemed more detached.

"What about you, Jackson? All well?"

"The main work's fine, LF, but as Habi suggests, the overall situation is not. And it's not just The Jockey. The Governor and Chief Secretary will both likely leave soon."

Yet more reasons for Le Fanu to decamp. Lord Willingdon, Governor since 1919, was a strong ally. So was Sir Charles Whitney. He might be from the conservative old school ICS but was also a realist who knew political change was inevitable.

"What are the rumours?"

"That Willingdon will be out in months, Whitney to be at Foreign and Political in Delhi soon."

"Those rumours've been around for months, of course, sir," Habi added, "but they're on the rise now. That makes smart people think they're going to happen."

Le Fanu did not tell them he would see Whitney that afternoon, or that the Chief Secretary had told him about the Delhi post weeks earlier. It should have been announced by now.

"That's what I love about this place," Le Fanu replied. "Rumour always triumphs over fact. Come on, the throng's departed. Let's get ashore."

Two

After just a few weeks away he had forgotten the crush of humanity that was Madras, and India. The porters took his bags and two constables cleared a path, but Le Fanu was still overwhelmed by people offering all imaginable and several unimaginable services. Three steps forward, one back and another to the side. No way through. He was suffocating, the terminal heaving, offloaded passengers bashing headlong into embarking ones. Harried officials tried to direct traffic, but the customers knew best, did whatever they thought necessary. Noise soared above logic, instinct above regulation.

He stumbled after the constables, faint, barely registering Habi protecting him ahead on the right and Caldicott behind on the left. Dazed, he wondered how he could have forgotten this. Crowded India had never bothered him. He loved it. Well, thought he did. In retrospect, he had blanked out his early days like this to recall order rather than panic.

Angry with himself, he straightened up, looked around.

"All right there, LF?" Caldicott seemed cheery.

"Yes. Just amazed I'd forgotten so quickly."

Habi turned around. "I hear very few people live in the Straits Settlements, especially in Penang. I have relatives there."

Of course he did. No doubt they had reported back. How much did Habi know?

"You're right, Habi," Le Fanu shouted, "but if India keeps

exporting so many labourers there, the population will grow quickly, and for the worse." That might have sounded too reactionary. "Well, you know, need to be careful …"

"Of course, sir, can't have too many Muslims in the one place, sir."

Le Fanu was not convinced Habi was joking. "Habi, I didn't mean …"

"Pay no attention, LF. Habi's been mixing with the Muslim League. He says he doesn't support them but I'm not so sure."

The other two laughed but Le Fanu sensed tension.

They struggled through the crowd towards a waiting staff car, an ostentatious black Landaulette. Le Fanu disliked riding in such a thing when the government was crying poor.

"Who bought that?" he asked, knowing the answer.

"The Jockey," Habi and Caldicott rejoined in duet.

"God Almighty, does he have no sense?"

"None," came the refrain.

Le Fanu's baggage barely filled a small corner of the storage trunk. The constables saw their charges into the car and the driver threaded out through the port onto the coast road towards the long beach stretch of the Marina.

"Where to, LF?" asked Caldicott.

He hadn't thought about that. "Ah, home, I think."

He feared that, like the port crowds, the house might betray memory and sentiment. It had been a tranquil retreat during difficult periods in his life, especially after Roisin McPhedren dodged his marriage proposal. She went to ground in Hyderabad, he to seed along with the garden in Mylapore. Then came Penang and Jenlin. He had not contacted Ro since.

"Tell me," he said, changing the conversation, "what's this about the Muslim League?"

He knew the All-India Muslim League formed in 1906, just after his arrival, Indian National Congress Muslim members fearing Hindu issues were being privileged. Since then, police reports had the group working well enough with Congress but noting the emergence of new Madras Muslim interest groups. He could not imagine Habi being involved, given his secular and police background.

"Sir," Habi responded, "there are many different Muslim communities in Madras. Some speak Tamil, some Telugu, others Urdu. Some are wealthy, others poor. There are over 50,000 of us here, so many differences. Especially now."

"Who are the most important groups?"

"The Urdu speakers, even though they pretend they're not from here."

Spoken like a true Telugu-speaking Muslim from the Andhra country north of Madras.

"What's their problem, then?"

"Habi, may I start?" Caldicott played the diplomat, or spy, Le Fanu was unsure which.

"Of course, sir."

"LF, remember Malabar."

"I do."

During 1921, the Moplah Rebellion had erupted along the Presidency's south-west coast following the British crackdown on a wartime Muslim movement that sought support from Turkey, an enemy power. Muslims, the Moplah community was about a quarter of the local population. At least 10,000 people died. The Raj hanged two hundred more and jailed another 50,000 with 20,000 of those transported to the Andaman Islands he had just sailed by. The jail there was among the Empire's most reviled. Coinciding with Mahatma Gandhi's Non-Cooperation campaign, the uprising was momentous and serious. The-then Chief Secretary told Le Fanu British power in the south had faltered.

"Well," continued Caldicott, "following that, a few Madras Muslim leaders became worried about the direction being taken by Congress and the independence movement. Some of them now want separate guarantees about the future. Opinion's divided and anxiety's rising."

"That division's always been there, surely?" Le Fanu responded. "Not so much here in Madras, perhaps, but out in your home town, Habi, there's always been a big history."

Habi came from Nellore, a north-of-Madras district with a sizeable Muslim population and a reputation for communal squabbles.

"Yes, sir. But people are more worried now. The non-Brahmins are being looked after here; Muslims worry they'll be left out."

The government had recently reserved several civil service positions for non-Brahmins, punishing the powerful Brahmin lawyers and professionals who dominated the Indian National Congress but remained in government service. Service diehards regarded them as traitors.

They were nearing Fort St George now. Le Fanu glanced back at the High Court's dominating spires built in the city's renowned Indo-Saracenic style. Muslim judges sat in those courts, had done for years.

"Habi, that makes no sense. The government has always looked out for Muslims."

"Malabar was bad, sir. Muslims are worried."

"That was a special circumstance, well out of the ordinary."

"We're learning much more about what happened, sir, and Muslims think they were targeted." Habi was unusually serious.

Le Fanu backed off. "Not sure I'm ready for such a serious discussion yet. I should read the files."

Habi looked underwhelmed. "Very good, sir. What'll you do when you get home?"

"Unpack, I think, then come into the office. I still have one, I suppose?"

That relaxed things, a little.

"We'll find you something, LF," Caldicott said.

"We will, sir," added Habi.

Was there an issue there?

"God, why'd I come back?" Le Fanu speculated aloud.

"We wondered that ourselves, sir. We concluded it was only because of us." Habi was straight-faced. That had not changed.

"Thanks, Habi, very touching."

The driver cut away from the Marina, passed the Madras Cricket Club and turned towards Mylapore, Le Fanu's suburb and heartland of the Tamil Brahmins who supported Congress. That location and his neighbours made many Madras conservatives suspect his loyalty. He had innumerable critics. The driver detoured past the towering *gopurams* of the Kapileswarar temple that had served Lord Siva for a thousand years. Le Fanu suspected he was being reminded that, in Indian eyes, the British presence was fleeting – a mere three hundred years or so.

They turned into his driveway and he was not sure what he thought. Recent memories were sad. When Ro went silent he responded in usual fashion, turning in on himself and shutting out others. His work suffered, so did his reputation. The Penang mission helped him escape house and office while Jenlin made him feel better about himself.

Would Jenlin like living here? That question and its implications worried him, too. Was she just another escape from his troubles and indecision?

The gardens were immaculate, the house exterior gleamed. All the servants lined up, women in matching saris, men in white uniforms with the sashes and badges of office crossing their tunics. He should dispatch that palaver if he really cared for his staff. Otherwise he was just another Raj hack with a tin ear culturally.

"Sir," said Habi, "we made arrangements for you. Food is available, the putting green has been cut, the mail culled."

"Habi, thank you. Very thoughtful. Will you join me for lunch?"

"Thank you, but no, LF," said Caldicott, looking at his watch. "The Jockey knows you're back, so we're summonsed before him in twenty minutes. First time in weeks. No coincidence. He's testing loyalties, playing mind games. Though I doubt he's read as much Freud and Jung as you."

"Give him my regards, or not, as you see fit."

"Can you imagine?" Habi appeared to think the risk worth taking.

The coming days would be difficult.

"I've a Secretariat meeting in about three hours," Le Fanu replied. "Shall we meet first thing tomorrow, say eight o'clock? We can compare notes. Everyone'll know I'm back by then."

"You underestimate your significance and the power of gossip." Habi was not joking. "Despite our best efforts, your arrival date has been public knowledge for days. The Jockey's already undermining you constantly and has lined up some really dirty work for you."

Surprising had it been otherwise, really. The Raj was at its best when devouring its own.

"Now I really do wonder why I came back," Le Fanu said.

"Come to my office first thing, LF; we've a heap of files for you." Caldicott looked grim.

He and Habi left, to what would be a Jepson grilling about Le Fanu's return. They would handle it well, but he felt sorry for them.

Le Fanu flicked through the post, mostly old newspapers and magazines, a couple of new books from London, messages from friends, including Chester Barnes, editor of *The Madras Mail*. While the *Mail* was past its rabid rag days, even Barnes had occasionally to keep the serious conservatives happy. Le Fanu rued the fact that most of those were now from the ICS rather than the commercial world. That odd twist on the old order lowered his mood even further. He resolved to read the *Mail*'s recent editions immediately.

He went out into the gardens, his favoured retreat. Habi was right. The putting green looked better than ever, but could he find his clubs? In recent weeks he had played the Penang Turf Club course with borrowed clubs. Flat and unchallenging like that he could handle, but it would be harder here. Le Fanu could not remember the last time he felt confident about his game.

Back inside he looked around the house then ate lunch. The servants had prepared his favourite foods. He would put up with Penang's average south Indian food if that meant he could live there, with Jenlin.

Upstairs he unpacked his few things, organised the wardrobe, lingered under the shower, rested. In fact, he nodded off to dream a jumble of exhausting thoughts, pressures, ideas and hopes. An hour later he woke feeling worse than ever.

Now for the Chief Secretary.

Three

It was like seeing the city anew. The driver went directly out to the Marina, traversing streets lined on both sides by tall trees whose merging branches canopied shade and tranquillity. Food vendors chased late lunch-takers and people needing a tide-over snack before the next big meal. Among the wandering ascetics, an archetypal holy man looked old but could have been otherwise, wearing just a voluminous loincloth. The ash-smeared face bore the sign of Siva. Unkempt hair and beard, spare frame, bare feet and walking stave confirmed years spent on the road. Piercing eyes stared out through the mane while the long fine nose and calm look made him a portrait photographer's dream.

San Thome Church on the Marina symbolised south India's complex European connections. The Portuguese built this Catholic church during the late sixteenth century, on the very spot where St Thomas died in 72 AD. Other missionaries followed, then the British, French, Dutch and Scandinavian colonialists. The British took root, but the others left only small enclaves, like French Pondicherry and Danish Tranquebar south of Madras.

It felt odd passing the long, white, two-level police headquarters building perched on the Marina and looking out to the Bay of Bengal. His first call would be at Fort St George, not here. That said everything about the situation and his state of mind. Looking at the second-floor balcony to the Inspector-General's office he had occupied so recently,

Le Fanu imagined Jepson terrorising staff and plotting the demise of upstart returnees. Unhappy memories. The Penang venture had allowed him to escape that office's paper mountains and flee The Jockey.

He marvelled anew at the University of Madras' Senate House and college architecture. R F Chisholm and Henry Irwin had blended English and European architectural styles to produce this unique one, towering Arabian domes sitting atop white-pointed red-brick facings. These buildings signified British power in the south. It was a pity that present political reactionaries shunned similarly hybrid reform proposals. Le Fanu had enjoyed London performances in Sloan Square's Cadogan Hall that Chisholm designed later, but Irwin stayed in India to produce other imperious buildings, notably the Viceroy's Lodge up in Simla. The Earl of Reading lived there now. Rumour had him and Lord Willingdon sparring. Le Fanu's supporter had coveted the post.

Traffic had thickened by the time they passed the Chepauk Palace for the second time today. Were there more cars, trucks and buses now than when he had left? Surely things could not change that quickly. He must still be culture shocked. The pony carts remained, tired animals pulling the high-wheeled and closed-box affairs that had patrolled the city forever. Bicycles abounded, and more motorbikes. He had not yet looked in on his own, the big Indian Power Plus that most Madras Europeans saw as yet another marker of his difference. He had not missed it while in Penang, hadn't needed the escape to solitude that so often drove him out on the roads here.

They reached Fort St George, stopping at the main entrance with its black marble columns that always looked misplaced. Some notable figures had entered here over the past four hundred years, including Elihu Yale and Clive of India, but none had faced anything like the present problems. Old hands thought Britain now had fewer years left in India than already spent. Gandhi bewildered a bureaucracy used to running on order and predictability. Indians ignoring British laws en masse confused officials in cities, towns and countryside across India, including Madras. Le Fanu admired the ingenuity but remained unconvinced about the immediate results.

He took the stairs to the second floor, remembering his way to the Chief Secretary's offices where he was greeted by a clerk and shown straight in.

"Chris, wonderful to see you; marvellous you're back."

Sir Charles Whitney was standing immediately inside the door, keen to shake Le Fanu's hand. "We've missed you, my friend, that bloody Jockey's a nightmare."

The familiar cigar smoke brume filled the room. Whitney *sans* cigar was a rare sighting. And he was as formal as ever. Heavy English suit, wing-collared shirt, pocket-watch chain across the waistcoat, groomed short grey hair, highly polished shoes.

"It's after lunch, too," he said, "so a celebration's in order." He went to an ice bucket standing on a sideboard. A bottle was already open.

"No ifs or buts, Chris, this is a good moment for me." He poured two glasses of champagne. "It's a Perrier-Jouet a friend brought over; been saving it for a special occasion that has now arrived. Cheers."

It was cold, crisp, full of flavour. The bubbles burst into Le Fanu's nostrils. Nice return.

"Very good, Sir Charles, thank you."

"For God's sake, Chris, drop the Sir. We know each other well enough by now. Besides, the bloody title's getting worthless. The head of the railways got one recently, and some Legislative Council lackey. Getting thrown about like confetti."

He blew the customarily perfect smoke ring then grinned. "Sounding like a right reactionary, no? But really, it sometimes makes one wonder if it's all worthwhile."

"In your case, Charles, it's all been very worthwhile and will continue so. And thank you again for this welcome back."

"Trust me, a choice between you and The Jockey is no choice at all. The man's impossible. Roughed up one of the Governor's aides a day or so ago, and you can imagine how well that went down. Well, roughed up verbally, anyway. Fool."

Whitney regaled Le Fanu with Jepson's escapades for several minutes, reporting police headquarters morale at historically low levels. An aggravated Willingdon was urging Delhi to dump Jepson. But the Governor had alienated key people up there so was getting no response. Meanwhile, Jepson became increasingly erratic.

One story had him visiting a suburban police station on a whim. A busy constable did not recognise or consider him. Jepson erupted, had the man paraded. After delivering a lengthy and vituperative tirade, Jepson placed a sign reading 'Donkey' around the hapless policeman's neck then consigned him to the city pound for twenty-four hours. The man's family complained, other station policemen, including a couple of European officers, went on strike, more city stations followed suit, and all hell let loose.

"Not sure how you'll go there, Chris. The madman's after you and has said so publicly."

"I can handle that." Le Fanu thought about the Penang job offer.

"Ordinarily I'd agree, but other factors are springing up."

"Like your departure?"

"Well, that should have happened a while ago, but some pompous ass in Delhi quibbled about removal costs and delayed things. All fixed now, though, and I'll be off soon enough. Not looking forward to it. Hate that lot up there."

He finished his glass, poured himself another and topped up Le Fanu's.

"Any word on your replacement, Charles?"

"All the usual jockeying. Sorry, didn't mean to scare you. There'll always be compromise candidates, of course, but Jepson won't figure this time. Couple of other names might alarm you, though."

Le Fanu waited.

Nothing. "Any clues?"

"Sorry, Chris, can't say anything. But the Chepauk Palace is in contention."

The Board of Revenue. That meant the First Member. Arthur Jamieson. Their mutual loathing began with a Crime Unit investigation into the murder of a visiting Englishwoman who disappeared from a Jamieson garden party. The man ranked his own abilities highly and everyone else's not at all but reserved special contempt for the police, Le Fanu especially.

"He's a serious possibility, Charles? Really?"

"Sillier things have happened. Not many, but even so ..."

"He'd be terrible."

"Oh, I'm irreplaceable, obviously, so whoever comes in will be inferior." The barely visible upturn at the corners of the mouth belied rare self-deprecation.

"Correct on all accounts." Le Fanu raised a glass, saluted his host.

"And to add more woes," responded Whitney, "Willingdon told me last night his replacement's decided. The announcement comes next week; the new man arrives in April."

"Can you tell me who?"

Willingdon's exit coinciding with Whitney's meant upheaval for Le Fanu, Habi, Caldicott and the Crime Unit.

"I can, confidentially. George Joachim Goschen, Second Viscount Goschen."

"Wasn't his father Chancellor of the Exchequer sometime back in the nineteenth century?"

"That's the one, merchant banker."

"And the son, what's he done?"

"Little to qualify for this post. My London friends consider him a surprise choice. He served the Governor of New South Wales in the 1890s. The family got him away from an older woman, but the ploy failed. Married her as soon as he got back. Went into politics but has spent most of his time in the City's financial circles. Had a cousin on the Bank of England board, too."

"Very different from Willingdon."

"That echoes several comments around here and the club, I can confirm. He'll be at sea for a while, and that gives people like Jepson opportunity."

Penang was looking increasingly attractive.

Whitney poured the last of the champagne. "Chris, I'm afraid that's not the only discouraging news." The Chief Secretary remained standing, uncharacteristically bothered.

Le Fanu wondered what was coming.

"I had a telegram from Hyderabad yesterday, from the General who employs Mrs McPhedren. She's very ill, in hospital. I decided not to tell you until now. The General called me a few minutes ago; her condition remains poor."

That was the last thing he had expected. "What is it?"

"Typhoid, I'm afraid."

Le Fanu remembered reading that eight million Indians had died from the disease between 1900 and 1920 but that new vaccines brought hope. "I thought we were controlling that more now?" he added, just to say something.

"Our doctors here have a few new things, but it's still pernicious."

"Any idea how she got it?"

"Nothing specific. Usual sort of thing, probably – through food or water."

"In the General's house?"

"He doesn't know. She'd been visiting other places, friends and so on."

Le Fanu's relationship with Jenlin made this even worse. He had not finalised things with Ro, procrastinating as always. In the silence that followed his proposal, Ro had never formally refused him, even if she did 'relieve' him of his obligation to her. So he'd left for the Straits Settlements with the proposal still standing, technically at least. Meeting Jenlin pushed that into the background. He meant to formalise things but had not. Now Ro was seriously ill.

"What do you want to do, Chris?"

Le Fanu did not hear Sir Charles immediately.

"Chris?"

"Sorry."

"Chris, my spies have told me about your new friend. I make no judgement on that. In fact, good luck; you deserve someone special."

Le Fanu wondered if Whitney also knew about the job offer.

"That said, my friend, you have to face this situation."

"I know. What should I do?"

"Well, *there*'s something new, you asking for advice. Sorry. Couldn't resist. Let's get another report from the General tonight, then reassess. You might have to go up there, depending on her condition."

Whitney was right, but Le Fanu relished neither trip nor meeting.

"What about Jepson?"

"Don't worry about him. If you have to go, I'll tell The Jockey to lump it. That'd be fun."

Le Fanu never connected the Chief Secretary with any sort of fun.

"I'd almost rather deal with Jepson than go to Hyderabad."

"You must resolve things sometime. You owe Mrs McPhedren that, at least."

When Ro had visited Le Fanu in Madras, the Chief Secretary took the trouble to welcome her publicly. In a society where mixed race Anglo-Indians like her were shunned, it was a bold step Le Fanu had and still appreciated.

"Sir, ah … Charles. I probably owe you an explanation."

"Your business, your life. You made an offer. It was not immediately accepted. You met someone else. And I hear she's special. These things happen, but you owe Mrs McPhedren support now."

"You're right."

"I'll telephone the General for a report and let you know. I'm assuming you won't join me at the club for dinner, given these circumstances?"

"I'll decline if you don't mind. I'll go into the office on the way back, then home. Could you telephone me there?"

"Of course, and I'm sorry to be the bearer of this news; it's a terrible welcome back."

"Thanks, Charles. I'd better be going."

"If you do go into the office, keep out of sight or Jepson'll be on you like an avalanche. Those are rare in these parts, and I wouldn't want you swept away."

Descending the stairs towards the car, Le Fanu could not order a thought. He had anticipated an awkward return, but not this. Penang was now far away and long ago.

Four

Le Fanu directed the driver towards headquarters but changed his mind halfway there and set course for Mylapore. Whitney was right. He was ill-prepared for a Jepson jeremiad. Madras passed by outside but he might have been anywhere, seeing nothing, later remembering nothing of the trip.

After the driver dropped him at the steps Le Fanu somehow found his golf clubs, pulled out a mashie niblick and a few balls, headed for the practice area. He didn't mind hitting shots poorly. This was the best distraction available. Golf balls disappeared to all corners of the garden and he trudged off to find them. The servants placed cold drinks on a nearby table but he didn't notice. An occasional blow came off the club face perfectly, but brought little pleasure. Two hours dragged by.

He felt guilty, irrational though that might be. He might not be directly responsible for her illness but he had left issues unresolved, complicated them, now had a problem. Well he might tell himself Ro's silence caused the rift, but if she was unsure about the proposal then he had failed to make his feelings clear. She would certainly question his sincerity once the Jenlin situation emerged. Right now, he was unsure what he really felt when he had proposed to Ro, or about Jenlin for that matter.

Frustrated, he took a full swing, flushed one over the trees into his neighbour's compound. What would that

Brahmin lawyer think when he found a golf ball marked 'St Andrews'?

Darkness drove him in to read the recent *Mail* editions. Nothing inspiring. He roamed about looking for something else to do. Dinner came and went, and five minutes later he could not remember what he had eaten. For once, a Sancerre was tasteless and he was off, not the wine. He showered, changed, came back down, but nothing improved. If anything, it deteriorated, like a Scottish North Sea haar rolling in to obliterate brain and vision.

Whitney rang just after nine. "Not good, Chris. No worse, but no better either, and that's worrying the medicos. They say she's extremely sick."

"Any predictions?"

"Well, you know typhoid. It sneaks up, gets hold, then refuses to shift. They've got all the latest medicines, and the top Indian Medical Service man up there has taken on her case at my request. He's on secondment from one of the Telugu districts, so that's lucky. The Nizam also has some great doctors on hand, of course." The Nizam of Hyderabad, among India's leading princes, one of the world's wealthiest people.

The Raj ruled princely states like Hyderabad indirectly, providing senior advisors to 'assist' decision-making. British counsel abounded, like Sir Maurice Wilson who now commanded the Nizam's unified police and military unit. As Inspector-General in Madras, Wilson had planned the Crime Unit after reading Hans Gross, then appointed Le Fanu its first leader. When Wilson transferred, he told Le Fanu a post was available for him in Hyderabad at any time. Le Fanu was tempted when Ro moved there, but resisted. Another indecisive moment brought on by personal confusion. But Wilson might help now.

"Charles, have they discussed her chances?"

Whitney paused. "In very guarded terms. You know what they're like. Typhoid moves fast so they're reluctant to predict. I've seen it myself over a long time here, sudden outbreaks and strange patterns. They're worried, though, Chris. Very. She's in a bad way. I'm sorry."

Le Fanu started to feel sick himself. "I'm not sure what to do."

"No surprise there. It amazes me how you're so competent at everything else but hopeless in matters like this." There was no malice in the comment.

Join the club, Le Fanu thought.

"However," Whitney continued, "here are the options. You stay here, wander round your house and garden and help no one. Or bury yourself in work and fight with Jepson. Or go to Hyderabad and support the woman to whom you proposed."

"But I've only just arrived back."

"Mere detail. This is an important thing in your life."

"I should go up. But I must make my excuses at the office, probably to Jepson in person."

"Christ, you're hopeless. When they understand the situation, people will expect you to go to Hyderabad. Well, most will. A few bigots still wonder why you consorted with an Anglo-Indian."

Le Fanu speculated about their thoughts on a Straits Chinese.

"But don't worry about them, Chris. Do what's best for you. Resolve this personal situation, otherwise you'll never make your mind up about anything."

He was right.

"You win, Charles. But I'll go into the office first, then

leave. Would you mind checking with Hyderabad in the morning then calling me here or at the office?"

"I'll do whatever's required, you know that. But don't let Jepson jab you. You need to go off in as good a frame of mind as possible."

They ended the call, Le Fanu poured a Laphroaig 18 kept for special moments. He needed the tang and taste of seaweed, smoke and oil to jolt him back. The first sip did that, as always. He found his address book on the side table under some papers, flicked through, stopped at a page, picked up the telephone, got connected.

"Sir Maurice, LF here. Sorry to ring so late."

"LF. Wonderful to hear from you but I'm assuming an emergency. Where are you calling from? I'd heard you were across the waters."

"Got back just this morning, but you're right, there's an emergency. I'm not sure you know or remember a friend of mine, Mrs McPhedren?"

"I do, for a host of reasons. Isn't she here now?"

"Yes, she works for the General up there. You've probably met him."

"Of course, see him at joint meetings of the British and the Nizam's forces. Sometimes at the Secunderabad Club and official dinners, that sort of thing. Decent enough chap, if not among my favourites. Why?"

"Ro, Mrs McPhedren, is in hospital with typhoid, and it's serious. Latest reports a few minutes ago were bleak. The top IMS man has taken on the case, thanks to Whitney. I wondered if you might telephone him and the General in the morning, see if you can get more detail. I'll go into the office first then catch the train up there about midday."

"Of course I will, LF, but is it a good idea coming here? I hear Jepson's after you. Word travels far and wide."

"Whitney persuaded me it's the best thing. A difficult decision, but I think he's right."

"Tell me the details when you arrive. Knowing you, there'll be a complication somewhere."

How was it they all said that?

"Ah, yes, there is."

"Knew it. But if The Jockey sacks you, or posts you to the back of beyond, or you tell him what to do with his job, the position's still here for you. That offer's permanent."

"Thank you, Sir Maurice. I do appreciate it."

Hyderabad or Penang?

By dawn he'd had just a couple of hours sleep. A long shower and several cups of more than usually strong south Indian coffee brought an artificial alertness to see him through the hours before the train. Anticipating the Jepson meeting he considered adding essence of Laphroaig to the coffee, but resisted. The heavy *idli* were a challenge, but the sinus-clearing *sambar* helped him finish.

The driver arrived at seven and they encountered little traffic. Devotees returning from the temples were bedaubed with devotional marks. Office workers rode bicycles, with briefcases strapped on rear wheel carriers. Street sellers were out, *pan* and *betel* shops doing brisk trade. Their customers went off chewing, then spitting the dark red residue most Europeans found revolting no matter how long they'd been in India.

A motor cyclist went by. Le Fanu had still not looked at his bike and would not until after Hyderabad, and he'd no idea how long that would be. His small case beside him contained just a few clothes because he intended a quick visit but it might not work that way. Perhaps he should get new clothes tailored in Hyderabad. Jenlin had quipped that he looked as tired as his wardrobe.

They reached headquarters, always impressive at this hour with the early light flicking off bright white stone. The driver passed the building, turned into Edward Elliots Road then immediately again in behind the offices and an annex added years earlier to what was originally one of the city's leading Masonic Lodge buildings. The Masons still bonded the city's leading European males. A senior ICS reactionary was the current District Grand Master and Jepson also a member. Le Fanu refused to join so was undoubtedly the subject of conversation.

He climbed the outside stairs at the back, turned into the corridor towards the Crime Unit offices. Habi was in.

"Good morning, sir. You look terrible."

"Thanks, Habi. To the point as ever. Is Caldicott in yet?"

"He's usually here by six-thirty. I'll call for him."

Habi summonsed a *peon* who hurried off. Caldicott arrived a couple of minutes later.

"Good morning, LF, no sleep then?"

"Don't you start. Fact is, I got some bad news yesterday. Mrs McPhedren has typhoid and is in hospital in Hyderabad. It's serious, very serious, according to reports. I'll get more news this morning but will go up there on the midday train."

Both Caldicott and Habi murmured sympathies but looked uncomfortable.

"All right, what's up?"

"Sir," said Habi, "The Jockey's demanded we all meet him at three this afternoon."

"We've no idea what it's about," chipped in Caldicott, "but it won't be pleasant. The I-G's been even more mysterious and mercurial than ever. He's up to something, and we think it concerns us, well you, certainly, and us as collateral damage in all likelihood."

"When did that order come in?"

"About five yesterday afternoon, sir, while you were with the Chief Secretary."

Jepson probably just wanted to deliver Le Fanu a verbal assault as punishment for not reporting immediately. Even so, this was worrying.

"Well, I have to go up there. What time does he get in? Not yet, I'll be bound."

"No earlier than nine, LF, and frequently later. Closer to ten."

"All right. Have someone keep an eye out and I'll go round there as soon as he arrives. Meanwhile, tell me what's on your desks."

For the next two hours, until a clerk announced Jepson's arrival at ten, Le Fanu caught up on all the current murder cases and Special Branch activities. Habi had three intriguing investigations that triggered his interest, given a notional connection between them. The victims were all prominent Muslims, but geographically spread. One was found in the Periamet district in Madras, another in the temple town of Tanjore south of Madras, and the third in the northern town of Guntur that had dominated Gandhi's passive resistance campaign in the Presidency.

"What are your thoughts, Habi?"

"I'm trying not to leap to conclusions, sir, but it's odd. There are small numbers of Muslims in both Tanjore and Guntur, so the obvious possibility is that those two were targeted. The Periamet one, on the other hand, could be the victim of a leather industry commercial dispute, either with a Hindu or another Muslim."

"But you think there might also be a political dimension."

"It's curious that these deaths have coincided with a rise in communal tension, yes."

"Quite right to think that way, Habi, but there's most likely a more banal explanation. Can you keep me advised on progress?"

"Of course, sir."

Caldicott had two priorities.

The first concerned the activities of a socialist group within the Indian National Congress, ignited by Russian developments. Some Russian-trained Congress members were now touring the districts, spreading communist ideas. Special Branch was under pressure with Jamieson and like-minded others stridently alarmed.

The second involved the Muslim League, with Muslim political sentiment rising at the very point Gandhi's more general campaign was on the wane.

As Caldicott explained, Le Fanu noticed Habi stiffening, holding back.

"We'll resume this later," Le Fanu said, rising, "I'll see you both before I leave."

"Good luck, sir."

"Go well, LF."

"Thanks, I'll need it, I think."

He followed the familiar route to his former office and, nearing the open door, heard the trademark whack of crop on boot, several times in rapid succession. Bad sign. A secretary sitting behind a desk guarded the inner sanctum.

Wanting to be more accessible, Le Fanu had removed that post. Jepson's restoration looked defensive, beleaguered. The secretary looked awkward.

"Please go straight in, sir."

Le Fanu turned into the Star Chamber.

"Le Fanu, you fucking disgrace. I hear you're shagging a Chinese bint now."

Jepson stood behind his desk in full dress uniform complete with ceremonial cap and gloves. The uniform was new, Le Fanu noticed, still shiny but necessarily several sizes larger than its predecessors. Jepson was now wider than taller, enormous. His face had swollen since their last meeting, jowls rolled over the shirt collar and around the tunic neck. The eyes were slits amidst a face more puce than ruddy.

Stunned by the vulgarity, Le Fanu attempted calm. "Good morning, sir. I do apologise for not having come yesterday, but I was commanded before the Chief Secretary and he gave me some bad news, I'm afraid."

"What, the bint toss you aside, did she? They usually do, I hear. Like a bit of variety, it seems. White men not good enough. And you're definitely not good enough."

This was awful, far worse than anticipated.

"Sir, unfortunately, that bad news means I must leave for Hyderabad on the midday train. I'll be back as soon as possible but can't say when. A friend is seriously ill in hospital."

"That would be the other trollop. Bloody hell, Le Fanu, you like a bit of colour, don't you? Must have a touch of the tar brush yourself. Helps if you're running a harem, I suppose."

The ringing in Le Fanu's ears and the tension in his gut reached previously unknown levels.

"Sir, this is uncalled for. I'm informing you of …"

"Fuck off, Le Fanu. I'm back, and you'll do what I tell you. You tried to steal my post, you and your Chief Secretary pal. Well, he's going, along with that bloody lunatic Willingdon, so you'll be on your own. You'll be out, I'll see to that."

"Sir, I don't have to tolerate this unprofessional treatment that I …"

"Le Fanu, I don't give a shit what you think. I'm telling you what'll happen. Consider this a warning to find another job. I've no fucking use for you. I'm sorting out your two bloody show ponies, too. They've had it too easy."

"You leave me no option but to make a formal complaint."

"Complain away. Your man won't be around to protect you, and my friends are ready to help kick you out, you fucking Indian lover. Fuck off to Hyderabad, I don't want you here. There are no cases for you because you're fucking incompetent. While you're up there, sort out which bint you want or find another one. I hear there's an unending supply. Get the fuck out of my sight."

He physically shoved Le Fanu out and slammed the door on his back.

Le Fanu stumbled away, stunned, vaguely aware of the secretary mumbling apologies. Caldicott was still in Habi's office. They had waited.

"You look worse than ever, LF. That bad?" Caldicott looked concerned.

"Appalling." He was shaking. "The man's off his head. Is it just me who makes him like this?"

"Oh no, sir," Habi said. "His staff hate it, and some have arranged transfers already. No one goes there unless they have to. Even then some avoid it. Several complaints have been made. And that's only the Europeans. He treats Indians even worse."

"It's like he has some sort of mental problem. He's not rational."

"He never was, it's just much worse," said Caldicott.

"Well, he wants me out of his sight, so Hyderabad it is. I'll see you when I get back."

"If we're still here, LF."

"You know he has both of you in his sights, then, because you're associated with me?"

"Oh yes, sir, we're reminded every day."

"Why'd you not tell me, even if I was away?"

"We're used to it now. Almost." replied Caldicott.

Five

Le Fanu somehow found his way onto the train. Normally he took in the Madras Central crowds and noise and bustle but not this time.

The more he thought about it, the more irrational Jepson's behaviour seemed. They were never trusting colleagues. Jepson hated the Crime Unit's modern methods; Le Fanu detested the man's attitude and lack of professionalism. But he honoured Jepson's rank, even if it was unearned. Le Fanu was there when the man's rash incompetence caused several deaths at the Marina Beach demonstration. He had tried to work with Jepson and modify whatever idiotic approaches came along, but nothing explained or justified this hysterical outburst. Habi and Caldicott suggested these episodes were multiplying and force morale plummeting. Once again, Le Fanu thought, he would have to make a stand, and that meant even more trouble.

It was late afternoon now, a few hours into the journey. Alone in a first class compartment, he looked out over the green, irrigated lands of the Telugu coastal districts as the train rolled towards Bezwada and a stop. They would reach Hyderabad after midnight. If not in such a rush, he might have stopped into Guntur and looked over Habi's murder case. Anything to prevent an early return to headquarters.

Invariably, when Europeans said they were going to Hyderabad most, like him, were actually headed for its twin city Secunderabad, known popularly as Lashkar or 'Army'. The huge military base there, one of the Empire's largest, was established in 1803 to consolidate British power across the Deccan and central India following the 1799 defeat of Tipu Sultan at Seringapatam. The twin cities were the different halves of the Raj whole with Secunderabad the outrider for British culture and attitudes. It even had a branch of Mappin & Webb, the great English silversmith firm. Hyderabad was the Muslim home to the Nizam, an outlier of the former Mughal Empire.

Despite everything, Le Fanu had brought books. He remembered buying Dorothy Sayers' *Whose Body?* at Higginbotham's on Mount Road before going to Penang. A friend had sent D H Lawrence's *Kangaroo* from London. Le Fanu still considered Australia a possible destination if he had to leave India.

However, he now started *Essentials of Hindutva* by V D Savarkar. Le Fanu wondered how Jepson would react to a senior policeman reading this. Savarkar studied law in London but began frequenting revolutionary circles there. His radical colleague, Madan Lal Dhingra, hanged for the 1909 London assassination of Sir William Hutt Curzon Wyllie, a former Raj Resident in several Indian princely states then senior India Office official whom Dhingra and colleagues thought personified Raj iniquities.

British authorities suspected Savarkar was involved in the assassination, had him arrested in France then tried in India. Sentenced to fifty years, he spent time in the notorious Andaman Islands' 'Cellular Jail' before being transferred back to India where he refined his ideas about a Hindu national state that would be immediately free of Britain and with little or no place for Muslims.

Like Jepson, most Madras Europeans would think Le Fanu a traitor for reading the work. But to his mind the British needed to understand such ideas if they were to deal with them effectively. The Savarkar movement worried him, and not just because it questioned British rule. Congress did that. This raised more dangerous possibilities. What *would* happen to Muslims? These views helped fuel the rise of the Muslim League, hence Habi's concerns. This critical moment might decide India's immediate political future, but instead of analysing developments, the British would crack down and send them underground to give their architects even more credibility.

Le Fanu fell asleep, waking as the train pulled into Bezwada and turned towards the Deccan Plateau. Amidst the platform's hustle and bustle, he took tea from a chai-wallah, enjoying the milky sweetness warmed by a disposable clay cup. Walking the platform and navigating the clash between boarders and leavers, he felt more comfortable back in the press. When the journey resumed he ate in the dining car then returned to his compartment to sleep fitfully, disturbed by images of Jepson in full cry.

The conductor woke him a few minutes before Secunderabad so he was ready to alight when the train stopped at the main platform. It was near one in the morning but a roar of voices, vehicles, announcements and hectic movement prevailed. A regimental relocation, gear-laden soldiers harried by regimental sergeant majors reporting to supercilious officers.

Le Fanu knew a local police officer and a porter would meet him but was astonished to see Sir Maurice Wilson himself.

"Good morning, LF. Nice to see you. How long has it been now?"

"Sir Maurice, this is a surprise, and I'm sorry it's so late. Almost two years, I think."

"That all? Seems longer, so many things have happened."

Le Fanu agreed silently. "All well with you here in Hyderabad?"

"Oh yes. Wish I'd come when I first had the chance. Would have reduced my time with that bloody Jepson. I hear he's even worse now."

"Given my session yesterday, yes, definitely. Habi tells me there's widespread unrest."

"Thought you looked a bit pinched. Otherwise you haven't changed much. Slightly thinner perhaps, a few more flecks in the hair. Happens to all of us."

A few months earlier and those comments might have been different, thought Le Fanu. "I'm all right, thank you, Sir Maurice, and you're obviously thriving."

"Ha, thank you. Now, I've booked you a room at Percy's, one in the front so you can look over the maidan and watch the cricket as well as the army manoeuvres. Bit of that going on right now, as you see. The Bolarum golf course isn't too far away, either."

"Very thoughtful, thank you, Sir Maurice."

"Not at all, glad to see you again. Hope we can have a chat at some point about the latest Crime Unit methods. And I could still use your skills up here."

"The unit's going well, sir. Habi's doing an excellent job, as you'd expect. Happy to have a chat any time."

"Excellent. The hotel's near the hospital and the military HQ in case you need to see Mrs McPhedren's employer. I've had a new report on her. No change. That's mixed news. The doctors had hoped for improvement, but at least there's no further decline."

They followed the porter into the warm, pleasant, early morning air. The sky was clear, the moon casting enough light to reveal the station exterior, a long, low, archwayed stone building set into the landscape of the extensive plains. As they travelled in Wilson's car, Le Fanu saw stars crowding the night sky. No wonder India had a long astronomical history. Almost twenty years earlier, the Nizamia Observatory was set up here, one of the world's best. That sky provided a benign welcome to a difficult visit, he thought.

Percy's was once the Deccan Hotel but Percival Parsons and wife Ethel now ran the twin cities' most popular establishment, thus the name. Le Fanu had heard the hotel's dance hall was popular, and that a cinema had opened next door. There was another change badly handled. The British distrusted this new entertainment form deeply. While Commissioner of Police, Jepson had also been the Presidency's official film censor. Now he directed the censor, and that did not bear thinking about.

It was a typical Raj hotel. Although built on just two levels it was unusually high, giving an exaggerated sense of space. The stone colonnades at the front reminded him of Fort St George's black marble extravagances.

He and Wilson passed beneath towering archways into a large reception area full of now-deserted lounge suites and casual tables. The alert clerk booked him in, his bags were sent up, Wilson arranged to pick him up in the morning and Le Fanu climbed the stairs to his room.

It was spacious and, as promised, looked over the maidan that Le Fanu could make out in the low light. There was a writing table, large wardrobe, comfortable looking bed, and attached bathroom where he immediately ran a bath to ease the stiffness accumulated in just a day. He been back less than two days yet so much had happened and little of it comforting.

He was not ready for the important decisions he might soon have to make. Jepson's outburst was his most unsettling professional moment ever, and Ro's illness rattled his confidence in the new relationship with Jenlin. Returning to India had been confronting. Expecting to be in Madras, he was now in a city he had found exotically confusing on one pre-war trip. Then there was the new Muslim political edge. And he was yet to have a decent meeting with his two strongest supporters, Habi and Caldicott. They deserved better. Because of him, Jepson was threatening both their careers. There was that problem again, Jepson.

Once in bed he couldn't sleep. He poured a Glenmorangie but it did not help. *Hindutva* was hard going but he got Savarkar's message. A Hindu-focused state would eliminate regional and cultural differences to unite India. Le Fanu disagreed. For one thing, the south would never fully understand or tolerate the north, while divisions inside the south were powerful. India's many major languages alone demonstrated the difficulty of creating national unity. And that was all before the Muslim role was considered.

Even the British were disunited, Le Fanu thought. The south was considered 'benighted' by the establishments in Delhi and elsewhere. People like Whitney rarely reached senior all-India positions because northern bosses thought they lacked skills and brains.

He did not have that problem, at least. No one in Delhi wanted him.

Six

The next morning broke clear and warm. Military drills and morning equestrian activity on the maidan provided colour and movement. The Secunderabad Hunt Club was out, another British oddity installed in the mistaken view it would civilise the locals. A steady line of cars, trucks, pedestrians, animals and bicycles paraded past the hotel. Most of Secunderabad's population served British India army units, so that line was making mainly for the barracks. It was more Aldershot or Woolwich than Indian city.

He breakfasted beneath courtyard trees, the odd grey squirrel scurrying after crumbs. Similarly solitary figures occupied the other tables, many reading old editions of *The Times.* Standard English food: porridge, bacon, eggs, even kipper. That last was surely not the genuine article. Le Fanu took toast and south Indian coffee, impatient to reach the hospital while avoiding the stodge.

Wilson arrived, and his driver then took them off through commercial thoroughfares whose shops were yet to open. Again, more like an English county town with neat standard shops, ordered streets and little traffic.

"Curious, isn't it?" Sir Maurice was taking it all in. "We deal with India by impossibly trying to make it more like England."

"I haven't heard you talk like that before, Sir Maurice."

"Maurice, please, Chris. This place makes it more obvious than Madras. There you have to deal with India, there's no escape. Most Brits up here simply stay in Secunderabad and reproduce a life they might have or wish they had at 'Home', as they insist on calling it. The really strange thing is that just a couple of miles away, Hyderabad is so much more interesting and different. I'm glad I work there and not here."

"I remember it as spectacular. Big wide streets, marvellous buildings."

"Including hospitals. I'm thinking we might shift Mrs McPhedren to the Osmania if she doesn't start improving."

"How'll that go down with the powers that be here, including the General?"

"Not sure that's relevant because the main task is to get her well. The IMS chaps are good enough, but Osmania has a strong European staff with the latest equipment and treatment. Better than here, the Nizam has more money."

"Agreed. Any more news?"

"Yes. She's still really sick but alert for the first time in days. She might not make much sense, but you'll be able to talk to her."

Le Fanu had not considered what he might say, apart from wish her well. "That's, um, that's very good."

"You've no idea, have you?" Wilson laughed. "Take my advice, talk about her health, she's not up to much else."

Embarrassed, Le Fanu nodded and looked out as the car passed under a canopied gate bearing the sign Station Hospital. Trimulgherry, one of the Empire's largest military hospitals, out in the middle of the cantonment, a huge, two level building in standard imperial design and colour.

Lieutenant Colonel Martin Statham, the chief Indian Medical Service doctor, met them at the main entrance. Technically, the IMS was no longer military establishment, but its medical staff were still ranking officers. Statham was short, slim, groomed, and to the point.

"Le Fanu, is it? I've heard about you in Madras but we've never met."

Le Fanu wondered exactly what he had heard. "Thank you for seeing me," he replied. "I know you're extremely busy."

"Yes, unfortunately we're amidst a typhoid epidemic. That's why I've been sent over from the Telugu country where I'm normally based. Need to lift standards here. Mrs McPhedren's not the only one afflicted but she's getting the best possible care. Friend of yours, I gather?"

The look was direct, eyes narrowed, mouth set. He did not approve, thought Le Fanu. And he had an attitude that matched the ego. Nothing new.

"Yes, she is. Looked after my household in Madras, then came up here to a similar post with the General."

"I see. Well, she's very sick. She was really bad initially, though has lifted a little. Nowhere near enough, however. We'd like to see improvement starting yesterday, but we're not getting it."

"Is there any assistance I might provide?" asked Wilson. "The Nizam and his Prime Minister are ready to help."

"I hardly think so," Statham fired back. "This is a British army establishment. We're on top of everything. No need for them to get involved." Imperious.

Le Fanu remembered his war days, bland assurances preceding every cock-up.

"I'm sure that's so," Wilson responded smoothly, "but if there's anything you need, please contact me."

Statham ignored the offer. "We'd better get you in to see her, then." He turned, stomped off down a long broad corridor, turned left into another, then up some stairs. He said nothing but eventually stopped at a door. "In here. No more than half an hour, she's not up to any more." He walked off.

"Pleasant chap," Wilson noted, drily.

"Indeed, the Empire's finest."

"I'll wait down with the car. Think you can find your way back?"

"Yes, of course. Thanks for all the help, Maurice."

"Not at all. Give her my best."

Wilson walked off, Le Fanu hesitated outside the door, on unsure ground.

After a minute or so he pushed open the door, entered. The curtains were drawn back slightly to admit minimal light, bed against the middle of one wall, chairs either side, a small corner cupboard complementing the bedside stand that hosted a water jug and a glass.

His eyes took a while to adjust enough to see her clearly. The sheets were drawn up to her chin. She looked tiny, eyes closed, as pale as anyone still living Le Fanu had ever seen. Given her skin was naturally olive, that was doubly worrying. The dark hair was shorter than before, lank around her face.

He stood there for about five minutes, helplessly realising just how ill she was. Her breathing was laboured, erratic.

Sensing someone present, she opened her eyes and also took several seconds to focus.

"Chris! What are you doing here?"

"Come to see you get better."

"I hadn't realised you were medically trained." It was forced, but the smile was there.

"And some things about you haven't changed."

"I thought you were in the Straits Settlements?"

"You heard that, then?" What else had she heard?

"You know how news travels."

"Well, yes. I got back day before yesterday, heard you were poorly so came up last night."

"I'm flattered." She reached for a glass. Le Fanu went to help, poured some water that she sipped.

"No need to be, you're one of my great friends."

"I see, I was wondering."

This he had dreaded. "I've been an awful correspondent but you're still a great friend, at least I hope so."

"In some ways, Chris, that's why I clammed up. I know that puzzled you. I wondered whether we really were ever more than friends, that we could be married. I was never sure what you thought."

"I had no doubts then, but the longer the silence, the more confused I became."

"So you changed your mind?"

"No. Not at the time. That is, not really."

"You sound confused."

"I am. I wasn't, but then I became confused. That was one of the reasons I went to the Straits. Escaping Jepson's return was the excuse, but I also had no idea where I stood with you."

"If so, that's my fault, but you were never that convincing." She took more water.

"Fair comment. I wish I'd expressed things more openly. It might all have been so different."

"Can you do it now?"

"Not as well as I'd like."

"So how are you? Found someone else?"

"How …"

"Oh, I'd heard and, really Chris, truly, I'm glad for you. But only if you're sure and know what you're doing."

Le Fanu did not know what to do, or say. "Ro …"

"Say nothing for a moment. It would have been nice to be together, but there was uncertainty. And honestly, I was worried about what it might all mean, especially for you in Madras."

She looked exhausted.

"Ro, you should rest."

"I will, once we're done. You've come a long way, and I'm grateful we can clear the air."

"Well, I met someone on the ship over to Penang. She's Straits Chinese and, like you, smart and beautiful."

"You're getting better at this. Well done."

That sounded genuine.

"Thank you. She's still in Penang with a business to run. I'm in Madras trying to work out what happens next, but we don't want to be apart. It'll probably be easier for me in Penang than for her in Madras, and we may even consider a third option."

"Chris, I do so hope it works out for you." She closed her eyes.

A nurse walked in, looked at him, consulted a chart, frowned, glared.

"Ro, I should go, you're tired. You need rest. I'm not sure when I have to go back, but I'll see you before I leave."

She opened her eyes, clearly in pain. "It was lovely to see you, Chris, and to talk. I'm still very fond of you, love you even, but it's better this way. Make it work."

She sank back into the pillow, lost consciousness. The nurse ordered him out.

He was both worried and relieved, navigating back through the corridor maze and avoiding streams of staff pushing trolleys. Worried because she looked so ill, relieved because she knew about and approved of his new situation. At least, he thought she did. Having botched one great relationship, he hoped desperately to make this new one work.

Seven

Wilson was waiting. "Well?"

"She's so ill, but we had a good talk. Things seem settled enough, but I'm worried about her."

"You really think it's settled, given these circumstances?"

"Well, yes." Le Fanu looked puzzled. "You think she might …"

"Christ, man, she's seriously ill, worried about what's happening. The last thing she wants is a long discussion about the meaning of life. She might be unhappy but not worrying you in case she doesn't make it."

Le Fanu slumped. Wilson was right. She had seemed certain but, instinctively, he knew she might not be. He wanted her to be certain because he wanted to move on.

"Come on," said Wilson, "let's get out of here and see if I can't persuade you to come and work with me. I'll make some inquiries at the Osmania. Not sure Statham's the one."

Le Fanu followed Wilson out. They said nothing but he thought a lot, most of it confused. He wanted Ro to be sure, but most of all wanted her well.

They left the hospital grounds and turned towards Hyderabad, away from Secunderabad.

"You know, Chris, two years here and I like it so much more than Madras. And I liked Madras well enough."

"What's the reason?" Le Fanu's question was routine rather than enthusiastic. He had little intention of coming here.

"You're going to make it hard for me, aren't you?" Wilson understood Le Fanu's mood. "Believe it or not, we're making progress here. The Nizam's a bit of a despot and doesn't like spending money, unlike most of his princely colleagues, but he builds public facilities and meets public needs better than British India simply because he can make a decision as he sees fit."

"How do the Hindus get on here?"

"There's the odd blow-up, as there is all over the country. But this family's been in power for two hundred and fifty years and done pretty well."

"Better than Ranji, then?"

"Ranji was a way better cricketer than administrator, sadly."

British India was aghast. The princely state of Nawanagar was in deep financial trouble. Prince Ranjitsinhji, its ruler, had been England's best batsman around the turn of the century and, more importantly, symbolised the idea that Britain could civilise India. Now he was just another problem.

"Swanning around Geneva at the League of Nations, isn't he?"

"Yes, with C B Fry as his secretary. Strange chap, that one. And an odd pair."

Fry had been Ranji's cricketing contemporary but now ran a controversial youth training establishment with his wife.

They entered Hyderabad, surrounded by Mughal-inspired architecture that differed vastly from that in Madras. Mosques displayed all the classical Arabian lines and styles, public buildings were stately and elegant. Roads were wider and better maintained than in Madras. Shops and offices were ordered, the masses of Mount Road in Madras at this time of the day nowhere in evidence.

"It seems deserted," said Le Fanu.

"You'll see the crowds soon enough, but town planning here is better, Patrick Geddes notwithstanding."

Geddes had reached Madras during the war to advise on urban development and town planning. The government expected him simply to praise the benefits of British rule, but he became a nuisance with his pro-Indian civic reform ideas. J C Molony, the bluff Irish Collector of Madras, had of late noted sourly that the lack of funds restricted what municipal authorities might achieve. Geddes had been ignored.

Le Fanu remembered uneasily, too, that Geddes' wife had died in Madras, of typhoid.

Wilson's office was not in the Kotwal Balda, the official police headquarters near the Nizam's residence, being an adviser to the Nizam rather than to the Chief of Police, the Kotwal-e-Balda, or to the military head. He was, however, located close by both of them, in an office near the Charminar.

On his previous trip to Hyderabad, Le Fanu had been impressed by the famous landmark that was both mosque and monument, built late in the seventeenth century. Some historians argued it commemorated the end of a severe plague epidemic. Local folklore was more romantic, claiming the Charminar stood where the then ruler first spied a beautiful Hindu woman who converted to Islam and married him. Le Fanu hoped the story was true, and that his own might be as successful.

They approached the marvellous building with its vaulted arches on four sides, three upper levels and four distinctive minarets, all constructed in elegant stone and standing against the skyline with the nearby Makkah Masjid, the other famous mosque that accommodated up to ten thousand worshippers. And they were soon in the surrounding markets, Laad bazaar with its bangle makers and Pathar Gatti's myriad of pearl dealers. The Nizam's ancestors had been passionate jewellery and pearl buyers so, now, hundreds of miles from any ocean, Hyderabad was a world-famous centre.

From there they drove through streets displaying smarter buildings than anything seen in Madras, their lower levels protected by sunshades to cool the shop interiors. Above those shades, living quarters had uniformly flat roofs that served as garden and drying areas. Here and there, restaurants served up biriyani, the distinctive Hyderabadi mixed rice and meat dish descended from Persia. Le Fanu remembered the spiced, nuanced dishes and hoped he might find time for some.

Wilson broke the silence. "Chris, do you need to shop for jewellery while you're here?"

Le Fanu had not thought about that. Of course he should. "If I had time later, that would be excellent."

"I'll arrange it."

They turned into a smaller thoroughfare lined with offices, then in through a stylish Mughal gate guarding a large compound. At the back sat a two-storey building in light coloured stone, surrounded by shade trees that reached halfway up the walls. Two other smaller buildings nearby had uniformed policemen outside cleaning their rifles, undergoing drill sessions or lazing about smoking on rattan charpoys.

Wilson and Le Fanu were saluted through the front door by two guards carrying smart new rifles, further beneficiaries of the Nizam's modernisation. At the top of the stairs Wilson turned left, then through a doorway into an office occupied by four clerks at desks. The clerks stood. Wilson steered Le Fanu through a door at the back where he immediately saw a familiar sight.

A large display case featured a sword, but was crammed with other objects as well. Wilson's famous collection of artefacts from Seringapatam, where Tipu Sultan died in 1799 and Britain took control of India. Wilson's grandfather had served there, the sword was one of Tipu's.

"The sword still has pride of place I see."

"Oh yes. Up here where Tipu's a hero, I can display it more prominently."

In Madras, the case had stood in a dark corner, sword hidden. For the British there, Tipu was a tyrant. Here, he was a Muslim freedom fighter who protected his realm and people.

"Having it must give you status."

"It does. And that allows me to collect other things I'd never have accessed otherwise." He reached into the display case, taking out a beautiful silver box, all swirling flowers and leaves, done by a repoussé craftsman. "Like this. Salar Jung the third gave it to me. He was once the Nizam's Prime Minister but more interested in collecting things. His house is an astonishing place. This was Tipu's pride and joy and in the house when I visited. Salar Jung just handed it over."

"You really do like it here."

"I do, it's civilised. And some smart people serve the Nizam. That makes the work pleasant and rewarding, like the pay."

He went to a small side table bearing plates of Hyderabadi sweets. "Coffee or tea?"

They both ordered coffee that arrived quickly, then sat across from each other.

"Chris, I'm serious. I really would like you here and, more to the point, I can use your skills. The Nizam's worried about Congress activists coming in from the Andhra country. You know all about that. You're the person to fix it."

Le Fanu was not sure he wanted to 'fix it'. The Nizam might be doing good things, but the Congress sought more Indian control over Indian affairs, and Le Fanu appreciated that sentiment. The Nizam and his fellow princes were just another set of long-term ruling elites, like the British from whose presence they had also benefited.

"Maurice, I do know a lot about what's going on in the Telugu country, although I have a few months of developments to catch up on, having been away. You know I'd work for you like a shot but I'm not sure I can be here."

"Because of Miss Koh."

"Yes, and because the Madras situation is complicated."

"Ro McPhedren has no bearing on this?"

Le Fanu felt guilty yet again. "No."

"Pity. I've met her a few times, nice person. I can see why you and she got together."

That did not improve matters.

"I'm still concerned about her, but she won't be in my life."

"And what about Miss Koh? Could you both be here? I'm assuming you're to marry?"

"That's the agreement." Le Fanu's chair now felt distinctly uncomfortable. "But no date set. She has her own property business and her father's antiques trade to look after. She travels a lot."

"She could easily pursue both here. I can connect her directly to Salar Jung. He's an inveterate buyer. And I can promise her a lot of property sales."

"Maurice, you're making it very attractive but I don't know how she'd settle in here. She's Chinese, you know."

"Easier here than in Madras. The Nizam and his people have very high opinions of their own importance, but value just about anyone who has the skills they need. We've all sorts here."

"Chinese?"

"Not sure."

"Besides that, I have to sort out my own ambitions. Yes, I'd be delighted to work for you, but how much longer will you be here? I have to think about what happens next, and where."

"You'll take over from me, obviously."

"Kind of you to say so, but I'm not sure that's what I want."

"Chris, a few years here and you'll be set financially. After that, you can do what you want."

That was a powerful attraction.

"I'll keep it in mind and discuss it with Jenlin. That's difficult, though, the mail's so slow."

"My telephone budget is large and I'm connected across the Empire. Let me know when you want to talk to her."

"I will, I will." He took a sweet, attempting to redirect the conversation.

A knock at the door produced one of Wilson's uniformed assistants. "Sir, a message for Superintendent Le Fanu, from Madras."

"What is it?" Le Fanu asked.

"Sir, a call from Assistant Superintendent Habibullah. He'd like you to telephone him back." The assistant handed over a note.

"Use my telephone immediately, Chris. I'll wait outside."

"No, please stay, Maurice, it won't be that confidential."

Wilson poured more coffee, took a sweet and went to an easy chair strewn with newspapers.

Le Fanu looked at the note, placed a call to Madras.

Habi answered immediately. "Sir, thank you for contacting me so quickly."

"Not at all, Habi. What's up?"

"Sir, some bigwig British industrialists arrive in Madras the day after tomorrow, and Mr Caldicott's Special Branch people have information about possible terrorist activity."

"Is that likely, Habi? There's been nothing like that in Madras so far."

"Correct, sir, but this information looks sound. The real problem is that the I-G's not listening to Mr Caldicott and won't even think about talking, let alone listening to me. People here are worried we won't mount a coherent response. There are some big names on the visiting list, and they're attracting leading business people from across the Presidency and elsewhere in India."

"You want me back, Habi? Will The Jockey listen to me any more than he does to the two of you?"

"Sir, he knows the Governor and the Chief Secretary back you. Given that support, he must listen to you. He's no choice, even though he wants rid of you. You're our only hope."

Le Fanu paused, wondering how he might evade it.

Habi sensed the hesitation.

"Sir ... I know it's a big request. Have you seen Mrs McPhedren? How is she?"

"Yes, Habi, I have. She's very ill so will be in hospital a while yet. I'd hoped to see her again before leaving, but let me check and I'll let you know what's possible."

"Sir, there's a train for Madras leaving Secunderabad tonight at ten, reaches here tomorrow at lunchtime. First class bookings are available."

Eight

His mind was mush by the time the train reached Madras punctually the following day.

He had spent the rest of the previous day with Wilson, who outlined the work and Le Fanu's role should he join the Nizam's staff. It was tempting, the pay twice that of the Indian Police Service, plus additional incentives like free housing. If he did five years he could afford a career change. But would Jenlin be there in Hyderabad for those five years? If not, the offer was worthless.

He then returned to Percy's for dinner, packed, visited the hospital. Staff there gave him leeway outside visiting hours. He could not enter the room, but watched her through a window. Still asleep, or unconscious, the nurses would not say which, she looked terrible.

After fifteen minutes, he wrote a note for her, left it with the nurses, returned to the hotel, then went to the station.

During the journey he slept fitfully, tried to read but failed, spent most of the time staring out into the dark. They soon reached the vast rice fields of the Andhra coast that brought landowners wealth and peasant workers a livelihood. The Indian National Congress was entrenched here, as much among landholders as their Gandhi-following labourers. Most owners, he thought, valued promised tax reductions more than independence.

Was he becoming as cynical as his European colleagues?

As the train neared Madras, Le Fanu felt exhausted but still had no solutions for his problems. He wearily surveyed the mix of shanty town roofs, permanent suburban dwellings, commercial houses, and the imposing buildings that proclaimed British power.

The splendidly ornate, shining white Victorian Ripon Building near the railway station was typical. It housed the Madras Corporation that now directed improvements to the city's local government, Molony's impoverished municipality. Described as neoclassical, the building's mixed Gothic and Indo-Saracenic features suggested the British could not choose between them. That definitely symbolised British rule. Open now for six years, the Ripon might just come to memorialise the end of the Empire in India and, perhaps, everywhere else.

Habi and a porter awaited. Le Fanu felt more comfortable than on his arrival at the port just, what, three days earlier? No wonder he was confused. They went out to the car, started towards headquarters, and he realised he had still not seen his office.

"How was the trip, sir?"

"Habi, I don't know how to answer that. I'm not sure where I am, except you're here so it must be Madras."

"Glad to be of reassurance, sir."

"What's the latest?"

"Not much. Assistant Superintendent Caldicott has Special Branch working day and night. They've fragments of information but little more. He'll brief you at headquarters."

It was warm and dusty now in the early afternoon with traffic its usual jumble of ox carts, pony drays, stray animals, bicycles, pedestrians, trucks, cars and buses. The city's roads, all three hundred miles of them, were crumbling under the pressure, and he now saw an even bigger contrast to Hyderabad. The Corporation, in its new building, was struggling already, a classic version of the gap between illusion and reality.

"Sir, have you eaten?"

Le Fanu was hungry. "Actually, no. I had something at the Bezwada station a few hours ago."

Habi diverted the car into a street near the Madras Club, disappeared into a small restaurant, then emerged with several containers. "Sorry, sir, no time to stop but I've bought lunch so we can eat back at headquarters. I need to get you there quickly."

The driver stop-started amidst the Greams Road traffic, then through smaller streets, before turning left onto Edward Elliots Road, towards the beach and the gleaming white building. Habi began striding upstairs as soon as the car stopped.

"We'll eat in my office, sir, and I'll get Assistant Superintendent Caldicott along."

They were soon eating vegetarian and goat curries and rice with their fingers, mopping up with roti. They finished, washed their hands and sat down to tea brought in by Habi's clerks.

"Thanks, Habi, I needed that."

"Sir, did you have some of that excellent Hyderabadi biriyani?"

"Afraid not, you dragged me back before I had a chance."

"Sorry, LF." Caldicott, out of uniform, was wearing a cream linen suit offset by a lemon shirt and dark tie. How did he look so relaxed and neat in this climate, and how was the linen not crushed? "We had to get you here quickly because Jepson's causing big problems."

"What do we know?"

Habi began. "You know the basics. A large delegation of important business and commerce people is here. Somewhere along the line, we learned our visitors might be terrorist targets."

"Where did the whispers come from?"

Caldicott lifted a file. "A couple of my plain clothes officers in George Town. First, they heard some suspicious looking individuals from the north had arrived. Then that an attack was planned."

"Where specifically did they hear this?"

"In a small restaurant near Elephant Gate, where the city's incomer communities gather."

"Sir," said Habi, "that's supported by news I'm hearing from Muslim communities. In particular, some Urdu-speaking Muslims heard that northerners had arrived here and were planning trouble."

"What have we heard from Delhi?"

"Nothing concrete," replied Caldicott. "My bosses there have passed on routine reports about troublemakers moving around the country. A couple of Punjabi and Bengali groups have been in and around Delhi, but nothing they have yet identifies Madras as a target."

"Any particulars?"

"Well," replied Caldicott, "you know the Bengali story from reports over the years. We missed all the wartime stuff that led to the Defence of India Act, then the Rowlatt Acts. The Bengali revolutionary groups challenged the legislation, so the inestimable Charles Tegart, as intelligence boss, charged into them head on."

"Hasn't he just become Commissioner up there?"

"Yes, still driving around with his Staffordshire bull terrier on the front of his car. No wonder someone took a potshot at him."

"I can never decide if he's a good thing or not."

"Much loved in Delhi, I can report."

"Hmm. What about specifics?"

"Sir," said Habi, "basic reports only, nothing detailed. The Anushilam Samiti organisation is still active among Bengali Hindus. Several of their members are now in the Congress, pushing direct action against the Raj. People like Subhas Chandra Bose of the youth wing are in that group."

"Didn't he qualify for the ICS?"

"Yes, sir, bright boy. Studied at Cambridge, finished fourth in his year in the ICS examination but turned down the job and came back to Calcutta to work against us."

"That's what we're up against, LF." Caldicott searched through some files, found one. "We have examples like that here in the south. We're losing support among people who would once have joined the administration. Now they're going to the Congress."

"And it's not only Hindus, sir," said Habi. "You know some Muslims lined up with the Ottomans and Germans, and even the Afghans against Britain here during the war. Tehreek-e-Reshmi Rumal is still active, mainly up north, but I've heard some Muslims here support its ideas."

"But we've found nothing definite yet? No arms dumps, no pamphlets?"

"No, LF, we haven't. But you can imagine the hysteria in the I-G's office. He wants to call out the armed police and the army to conduct house-to-house searches across the city, even though we've no addresses or names. So we needed you back here to modify advice going to the Governor."

"Willingdon needs no advice from me about The Jockey."

"Agreed, but several senior ICS people support Jepson. Your advice will counteract that."

"Fair enough. I'll see Whitney later."

"Sir," said Habi, "we must move quickly. A friend tells me senior military officers support the I-G's ideas about tough action. If we're not careful we'll have raids all over the city. That'll mean demonstrations in response. If revolutionaries are here, they'll exploit that and create serious problems. And we know what The Jockey's like under those conditions."

Habi was referencing Jepson's infamous handling of the Congress beach demonstration near headquarters a couple of years earlier. He'd panicked. Several demonstrators died when he ordered police to fire. That and his subsequent promotion alienated prominent Hindus and Muslims.

"Indeed we do, Habi. I'll talk to Whitney and discuss it with the Governor as well, if I get a chance. I'd be surprised if they're not on alert already. I'll call them. Not that I know where my office is, it occurs to me." He had occupied the I-G's office before going to Penang and now had no idea where his place was.

Habi and Caldicott looked at each other.

Caldicott spoke. "LF, we need to talk to you about that."

"You won't like it, sir. We're sorry."

"What are you talking about?"

The other two looked at each other again and signalled for Le Fanu to follow them.

They left Habi's second floor office, followed the corridor towards the rear of the original building, then across the connecting passageway to the annex. Habi descended the stairs then turned left into a narrow passageway strewn with boxes, broken chairs, the odd bookcase and even an old bicycle. Caldicott walked towards the dead end, took a key from his pocket and opened a door.

The door could not open completely because the space was more cupboard than room. There was no window. A desk was jammed against the side wall, too wide to fit in the room crosswise. It was further hemmed in by a chair, a battered filing cabinet and a small bookcase overflowing with volumes and reports. Le Fanu recognised his copy of Hans Gross's *Criminal Investigation,* the book that inspired Sir Maurice Wilson's Crime Unit.

"What's this, then?"

"LF, sorry, but it's your office. The Jockey arranged it specifically. We've cleaned it up as best we can, but this is where he wants you."

The man had organised the most humiliating arrangement possible. Le Fanu was almost impressed by the ingenuity. He was transferred from the building's most prestigious room to one beneath the dignity of the newest probationary constable.

"No staff, then?"

"Sorry, sir, The Jockey made that clear. He's making an example of you. We challenged him but ..."

Le Fanu did not doubt that. "Habi, Caldicott, thanks for trying, but don't do anything more on my behalf. He's looking for an excuse to punish you. I expected a slight, but I wouldn't have predicted this. Jepson's given it a lot of thought."

He looked around. That took no time. "Don't think I'll even bother with a picture because I doubt I'll spend much time here. Whitney'll fix me something. Meanwhile, we'll meet in your offices or back at my place in Mylapore, or somewhere in town."

"Chris, we're really sorry." Caldicott flapped his arms. "But it shows you his priorities. He spends most of his time plotting against you, and what little is left he uses to dream up attacks on these terrorists he's obsessed with. He's dangerous."

"I can see that, so we three must keep in close touch. Though I see there's not even a telephone. Typical, eh? I just get used to using the thing then it's taken away."

He closed the door, locked it and pocketed the key. "I might contrive to lose that and give him a requisition for another one."

They walked back along the passageway, squeezing past the boxes – and the bicycle that Le Fanu now noticed had flat tyres.

Nine

As soon as he reached Mylapore, Le Fanu called Whitney. "Charles, I'm back in Madras and have spoken with Habi and Caldicott. If you like, I can see you immediately."

"I'm very glad to hear that, Chris. I'll be in the office for some time so come on over."

Le Fanu ate a quick meal, drank a couple of strong coffees then had his driver make for Fort St George.

Sitting in the back of the car that hurried through now deserted suburban streets, he wondered how the Raj contrived to promote people like Jepson at a time when patience, diplomacy, understanding and skill were needed to handle the escalating Indian political sentiment. People now no longer simply accepted everything dictated to them by British rulers. Questions were asked, sensible answers demanded. Jepsonian crassness might have been acceptable once, barely. Now, it was a dangerous liability.

And that risk was both personal and professional. Jepson's hysterical attack suggested some mental problem, and the Raj handled such things poorly. Alcoholics and the troubled were sometimes bundled off back Home, given little or no treatment and left to sort themselves out. All too often, however, they were left in post to wreak havoc on those around them. That was effectively how Jepson was being handled, threatening Le Fanu's immediate Indian future at a point when he was already considering his options. It also threatened the Raj's reputation in the south.

It was not the first time Le Fanu was stretched between protecting his own best interests and remaining loyal to the system. British rule in India was flawed, yes, but his duty was to do everything possible to prevent Jepson from causing chaos.

A couple of clerks and a junior ICS man were hovering near Whitney's office, but the building was otherwise deserted. Order must prevail. Most Europeans would be dining at home in full formal dress, observing the niceties. It was a wonder anything ever got done.

Evidently, the Chief Secretary's day had been long. The windows were open but eau de cigar and smoke filled the office, the man himself scarcely visible through the haze, hunched over a file of papers, whisky at hand beside an ashtray that had long ago given up trying. Butts and ash spilled into an ever-widening ring that Whitney tried now to sweep aside with his sleeve.

"Not one of the great days, Chris." He rose, extended one hand in greeting, pouring whisky into a spare glass with the other. "*Sláinte*."

Le Fanu raised his glass. "How bad is it, Charles?"

"As bad as anything I've ever fucking experienced here, and that includes the height of Gandhi's campaign."

The obscenity reverberated off the walls. Le Fanu had never, ever heard the urbane Chief Secretary swear.

"I see."

"I doubt you do, fully. Jepson's given us what is now an officially serious problem. An hour ago he had some lackey inform the head of this business delegation that the entire group was in grave danger of being killed. You can imagine how fast that reached Willingdon's ears, and how soon he called me demanding Jepson's arse on a plate."

"Bit late for that."

"Agreed, and we all know why. Chain of command. Again. Even Willingdon couldn't get the heaven-born in Delhi to see sense and dump the fool."

"Where is our police force star at present?"

"Gone home, I gather. Had a hard day, he said to one of his people; needed a rest. Been in for all of five hours. During which he's caused total uproar."

"If he's asleep, at least that gives us a chance to catch up."

"Ha, optimistic as ever. I'm just not sure exactly which bit of the mess we might catch up on."

Whitney lit another cigar and refilled the glasses.

"Charles, what's the situation now?"

"The business delegation is holed up at the Connemara and afraid to leave. Willingdon's given the management there strict instructions to serve up whatever the scared visitors might demand, at government cost. Their appointments for the next two days have been cancelled."

"That's going to upset our own box wallahs who'll be sniffing money."

"Already has, but can't be helped. Jepson's put the fear of God into these people, bloody idiot. At least the business house heads also want him out now." He sipped at the whisky.

"We have guards at the hotel?"

"Yes. Police posted there and around the immediate perimeter, armed constables and four European supervisors. An infantry company from St Thomas Mount is covering the wider grounds with road blocks set up two streets away in all directions."

"You mean Mount Road's blocked off?"

"Yes, inevitably."

The prestigious Connemara Hotel fronted onto the city's most prestigious road, surrounded by the leading retail and commercial houses.

"I guess we had no choice," Le Fanu said, "but that's a very big signal to the city that we have an equally big problem."

"Perceptive. Jepson's really buggered this up. Any thoughts?"

"We're stuck with the police and military arrangements. But what's Jepson doing about the apparent threat itself? I haven't seen the latest intelligence assessment."

"You know what Jepson's done. Nothing. Apart from cause panic."

"What's your present assessment of this alleged threat?"

"Fair question." Whitney pulled a couple of ash-marked pages from a pile of papers. "In all honesty, we've nothing solid. There could be up to half a dozen visitors, maybe more. Possibly Bengalis, come to cause trouble. Jepson immediately concluded the businessmen were their targets."

"Because they were the most obvious ones."

"Of course. He's neither subtle nor thoughtful."

"You've some other ideas?"

"None you wouldn't immediately offer up. We've a couple of Congress hardliners here in Madras, but it's unlikely they'll resort to armed violence. Some of our criminal gangs might have hired in outside assistance to help settle scores. There are a few Hindu zealots with outlandish ideas but, again, I don't see armed action being likely."

"Habi tells me some Muslim groups are more than normally anxious."

"True, but that's being expressed mostly through normal political channels. We don't have a history of armed protest down here, you know that."

"Apart from Ashe."

"Well, yes."

ICS officer Robert Ashe, as Acting Collector of Tinnevelly district in the far south of the Presidency, had been assassinated in 1911, his killer belonging to a secret society that pledged armed action against Europeans and with connections into Bengali activist circles. The death sharpened local European sentiment against nationalist developments, and was wheeled out frequently as evidence of what would happen if British rule became too liberal.

"Come to think of it," Whitney continued, "I hear Jepson mentioned Ashe a couple of times."

"Typical, and seriously unhelpful."

"Bombast and bluster against rationale and reason, as always."

"So there's no reliable evidence this is a genuine armed threat posed by outsiders?

"None I've seen."

"Then the best thing now is for me to talk with Caldicott. May I use your telephone?"

A few minutes later Le Fanu was en route to a secure intelligence service office buried away in a nondescript George Town building a couple of streets back from First Line Beach. Caldicott had set it up as soon as he took over the service, and it was now an obvious place for them to meet. The broom cupboard back at headquarters would not do and, besides, Jepson had supporters there.

Le Fanu walked up some rickety stairs, knocked at an

unmarked door and was shown in by a plain clothes officer who led him to another office.

"Good evening, LF." As always, Caldicott looked unnaturally immaculate and, at this time of night, alert.

"You look on top of things, Jackson. Whitney will be pleased. He's pessimistic about the situation."

"Understandably. Jepson has set off a stampede."

"Any justification for that?"

"Not to this degree, no, but odd things are going on."

"Like what?"

"We've had several unusual people reach Madras from different northern centres over the past ten days or so. One or two are from Calcutta and have had tenuous links with the more radical groups up there over the past five years. Then there are a couple of Delhi people, and a handful from Bombay. That's without three or four more from an extremist outfit based in one of the smaller Rajput princely states."

"That's clearly suspicious."

"Definitely, but it's not clear that this business delegation is the target. If anything, Jepson's actions have tipped off these newcomers so we've had a tough time tracking them over the past twenty-four hours. They're all over the city and don't meet as a group, more like a collection of cells."

"What do you think?"

"You want coffee? Food?"

"Coffee yes, food no, thanks."

Caldicott had a servant go off to make coffee, then extracted some files from a drawer.

"I doubt the businessmen are the target. There may be *no* specific target. The visitors might've come simply to escape the limelight for a while. Which they'd have done but for our fabulous I-G."

"There are some prominent figures in that business delegation."

"Agreed, but only in the business sense. Our visitors are strictly political. Everything they've signalled recently has concerned political reform or the lack thereof. They hate Gandhi's passive resistance, want more direct action. If they're here to cause trouble, it'll most likely be political. I've already upped security around Willingdon. He knows about all this but no one else senior does."

"Excellent. Any other obvious targets?"

"I've got people watching Whitney, the First Member of the Board of Revenue, the Governor's family and private staff. And some poor sod is trying to look after Jepson."

"Who's that?"

"A good man I've promised to look after in return for this persecution."

"Is The Jockey really a likely target?"

"Could be. They shot at Tegart up in Calcutta, after all, and The Jockey's prominent here, makes himself obvious. He's a *large* target in all senses of the word."

They exchanged grim smiles.

"What else do you know about these agitators?"

"We've some background on a couple of them, and it's not great reading. There's a definite link into extremist outfits like the Ghadar movement to add an international tinge."

The Ghadar movement arose among Sikhs to support nationalism with an extremist edge and a reach into Europe, Canada and the United States. Its emergence had prompted the establishment of formal intelligence organisations in India alongside what were now MI5 and MI6.

"That all?"

Caldicott hesitated, shuffled some papers.

"I've been waiting to raise this. You'll have sensed tension between Habi and me?"

Le Fanu nodded and drank some coffee the servant had brought in.

"There's a growing Hindu–Muslim divide here in the south. Habi sees it from his perspective, but I've reports that Muslim hardliners are gaining traction, notably among Urdu speakers linked to the north. They're reacting and/or responding to developments like Ghadar, and to mounting Hindu nationalist pressures driven by people like Savarkar."

"I was reading his thoughts on the train. Should we worry about that down here?"

"He's gaining support among conservative Hindu hierarchies here, especially in places like Madurai and Tanjore with their major national shrines and the myriad of pilgrims from the north."

"Any evidence of local action on this front?"

"Not yet, but a couple of our targets have visited the big temples in both those places and in Mylapore. They're being tailed currently."

"And The Jockey knows none of this?"

"Of course not. That would involve listening and reading. He can only handle one thing at a time, like voicing ideas uninformed by anything I've just outlined."

"Thoughts on what we do now?"

"If you could get to Willingdon, that'd help. If he shouted sense into The Jockey, that would be marvellous. Ideally, if Willingdon empowered you we'd be far better positioned."

"Thanks for the vote of confidence."

"My pleasure, LF. Could you get something done tonight? We've lost a lot of time and potential information thanks to Jepson, and I don't want these suspects disappearing into the woodwork. They're potentially dangerous."

Le Fanu telephoned Whitney again, and he agreed to call the Governor. A few minutes later the Chief Secretary called back. They would meet at the Governor's mansion in an hour.

"Excellent, LF," said Caldicott. "Thanks for that. Now tell me, how's Mrs McPhedren, and what are you doing about all that?"

"You mean this evening's not complicated enough?"

Caldicott shook his head. "Hopeless. You must know one of Habi's relatives reported all your activities back from Penang? And I mean *all* activities."

"I, um … well, guessed that might be the case."

"So yes, we know about the delightful Miss Koh."

But did they know about the job?

"Well, Ro's extremely ill and I should return there as soon as possible. And Miss Koh, Jenlin, and I do have plans, but for the present I'm here and she's there."

"And you have to work out what to do. Habi and I both know what that means. Just so you know, you can talk to us if it would help."

"I appreciate that, and I will. But can we just focus on this mess The Jockey's created?"

Ten

By now the city lay in darkness, people and animals alike huddled by the roadsides. The car lights picked out lean-to shanties backed up against walls, trees and anything else that provided support. Le Fanu wondered how his Raj colleagues could experience this day after day and still believe nothing needed to change in India. There were perhaps two hundred slums in Madras now. Gandhi and the nationalists wanted to improve life for ordinary people, the same objective those British officials spouted endlessly. Agreed on the goal, the warring parties differed only on how best to get there. The British plumped for more of the same, even though past failed policies had caused the present problems. The nationalists' solution began with the need to run their own affairs. But democracy in India, with its myriad of languages, cultures and histories, would be a complicated beast.

The driver crossed Napier Bridge, named for a mid-nineteenth-century governor, then turned right to follow the Cooum River. Across on the other bank, the Gymkhana Club, with its golf course, was a constant reminder of Le Fanu's difficult place here. He loved the game but felt awkward at the Gymkhana and even more so at the elitist Madras Club. The Cosmopolitan was supposed to help bridge the East-West social divide but, these days, he seemed to be the only European member. London's push towards political reform had driven even moderately minded Europeans into defensive positions. The elite clubs now provided a greater haven than ever.

As they turned into Government Estate that contained the Governor's mansion, the Banqueting Hall and other administrative buildings, Le Fanu thought it ironic that Lord Willingdon, the principal Raj representative here, was probably the most liberal senior official, excepting the ever-intriguing Whitney. Willingdon was a career imperial servant who had seen much change and knew something must shift in India but commanded little support, hence the widespread joy at his imminent departure.

Two liveried servants waited at the grand entrance to a residence designed to cow locals, and led Le Fanu into a waiting room where they plied him with more coffee, but he refused the sweets. The room was another exercise in imperial superiority. Paintings and photographs of every British governor over four hundred years lined the walls. Some were illustrious, others less so. The second Lord Clive, son of Clive of India, began both life and career here. Grant Duff's 1880s marital disasters caused a huge scandal. Willingdon would rank among the most able, despite his wife's eccentricities. At least Willingdon had a wife.

Le Fanu's musings were interrupted by Whitney who hurried in, trailed by the ever-present smoke. "Thanks for arranging this, Charles."

"Oh, don't worry, HE is keen to talk to you." Another piece of colonial shorthand: HE for 'His Excellency'.

A servant announced the Governor was ready, spun immediately about and sped off up a corridor, around a corner, through several doors then ascended a staircase to arrive at a grand set of doors guarded by yet another servant who bowed then admitted them.

Willingdon was all smiles, spare and angular, long face dominated by the big moustache and impressive brows over eyes that always seemed half hooded. He advanced, hand thrust out. “Chris, delighted to see you. Sorry you’ve been foisted into this so quickly. Especially when you’ve personal things that need attention. I appreciate your help.”

Did anyone not know about his affairs, Le Fanu wondered.

“Thank you, sir, always happy to assist. And this is a special matter.”

“It is that. Now, I’m having a drink. Join me?”

He poured large measures of Glenmorangie into three crystal tumblers. Whitney offered cigars that the Governor accepted but Le Fanu did not.

“Now, LF. How much do you know?”

“He’s spoken with me, sir,” Whitney cut in, “and, since then, with Caldicott, so he probably knows more than we do presently.”

“As it should be, Charles.” Willingdon took in a large breath of smoke.

“Sir,” Le Fanu said, “Caldicott confirms there are suspicious northerners in the city. Some are from Bombay, others from Calcutta and Delhi, with a few from the Rajput states. But Caldicott’s far less convinced than the I-G about who or what might be the target.”

“Jepson’s not an I-G’s arse!” Willingdon half choked on the smoke. “Sorry about that, but the man’s impossible.”

Le Fanu managed a straight face.

Whitney took a second or so to comment. “Sir, we know the problem. Given that LF’s back, why not second him to your staff, as your personal law and order advisor, possibly? That way you’ll get accurate information and be able to issue sensible instructions to The Jockey. That'll hamstring him." Another perfect smoke ring floated serenely upwards.

Willingdon began laughing. "You're a devious bastard, Charles, and I'm really glad you're *my* devious bastard. Brilliant. I'll sign an executive order immediately. A courier can take a copy to Jepson first thing. That'll be a terrific start to his day. Why does he hate you so much, LF?"

"You know some of the story, sir. He hates change, ignores popular opinion, loves power, despises delegation. I questioned his decisions a couple of times, was present at the beach tragedy, and he sees me as a nuisance. More recently, it's become far more personal."

Hesitantly, he recounted his most recent experience. "Sir, he has a psychological condition, and that should be dealt with officially. His behaviour's irrational, at least towards me."

"God," said Willingdon, "Delhi'll love that. There'll be an entire flock of ostriches strewn across Lutyens' new lands. I'll keep it in mind, but I'm more concerned about what we do here immediately."

"Charles has made good provisions already so we don't need to do anything more tonight. Caldicott'll have his people keep close watch, but I suggest we immediately mollify the business tycoons and get them on a full programme first thing in the morning. That'll keep them happy but also calm our suspects. If they go to ground now, we're in strife."

"Good advice, LF. Charles, can you both go to the Connemara first thing, reassure that lot back onto their original itinerary. Tomorrow afternoon they're to tour the Buckingham Mills. Make sure that happens. Get onto the management there, too, smooth out any concerns."

"Certainly. And The Jockey?"

"Leave him to me. I'll enjoy that after all the bloody trouble he's caused."

"Sir," added Le Fanu, "he has a few senior officials on his side. You probably know that, but it's worth keeping in mind."

"You mean like Jamieson?"

"Yes, and others. They fear making political concessions to Indians so are digging in. I'm not sure how deep they've gone yet, but my friend Barnes at the *Mail* will know."

"You do have odd friends, Chris."

"Thank you, sir. They come in handy."

"They most certainly do."

"Besides, Chester's no mad reactionary. He writes reason for his readers."

"I know, and I'm grateful. Tell him so, if you like. But what's your thinking on the Muslim angle? I speak with some of their leaders who seem confused."

"I've no direct evidence yet, sir, but Habi tells me there's a worry. He and Caldicott are at odds on the matter, so something's brewing. Some Muslim leaders doubt Congress's long-term intentions, and are bothered by government's lack of focus on their concerns. You talking with the leaders will help. Might not change the bigger picture, though."

Whitney intervened. "I should also say that privileging the non-Brahmins sent shock waves through Muslim circles. They think they're missing out. It seemed smart to bash the Mylapore Brahmins, but some of us thought the ramifications weren't calculated deeply enough."

Willingdon nodded. "The Muslims here have always been divided, though. Any signs they're teaming up more effectively?"

"Not yet," Whitney replied, "but we should encourage them to do so."

"I'll have my people set up meetings," the Governor replied. "So we've got a plan and some things to do. I'll drink to that."

They toasted each other.

"Tell me, Chris, how's Mrs McPhedren? On the mend, I hope."

Le Fanu could not read the tone. "She's extremely ill, I'm afraid. Sir Maurice Wilson is up there, as you know, and he's ensuring she has the best possible care. But she's not in a good way."

"I'm most sorry to hear that. If I can help exert influence anywhere, just ask. I mean that, sincerely."

"Thank you, sir, I will."

It was late. The conversation stumbled. They finished their drinks, and Le Fanu and Whitney stood to leave.

"LF," said Willingdon, "great that you're here, we need you. Don't worry about The Jockey, but do worry about Mrs McPhedren. If you need to get to Secunderabad in a hurry, please let me know and I'll make all arrangements."

"Thank you, sir, I'll update you tomorrow once we've calmed the delegation."

He and Whitney made their goodbyes and were shown back to the entrance by the servants. The drivers awaited.

"Chris, may I add my thanks? If you weren't here, we'd be in serious trouble. Caldicott and Habi are very good, but Willingdon's better able to work with you to sort this mess."

"How long have you been working on that secondment idea? Genius, Charles. Willingdon gets decent advice but belts Jepson's incompetence at the same time." He thought of Caldicott's request, hadn't even needed to ask.

"Sad thing is The Jockey might not even notice. But thank you. I've had it in mind for a couple of days but didn't want to say anything in case it fell through."

"Well played. I'd better get some sleep. Still not entirely sure where I am."

"Fair enough. Good night, then. Get to my office early and we can plan the Connemara meeting."

Le Fanu drowsed in the back of the car as they sped home through the back streets. He was not sure whether he was dreaming or recalling scraps of the conversation with Whitney and Willingdon as they rolled along, headlights again revealing sleeping figures laid out on charpoys or simply on mats spread on the ground. Was he noticing this more now? And if so, was that a change in attitude towards his work, his life even? Small temples flashed by, crammed in among shops, offices and the palatial houses of the better-off residents in this changing neighbourhood.

By the time they swung into the driveway, Le Fanu was ready to fall into bed for at least a brief sleep before meeting Whitney back at Fort St George. The car lights illuminated the gardens as the driver navigated the circle in front of the entrance, then picked out a figure sitting in a planter chair on the veranda, glass in hand. Jackson Caldicott.

Eleven

"Sorry, LF, you're probably exhausted." Caldicott looked apologetic but worried.

"Yes, but you're not here on a whim. How bad is it?" Le Fanu squeezed a hand over tired eyes.

"About eight out of ten. Habi might be right. My people have discovered potential links between his Muslim murders and our raiders from the north."

"Have you told him?"

"Not yet. Only found out myself half an hour ago and thought you needed to know. I didn't want to disturb Habi so late, and I'll see him early tomorrow anyway."

"Are you two all right? You're not as close as when I left."

"Oh, I *think* we're fine, we just disagree on a couple of things. I think he's overplaying the Muslim discontent."

"Habi's no one-eyed Muslim."

"And he's a friend as well as a colleague, but I think he's wrong on this."

"Except there's now a suggestion he might be at least partly right."

"There is that."

Out came more coffee and snacks. Both took some of each, and the momentary silence was pierced by a barked screech from a nearby tree.

"What was that?" asked Caldicott.

"A hungry short-eared owl. Haven't heard it for a while, obviously. Glad it's still here. We've had a breeding pair in the trees for a few years now."

"Very rural."

"The city's changing, Jackson, and not for the better. But if the birds remain, there's still hope."

"If you say so." He looked doubtful.

"So what are these links your smart people have discovered?"

"Probable rather than definite, so far, but significant. Thanks to a friendly boarding house desk manager, we retrieved a list of names and addresses that just happens to include the Muslim man murdered here in the city."

"Who was he? I haven't got those details."

Basic. Not having that information suggested he was not on top of this.

"Mohammad Reiza Khan, an Urdu-speaker and prominent grain merchant who's traded across India, especially around Delhi and through the United Provinces. A leading official at the Hafiz Ahmad Khan Mosque in Chepauk, as well. And he was big in the Muslim League branch here."

"That last point alone makes this look like a strong connection."

"That's why we're looking deeper. He's the only victim on the list so far, but his presence looks more than a coincidence."

"Any obvious reason he was on that list?"

"We're thinking it was created by a known Hindu nationalist amongst our visitors, and now treating this murder as a possible communal campaign. Hindu organisations here weren't bothered by the Muslims' pro-

Turkish moves, but those up north were. They might have targeted Mohammad Reiza Khan because he was on the League committee here that mainly supported Turkey."

"Meaning these visitors might have killed him, or were beaten to it by someone else."

"Technically correct, Chris, because we don't yet know when that list was created. And I haven't checked Mohammad Reiza Khan's time of death with Habi. It's not my case so …"

"Oh, understood. Habi will have that detail, but it won't tell us when the list was created. We should find and interview these visitors."

"Slight problem, LF. They've moved from their original accommodation. They're either routinely cautious, which makes them serious players, or they've worked out they're under surveillance. We're trying to find them now."

Le Fanu fell back in his chair, drained.

The owl squawked again.

Caldicott looked into the trees. "Persistent."

"Stalking her quarry. Hope we're as successful."

"Rough return to Madras for you. How're you coping?"

"Tired, and confused."

"You never did deal well with personal and professional issues at the same time."

"So everyone keeps telling me."

"Sorry."

"Didn't mean to sound sharp."

"Didn't take it that way."

Another short silence.

"What now?" asked Le Fanu.

"Sleep for you. I'll get back to the office and see if there's anything new."

“Let me know first thing in the morning so I can inform Whitney and Willingdon.”

“Of course, and I’ll check with Habi.”

“Terrific. Thanks for coming around. I appreciate it. My driver’ll take you back.”

Caldicott went off to the car but Le Fanu remained on the veranda, sleep beyond him. The t–Muslim conflict was worrying, especially here in the south where it was unusual. If these newcomers were trying to upset the natural balance, that had to be premeditated.

Habi was as much friend as colleague, so Le Fanu did not want him upset but, more broadly, Le Fanu admired the Muslims. His wartime Mesopotamian command included both communities, and he respected them all as soldiers and people. He worked hard, with opposition from senior officers, to ensure that all were treated equally and with respect, and that the communities dealt with each other similarly. That worked, mostly. Given present political difficulties, poisonous communal relations would be disastrous. Raj policies did not help, drift reigning rather than purpose.

Next morning, he could not remember going to bed but knew he’d not been there long. Breakfast and coffee helped marginally, and he snoozed en route to headquarters. He hurried towards Habi’s office to avoid meeting people, especially Jepson, even though he was unlikely to be in by seven.

Habi looked like he had not slept either. “Good morning, sir.” More subdued than normal.

“And to you, Habi. I’m really sorry we haven’t had the chance for a long chat.”

“No matter, sir. How’s Mrs McPhedren?”

"No reports today yet, but I'm hoping for good or at least not terrible news."

"Worrying illness, sir. My friends tell me there's a lot of it around Madras now."

"Your family's not affected, I hope?"

"Oh no, sir. All fine. I can focus fully on my work." Was that a rebuke?

"Habi, I know you're concerned about what might be happening to Muslims here. But why are you so worried? I trust your instincts, but haven't had time to hear your full explanation." That came out badly.

Habi thought for a moment, looked at Le Fanu, then stood up. "Sir, you'll have had breakfast, but could you take a little more?"

"Of course."

"Come on then."

Habi led the way out to the yard and commandeered a car. He whispered to its driver who saw them into the car, climbed in himself and steered out onto the Marina then towards George Town.

"Sir," said Habi, "best if you judge for yourself, so I'll get you to talk to some people. Now please tell me more about Mrs McPhedren."

All the while wondering where this might lead, Le Fanu gave Habi a full account of his Secunderabad trip and what he had heard since.

"A troubled return from the Straits Settlements, sir. I'm sorry it is so worrying, and I hope Mrs McPhedren gets well. But what was it like over there in Penang?"

Le Fanu sensed a baited hook but had known Habi a long time so told him all about his experiences. That helped him remember how much he had enjoyed the place and not only because of Jenlin Koh. The work and his colleagues were also interesting.

"Very good, sir. I'm guessing they want to keep you."

There was that hook.

Le Fanu laughed. "Habi, you're the best informed person here, so I'm sure you know I have a job offer. No one else here does, yet. I'm still considering, but it is attractive."

"And I'm sure there are other attractions as well."

"As I'm sure your relatives there have told you. I thought so."

"My apologies, sir. I'd prefer you to stay here, for purely selfish reasons, but I understand the attractions. I also understand the difficulty of making a final decision. If you do go, I hope we can resolve these communal troubles beforehand."

"And I'll do my absolute best to ensure your future is secure, Habi. You know that. And I'm assuming you couldn't come with me even though I could really use your skills."

"Thank you for the thought, sir."

Did that mean he wasn't ruling it out?

They were now in the middle of George Town, outside a Muslim restaurant, judging by nearby dress and appearance. Habi asked the driver to wait, went to the desk and spoke to a tall, bearded, distinguished looking man. The man looked towards Le Fanu whom Habi beckoned in, and they went to a table in the middle of the room.

A stream of waiters arrived with trays of food in steel bowls. Everyone else stared at Le Fanu. They apparently all knew Habi as a policeman but were puzzled by his European colleague.

Habi addressed them. "You have heard of Superintendent Le Fanu. He was the Inspector-General of Police here recently. He's come with me to hear your thoughts on how things are now for Muslims in Madras. I've told him there are problems, but he needs to hear it from you. Don't be afraid to speak. He'll listen. And if he thinks some things are wrong, he'll try to fix them. Superintendent Le Fanu commanded Muslims and Hindus alike in the war and was well respected. This is your chance to tell someone what you think. Don't waste it."

As soon as Habi finished, a bearded man wearing *shalwar kameez* and a *haji* cap stood and looked around. He must be a leader, Le Fanu thought, because the others all deferred to him.

"Sir," he said in Tamil, "we are most pleased our friend Habi has brought you here because this is a difficult time for Madras Muslims. There have been mysterious deaths, including that of our honoured community member Mohammad Reiza Khan. Madras Muslims have felt more under threat during the past few months than for many, many years. And the government seems not to care."

All present murmured approval, a few expressing loud complaints. At least fifty people were there, and this conversation had obviously occurred often.

Another man spoke up. "We work hard and support the government. Some of us support the Congress but most have not joined the protests. Now we feel victimised."

More approval and protest.

Yet another man stood, arms akimbo. "Hindus here have been tolerant in the past, but they're being stirred up by strangers come from across India. The government must act."

Le Fanu sensed the temperature rising and noticed Habi watching him closely.

Two men began shouting at once.

"Protect the Muslims!"

"Prosecute the troublemakers!"

The original speaker lifted his right hand and the place fell silent.

"Remain calm," he said. "We're peaceful and must stay that way. Violence is not the answer. But, Superintendent Le Fanu, the government must help us. Habi says you were a leader in the war. You know that we're disappointed our service has not been better recognised. We feel used. Our friends who served have not been looked after. Our goals and ambitions are ignored. The Muslim League speaks of these things and the people are listening. We want to be left alone in peace, but if we're not protected by you then we'll protect ourselves and follow those who promise help."

Habi spoke up. "Superintendent Le Fanu has heard you and will investigate. I know him and can promise you that. Now we'll have some food before we leave."

As they ate, several men came up and gave Le Fanu detailed examples of recent incidents. Some offered information about the troublemakers, others reported the fears developing among families, especially those living away from the main Muslim enclaves.

Le Fanu knew none of this was stage managed. Habi had needed him to hear this, because Muslim concerns were not being heard by government or police. That made the situation more volatile, drove support towards the Muslim League and even more radical wings, at a time when the Raj needed to strengthen its support. Habi was right to be concerned.

When they emerged, the traffic had intensified as the work day loomed. The driver set course for the Marina and the office.

"Habi, thank you. Clever idea. I now understand why you're worried."

"Sir, I've not seen it like this before. Muslims are frightened. The murders have unsettled them, so have these visiting agitators. Those things are connected."

"When we get back, Jackson will immediately tell you his people have found possible confirmation of that link. He was waiting at my house late last night to tell me."

"I'm very glad to hear that because I was thinking he doubted my intelligence."

"He'd never do that, Habi."

"It has been hard with you away, sir, and that makes it doubly worrying to think you might leave permanently."

Nothing Le Fanu might say would help, so they travelled silently for the last few minutes.

Twelve

The convoy of trucks parked along Edward Elliots Road outside headquarters, packed with armed policemen, immediately brought back bad memories for Le Fanu. He looked across. Habi obviously felt the same. They shook their heads simultaneously.

"You're thinking what I'm thinking, Habi?"

"About that disaster at the beach? Yes."

"What is this about?"

"I've a bad feeling it's about our northerners. The Jockey's taken to the whip again."

Inside, the corridors resembled what Le Fanu had imagined Bedlam might have been like. Deafening noise. Officers, constables and clerks charging about, all carrying pieces of paper and shouting instructions no one else heard. Policemen arming up, a conga line from the armoury where one harried officer was signing out rifles, pistols and ammunition.

Habi helped Le Fanu thread through the pack to his office where Caldicott was sipping tea, relaxed as ever.

"Enjoy the show?" he asked.

"No," replied Le Fanu, "it can only mean bad news."

"Confirmed."

"The Jockey's going after the suspects," Habi threw in.

"Of course," Caldicott responded, "can't help himself. No one knows what they're doing because he's yet to issue an operational running sheet. A couple of officers have been told what they must achieve but with no instructions on how to do it."

"Typical." Le Fanu ran a hand through his hair. "And he's not called either of you, of course, even though you're the only ones who know anything about the matter."

"We're the last people he needs. You know The Jockey's approach: never let information inform action."

"Sir," said Habi, "we have to do something or our own avenues will disappear." He and Caldicott looked at Le Fanu.

"What, you want me to try and talk reason into Jepson? Now?"

They smiled.

"You can do it, LF. Nothing's too hard for you."

"Sir, you're our only hope."

"And you want me to do that then stay on here long term, is that it?"

"Sir, we suspect you'll leave anyway, so this might be your last chance to help us."

"Habi, even for you, this is pure evil genius. I've no choice, have I?"

"Afraid not, LF."

"And what's the best possible result from me risking life and limb?"

"Stopping the madness, obviously, LF. Only you can do it."

The strained laughter reflected anxiety about the likely consequences of Jepson's intemperate action.

"Wish me luck, then."

He pushed back through the packed corridors, around to the front of the building where the crush was reduced but the atmosphere gloomier. Senior officers here were more alive to the possibilities. He spotted one who had worked for him directly on earlier cases.

"Cuthbertson, nice to see you. Any idea what's happening?"

"Sir, nice to see you, too, and no, except that the I-G has ordered a mass arrest mission."

"Of whom?"

"Visitors from elsewhere in India, apparently, who may or may not be causing trouble here."

"And where will these arrests occur?"

Cuthbertson stretched up awkwardly on the balls of his feet. "Sir, I'm not in direct charge."

"Who is?"

"Not entirely clear. Neither are the locations, if I'm totally honest."

"Thanks, and good luck. Be careful. Habi and Caldicott think these people are potentially dangerous."

"Appreciate the caution, sir. Great to have you back."

Le Fanu walked into Jepson's reception area.

A uniformed European looked up from the desk, immediately worried. "Is there some way I can help you, Superintendent Le Fanu?"

"I don't want to make your life difficult, but would the I-G have a couple of minutes to see me?"

Raised voices emanated from the inner office, and the man looked despairingly at Le Fanu. "I'll see what I can do, sir. No promises."

He rose slowly, then moved even more lugubriously towards the office where the voices were becoming louder. Glancing towards Le Fanu, the clerk knocked hesitantly.

"What the fuck is it now?" came the immediate

response. "I'm trying to organise a complicated bloody manoeuvre here."

The man slid inside.

A brief lull followed.

"Le Fanu? What the fuck does that useless lowlife want?"

Another lull.

The man reappeared, face strained, and gestured for Le Fanu to enter.

"Stop wasting my bloody time, Le Fanu. You know I want you gone. What d'you want to complain about now, before you get back to your shagging?"

Le Fanu ignored that bait but knew he might lose control should more appear. "Sir, I understand you're organising a mass arrest of some individuals from the north?"

"None of your bloody business."

"I quite agree, sir, but last night Caldicott received additional information about those visitors and I wanted to make sure you had that for your planning."

"How fucking thoughtful of you. Slimy bastard. What possible information conjured up by that fashion plate could help me?"

"Sir, some of those suspects are almost certainly connected to the murder of Mohammad Reiza Khan here in Madras. That, in turn, suggests connections to the other Muslim murders in Guntur and Tanjore."

"Bloody Muslim-lover now, as well as half-castes and other sundry Asians, eh? You're getting worse as you get older, Le Fanu."

"Perhaps so, sir, but there's a possible criminal conspiracy here. We should be rounding up the entire gang rather than just a couple of functionaries."

He took a breath, awaiting the onslaught.

"You really are an arrogant bastard, aren't you, Le Fanu. No one else knows anything. We're all idiots to you. Useless fools requiring your instruction. Well, why don't you just fuck off? I've got this in order and it's ready to go."

"May I inquire as to the targets, sir? I can help Habi and Caldicott gather further information."

"No, you may not. You don't need to know anything. Read the bloody papers tomorrow. Knowing you, that'll be *The Hindu*, what with you being an Indian-lover."

Le Fanu remained calm, just.

Another tap at the door, and the hapless clerk came in. "Sir," he said to Jepson, "the First Member of the Board of Revenue would like a word."

"Of course, show him in. He'll love seeing who I have in here."

Arthur Jamieson. Apart from Jepson, the last person Le Fanu needed to see.

The man swaggered in, hubris in a suit. He saw Le Fanu. Stopped. Disdain. He turned towards Jepson. "Arthur," he said, "I'd have come earlier had I known you were entertaining this shit. Not that you need assistance to deal with the Indian-lover, I hasten to add."

"Ha, thanks for the thought. This shit, as you so aptly describe him, is about to leave, having attempted to give me the benefit of what he imagines to be his expertise. Mission failed, obviously, given he has no expertise."

"Predictably so," continued Jamieson. "Some things don't change, although I gather his choice of companion does, rapidly."

"Le Fanu's always attracted by colour and movement."

They laughed uproariously.

Le Fanu tried to stay silent and look calm when he was neither.

Jamieson maintained the barrage. "Must be his continental heritage. Prone to flights of fancy and compulsive behaviour. Never was sure how he got into the service with a name like Le Fanu. Foreigner. Bound to be a problem. Like bloody Galletti. That man's a menace, too."

Arthur Galletti was a legendary ICS square peg in a round hole, famed for siding with Indian leaders in his districts and forever being in dispute with anyone ranked above him. His Italian heritage and citizenship became a cause célèbre during the war, especially after he published an article apparently supporting Germany, where he had studied and spoke the language fluently. War warp excepted, Le Fanu didn't mind the comparison. Galletti had a soul and a brain.

"Galletti!" shouted Jepson. "Galletti. The man who refused to toast the King Emperor on Empire Day! What with him and this miserable fucker, no wonder the Raj has weakened. Get rid of *them* and we'd sort out these bloody Indians immediately."

"If you'll excuse me." Le Fanu walked towards the door. "I take it, Inspector-General, you are ignoring the additional intelligence now available. You imagine your plans are sufficiently robust. I am informing you now, officially, that at least one senior officer out there knows neither what is planned nor how it is to occur. You must ensure your senior officers know your plans so they can better command the policemen whose lives are in their trust. We don't want old problems repeated, do we?"

He genuinely feared Jepson might expire, because the man coloured to a degree Le Fanu had never before witnessed.

"You can't speak to your commanding officer that way," spluttered Jamieson.

"I've simply confirmed he has refused relevant advice that might help avoid potential conflict and ensure the safety of those under his command. If you consider that to be disrespectful or insolent, then good luck explaining it before any formal inquiry."

"Get the fuck out of here, Le Fanu, and don't fucking come back. Run off to your protectors, who are also on the bloody way out. We'll get this bloody Presidency back under control as soon as you soft bastards fuck off into a hole somewhere."

The rant continued as Le Fanu walked towards the now strangely quiet corridors.

As he passed by, the clerk looked up. "Thank you, sir. For what it's worth, I'd rather you were still in command."

Nearby voices muttered approval.

Le Fanu walked away, giving himself a mental pat on the back. He'd remained calm under full scale attack from his two main opponents. In earlier days he would have reacted more impulsively. This time he had undermined Jepson and involved Jamieson. Jepson would be held responsible for whatever failures might eventuate, because those witnesses outside had heard the exchange. Jamieson might collude with Jepson, but the clerks had heard it all. Jepson's track record and the fact he and Jamieson were known to despise Le Fanu would further weaken their position.

By the time he reached Habi's office, Le Fanu was almost completely relaxed. It must have shown when he walked in.

"LF, you look like you've actually had a good time."

"I wouldn't go that far, Jackson, but Jepson and Jamieson now have more to think about."

"Jamieson was there, too, sir?" asked Habi. "They've spent a lot of time together while you were away. Around here now they're known as DBT - Double Big Trouble. What happened?"

Le Fanu reported what had happened and what might occur next. "Jepson's a coward," he said. "If there's any chance of something going wrong, he'll blame someone else or call it off. Jamieson's as bad, and Jepson knows he'll get no support if the First Member believes his own interests are at risk. And I've advised them senior officers know next to nothing about what's planned. People in the office and the corridors heard it all and will remember."

"Brilliant." Caldicott looked genuinely impressed.

"Please don't think it was planned, and it might not work. I was just willing myself not to hit Jepson. What my voice said had almost nothing to do with me. Very strange."

"Sir," said Habi, "if this operation gets cancelled, our inquiries are still alive. If The Jockey goes after our targets, we'll almost have to start again, so I hope he sees sense. Otherwise ..."

Caldicott moved in. "Habi, you're right, as always, so let's hope sense prevails. If Jepson backs off, the reactionaries and conservatives will be belted, and that'd be a great thing."

"Don't be too optimistic," Le Fanu warned. "Those two blowhards can still make dumb decisions, but at least they now have a problem. More importantly, what new information do we have, if any?"

Thirteen

Having to meet Chester Barnes that evening, and having done as much as he could with Habi and Caldicott, Le Fanu had the driver take him to Mount Road and the new *Madras Mail* building that stood beside its great rival, *The Hindu*. This had to be one of the Empire's most unique newspaper situations, the *Mail* serving the Raj and *The Hindu* increasingly promoting the Indian National Congress.

The *Mail* was the perennial voice for the city's European conservatives, and that was most of them. Over the years, that rule had been proven by the odd exception, like Eardley Norton. He remained among the city's greatest lawyers, having helped establish the Indian National Congress and despite marrying the woman with whom his 1890s affair ended that political link. But people like Norton were rare, and unloved by most *Mail* readers.

Le Fanu entered the imposing entrance of the two-storeyed cream building and went upstairs to be shown into the editor's large office. Barnes stood with a smile, jacket off, red braces creasing the cream shirt that was complemented by spotted bow tie and linen trousers.

"LF. I've missed your penetrating insights into the failures and foibles of my readers. Welcome back."

"Chester, you're as bad as ever. Still looking for gossip. But likewise, wonderful to see you."

"Coffee and vadas on the way."

"Whatever would your readers think?"

"I know, you're a bad influence. First comes the Indian food, then, you know, next thing I'll be supporting the Congress."

"And how are your readers seeing things at present?"

"Same as when you left, only worse. Still angered by Indianisation of the ICS and any potential political concessions. Many senior ICS men around the club are complaining to their business colleagues they're all being sold out by London."

"No future in that thinking."

"Agreed, but they don't see that."

"Are they saying anything about Muslims?"

"This have to do with those murders I hear Habi's investigating?"

"Obviously, and, yes, if I hear anything you can print, I'll let you know immediately."

Barnes turned up his hands in appreciation as the coffee and snacks arrived. There was a lull as the servant fussed about pouring and distributing. They sat at a side table as soon as he left.

"Habi's worried the Muslims are getting restive," said Le Fanu.

"He's right. Their senior leaders think they're being deserted by the Raj."

"You agree?"

"That's what they're telling me, and I can see why. At best they're scarcely mentioned in dispatches; at worst described mostly as expendable."

"That's a bit over dramatic."

"You haven't been away long, Chris, but attitudes have turned harder here very quickly. Everyone's out for themselves. More than ever."

"That you or your audience speaking?"

"Me, as it happens. Anyone who supports even moderate reform these days is ostracised, so watch it next time you're at the club."

"I won't be rushing there."

"Then you'll be ignoring an important information source, especially about attitudes."

Barnes was right, Le Fanu knew. At some point he'd have to front 'the longest bar in the East' and its perennial pretence of being in Mayfair.

"More importantly, LF, how's Ro? I hear you've been up to see her."

First Habi, then Wilson, now Barnes. Their insider knowledge made them good at their professions, he knew, but really.

"Unfortunately, not good. Typhoid with all its usual worries. Looked terrible when I arrived and only marginally better when I left."

"And you were up there … why?"

Le Fanu was stunned. Not by the question, but because he couldn't answer it logically, or convincingly.

"Um, obviously …"

"Obviously you've no idea, which is what I suspected. Are you still in love with her?"

"God, Chester, what sort of question is that?"

"If you don't know, then it's even more odd you went, especially given your new interest."

Stunned again. "Now how the hell …?"

"Jackson and I kept in touch during your absence. He accesses Habi's extraordinary intelligence network as well as his own, so here we are."

"Bloody hell, no chance of a private life here, then."

"You should know that by now. Shipboard romance?"

"Not at all, I …"

"Who found whom?"

"She found me."

"What's her story?"

"Travels for business, her father's an antique trader. It was at his shop where our escapee ICS man attempted to sell all his treasures."

"So you had to see her professionally?"

"Yes."

"And that turned into a more social arrangement."

Le Fanu nodded.

"Ye gods, remind me to find you a chaperone next time you leave Madras."

"No need."

"It's serious?"

Le Fanu stood, crossed to the window, looked out over Mount Road then turned back to Barnes. "You know, Chester, I haven't had to explain it to anyone else but, yes, serious."

"It's a bit sudden, you'll admit."

"After Ro? Yes, but Jenlin's special – smart, educated, independent and ambitious."

"Sounds like Ro but more exotic. Straits Chinese looker, I hear."

"There's more to her than that. She has her own property business to run now as well as her father's."

"Does he approve?"

"Jenlin has told him she's serious."

"But she's there and you're here."

Le Fanu hesitated. "The Straits police chief and the Governor have offered me a post, I'm really back here to resign."

"Because of Jenlin."

"Yes."

"Yet you hare up to Secunderabad the moment you hear Ro is ill."

"I owe her …"

"Support, yes. I hear the words, but you're the only one who doesn't think there's more to it than that."

"Ro …"

"Still cares. She didn't want to complicate your life."

"I care for her."

Barnes stared at him. "So which is the chosen one?"

Le Fanu wilted. "If only I knew."

"We need something stronger than coffee." Barnes got up and reached into the furthest corner of a large cupboard to pull out two glasses and a bottle. An Auchentoshan. "It's a lowland malt, so probably not enough bite for you, but it'll have to do."

"Lovely drop. It'll do nicely."

A touch of water, a toast, smooth warmth on the palate. Barnes poured new measures.

"So, LF?"

"I've no idea."

"Let me write that down. A rare moment."

Even Le Fanu had to laugh. "And you call yourself a friend. Lucky I know you mean well."

"Are you sure?"

"About anything? No, and especially not about this."

"Guilt's a powerful thing."

"I suppose so."

"Take some time, would be my suggestion. You have to sort out what you really want to do."

"That's true, but I can't abandon Ro while she's like this."

"And there's the man some of us know and admire. Call me anytime if I can help."

"I will. No promises."

"Goes without saying. On another matter, which horse is our favourite jockey riding right now?"

Le Fanu was not sure he wanted to remember. "I've just been listening to him and Jamieson analyse my incompetence and my taste in women."

"Great sources of advice there."

"I know. Jepson had arranged for a convoy of armed policemen to go and arrest some potential problems from north India. No other officers knew the plan, the exact whereabouts of said problems, or what they've done to warrant arrest. Another Auchentoshan please."

Barnes obliged. "The usual, then. Should be plenty for me to write about?"

"Unless he changes his mind. By the way, the visitors might be connected to the Muslim inquiry."

"Are you giving me a clue? Where's my friend Le Fanu and what have you done with him?"

"Funny. You'd have found out anyway, and faster than Jepson. There's a possible link between Mohammad Reiza Khan's death and some of the newcomers."

"He was a player in the local Muslim League."

"Well, there you are. Something to follow."

"Thanks, LF. I'll let you know if I find anything or, rather, if my Muslim journalist does."

"You have an Indian journalist at the *Mail*? How many subscribers have you lost?"

"None, because they don't know. Harder to get good journalists from the UK now finances are tighter. Locals are better anyway, more connected to what's happening. So I've hired her on the quiet and she never comes to the office. We meet occasionally but otherwise correspond by notes."

"*Her*?"

"Wondered if you'd pick that up. Might shock my readers more than being Muslim."

"From Madras?"

"No, which is why I suspect even Habi doesn't know yet. She's been here a few weeks, comes from an important Hyderabadi family. Had a fallout with them when she returned from America. She did journalism at Columbia University in New York. The family thought she'd simply marry whomever they lined up. She refused. Wanted to use her new skills. Contacted me through some friends and she's done great work already."

"Things really are changing."

"Oh, yes."

"She have a name?"

"Not for you yet, no."

"Fair enough. I'd better get going, but if I hear anything I'll let you know and you can tell your new star."

"Much appreciated."

"And thanks for the Auchentoshan."

Le Fanu considered going home but knew he should brave the office first. The driver cut across Mount Road and into Triplicane, through a couple of shortcuts for a quick run towards the Marina and headquarters.

The convoy was gone.

Habi was still in his office, with Caldicott. "Good evening, sir, we didn't expect you back today."

"Couldn't keep me away, Habi."

"No good news, LF. Senior Secretariat and Board officers ran about madly, lots of shouting. But The Jockey wouldn't be budged. The convoy's off on its mission."

"Damn it. When?"

"Ten minutes ago, no more."

"And you two weren't invited?"

"No, sir."

"And do we know where the convoy is headed?"

"Officially no, sir." Habi was straight-faced.

"But …?"

"A friend of mine on his way out to the trucks happened to call in here on another matter and accidentally told me the destination. Sir."

"How unfortunate, Habi. But well done."

"It was, sir. Don't want to get him into trouble."

"Of course not."

"LF, Habi and I were thinking about dropping by that location to see if we could help. Interested?"

"It'd be the right thing to do, wouldn't it? How're we getting there?"

"Sir," said Habi, "best to be inconspicuous, so another friend has kindly offered us his driver and car that should be outside about now."

The risks were high but they could not resist. Besides, this Jepson jape had the potential to go very wrong, and its senior officers were woefully under-briefed.

The car was a dark coloured Citroën B2, just a year old. It might stand out a bit.

"Nice car, Habi. Who's the friend?"

"A businessman, sir. He trades with the French, thanks to some Pondicherry colleagues, and he bought this more cheaply than he could a British or an American car."

"Better tell the driver to be careful."

"Yes, sir." Habi spoke to the driver in Urdu.

"Where're we going, anyway?"

"The information, LF, is that some of the visitors are out near Saidapet on the edge of The Long Tank. Some village near there."

"Sounds imprecise."

"Agreed."

They followed the roads that bordered the tank from Nungambakkam towards the outer reaches of the city. Settlements thinned, but no sign of the convoy.

Until they turned the next bend.

The lead truck was on fire, police bodies slumped across the sides of the tray.

Remaining police hunkered behind the other vehicles, firing indiscriminately at non-apparent targets. No officer in charge, it appeared. Chaos.

"Jesus, LF, this looks really bad."

"Well, surprise, surprise. I'm guessing Jepson's not even here?"

"Still in his office, last I heard."

They got out and Habi sent the driver back. No point damaging the Citroën.

Le Fanu took off in a crouching run and reached the first vehicle. The other two followed. They attracted some shots, and the rattled policemen kept firing, Le Fanu could now see a few huts huddled beneath palm trees. A small temple nearby. No one else in sight.

The policemen reloaded.

"What are you firing at?" Le Fanu asked.

"Not sure, sir. We were ordered to fire over there, so we are. No one's told us to stop."

"Who's in charge?"

"No one here. Our officer went ahead."

"What happened?"

"Again, not really sure, sir. We came around that bend and the gunfire began. Then the first truck caught fire. That's when we got the order to shoot back."

"Habi, come with me. Jackson, stay here, stop the shooting and get the men organised."

"Right you are, LF."

Le Fanu and Habi raced towards the second vehicle. Same story. Indiscriminate firing, no one in command. Two more vehicles to go before they reached the one on fire.

They found a junior officer at the next one.

"Not sure where you came from, sir, but very glad you're here. The two senior officers went forward and haven't returned."

"What's your name?"

"Rutherford, sir."

"Right, Rutherford. Regroup these men, then wait to hear from me or from Assistant Superintendent Habibullah. Assistant Super Caldicott is back there, so there's plenty of support. Keep your head down. There's not much coming our way now so have your men hold fire."

"Sir, when we rounded the bend our lead vehicle came under fire. The senior officers ordered return of fire then went forward. That's when the lead truck blew up."

"Any idea what happened?"

"One of the men thought he saw something on fire come through the air."

"Firebomb." If so, this was a serious encounter.

Le Fanu and Habi advanced towards the next vehicle. And found bodies. The two senior officers, five constables. Le Fanu's old phobia returned instantly and he felt nauseous. He tried to avoid looking at the blood. Took a deep breath.

The remaining five men were cowering behind the overturned and burning truck, heads hunched in arms, uniforms scorched, rifles cast off.

Habi touched one on the shoulder. The man looked up.

"How are you, constable?"

The young man nodded. "Good, sir. Shaken only, but we don't know what to do."

"Don't worry, we're here now. Superintendent Le Fanu will take over. Tell me what happened."

"We came around the turn and shots went over our heads. We don't think they were aiming at us, more scaring us off. But our officer ordered us to fire back, so we did. Then a couple of objects were thrown out from the trees and landed underneath the truck. They exploded, the truck tipped over and some of us were thrown out. The others were not so lucky. Then the two officers came up from the rear, got caught out in the open and shot."

The man and his cowed colleagues looked numb, eyes glazed, limbs shaking.

All the hallmarks of a poorly planned and led expedition, Habi thought.

Le Fanu had calmed the others. Over the next few minutes they despatched the wounded to hospital, transferred bodies to serviceable trucks and gathered the remaining policemen.

Le Fanu remained queasy. It was a long time since he had seen wounds and blood on this scale, and the old wartime phobia had resurfaced with a vengeance. He survived by looking steadfastly away. On the few occasions he had to look, more deep breaths helped, a little. Faint, clammy and dizzy, he somehow held on.

Habi knew. "Need a break for a minute or two, sir?"

"No thanks, Habi, this is under control. Get someone back to Caldicott, and we'll organise the contingent to get on with the next steps. But I need five volunteers now."

"To go into the village?"

"Yes."

"Well, we'll come with you." Habi looked concerned.

"I'd be glad of that."

Habi ordered what remained of the contingent to stay with the trucks, under Rutherford's direction, until the search party returned. Then five volunteers were found. Caldicott inspected their rifles, and their ammunition was replenished from the remaining constables' supplies.

Le Fanu wondered if he was about to aggravate Jepson's errors.

Fourteen

There had been no firing for several minutes but the volunteers still looked nervous. Le Fanu couldn't blame them. There were sixty yards of open ground to cover before reaching the trees and shrubbery at the village's perimeter. Were the gunmen in there? He had no idea, his throat drying in anticipation. Wartime memories of Mesopotamia.

"Ready?" he asked, with no great conviction.

Habi and Caldicott nodded, checking their pistols. The five constables fiddled with their rifles, raised their hands in acknowledgement.

"Good. I'll lead off. Habi and Jackson, you take the wings. Constables, spread out behind me in a half circle about ten yards apart. Keep low. I'll give the signal to start."

He spoke with each of the men, checking their weapons. All in good order. He reassured them individually. They should not be in this position, and he hated exposing them to danger.

After a final look at the relieved-looking troops being left behind, he led the volunteers out from behind the vehicles, crouching low, pistol drawn. The constables fanned out, presenting the smallest possible targets. Jackson Caldicott took the right flank, Habi the left.

Five yards in. No sign of anyone ahead. Importantly, no gunfire.

Twenty yards. The same. Sweat ran down inside his clothes, standard work suit little cooler than the service uniform, even with his tie loosened. Kites in the trees, others wheeling high above. Chickens and pigs around somewhere, too, judging by the noise. No human sounds other than his search party.

It seemed like a mile still left to cover. They were in a killing zone.

Forty yards. Apprehension rising. A crucial point. Gaps appeared in the vegetation ahead, and he glimpsed thatched village huts, a well to one side, two fire pits in a sort of village square. Washing strewn over rough frames outside houses. Still no sign of people. A good thing, possibly. Any defending force would have revealed itself by now, surely.

Ten yards out from the tree line he saw the first body, blood streaming from a chest wound. The nausea returned immediately. Le Fanu looked away and spotted Habi in his peripheral vision who had realised what was happening.

Le Fanu nodded back assurance but felt terrible.

Then they were in the trees and found half a dozen other bodies. His condition worsened. Sweating profusely, he could scarcely stay upright. Pulse racing. Vision blurring. Dizzy. He fell to a squat, feigning interest in possible clues near the bodies.

A hand on his shoulder.

Habi. "Well done, sir, we're in. No problem." He handed Le Fanu a water bottle. How had he remembered that?

"Thanks, Habi." Le Fanu swigged at the water, poured some into his palm, sloshed it over his face and felt little better.

The constables regrouped inside the tree line, checking bodies for papers. One came up with a collection of weapons and laid them out on the ground.

"Bloody hell, LF." Caldicott had materialised out of nowhere. "Those look like Fedorov M1916s. I've read about them but never seen one."

"And that's important?" Le Fanu had avoided all weapons whenever possible since the war.

"If I'm right, our culprits are suddenly more significant, assuming they're involved here."

"Why's that, sir?" asked Habi.

"See the shape of that rifle? During the war, Fedorov served in the Russian Imperial Army that used French-made Chauchat machine guns. Terrible things, scarcely worked. So he designed an automatic that could fire multiple rounds and increase the impact of every infantryman. Bit like our Lee–Enfield No. 1s."

Habi picked up one of the rifles and turned it around.

"Very effective," Caldicott continued, turning to Le Fanu. "Oddly, this model uses Japanese shells. That puts less strain on the internal components than Russian ammunition does, apparently."

Le Fanu got the drift. "So if our suspects are involved, they're armed with Russian rifles that require Japanese ammunition. That means they're organised and well supplied."

"And," Habi chimed in, "have scarcely come to quiet Madras just for a meeting."

"Indeed so, Habi."

"Any idea who we have here?" Le Fanu jerked his head towards but did not look at the bodies being rowed up by the constables.

"The men have done a quick search, LF, but no papers. At least, none with names on. These people didn't want to be identified."

"Which again suggests a planned mission. We'd better push on."

Ordering a constable to stay with the bodies, Le Fanu led his team into the village from which no sounds had emerged so far. Everything remained quiet.

As they neared the huts, a child's face peered around then snapped back from a doorway. An adult's showed briefly at another. Gradually, stunned and frightened people filed out to greet the police. Le Fanu remembered that look.

Then he turned into a laneway and found a pile of perhaps a dozen bodies. Men and boys at first look. All shot, wounds and blood everywhere. Those Fedorovs had almost shredded some bodies. The bile returned.

Habi raced up, distressed. "Sir, this is a Muslim village. A man tells me the gang arrived this morning, pulled out these males and executed them. That happened about half an hour before the first police trucks arrived and distracted the killers. Otherwise they'd have killed even more."

"This is bad, Habi. Tell the headman we'll get more police here immediately to protect his people, and to go after these killers because some escaped, that's obvious."

"I've done that , sir. Can I bring him over to tell you what happened?"

Without waiting for an answer Habi beckoned an elderly man over whose short, gaunt frame looked drained. The chiselled face was expressionless, but the dark eyes angry.

"He's a Tamil speaker, sir, so you can talk with him directly."

By now, more villagers had left their huts, most going straight to the pile of bodies from which individuals were claimed by families amidst grief and despair. They would be buried by nightfall, a terrible end to a terrible day.

Le Fanu learned a gang of perhaps fifteen had arrived early that morning, on a lorry that parked up out the back. Armed men roamed the village, captured the young men and boys, lined them up then shot them sequentially. None of the shooters spoke. They completed the killings and were looking for more victims when the police arrived. The gun battle followed.

Given this ruthless planning and prosecution, similar attacks must be in the offing. They had to find this gang.

"Jackson, gather any other information you can here, then get back to your office and see if your team can drum up any more. Something must point to whoever it is we're dealing with."

"Of course, LF. I'll use one of the constables, if I may." He began walking toward the bodies in the trees but did not get far.

"What the fuck have you done now, Le Fanu, you useless bastard?"

Jepson swaggered out of the trees, thrashing the whip against his boots. Face flushed from the exercise, cap falling over his eyes and uniform jacket wide open in a vain attempt to beat the mild heat, he looked out of control. Two fraught European officers trailing in his wake looked apologetically at Le Fanu.

"Sir, good you're here but we've a scene of offence to secure, so if you could …"

"Fuck off, Le Fanu. Scene of offence. Same old rubbish. Same old Austrian mumbo jumbo. Never solved a bloody crime yet."

"Sir, you'll find it has, if you check the records, and more than one over the past four years."

"Insolent shit. How dare you reprimand me in front of the men."

"No reprimand, sir, just a request to stay out of the scene of offence, and a reminder the Crime Unit has an excellent record."

"That any of our dumb Indian constables would have done cheaper and faster."

The nearby Indian constables looked uncomfortable and angry.

"Habi," said Le Fanu, "take the men off to double check the village and perimeter in case we've missed anything."

Habi understood immediately and led the constables away.

"Sir, I really must …"

"Fuck off. Excellent idea. Go and pack your bags, even better one."

One of the European officers tried unsuccessfully to divert Jepson who, however, was in full cry. "Sooner we get rid of this native-shagging shit, the better," he boomed.

The villagers looked confused and scared.

"Sir," Le Fanu persisted, "we've several innocent villagers murdered here by a well-armed gang with a clear plan. We must find the remaining killers quickly. Otherwise we'll have even more deaths, and that'll look bad in the *Mail*."

"No doubt your poof editor friend will blame me to make you look good."

"Sir, you really cannot go around …"

"I'll do and say exactly as I want, Le Fanu, now fuck off so I can clean up this mess. How many dead Muslims have we got? Probably not enough."

Le Fanu heard Habi suppress a protest. He looked around, shook his head. A couple of villagers heard and understood, too, and were telling their neighbours who began mumbling.

"Sir, I'm leaving here, taking the men back to headquarters. You're now officially in charge. But I must inform you I'll be immediately laying formal complaints against you and this unwarranted behaviour."

"Do whatever you want, you're fucked. I'm in charge. Time for some straightforward police work."

Jepson barked orders at the two officers who clearly wanted to be anywhere but here.

Le Fanu began walking away, followed by Habi and Caldicott, then turned back. "Is it vaguely possible, Jepson, you've any idea of the damage you've done? Get medical help at the earliest possible opportunity. Your behaviour's disgraceful. That shambolic raid killed several good policemen who deserved better than being commanded by an incompetent fool like you."

A further spray of Jepsonian invective followed them away.

No one spoke until they had returned through the trees and across the clear ground to the vehicles where the remaining police awaited.

"Sir?" Habi broke the silence. "What are you going to do? His references to Muslims were outrageous. I cannot let that go unreported."

"Habi, I fully expect you to report it. Give me your account and I'll verify it with whoever you want. I'll give it to Sir Charles Whitney, along with my full report. I've never experienced anything like that."

"Careful, LF, you don't want to play into his hands."

"Jackson, I appreciate your concern, but this must go the full distance. Jepson's problem is giving the rest of us an even bigger one that's worsening by the hour. He's endangering more police lives, and I'll not have Habi and Muslims maligned like that. Nor will I tolerate such Neanderthal approaches to police work. It undermines the entire force."

"I understand, but we can't risk you being pulled out, we've enough problems now."

"I'll try to avoid provoking him, Jackson, but I'm sure as hell following this up."

They climbed into the trucks, one carrying the police bodies, another the dead gang members. Several truckloads of incoming armed police arriving were clogging the road, along with thousands of curious people from nearby villages. Le Fanu also saw *Mail* and *Hindu* reporters, along with others who provided stories to newspapers across India. This would be banner headlines tomorrow, more bad news at a time when proven government leaders like Willingdon and Whitney were about to disappear. Jepson could not go untouched.

The slow journey back stopped first at the Madras General Hospital morgue. He would contact his friend Dr Ramachandran tomorrow. Their first meeting since Le Fanu's return would have been better over lunch than an autopsy, but Rama would be stretched over the next twenty-four hours.

It was not until they reached headquarters that Le Fanu remembered he had no office in which to write his report. "Fuck Jepson. He's not going to win this."

Habi and Caldicott, sharing the back of the car with him, jumped. They had all been silent throughout the journey.

"LF, you can handle this. But stay calm. Let him blow up on his own."

"No, I'll give him some help. Do me a favour, Jackson, will you?"

"Certainly. What?"

"Draw up an account of what just happened with Jepson. Then do a report of the whole incident and review all the evidence to this point."

"Of course."

"Habi, now you."

"Sir?"

"Once Jackson's finished the Jepson report, bring it to me."

"Of course, sir. Where'll you be?"

"Talking to the Chief Secretary who'll arrange a meeting with the Governor."

"How'll I get in to give you the report, sir?"

"I'll clear you, Habi, right up to the Governor's level. It's time they heard you on what's happening, and what Jepson said about Muslims. Sorry not to include you, Jackson, but we need that intelligence report urgently."

"Understood, LF." But he looked doubtful.

"Could be a long night," said Le Fanu as he walked out.

Fifteen

He returned to Mylapore for a break. Besides, it was easier to work there. Still no word from Whitney about a Secretariat office. A servant brought a fresh lime soda and a note. Sir Maurice Wilson had called.

"Maurice, sorry I missed you."

"Not at all. I hear you're busy down there."

The man's informer network matched Habi's.

"There's news?"

"She's marginally better but the doctors are concerned about the lack of serious improvement. Because she can't eat, she's losing weight. That doesn't help. Bit of a vicious circle."

"Are the drugs helping?"

"They're probably what's keeping her alive."

Le Fanu remembered the frail figure he left at the hospital what seemed like days ago. "I'm not sure what to say, Maurice, apart from appreciating the update."

"Not much to say, Chris. Just wanted to keep you informed. And to let you know the job is still here. I'm a way better boss than The Jockey."

"How did you …?"

"You know I've still got friends there. The telephone now spreads gossip so much faster. Your spat with the brat's all over India already, and most people in the know support you, if that helps."

"It does. I'll remember that next time he's screaming at me. Thanks again for letting me know about Ro."

"I'll keep doing so."

Le Fanu checked the time, telephoned Whitney, who would arrange a meeting with Willingdon and call back.

The cook inquired about dinner but Le Fanu asked for something light. A sandwich arrived soon after. He'd never really adjusted to India's sugary bread that more resembled cake and was ill-matched here with corned beef. He took a couple of bites, cast it aside and poured a whisky. Better way to take grain. He picked up the *Mail.*

Barnes's lead story featured an up-country rajah who'd imported a Rolls Royce but lacked a local regular petrol supply. So the car sat motionless outside the mansion with the Rajah inside, waited upon hand and foot and receiving visitors there.

Le Fanu thought he might chip his friend. He did not sympathise with the big landowners, many of whom treated their workers poorly, but this reinforced Britain's condescension towards India that found its sharp end in opposing political reform. It demeaned the talent and service of people like Habi and many others.

He called Habi to alert him that there might be a meeting later on.

The serious story, the Muslim murders, was buried away in the middle of the paper. Tomorrow's edition would highlight the village attack, no doubt.

Le Fanu spoke to Chester Barnes for several minutes. Something approximating the truth would now appear to balance *The Hindu* account that would emphasise British perfidy. Few Madras citizens read both papers, so most were left with a view nuanced ideologically and politically. Nationalists would 'see' another incompetent British handling of a local problem, diehards another escalation of communal feuds and a valiant British attempt to make peace. Reality lay somewhere between the polarities.

The sandwich remained abandoned. He hesitated, then poured another whisky.

Whitney called. The meeting would be at the Secretariat in an hour. Le Fanu finished his drink and advised Habi, who agreed to meet him there.

For thirty minutes Le Fanu rifled through mail, skimmed earlier newspapers, ate fruit, tried to stay awake, then from the car watched the familiar but never dull sights slip by. Despite everything, he still liked the place. The driver dropped him at the Secretariat steps where Habi awaited.

"Good evening, sir. We're meeting the Chief Secretary, then?"

"Yes, Habi, and Willingdon, too. He's probably been here all day, given what's going on."

Habi looked nervous.

"Just be your normal efficient self, Habi, Willingdon appreciates intelligence."

Habi looked doubtful.

They climbed the stairs and turned towards Whitney's office where they found the Chief Secretary waiting. "Good evening, LF. Habi, excellent to see you. Doesn't happen often enough."

"Thank you, sir."

"Willingdon's been in his office since this morning. Big day here, thanks to you chaps."

They walked through the corridors, a succession of peons making way for the travelling smoke cloud that masked three eminent persons.

Whitney stopped before a massive double door and knocked. A servant opened it, showed them in and across a short hall to a small office where the Governor's Private Secretary, a young, on-the-rise ICS man, hastened them into a huge room lined floor to ceiling with books, pictures, trophies, animal heads and other colonial trappings.

Le Fanu hated the heads. The rate things were going, the Raj would leave few animals, birds or fish in India, or anywhere else for that matter.

Glass in hand, the Governor was at a huge bay window, looking out to the ocean. "Charles," he said, "I've seen too much of you today. But LF, great to see you."

"Good evening, sir. Allow me to introduce Assistant Superintendent Habibullah who commands the Crime Unit."

"I'm honoured to meet you, Assistant Superintendent. I've heard of your excellent work and congratulate you on your successes."

Le Fanu could swear Habi was blushing beneath beard and dark face.

"Thank you very much, Your Excellency. I'm honoured to be here."

"Don't be, we really need your assistance, and I'm only sorry we haven't met sooner."

Willingdon crossed to a large table strewn with maps, charts, papers, reports and books. He directed them into the surrounding chairs. "I'm revising my knowledge of the Presidency's Muslim story, given recent events. Are we in for trouble?"

"Your Excellency," Whitney said, "we should hear Habi first. LF, you agree?"

"I do."

"Habi, over to you."

"Sir Charles, Your Excellency, thank you." Le Fanu had never seen Habi so nervous. "I'll do my best."

"Relax, Habi." Willingdon came around the table and sat by him. "I need your honest view, don't hold back. Talk to me as LF says you talk to him. Too many people already tell me what they think I want to or should hear. I need the truth."

"Certainly, Your Excellency. There's definitely a rising problem. The three recent Muslim murders do connect to the village events where even more Muslims were killed. These visitors from the north are linked to Mohammad Reiza's death. Today's killings were carried out by at least some of those from the north."

Whitney intervened. "Habi, LF. Do we have any identities from today yet?"

"Not so far," answered Habi. "No identifying papers on the bodies. That was deliberate, and suggests the venture was planned, not random. The victims were Muslim, so one obvious conclusion is that the attackers were Hindu."

Willingdon looked uncomfortable. "Habi, forgive me, but could this just be a difference of opinion amongst Muslims?"

"That's a fair question, sir. Yes, there are differences between Presidency Muslims. Tamils, Telugus and Urdu speakers often disagree on business interests, religious views and political objectives. Historically, however, those differences have never produced an atrocity like this. There's been the odd murder over the years, heated moments of madness, rage or jealousy. But never such a deadly, planned mass attack. Elsewhere in India, that sort of attack has usually resulted from Hindu–Muslim clashes."

Silence prevailed, interrupted after a while by Le Fanu. "Habi, what do we know about these characters from up north?"

"Not as much as we'd like, sir. But we do know that a quasi-Hindu nationalist movement is on the rise up there and across in western India. You know of Vinayak Damodar Savarkar's writings."

Le Fanu remembered his train trip to Secunderabad.

"I thought he'd gone quiet since his release from jail," said Willingdon. "Didn't he agree to renounce violence and stay away from politics?"

"Yes, sir, but there's some debate about his sincerity. He's still promoting Hindu rights and was a renowned critic of Muslims as a kid."

Whitney puffed more smoke upwards. "Habi, is there any possibility your Muslim sources have, shall we say, certain predisposed views?"

Habi grinned. "Sir, we Muslims are as biased as anybody, but Savarkar's views are reported widely. He says consistently that Hindus must dominate Muslims."

"Writing's a long way from doing." More smoke spiralled up.

"Agreed, sir. But many Hindus are listening to and reading him. And some are developing big ideas. Dr Hedgewar, that Nagpur medical man up in the Central Provinces, is building a paramilitary group to promote Savarkar's ideas. They're both Brahmins, have histories of nationalist activity, and are disillusioned with the moderate Congress approach. These new movements are getting support."

"I've heard that from Frank Sly, the CP Governor. And he's no reactionary, strong supporter of the Montagu-Chelmsford Reforms that so many of your people oppose, Charles, sorry to say."

"Can't disagree, I'm afraid, Your Excellency."

"So, if Frank's worried about Savarkar and his acolytes, then I am, too. Is there any evidence of a connection between all that and what's going on here, Habi?"

"Not yet, but Assistant Superintendent Caldicott's team and mine are both searching hard because these cases definitely overlap."

"LF," Whitney asked, "do you have any views?"

"We should chase any possible connections, and Jackson's people are checking their contacts elsewhere, including Nagpur. Habi's right. Most problems like this are straight out Hindu–Muslim clashes rather than disputes within one community or other. And we can't ignore the possibility of links to developments elsewhere. Though why they'd choose Madras is a puzzle."

"Sir, not if they thought we were unprepared, never having dealt with that sort of thing."

"And they'd be right, Habi," said Willingdon. "Maintain this line of inquiry until proven wrong. I'll check with my provincial counterparts and see if they can enlighten us."

Whitney stood. "Very good, Your Excellency."

"Habi," said Willingdon, "thank *you*, especially, for coming. I know it hasn't been easy. And I know that explaining your views hasn't been easy within the police."

"Thank you, sir."

"Your Excellency," Le Fanu intervened, "the main reason for that is the Inspector-General. He's created an atmosphere in which it's impossible to debate anything. Habi's views are unpopular. He and Caldicott have disagreed, and that's rare. But those views must be considered, and that's impossible in the force at present."

"Fuck the man! Apologies for the language, Habi." Willingdon was angry. "Delhi won't let me touch him, too scared of publicity, here and in England. The really worrying thing is his support here among ICS members who should know better. Like that ass Jamieson. I hear they're close."

Le Fanu reported his meeting with the pair.

"As I say," Willingdon added, "Delhi's too scared to break those chummeries, and the longer they survive, the more dangerous they become. Especially when the likes of these killings comes along. Jepson's incapable of dealing with them. Any ideas, Charles?"

"Only the obvious one. LF should be in charge."

"Of the police? Of course. But I can't swing that."

"I was thinking more of perhaps extending LF's current brief to include full Presidency oversight of Hindu–Muslim matters? All of them, not just crime-related. Although I hear writers these days suggest everything is crime related. Anyway, that would give him free rein."

"You'll be missed, Charles. Brilliant. LF, consider yourself appointed."

"And I've an office for you here in the Secretariat, already stocked with the necessary materials. I'll show you once we leave." Whitney looked smug.

"But before you do leave us, Charles, I'd relish the chance to best you, just once." Willingdon saluted his Chief Secretary, who returned the favour.

"Thank you, both," said Le Fanu, "and you, Habi, for persisting with these unpopular views that are obviously more right than wrong."

"You've taught me well, sir."

Le Fanu doubted he'd taught Habi anything.

As they left, Le Fanu wondered how Jepson would react. He'd just lost significant power, Le Fanu again the cause. The war would escalate.

Whitney, Habi and Le Fanu walked back along the corridors, silently at first, sensing major confrontations ahead.

"Come on, LF, I'll show you the new office. You come along too, Habi, you'll be spending a lot of time here." He walked around to an area close to his own office, Le Fanu realised. An outer door revealed a waiting room and a desk.

"There'll be a clerk here in the morning."

Whitney showed them through into a spacious office with large windows overlooking the harbour. As Whitney had suggested, it was already full of materials on the Presidency's Hindu–Muslim relations, and one wall carried a large map locating Muslim communities.

"This'll be a start," said Whitney, reprising the smug look.

Sixteen

Having finally fallen asleep around 3 am, Le Fanu was bleary when woken by the birds three hours later, sunlight streaming in to make the room hotter than normal because he had forgotten to close the wooden shutters. He lay there for a while, mentally reviewing that day's priority list which seemed far too long. A cold shower helped wake him, the cook's excellent breakfast added more cheer. His old cook had retired home to the country when Le Fanu left for Penang and Varna, the new one, came on recommendation from Krishna Rao, his restaurant friend. A brilliant choice. That reminded Le Fanu he still hadn't eaten any of his friend's Udipi food. He should fix that.

"Varna, wonderful breakfast, thank you. Could I have more coffee, please?"

The cook beamed and hurried away as the telephone rang.

Jackson Caldicott. "Good morning, LF, sorry to call this early."

"It must be important."

"We might just have picked up the suspects' trail."

"That is a good start to the day."

"Thought you'd like it. I hear you've a smart new Secretariat office, so why not call in to mine on your way there so I can fill in the detail?"

"Twenty minutes? I take it The Jockey won't appear until much later?"

"Naturally."

There were more people living on the streets than when he left, he reckoned as the driver headed towards the police offices on the beach road. Times were harder. The monsoon had failed, country crops followed suit, so merchants had less product, prices rose, labour demand slowed and people made for the city in vain search of work and income. Shanty towns were mushrooming in Madras, especially along the Buckingham Canal. It still amazed Le Fanu that entire families could emerge from these makeshift homes looking as immaculate as he did coming out of his mansion.

That this was still happening was another blot on the Raj, even if the task of improving life for well over 250 million people across India was close to impossible. And that figure ignored the 17 million who died during the Spanish influenza epidemic at the end of the war.

As they turned into the police compound, he feared for the future given the Raj's poor handling of Congress and the Muslim League. Mohammad Ali Jinnah, the League's leader, had resigned from Congress to champion India's Muslims, prompted among other things by the allies' post-war demolition of the Ottoman Empire and its Caliphate. The Caliph had been the Muslims' spiritual leader, now they sought a new direction. For Le Fanu, that made Jepson's village outburst even more shocking. It suggested that Muslims did not matter to the British.

He went up to Caldicott's office. Le Fanu wondered how much time his friend spent here now. The George Town one was more removed from the Jepson jeremiad.

As he approached, he heard Caldicott and Habi in animated discussion.

"Good morning, gentlemen. An argument? I hope not, because right now I've enough challenges."

"A spirited discussion only, sir." Habi looked unconvinced by his own comment.

"You two debating the Muslim question again?"

"Afraid so, LF. I think Habi's overreacting."

"National Muslim leaders might disagree. And given Jepson's outburst, I understand why Habi's worried. There's too much Hindu–Muslim tension about. We must treat yesterday as a Hindu attack on Muslims until we see evidence to the contrary."

Habi looked vindicated.

"I accept things are difficult, but there's no intelligence to suggest something big is imminent."

"But," shouted Habi, "there are several dead Madras Muslims in the morgue following a planned execution! How can that not be big?"

Le Fanu paused. "The best way to find out what's really going on is to focus on the evidence. Jackson, you've got something new?"

"Thanks to your journalist friend. He called last night to pass on new information."

Caldicott did not know about the secret Muslim source. Le Fanu wondered if Habi did yet.

"Interesting," Le Fanu said. "Where'd he get it from?"

"No idea," Caldicott shot back. "Said he'd been talking to someone."

"And I have to admit it does sound credible, sir."

Perhaps Habi did not know.

"Tell me."

Caldicott pulled over a sheet of paper. "A group of men registered at a small hotel in Perambur two days ago, and stood out because they spoke almost no Tamil."

"Could anyone make out what they did speak?"

"Hindi in some cases, and probably a couple of Bengali speakers."

"That worries me. Habi?"

"Sir, it does suggest some sort of Hindu organisation. If they've come from different places they must have been in contact before arriving, and that indicates a plan. That's what Assistant Superintendent Caldicott and I were, um, discussing."

"Jackson, you don't see it as a plot?"

"Not really, LF. Yes, it's odd but, again, there's nothing worrying in the intelligence. Or anything to suggest Madras is a target."

"Sir, at least one of them comes from Nagpur."

"And you think immediately of Dr Hedgewar."

"Yes, sir."

"I assume Barnes's informant gave us an address?"

"Yes, LF, we have it under watch."

"Any suspicious activity?"

"Not so far."

"I'm worried. There's no reason to think they'd be a target but large numbers of Anglo-Indians live in Perambur because of the railways." Le Fanu was thinking of Ro who came from a railway family. The Anglo-Indian public taint had been a factor in their relationship.

"LF, I've sent officers to check if the Anglo-Indian leaders have encountered any threats."

"Good work. Is that all?"

The other two nodded.

"In that case, we won't make progress sitting here. Jackson, get back to your real office before Jepson arrives.

Keep in touch through the day. Habi, you drew the short straw. We'd better visit Dr Ramachandran."

At least the other two agreed here, laughing simultaneously.

"Sir, are you up to this? Perhaps I should go alone."

"Good idea, Habi. LF might not be ready, he's been away a while."

"Quite right, don't want to make things too hard for Dr Ramachandran."

"I'm glad I can make you two laugh. Thanks for your concern. I'll be fine."

"Of course you will, sir." They would not let up, Le Fanu realised.

"Good luck, LF. I'll look forward to your reports later."

"Please go and do something useful."

The nearer they got to Madras General, however, the less confident he became. Habi tried to distract him with a constant commentary on passers-by, Raj gossip, local restaurants, newspaper articles and anything else he could think of.

"Thanks, Habi, but I think I'm overloaded now."

"Of course, sir. Once we're there, let me know if you need anything."

Someone must have telephoned ahead because Rama was waiting at the rear of the hospital, near the shortcut to the morgue. Le Fanu thought his friend looked older, more drawn, though it was only a few months since they'd last met.

"Chris, Habi, lovely to see you, though I'm sure we all wish it were somewhere else."

"Hello, Rama. Are you healthy? You look more tired than I feel."

"It's been busy these past few weeks, and yesterday topped it off. We've been here all night."

"Sorry about that," Habi said, "but we have a real problem with this."

"Of course, Habi, I understand. As a Hindu, may I say I'm very sorry this has happened. Hindus and Muslims have always got along here."

"Thank you, sir. I agree. That peaceful background makes this worse, especially following those other murders."

"What would you like to do first?"

"I suspect Superintendent Le Fanu should get the autopsy over first," Habi replied.

Le Fanu nodded.

Rama turned through the door into the corridors that Le Fanu immediately remembered for their smells and abhorrent shelves of specimens. Twenty paces in and it was getting to him. He was sweating, faint. Head down, watching his shoes. That probably made it worse. But he could not look at those jars. Habi slid him a water bottle. Le Fanu sipped at it while Rama hurried past the worst exhibits to reach his tiny, cluttered office where a fan belted about tepid air and errant papers.

"Rest here while I finalise the lab. Habi, can you keep time and come in after ten minutes?"

"Of course, sir."

Le Fanu swigged more water and swiped his forehead with a handkerchief taken from his pocket. "The worst thing, Habi, is getting out of practice and having to start all over again."

"I understand, sir. Once you're back here permanently, Dr Ramachandran will retrain you."

Le Fanu couldn't tell if Habi was being provocative or disingenuous. It was rarely the latter.

A few minutes later Habi was steering Le Fanu towards the morgue. Bodies lying under sheets on trolleys everywhere. That did not help. Through the green swing doors. Several deep breaths. More water.

Rama's entire team looked exhausted. Every table was occupied with Rama at the closest one so Le Fanu did not have to run the gauntlet. Even so, he felt the room closing in and started shallow breathing, which Rama noticed.

"Over here, Chris. I've reserved a place for you." There was a chair strategically placed so Le Fanu could not see the worst of the body.

"Thanks, Rama, I'm surviving." The shallow breathing had passed. "What can you tell us?"

"The bullets were all Japanese, and we're told that's consistent with the weapons found out there. Russian, I believe?"

"Yes," Habi replied.

"Those bullets were modified to cause maximum damage. Whether they hit body or head, they literally exploded on impact, causing catastrophic injuries."

He lifted the sheet on the body. Habi took a long look, Le Fanu glanced then looked away.

"I see what you mean," said Habi. "They'd have died instantly."

"Yes, but they weren't all shot immediately."

"What do you mean?" Le Fanu was puzzled. "It looked to us like they were lined up and executed."

"They were, more or less. But some were severely beaten beforehand."

"Why do that if you were going to kill them?"

"To humiliate them." Habi's voice shook. "This was a message to Muslims."

"Are you sure?"

"Unfortunately, Chris, I agree with Habi. This shamed the victims, humiliated them, as Habi says. That gives the attack clear intent."

"So this was an attack by Hindus on Muslims based on faith."

"That's what it looks like. Now, let's get you back to my office."

Le Fanu somehow made it there. Rama took a bottle of Talisker from the cupboard, poured a measure and handed it over. "I laid in the stock especially."

Le Fanu downed it.

"Dr Ramachandran, what can you tell us about those other Muslim murders?"

"Habi, I've only seen the Madras victim, Mohammad Reiza Khan, but there's something odd about that now we've also seen yesterday's unfortunates."

He pulled a file from a drawer, selected a page and handed it to the policemen. "This copy's for you. The murder victim was also beaten up before being killed. Shot with a rifle similar to those used yesterday. Similar ammunition, too. One bullet caused massive damage."

Habi exhaled heavily. "Sir …"

"I know, Habi. We likely have an execution squad in Madras, targeting Muslims."

"Sorry to confirm that bad news, but the evidence looks conclusive." Rama stood behind his desk. "We've completed the autopsies. Not all victims were beaten, but they were all shot with the same ammunition used on the Madras murder victim, who was also beaten. I suspect you'll find similar wounds on the other two victims who may or may not have been beaten."

"Thanks, Rama, I think. The hardest task will be getting Jepson to take this seriously, given his comments about Muslims yesterday."

"What was that?" Rama was surprised.

"That not enough of us had been killed," Habi said quietly.

"Why doesn't Willingdon sack the fool?"

"Can't get support in Delhi, and because Jepson has Secretariat and Board supporters."

"He belongs back in the nineteenth century," said Rama.

"That's too modern for him," Habi replied.

Seventeen

Le Fanu, Habi and Caldicott were in the Connemara lounge at seven the next morning, having first inspected the road blocks then checked the police contingent around the hotel. The constables guarding the swimming pool were enjoying themselves the most, though their presence bothered some guests, especially the European women.

Le Fanu preferred the D'Angelis because the Connemara was long on starch, lost on service and lamentable on atmosphere. Surprisingly, Whitney seemed to feel the same way when he arrived with a couple of junior officers.

"Good morning to you all." A cigar was already at work. "Pity we have to meet here but there you are, the box wallahs enjoy it." Whitney flicked ash at a nearby tray, missed.

"Good morning to you, Sir Charles," Le Fanu replied, "I assume you've had breakfast."

"Good God, yes. Bad enough having to come here, without eating at the wretched place."

Habi and Caldicott did not know where to look.

Whitney noticed. "Never mind me, you two. Been here too long. That said, it's still better than Delhi."

"Yes, sir," they chorused.

"Now," Whitney continued, "we meet this lot in the library in about half an hour so let's get ready in there."

They traipsed through several corridors past smarmy servants and syrupy European managers, trooped up to the second floor and in through a door marked 'Library' to find a room that had a few old copies of *The Times*, *Country Life* and *Punch*. Nothing else.

"Some library." Whitney picked up a tattered copy of the latter and thumbed through the pages. "Wonder if 'HB' gets a run in this?"

"One of your favourites, Sir Charles?" Le Fanu tried to sound neutral.

"Hilton Brown? Damned good writer, troublesome ICS man, keeps asking questions and raising alternative ideas. Bloody nuisance."

The other three grinned. "Can't have that, sir," Caldicott remarked.

Whitney returned the smiles. "I know, bloody reactionary, eh? HB's a good man who's uncomfortable with the directions taken by some of his colleagues, and he's right. But he'd be more effective if he found other ways to deal with it. Like all of us, I suppose." He pounded a butt into a silver tray and lit another cigar.

"Sir," asked Habi, "who exactly are we meeting?"

A trailing junior handed Whitney a page that the Chief Secretary scanned.

"Thanks for saving me, Habi. Twenty-five in all. Lancashire cotton mill owners, garment manufacturers, a few engineering companies with railway interests, a couple of jewellery suppliers, then there's some mineral dealers, a gold company representative, shipping agents and, believe it or not, two horse dealers. Those last two'll have trouble beating off the Aussies. They've dominated the market here for fifty years."

"I can see why the Governor's worried, Sir Charles," Caldicott slid in, "that covers the gamut of our British trade."

"It does, indeed, and right now they're an unimpressed gamut, if you can have such a thing."

The door opened and the aggrieved contingent filed in, spearheaded by a tall, distinguished-looking elderly man. He was followed by a motley crew of largely middle aged men of various shapes and sizes ranging from cadaverous to elephantine.

To Le Fanu's surprise, the group was joined by three elegantly turned out women in their thirties and forties, a sharp contrast to their male counterparts.

"Gentlemen," the leader intoned in a perfect Oxford college accent, "to whom do I have the honour of speaking?"

Le Fanu noticed one of the women rolling her eyes.

"I am Sir Charles Whitney, Chief Secretary to the Government of Madras. This is Superintendent Le Fanu, Special Advisor to Lord Willingdon, Governor of Madras." Whitney was laying it on. "Then we have Assistant Superintendent Mohammad Habibullah, who is head of our special Crime Unit that employs the newest European approaches to criminology. And last but by no means least, Assistant Superintendent Caldicott who is Head of Special Branch here so liaises with MI5, MI6 and Scotland Yard. Now, who are you?"

The eye-roller was smiling now. This group had internal challenges.

"Oh, well, I'm Jeremy James, from the White Rose Mills in Lancashire."

"Your position there?" pressed Whitney.

"Oh, I assist our General Manager."

That game to Whitney.

"And your colleagues?" Whitney turned away dismissively and invited the rest to introduce themselves.

There was the odd managing director and general manager, but after Whitney's performance they stumbled through their recitations.

Except for the women. One was senior partner in a London law firm establishing connections across India. The second was principal of a leading London fashion house. Le Fanu wondered who in Madras might afford and wear her clothes. Number three owned an engineering works in Glasgow and, undaunted by the male posturing, had obviously been in India a lot.

"Very good," said Whitney. "Now, we're extremely sorry you've been confined to the Connemara but hope you understand it's been necessary. My experts here will give you the details, but we've had some unusual incidents in the city recently, so we're taking all precautions, especially with such a notable group as yours."

He paused. Le Fanu wondered whether that was to underline irony or sincerity.

"But," Whitney continued, "we've arranged for you to begin your visits today. I understand you have both group and individual appointments so we'll accommodate all of those. One of my assistants here will be with you full time to make all arrangements."

Whitney pointed to one of his juniors who looked unimpressed at being designated babysitter. His attitude was returned by his charges, except the women who looked kindlier.

"Now, Superintendent Le Fanu will give you the overall picture. He'll be followed by Caldicott and Habibullah who'll fill in the detail. Gentlemen."

An hour later, the three of them left the Connemara together while Whitney went to the Secretariat.

"The Chief Secretary put them in their place quick smart." Caldicott was enjoying the memory.

"But they were still unimpressed at having their travel interrupted," Habi said, "and they weren't pleased at being chaperoned."

"They'll get used to it." Le Fanu changed course. "What next for us?"

Caldicott would return to his George Town lair and check the latest intelligence reports; Habi to headquarters for updates on the murder cases and the village shootings.

Le Fanu was suddenly irresolute, because he had no immediate concrete task. "I'll walk to the *Mail*." It was close by, and he could also view the new books in Higginbotham's. Barnes might not yet be in the office but it was a worthwhile risk. "If Chester is unavailable, I'll call for a car."

He set out on the short stretch to the office, feeling the morning temperature rise along with the noise and smells of a working day. A couple of beggars asked for money, itinerant sellers offered him woven brooms, and off in the distance he saw some provincial pottery sellers surrounded by buyers or the curious, or both. He stood out himself because few Europeans walked anywhere.

By the time he reached the *Mail* building and climbed the stairs he was in a sweat. Luckily Barnes was in so he was soon in front of a fan with a fresh lime soda at hand and another being prepared.

"Most welcome, LF, but it's unlike you simply to drop in."

"We were up at the Connemara with Whitney soothing stranded industrialists."

"Anything for me there?"

"Couple of interesting stories. There's a woman here

from a London law firm doing interesting work across India. Might be a different angle."

"Certainly is. I'll follow that up. Now, why are you here, really?"

"Filling in time. I wondered if you'd heard more from your mystery journalist."

"You must be psychic, but can I get you anything more after that arduous walk?"

"Less sarcasm for a start, but nothing else."

"Fair enough. She has just reported in again. Last night, the local Muslim League bigwigs received detailed information on the people who carried out the village raid. Names, home towns, local addresses, the lot."

"I wonder if Habi has all that?"

"Good question. He may not, because her other news is that the Muslim League's now wary of the police, thanks to Jepson's remarks."

"I knew that couldn't be good. Anything else?"

"Several Muslim leaders are suggesting their best protection will come from within."

"Vigilantes."

"Rather like that Hindu chap in Nagpur is suggesting on his side."

"You know about that?"

"He's becoming big news. Gandhi's backdown on mass action opened the door for someone like that. And the Muslim uproar over losing their Ottoman leaders pushed it wider."

"Hedgewar's not getting much support, though."

"Enough to attract attention. He's now being pursued by journalists, and that's a sure sign."

"So am I, but my name's not front and centre."

"Sorry, mate. You're not news, first. And I keep you to myself, second."

"Should I be flattered?

"No."

"Right, I'll be off. Doing anything for dinner? I'm overdue at Krishna Rao's."

"Can't tonight. Tomorrow?"

"At the moment, yes. Any problems I'll let you know. Thanks for the information."

He called a car, descended the stairs, waited ten minutes, got collected and soon arrived at his new Secretariat office where the document piles had proliferated. Some were from Whitney, the rest from Caldicott and included further information on several Hindu and Muslim organisations as well as many of the suspects. And Habi's team had identified three of the dead raiders.

Le Fanu arranged to see Habi later, telephoned Caldicott for a further update, then thought it time to talk further with Whitney.

As he walked towards the Chief Secretary's domain, several people addressed him by name, warmly. Le Fanu knew almost none of them, but they seemed happy to see him. Whitney got him straight in, and he passed two cross-looking young ICS men on their way out.

"Come in, Chris. I need knowledge and common sense. Someone has corrupted the ICS examination, I think. Our new people are hopeless, including those two miscreants you saw leaving."

"You're changing, Charles, more jokes these days."

"That wasn't one of them. Those two produced an economic report so far off the mark it might have been one of Lenin's propaganda magazines."

"Not that bad, surely?"

"The socialists are sneaking in. Those two were quoting John bloody Maynard Keynes at me, huge slabs from *A Tract on Monetary Reform* and his pre-war *Indian Currency and Finance.*"

"He does have a following."

"Even here, yes. But none of it makes sense for Madras. We're just here to balance the books. But you didn't come about that, you've enough problems."

"Were you happy with this morning's meeting?"

"Enjoyed myself. Took that poseur down a peg or three."

"You did. But the women seemed smart."

"Couple of Girton girls, one of them among the first women recognised by the Law Society. Different world now."

"If those three are typical, that's a good thing. Far more impressive than the men."

"Going a bit suffragette?"

"No bad thing." He thought of Jenlin.

"Actually, I agree. Have a couple of daughters myself who got blocked from doing things for which they were highly qualified."

It occurred to Le Fanu he knew nothing about Whitney's private life, nor about anyone else's, apart from Jepson.

"Where are they now, Charles?"

"Another day, Chris. Anything I can help with?"

"Just checking if there was anything to follow up from this morning. And to say Barnes has given me good information that Habi and Caldicott will get onto."

"HE will be delighted. Join me at the club tonight?"

It was expressed as, but not, a question. Le Fanu did not want to go but the answer was obvious. "That'd be excellent, Charles, thank you."

"Good, I need some decent company. Turn up about seven."

Le Fanu traipsed back to find a clerk outside his office, sitting at a desk and arranging papers. A very junior ICS man who stood when Le Fanu arrived.

"Superintendent Le Fanu? Honoured to meet you, sir. Douglas Gaines, sir."

"Thank you, Gaines. How long have you been in Madras?"

"About three months, sir."

"Background?" Le Fanu feared he sounded like someone from the nineteenth century.

"Hampshire, sir. Landed family, I'm the youngest son. Sent off to Winchester, hated it. Then to Edinburgh University."

Whitney had done his homework.

"So did I. Loved it. You?"

"I did, sir. And St Andrews."

Whitney really had done his homework.

"Good start, Gaines, good start. Any messages?"

"Some routine calls from Assistant Superintendents Habibullah and Caldicott. Another from Sir Maurice Wilson, I think, Hyderabad?"

"Indeed. Well done."

"Another from the office of the Inspector-General of Police, sir."

"In future, Gaines, keep those from me until very late in the day."

"Understood, sir."

“And when we’re here like this, drop the ‘sir’.”

“Understood. Sir.”

“You’ll do.”

“And there’s a telegram on your desk, sir, ah, Superintendent.”

“I’d better look at that.” Wilson had called, now a telegram. Le Fanu dreaded the news.

He walked into his office, looked approvingly at the organisation Gaines had imposed. Nothing on the desk apart from the telegram. It was from his Singapore spy friend, Watson.

Jenlin Koh was listed as a passenger on the *Asiatic* sailing from Singapore to Colombo where she would disembark. Watson concluded she would then sail for Madras.

Eighteen

He sat for several minutes, not knowing how to interpret this, trying to fathom what she was doing. Having yet to receive a letter from her made it more puzzling but he was still just back in Madras a week, despite all that had happened, so perhaps that was not surprising. After the day's earlier confrontation, he was certain his brain had slowed.

Gaines entered bearing tea and food. "Hope you don't mind, Superintendent, but I thought you might need sustenance."

"I do, thank you. Now what's your view of present events?"

Gaines hesitated, hands clasped behind his back, head up, looking straight ahead.

"At ease, Gaines. Feel free to speak."

"Thank you. Superintendent, we're getting ourselves in a policy bind. The civil and police sides are fundamentally at odds. Specifically, I should say the Board and the police, because the Secretariat and the police get on well, as your presence here confirms."

"And what are your spies saying about the Board?"

"Superintendent, I'm a very junior person."

"From where I'm sitting, you're doing fine. So?"

"Bluntly, the First Member's priority is to become Chief Secretary. He thinks lining up with Jepson against you and Sir Charles will win favour among conservative police and ICS officers."

"But Whitney's a conservative."

"These days perhaps more a realist. Some think that because he and the Governor turn to you for solutions during these reform days, the Chief Secretary is softening. Silly, I know, but these are silly times."

"Gaines, we'll get along well. Anything lined up for me?"

"Sir Charles asked me to remind you about dinner at the club this evening, and that the Governor will see you both after. And a friend in the I-G's office tells me there are differences of opinion about how to report the village events."

"No surprise there."

"There's one other thing you may not have heard. Word came from Delhi late last night. The Chief Secretary will remain here for the next week but move up there soon after."

"So get our skates on and fix this mess, that the message?"

"Yes, Superintendent."

Le Fanu sifting through everything in his head, personal and professional, for an hour, and even attempted to chart it on paper. That made it look even more complex. Jenlin might arrive in Madras while Ro was still ill in Secunderabad. Jepson and Jamieson were waging a vicious campaign. Whitney was now definitely on the way out, Willingdon close behind. Hindu–Muslim tension in Madras was on the rise, instigated by an armed and organised outside force. And that tension was fuelling friction between Habi and Caldicott. He felt tired just looking at the pages he'd created so filed them under 'bin'.

Through what remained of the afternoon, he constructed case notes on the village incident and the murders, pointing to the potential links between them. Le Fanu realised that, while Habi had passed on some Mohammad Reiza Khan case information, he knew little about the other murders.

He called Habi and asked that the case files be sent over.

"Of course, sir, but why?"

"Because I think increasingly that you're right. There's a clear link between the murders and the village episode. And I fear more of the same, so I want to have a look and see if I can help."

"Excellent, sir. Assistant Superintendent Caldicott is here and would like to speak with you."

"Hello, LF. New office suiting you?"

"Far better than my official one over there, yes. What's up?"

"We've confirmed all the names and addresses Barnes passed on to you and we're planning a raid tonight. Care to join in?"

"I've dinner at the club with Whitney. Can't escape that. What time?"

"Midnight or so. We reckon they're more likely to act through the day, given what's happened so far. Always a risk we're wrong, but that's the plan."

"I should be free by then. We will see Willingdon after dinner but I should be clear by midnight. I'll let you know if there's any change."

"Good, we'll leave from headquarters but could pick you up wherever you like."

"Make it here, then, save time."

"See you then."

It would be difficult for Habi and Caldicott to mobilise this inside headquarters, he thought, given Jepson's belligerence. He felt guilty not being there to help.

Le Fanu read and reflected on the Hindu–Muslim developments across the Presidency and came away concerned. He saw the same patterns that bothered Habi. Muslim leadership was distancing itself from the Congress, and some Hindu groups welcomed that. Locally, all the usual niggles were becoming more serious, disturbances had arisen in places not normally affected, and communal sniping was becoming an everyday occurrence. That was a worrying backdrop.

Whitney had offered to take him to the club but Le Fanu cancelled that, explaining he would need to move quickly later, given the planned operation. His own driver took him from the Secretariat to Club House Road off the central section of Mount Road, near the Connemara. He wondered how the day had been for the British delegation.

He climbed the steps into one of the Empire's largest clubs, a sprawling, elitist citadel in a city undergoing great change. Women were consigned to their own pavilion, set off to the side of the main building into which they were not permitted. That was why women preferred the Adyar Club, where they could become members, and one of several reasons Le Fanu avoided coming here. Women got the vote in Britain in 1918 yet could still not join this club in Madras.

In truth, Le Fanu had come to hate the place. He had tolerated its set ways, anti-Indian sentiment and terrible English food before the war but, afterwards, those flaws magnified into the Empire's obvious problem, especially in India. A few thousand whites could not hold down millions of Indians forever, so change was needed. Club denizens, however, simply closed the doors and pretended everything was its normal nineteenth-century self.

It was almost a year since his last visit but the atmosphere was instantly familiar. Clouds of cigarette, pipe and cigar smoke created a fog in the bar. Men all dressed the same were hived off in corners swapping notes, gossip and information. Several looked at him, one or two called cautious greetings, many chose not to see him.

Whitney materialised at his elbow. "Been on the lookout for you, LF. The natives are restless. The Jockey's in attendance with Jamieson, and they're off dining somewhere with a coterie of conservatives. I know, marvellous coming from me, eh?"

They walked the length of the bar and into the dining room where Whitney had a small table in a secluded corner.

"Should be able to eat in peace here. And drink." He signalled a waiter. "What'll you have, LF?"

"Just one glass of wine, thanks. A Chablis. I'm on a raid later with Habi and Caldicott."

"The village vandals?"

"Yes, Barnes got some additional information, and we want to grab them while we can."

They consulted the menu and placed orders for food and wine.

Whitney lit up, as usual. "The Jockey know about this?"

"I assume so. Normal procedures would ensure that, but there's always the chance he doesn't read anything put in front of him."

"It's just that I heard him bragging earlier you're banned from all operational activities and Habi and Caldicott must get every move approved by him."

"News to me and, I suspect, to them. Would you mind if I telephone to confirm?"

"Go ahead, there's a chap there I need to bother, anyway."

Ten minutes later Le Fanu was back. Whitney appeared not to have left the table.

"Habi and Jackson knew nothing about that, either, but the plan will proceed tonight."

"As it should. But we'd better have a contingency."

"Like what?"

"I'll issue an order confirming the operation's under your command at my specific instruction. Part of your new responsibilities. Habi and Jackson are seconded to you along with all the men involved. Technically, it's not even a police matter."

"Can you do that?"

"No idea, but it's worth it. Upsets The Jockey and Jamieson simultaneously. Excellent result."

"I hear you're to leave sometime after next week."

"Gaines beat me to it. I was going to tell you after we finalised this administrative matter."

"Are the two things linked?"

"They might be, now I think of it. It might help cruel Jamieson's pitch at becoming my replacement. The more we tie him to Jepson the better. Willingdon'll confirm the new Chief Secretary soon, and I can tell you it's not that bloody First Member."

"There's more at stake here than a mere raid, then."

"Oh yes. I'll write the note when we finish dinner, and you head off for the fun and games."

"Who'll replace you?"

"Can't say, but don't worry. You'll be safe."

Dinner and drinks arrived, over which Whitney recounted fascinating stories from the old days when Madras had even more eccentric characters than now. That seemed hardly possible.

Just as dessert loomed, a shadow fell over the table and they realised things nearby had gone quiet. They looked up.

Wine glass in one hand, bottle in the other, Jepson was swaying unpredictably, face flushed, hair awry, tie loosened, shirt flap showing under a jacket threatening to burst any moment. "Bloody Le Fanu. Heard you were fouling the building, thought I'd come and clean you out."

Whitney stood abruptly. "Inspector-General, I suggest you leave immediately."

People at nearby tables stood, some hurried away. Servants stood fixed, uncertain what to do.

"Well you can fuck off, too, Whitney."

The room stilled.

"Jepson," Whitney replied in steady voice, "best run off before you do irreparable damage to what little is left of your reputation."

"I repeat, fuck off. You're as bad as he is."

Le Fanu stood. "Sir, please let's take this elsewhere. I'm happy to discuss it but not here."

"Sanctimonious shit. I'll have you out of here. Fucking blight on the police service and the Raj. Deliver us to the Indians, that's what you want. Sell us down the fucking river. Probably lusting after an Indian bint now, too, are you? What do you want, Hindu or Muslim? Long as they're coloured, that's you, isn't it?"

Voices elsewhere started to rise, and Le Fanu sensed not all were supporting him even if Jepson's behaviour breached all club rules and traditions.

"Jepson," Whitney cut in, "I repeat, leave now or you'll regret this. The club has clear rules on this sort of thing, and you're breaking them."

Some agreement from nearby.

"And I repeat," Jepson shouted, brandishing the bottle, "I'll have you out of here as well. Fuck off to Delhi. They'll know how to chew you up and spit you out."

The manager arrived with half a dozen well-dressed but large servants who might have been trained for this rare moment. But he seemed hesitant to order them into action.

"Sir," Le Fanu pleaded, "let's go somewhere else. Don't escalate this by getting these gentlemen involved. The members want to get on with their meals."

"The members want rid of bastards like you and your toady pal here, and I'll do that for them."

Jepson lurched forwards, upsetting the table and sparking more protests nearby. He swung the bottle towards Le Fanu who swayed back then grabbed it. Jepson swung his free hand and let go of the glass that careened into the wall.

Protests were now in full force. The large men looked to their boss who nodded. They moved in, Le Fanu and Whitney retreated. Jepson took a swing at one, connected, then kicked two others. Chairs went over, the table upended. Glass, food and cutlery flew everywhere.

Le Fanu was surprised to see Whitney smiling, then looked across the room to see Jamieson had arrived, looking furious. This was not part of his plan.

The large men tried to immobilise Jepson, but to his drink-inspired mind defeat was more an opportunity than a reality, so he continued to thrash about on the floor while they tried to subdue him. More tables and chairs went flying, along with their accoutrements. Jepson continued to abuse all and sundry while the manager tried to placate his aggrieved clientele.

It took fifteen minutes to restore calm. Jepson was escorted to the manager's office, servants scurried about righting things while bar stewards served complimentary drinks to soothe the offended.

"That was entertaining." Another cigar was lit.

"Jepson has a problem, that's clear. I doubt anyone here has seen anything like that before."

“Some older members will have, happened a bit in the good old days, but I admit, the club has become more civilised in recent years, or less depending on your point of view. Still, this does us some good.”

“How’d you mean?”

“A performance like this from the head of the police? Very bad form. Jepson’s really blotted his copybook now so my inquiry into the village fiasco doesn’t matter, irrelevant. Delhi can’t block this. He could even be expelled from the club. That’ll be the end of him. I’ll report to Willingdon who won’t be able to ignore it and won’t want to anyway. That’ll clear your way to becoming I-G again. And Jamieson is damaged comprehensively by association. I see he shot away quickly.”

Le Fanu was fairly sure he did not want the I-G position. An offer would further complicate an already muddled life. He was happy to see the back of Jepson, but he remembered the boredom and frustration of the top post.

“We should proceed carefully, Charles. We don’t want to rush things.”

“Chris, there are times when you’re so bloody transparent it’s not funny. I know you don’t want the job, but I have to make sure you get it, because that’s what’s good for the rest of us.”

“I appreciate the vote of confidence, but you know I’ve got a few complications in my life.”

“Not the least of which is this raid in the next couple of hours. Hadn’t you better focus on that? I’ll do the cover note.”

The manager arrived offering drinks. Whitney accepted but Le Fanu refused.

“LF, given this kerfuffle, don’t worry about seeing Willingdon. I can handle that. He and I’ll discuss the consequences then we can all convene more calmly tomorrow."

"Thanks for that, Charles. And for dinner."

"Wouldn't have missed it for quids. Not every day you get to see The Jockey make a complete ass of himself. Not in public, at least."

As he walked away, Le Fanu saw them back in all those far corners animatedly discussing events. The news would be all over the city already.

Back at the Secretariat he went up to his office, footsteps echoing in the deserted corridors. Gaines was still on hand. Did he have a home?

"Eventful evening, I hear, Superintendent."

"The news does travel fast, eh?"

"News like that, certainly. Habi has asked that you telephone him at his office."

"Habi, you've heard then?"

"Certainly have, sir. This place is in an uproar, and no one can talk about anything else. They've all lost focus. Sir, Assistant Superintendent Caldicott and I are reluctantly thinking we might postpone the raid."

"Really?"

"Yes, sir. Sounds silly but it might be risky to run the thing in these circumstances. For two reasons. All our personnel are distracted. And if it goes wrong it might give credence to Jepson."

"I hadn't thought of that, Habi, but if you and Jackson are worried I'll certainly accept your advice. But is there a risk we'll lose these characters again?"

"Unfortunately, yes, but we'll just have to increase our surveillance."

"Fair enough. I'm happy with an early night after all this."

Nineteen

Gaines was already in the office when Le Fanu arrived at 6.30 am. Clearly without a home, he had produced several files with colour coded tabs denoting each Muslim murder case, reports on the village killings and intelligence reports on the northern visitors.

"Good morning, Douglas. You ever leave the office?"

Gaines ignored that last bit. "Thank you, Superintendent, and I'm already hearing even more colourful accounts of last night's event."

"Madras is just an overgrown village."

"Afraid so. But will this change our approach to these cases?"

"I hope not. Jepson still has friends in the service branches. Most of them and a good slab of the commercial community loathe the idea of political reform. Jepson's extreme but typifies the really conservative forces. The First Member, for one, remains in his court. Do sit down, Douglas, I'm getting a sore neck looking up at you."

"Thank you, Superintendent." Gaines carried a chair from the wall and sat on the other side of the desk. "Given reform of some sort is inevitable now, shouldn't we be trying to shape it and maintain influence instead of being obstructionist?"

"Why aren't you running the political branch?"

"It's plain obvious to me and my generation. Most of us reckon our Indian careers will end well before we're due to retire. Gandhi's backed off but he'll return with millions of supporters. And things are changing at home. Take that Parsi chap, Shapurji Saklatvala. He's in parliament for the Labour Party but is really a Communist. There's growing support for some sort of self-rule in India. You'd have to be blind to ignore all that."

"As I say, you should be running political. I'll have a word to Whitney before he goes."

"I've work to do for you first, Superintendent."

Le Fanu spent three hours reading Gaines's papers, especially those on the Muslim murders, seeing again why Habi connected them with the northerners' arrival.

The Tanjore victim, from the Rowther community, was a local Muslim leader in a major Hindu pilgrimage centre. He was also connected indirectly to the Muslim League, his brother in Madras an officeholder. The Guntur patterns were similar, the victim a well-known merchant who had resigned from Congress over concerns that Muslims were being forgotten.

This political dimension to the murders could neither be ignored nor put down to simple coincidence. Le Fanu couldn't remember doing it, but the only thing he brought from the broom cupboard office was his copy of Gross's *Criminal Investigation*, the book that had inspired Sir Maurice Wilson to create the Crime Unit. Two local lawyers produced the edition because they wanted to see more advanced investigation methods used in Madras.

Little did they know, thought Le Fanu, how much trouble they had caused. Senior police like Jepson still opposed the new methods, despite the success, despite widening adoption around the world and despite younger policemen routinely being trained in the methodology. That antagonism mirrored the overall resistance to change that Gaines had observed. Perhaps Gaines should be drafted into the IPS. Not until after Jepson was out of the way.

As he thumbed through the well-worn sections of *Criminal Investigation*, the more Le Fanu believed Habi to be right.

"Gaines, could you telephone Habi and ask him to meet me? Probably best at Caldicott's office. Say in an hour."

As his car passed through Fort St George's narrow wall gate to the coast road, Le Fanu was reminded, again, how cloistered the British were in India. Less so in the districts than here, perhaps, especially in the punishment stations. Out there, Brits were forced to meet locals because there was no one else. Those posts were particularly tough on British women. A few intrepid ones learned the local language and worked hard to improve things for local women, but others clung to a sparse club life and longed for leave back Home.

In bigger towns and cities, it was easier to retreat into a sheltered life, as he had seen in Secunderabad. He thought again of Ro. He might well be accused of taking shelter here in Madras. Jepson's implosion was one manifestation of closed community thinking, where different thoughts and approaches were dismissed. The man's contempt for Indians was regrettable but, sadly, not unusual, even if ICS and European police officers had to be proficient in a local language or two. Somehow, cultural sympathy did not automatically accompany language facility.

Besides which, Le Fanu had still not contacted Krishna Rao, someone he called a friend. Was he supposed to be going there tonight, with Barnes?

He sensed paradox. Some of the best investigations into south Indian language, history and culture over the past century were produced by European officers. Gordon Mackenzies' 1883 *A Manual of the Kistna District, in the Presidency of Madras* remained a model. The renegade Galletti's Telugu language skill was unparalleled, his work on the Dutch East India Company unsurpassed. However, service colleagues of thinkers like that produced the blindest, most belligerent and retrogressive views of Indian society and ambitions possible.

By now, the temperature was rising towards 90 degrees Fahrenheit. He opened a car window to catch the sea breeze and all the sounds. Passing through George Town streets, he heard the commercial patter, deals argued and done. Progress slowed as those streets narrowed so that the upper storeys of buildings on both sides seemed somehow to lean towards each other and almost meet.

Back at street level, wandering cows blocked the way. So did laden handcarts pushed by lightly clad, spare, wiry figures eking out a living. The flower market was quiet, vendors on a meal break before the next onslaught of customers seeking devotional flowers that would swamp the area's many small temples.

He clambered up the stairs to the nondescript office that was already the Presidency's main source of criminal and political intelligence, and one of the best in India. Caldicott had a flair for this work so he, too, no doubt, would soon be earmarked for a transfer.

"Good to see you, LF. None the worse for last night?"

"Oh, I'm fine. The Jockey will have a really sore head and sore ears. I haven't heard from Whitney yet, but he or Willingdon or both will have had several words with Jepson. It was unpleasant but not difficult. Even most of his supporters thought he went too far."

"And the rumour mill suggests Whitney even enjoyed the contretemps."

"You have to hand it to him. In the middle of that fury he was reckoning the odds turning in his favour. Whitney's leaving is a big blow for us."

"Agreed. But Jepson's not done yet."

"What do you mean?"

"His pal Jamieson's pulled a clever stroke. Announced this morning he's appointing The Jockey to a special committee that'll make recommendations to any reform committees dealing with service conditions on either the police or civil side."

"Can he do that?"

"Technically, yes, though the normal course would be to negotiate agreement with Whitney then get approval from the Governor beforehand. By not doing that, he's declared support for Jepson and war against the departing senior officials."

"Bold for Jamieson. Reckless, or desperate?"

"Not really, when you think about it. He stakes a claim on a major policy area, just like he's making a pitch to replace Whitney. Momentarily, Jamieson's the senior man thumbing his nose at Willingdon who's not that dangerous because he's also about to go. The odd shouting match might eventuate but it's worth coping with to get where you want to be and have Jepson in your pocket as a bonus. Few people would consider that last point a bonus, I agree, but you'll get the point."

"Bloody hell. This just gets worse."

Habi came in carrying a bag full of documents and parcels of food. "Thought we could have lunch as we talked, sir."

He revealed banana leaves, rice, pickles, a goat curry, several other accompaniments and jars of lassi, the sweet milk drink Le Fanu had never really liked.

While they ate, Le Fanu repeated the club tale to Habi, who'd heard several versions from people who'd not been there but whose accounts were remarkably accurate, it turned out.

"Any other news this morning, Habi? I've now read through all the Muslim murder files, and I think you're definitely on the right track."

Le Fanu sensed Caldicott stop eating as Habi savoured the moment.

"Thank you, sir. Other news this morning suggests further links, too."

"Like what?" Caldicott's comment was more sneer than question.

Le Fanu hoped he would not have a management problem here.

"Like more information from Guntur. The victim there was Ashraf Haider, another merchant who helped fund local Congress activities during Non-Cooperation. He fed Gandhi's passive resistance strikers and volunteers there, and paid the fines for all of them. Had several freed from prison. He was a very big wheel."

"So?" The edge remained.

"So his name was found by police on a list among more papers held by some new Hindu organisations in Guntur. There's no indication what the list was for or why it was created, but again it's too much of a coincidence."

"Someone's list of likely donors?"

Caldicott was belabouring the point, Le Fanu thought. "Jackson," he said, "it does need following up. A Hindu nationalist lot is not likely to have asked a Muslim for donations, surely."

"Fair enough, but I'm not immediately accepting this as a big Hindu–Muslim flare-up when there may be other explanations."

"Fine, but we can't ignore this."

"No."

Le Fanu turned to Habi. "What else have we heard from Tanjore?"

"Local police reports. What you'd expect. The officers down there can't see the bigger picture. For them, it's a random killing done on the spur of the moment."

"Which it could be." Caldicott couldn't help himself. "Sorry."

"They could all be random," Le Fanu conceded, to lower the temperature, "but the broader patterns suggest otherwise. Jackson, what more do we have at the national level on these people who've turned up here?"

"I'm expecting more reports today but there were communications between the different groups before they travelled to Madras, plans for where they'd all stay, and regular communication between them once they arrived. That's how they wound up at that village. We've no explanation for why they went there, but my people are still sifting materials."

"Any additional evidence to connect the three murders to these gangs? They almost look like cells of the one gang to me."

"Possible, LF, but the answer so far is no. We've no more than we had yesterday."

"Any thoughts, Habi?"

"We should look more into the two murders that

occurred outside Madras, and start with Guntur. The additional information there is stronger than for Tanjore."

"Who do you need?"

"I can handle that alone, sir, with local assistance. I've three friends up there from the old Police School days. They're checking additional information and will report back tonight. If that looks significant I'll go up tomorrow for two or three days."

"That sounds good. Jackson?"

"I've these new reports coming in so I'll deal with those, update you and plan from there."

"Fine."

They finished the food, washed their hands and set off, Habi and Le Fanu leaving together.

"Habi, not too hard being out at headquarters on your own?"

"No problem at all, sir."

"You're doing great work, as usual. Keep it up. Don't mind Caldicott. This is a difficult time."

"No one wants to think about a Hindu–Muslim struggle, but it's possible and we must head it off."

"I agree."

It still bothered him, walking back through the Secretariat entrance guarded by those massive black marble columns. They honoured British ostentation. He climbed the similarly ornate stairs and found Gaines waiting for him.

"Superintendent, sorry. Sir Maurice Wilson wants you to telephone him urgently."

Twenty

He was back on the train to the twin cities by midnight, slept little and survived on tea and coffee provided either on the train or by sellers at various stops that he could not remember. Yet another blur. Those stations were usually highlights for him because this was real India, life outside the Madras bubble, with people whose views and attitudes determined Britain's success in holding the Indian subcontinent.

Through this long night, though, none of that mattered.

It was early afternoon before he reached Secunderabad station where Wilson was again waiting. They said little, exchanged handshakes and nods. Le Fanu handed his bag to the driver who pushed a way through the crowds, got them into the car and set off. They drove in silence for a few minutes.

"Chris, I'm sorry for dragging you back so quickly."

"Goes without saying I'm glad you did, Maurice."

"You need a break first? Sorry to say, you look terrible."

"I'd be lying to deny that. But no, press on."

Silence returned as they made for the hospital, Le Fanu wondering how it could all look so normal, when for him it was not. He doubted he could handle the next few hours. His mother was still alive, and his brother, even if they did not speak. It had been odd when his father died. Once Le Fanu turned down the Foreign Office in favour of the Indian Police Service, his father cut him off. But at his death, Le Fanu felt remorse for having let the rift continue, for not having spoken or communicated with his father at all. In his darkest moments still, that regret remained.

Wilson accompanied him into the hospital's reception area, got the necessary clearances and met the doctors, Statham again their leader.

"Good morning, Le Fanu, sorry to be seeing you so soon again."

In his shaken state, Le Fanu had no idea how to interpret that. "I won't prevaricate. We've almost certainly lost her. Hasn't responded as we wanted, and we've tried everything. Sorry to say we're just awaiting the inevitable. Shouldn't take long."

Le Fanu was unsure whether Ro's imminent death or Statham's insensitivity hit hardest.

"Might we have a quiet word?" Wilson grabbed his elbow, steered him to a corner, sat him in a wicker chair and took the one opposite. He leaned forward, elbows on knees. "Chris, we need action, and you must help me. I've got the Nizam's medical people on standby at the Osmania. We have to shift her, it's our only chance. This bombastic buffoon's expertise stops with leeches. They've tried everything and failed. Help me get her out."

Le Fanu nodded vaguely. "Of course, but we …"

"No, I need you to concentrate. Demand her release, now. Do that while I telephone the Osmania team and get them ready. Do it. Now."

Le Fanu struggled to stand, Wilson again with hand at elbow steering him back to the knot of impatient doctors looking at watches, ready to get on with their day that allowed nothing for a dying Anglo-Indian woman.

"Dr Statham, I …"

"Lieutenant Colonel, actually."

That transformed Le Fanu, rage replacing remorse.

"Right, *Lieutenant Colonel.* You're an abject failure …"

"Look here …"

"No, you look here. I repeat, abject failure. So you'll now release Mrs McPhedren to a team incoming from the Osmania."

Wilson slipped away.

"And," Le Fanu continued, "you'll hand over all Mrs McPhedren's records, updated to the minute of her departure."

"You cannot …"

"I can and I am, and will continue to do so. Now make the necessary arrangements. Have her ready to go within the next ten minutes."

"You're not family and have no …"

"Right now I'm the only family she's got. This is my decision. Get her ready to leave. Now. Take your reprobate retinue with you in case you have trouble finding the files. You'd struggle to find your backside. Or her room for that matter, you haven't taken this at all seriously. Once this is over, I'll be writing to your superiors."

"Of all the damned …"

"Never mind that. Just fuck off and follow my orders."

Statham tried to regain authority by ordering his staff away, and they all moved off, hopefully to her room to prepare her for the move.

Le Fanu was shaking either from rage, relief, anxiety or sheer frustration, and had to sit again. A nurse came from behind the desk and handed him a coffee.

"Superintendent, I hope this helps. And may I say thank you."

He looked up. She was English, about his age, smiling. "I know it's hard," she said, "but what you've just done has been needed ever since Dr Statham arrived. Status matters more than care for him, and that's rubbed off on his team. The nurses have hoped for something like this for weeks."

"I …"

"No need to say anything. I have three nurses getting Mrs McPhedren ready for the trip to Osmania. They're very good over there. If anyone can help, it's them."

The shaking returned. And tears. Relief, definitely.

Somehow over the next hour they managed it all. Wilson brought in two doctors and three nurses from the Osmania, all English. They'd come over in an ambulance, charged in with a wheeled trolley and been directed to her room by the nurses who had readied her. Within ten minutes Ro was on her way.

Statham was nowhere to be seen.

"Very well done. Now let's follow her." Wilson made for the door.

Le Fanu crossed to the desk and thanked the nurse again.

"Thank *you*," she said, "but good luck for what comes next."

He followed Wilson into the waiting car that took off before he closed the door. They caught the ambulance that raced through Secunderabad into Hyderabad before pulling up at the front of an impressive, three-level white hospital in Islamic style topped by Arabian domes. Near the river and flanked by gardens, the Osmania outdid Madras General by a very long way. It dazzled, sunlight reflecting off the surface. It was better than anything Le Fanu had seen anywhere in India.

"Impressive, eh? Especially with the library and the High Court nearby. The court's like Madras, oddly enough, red and white stone and Arabian domes." Wilson was beside him as they got out of the car and passed under the towering, shaped entrance. "The Nizam had a Calcutta-based Englishman design this and several other buildings after some big floods here a few years ago. Vincent Esch, designed the Bengal Club in Calcutta. Wonder what they think now he's working for the opposition?"

They reached a spacious reception area, and Le Fanu watched Ro being wheeled up a corridor. A dark-haired block of a man in a white coat approached them.

"Sir Maurice? Superintendent? I'm Rory Metcalfe, I'll be looking after Mrs McPhedren." A Scots lilt.

"Dr Metcalfe, we've spoken on the phone. I'm Wilson."

They shook hands and Metcalfe turned to Le Fanu. "Superintendent, I know you've raced up from Madras and that this is an ordeal, but let me assure you, not only is this building new, so is all the equipment. The Nizam made sure we have the best in facilities, staff and treatments. We've all the latest typhoid drugs and all the latest knowledge, so she won't get better treatment anywhere, full stop, let alone in India."

"Thank you, Dr Metcalfe. I'm most grateful you've come to her aid."

"Rory, please. Glad to help. Now, she's unconscious so there's nothing you can do here for the moment. We've got her records, my team is already looking at her and deciding what we do immediately, so we'll start treatment in the next few minutes. I suggest you get out of here, have a break, then come back at, say, seven?"

Four hours away. Seemed a long time.

Metcalfe sensed the concern. "I know. It'll take a couple of hours for the first treatment effects to show up so no point you hanging about and getting even more tired. I'll be here at seven. We can advise progress then before you get dinner and a sleep."

"He's right, Chris, come on. Thanks, Rory." Wilson dragged Le Fanu away and they returned to the car still parked at the entrance.

"Impressive enough for you?" Wilson asked as they drove away.

"The only thing I regret, Maurice, is not listening to you in the first place. Can you imagine a greater difference between Statham and Metcalfe?"

"Ha. No. But bear in mind there's a world of difference between the military and the Nizam's civil service. Statham's caught up in all that Raj rank pomp and circumstance we know so well. India might well have been Elgar's model. I quite like the man's music."

"Where are we going?"

They were deep in Hyderabad, wide and orderly streets with substantial buildings everywhere, so different from Madras.

"A friend of mine turned a local mansion into a private guesthouse, and I've got you a suite there with a small office attached, and a telephone. So you can work while you're here. If nothing else, that'll fill in time for you. And the place is literally around the corner from my home and office. I've also assigned you a car and driver. Come and go as you please."

"Maurice …"

"Say no more. But be warned, I'm still intent on getting you here, so consider this a bribery attempt."

The car stopped at a guarded gate set in a high wall. They were waved through, and the driver stopped under a covered entrance way to a large two-level house that looked more English countryside than Indian princely state. The gardens were extensive and a host of white-uniformed servants fetched food and drinks for a few guests seated at wooden folding tables shaded by huge, colourful umbrellas.

"C'mon," said Wilson, "let's get you settled in."

The foyer was cool and spacious, in marble, elegant ornaments placed carefully to complement the expensive furniture. A young Englishwoman registered him efficiently and called a servant to take him upstairs. Wilson came along.

As they followed the servant up the wide wooden stairway, Le Fanu realised there were just a few rooms in this large house. This catered for the elite. How would he justify these expenses? Might have to talk to Whitney.

Wilson was a mind reader. "Don't worry about the bill, all taken care of."

"But …"

"As I said, treat it as bribery."

They stopped outside a dark-coloured door guarded by two large Chinese palace floor vases. The big reception room contained two sofas and a couple of tub chairs placed around a low table. Paintings of Hyderabad graced the walls, and a window let in filtered light. Off to one side, a large bedroom with attached bathroom. On the other, a small kitchen with tea and coffee making facilities and a stock of local delicacies. Through the back, an office that looked over the gardens.

"This is marvellous, but you can't pay for it. I'll …"

"For God's sake stop fussing. This costs me nothing. I did the owner a favour, he's doing me one back. Now, I'm going to the bar. Have a shower, meet me there in fifteen minutes. We'll have afternoon tea, be at the hospital by seven, then have dinner at an Udipi place you'll like."

An hour later they had finished coffee, savoury snacks and a couple of sweets.

"Drink? I'm having another whisky."

"Small one."

Two Aberlours arrived in Stuart crystal tumblers.

"*Sláinte*," they said in unison.

"Maurice, again, thank you."

"In some ways, I'm paying you back. You really have no idea how much opposition I faced back then, establishing the Crime Unit. You making it a success saved my career in Madras, and I'm not exaggerating. And its success played a big part in my getting this post. The Nizam interviewed me and asked several questions about it. So see this as returning a favour, as well as a normal human attempt to help a nice woman."

"What can I say?"

"That you'll join me here would be an excellent start. Sorry. Make no mistake, though, she's extremely ill. There's no guarantee she'll survive, but she has a far better chance with Metcalfe, that's certain."

Le Fanu wondered how long he'd be in Hyderabad, and how he might deal with whatever came along. "Maurice, she's a fighter, has had to be all her life for all the reasons you know. With good care, she's as likely as anyone to make it. She deserves to."

"I agree, so let's do all we can to help that happen. Now, we'd better get going."

Twenty-one

Thirty-six hours in a whirlwind.

Rory Metcalfe spoke with them for an hour when they returned. Yes, she was extremely ill. The army doctors had probably done their best without the latest available drugs that Osmania had administered immediately. It was too early to be optimistic but she had stabilised. A nurse would be with her throughout the night, and Ro might regain consciousness by morning.

Le Fanu and Wilson dined at the Udipi place where the food matched that of his friend's in Madras. Wilson had a drink with him at the hotel later and chatted about nothing in particular. Le Fanu slept surprisingly well, partly because he was too exhausted to do anything else and partly buoyed by Metcalfe's cautious optimism.

Nine the next morning, he was back at the hospital. Ro still sleeping, her breathing strengthened and fever reduced if not yet enough. She was responding to the drugs.

Wilson had commitments until mid-afternoon so Le Fanu returned to the hotel and rang Habi and Caldicott. Both reported progress. Most of the suspects had changed locations again but followed by Caldicott's Special Branch undercover officers, who reported nothing notable. Any further armed actions seemed either delayed as a result of the village battle or because they were part of a longer-term plan.

Habi had also worked up additional case file materials on all three Muslim murders, especially those in Tanjore and Guntur.

"Sir, all the victims had stronger political links than we thought initially. They were active locally but with connections right across India. We don't know if they met up at any stage, but they would certainly have known about each other. Assistant Superintendent Caldicott is asking Delhi to give us anything they have on them."

"Good work, Habi. I'll ask Sir Maurice to dig out anything here. Muslim Leaguers have been talking with the Nizam, given his significance within the community, and a formal organisation for Hyderabadi Muslims is developing. You never know, there might be some new intelligence here."

"Thank you, sir, we need every scrap possible. Now, is Mrs McPhedren any better?"

"She is, Habi, but early days. At least there's a start."

"I hear the Nizam's new hospital is excellent."

"You've heard correctly, Habi, and the staff are excellent, so she will recover."

Caldicott also asked about Ro but moved on to Jepson quickly. "He and Jamieson are still out and about, pressuring everyone they can. The First Member is campaigning openly for the Chief Secretary's position. Luckily for us, that's going down badly. The old hands can't remember this ever happening in such a blatantly self-interested way."

"Change takes many forms, Jackson, and the old hands oppose all of them."

"They're right on this one. Jamieson's shameless. And taking The Jockey along simply to gain reactionary support."

"That'll come back to bite him."

"Hopefully. Whitney and the Governor are countering the nonsense, and Whitney's still threatening a full formal inquiry despite Delhi's opposition. That should rattle Jepson, and there's big support for it within police ranks. They've heard from colleagues about what happened. There's huge resentment that incompetent planning killed innocent policemen. I'll keep you informed."

It was lunchtime as Le Fanu finished his notes, updated the files and read the new information, so he went out to a garden table and ordered mutton biriyani. It was excellent. So was the ice cream, made locally by a transplanted Gujarati family, apparently. The world seemed a better place.

Back upstairs he tried to read more Savarkar but awoke a couple of hours later to find he'd lasted just two pages.

Wilson called and suggested they return to the hospital. Metcalfe advised them that progress was still good. The team had the drug regime organised, and treatment would continue. Ro had woken briefly twice, a good sign. They should call again next morning.

By five they were in Wilson's office or outside it, more accurately. Full-length shutter doors opened onto a roof terrace where coffee was served in the late sun under a clear sky.

"I see why you like being here, Maurice, this is very pleasant." Le Fanu leaned back in a lounger, feeling the warmth ease physical aches and pains. Mental ones remained.

"And the work's interesting, as I keep telling you. The Nizam has his critics. Don't we all? The British Resident thinks too many royal decisions reward those who provide the largest gifts. I haven't seen that myself. The Nizam's doing good things, like that hospital. Ordinary Hyderabadis get better services now. British India struggles to make anywhere near the same progress."

"The opposite might well be the case in Madras."

"Careful who you say that to. Anyway, my intelligence people have those names of yours and are checking them against our records. Should have any results soon enough."

"That'll be helpful. What's the general political climate here like?"

"Not as far gone as in British India. The Congress is weak and the Nizam's keen to keep it that way. That's why he could use your expertise. Some Muslim groups are trying to mobilise but they don't really oppose the Nizam. They're more interested in social welfare improvements than politics. But we know that sort of thing can get out of control quickly."

"It can, but we have an important part to play. Jepson killing people hasn't helped. Dyer's troops shooting those people at Jallianwala Bagh boosted Congress membership immediately."

"God, that was a mess. And aggravated by all the support he got from the reactionaries. My Punjab friends tell me well over a thousand died that day. And some idiot complimented Dyer for being 'the man who saved India'. More like helped lose it, I reckon."

"You think so?"

"Chris, you're a sensible fellow. We'll lose India at some point. Leave it, at any rate. The question now is when, not if, despite the mad views of people like Jepson and Jamieson."

"I hadn't thought about it that way, but it makes sense."

"So you must think hard about your own best interests. We won't be out on our ears in the next couple of years, but it will become increasingly uncomfortable and there'll be complications. Indianisation will only increase. My advice is to get here quickly for some profitable years then go off and enjoy the rest of your life."

"Well done. I really will think hard about your offer. It's tempting."

"Just say the word, there's plenty of interesting work."

Another enjoyable evening meal, and Le Fanu slept through for the first time in a month.

Twenty-two

Rory Metcalfe reported Ro fully conscious and taking food. Wilson took Le Fanu from the hotel to the Osmania where the medical team directed them to a small staffroom off the main reception then handed over some reports.

"You won't understand the full details," Metcalfe said, "but you'll get the drift. Mrs McPhedren's still seriously ill, but we're hopeful she's through the worst. Not confident, just hopeful. She's definitely better than when you brought her in."

"Rory, that's magnificent."

"Thank you. Luckily we've got the drugs and equipment to go with the care. That's our only advantage over the military."

Wilson looked at Le Fanu but said nothing.

"Now," Metcalfe continued, "we must consider what happens next."

Le Fanu did not understand. "I'm not sure …"

"My mistake, didn't make myself clear enough. Mrs McPhedren will remain here until we're sure she's well enough to leave. Right now, that's at least a week away, possibly longer. So that time's accounted for, but what happens then?"

"Chris," Wilson prompted, "Rory's asking where she goes next, who looks after her."

"That's it," said Metcalfe.

"Put directly," Sir Maurice continued, "does she return

to the General's and, even if she can, will that be the best place for her?"

"She's nowhere else to go that I know of." Le Fanu worried that sounded callous. "I mean, most of her relatives are distant ones, and spread all over the south. I doubt she'd want to bother them, or even be with them."

"Which is Rory's underlying question. Where does she go from here? She'll be weak, and on these drugs for a while."

"That's correct." Metcalfe consulted the notes. "If we say another week, perhaps two here, it'll be three or four months before she hits best form and won't be able to work until then."

"I see." Le Fanu had not anticipated this. "Well, let's give it some thought and …"

"Chris, you know my wife and I will be glad to help."

"I do know and appreciate that, but it's obviously not the long-term solution. Rory, may I speak with Ro?"

"Come back around five, she should be alert by then. Typhoid hits hard, you know."

"I do. You and your team have kept her alive, really."

He turned away, suddenly emotional. Until then, he'd denied the idea she might die. The other two placed hands on his shoulders.

"Natural reaction, Chris," Metcalfe said. "You'll feel better when you see her later."

Now Le Fanu felt cross with himself.

"Come on," Wilson had his hand at Le Fanu's elbow, again. "I'll get you back to the hotel, take a break, then we return later."

By the time he was back in the room, Le Fanu was an emotional wreck. He could not escape the thought she might have died, and that hit him emotionally harder than he had expected. Having spoken to her on the previous trip, he thought their relationship was resolved and he could get on with developing a life with Jenlin. Now, the last few minutes made him think it might not be that simple. He'd read enough Freud and Jung to expect some residual concerns for Ro, but not this.

He drifted until mid-afternoon, ate lunch without noticing what it was, walked in the gardens and tried unsuccessfully to order his thoughts. He picked up an old English magazine but became bored after about two minutes. All the while he drank too much coffee.

Then came a note from reception. Would he please telephone Sir Charles Whitney.

"Nothing in particular, LF. Well, yes, there is, but tell me about Mrs McPhedren first."

Le Fanu recounted developments.

"And you're feeling like you've been hit with a wet sandbag."

"How …"

"Oh, I've been through it with my wife, twice. Terrible business. The first time I thought seriously about resigning, going back to England and some sort of normal life."

"Really?"

"Of course. It happens to a lot of people. But my wife talked me out of it, knowing I'd be hopeless and just bother her. She thought putting up with that'd be worse than having typhoid. Remarkable woman."

Le Fanu knew Whitney was trying to tell him something, equating his wife to Ro.

"You'll have things to consider, Chris, so if you need anything just ask. Just do it quickly because I really am off to Delhi soon. But there's something else."

Le Fanu wondered if he could cope with anything else.

"The Jockey's persecuting Habi and Caldicott. They won't tell you that themselves. He's turning up in their offices unexpectedly, asking for all sorts of reports to be delivered immediately, criticising progress publicly, having others do the same. Especially that bloody Jamieson. He's undermining them, and people are deserting them out of self-preservation. And to make things worse, Delhi is still blocking my formal inquiry. They don't want public speculation."

That added to Le Fanu's weariness. They were more friends than subordinates, difficult though that was in British India. He had championed Habi who more than repaid that debt. And Caldicott was only in the IPS at Le Fanu's suggestion. Otherwise he'd be making a fortune in business. Now they were suffering because of him.

"I expected this, but not so quickly. What do you suggest, Charles?"

"Get back here as fast as possible to start with but that, of course, depends on Mrs McPhedren."

Le Fanu felt like an industrial press had been dumped on his shoulders. "I'll talk to her then call you back. Things might be clearer by then." He doubted that, but it was the best he could manage.

Another hour of indecision followed before there was another request from reception, this time to call Habi.

"Sorry to bother you, sir, I realise …"

"Don't apologise, Habi. Things are tough, I know, so …"

"A little more than normal, sir, but nothing …"

"I'll be back as soon as I can, but how can I help now?"

"I'm going to Guntur tomorrow morning. We've more information on the victim there, and on the visitors and their Guntur connections. The Muslim League might be a target so I think we should move quickly."

"If it looks serious let me know immediately. I'll be returning to Madras sometime over the next couple of days. I could leave the train at Bezwada and have a car take me on to Guntur."

"Sir, that'd be excellent."

"If you need me, I'll be there. And I really am sorry things are so tough. It's all my fault."

"I'd like to agree with you, sir, but can't. The Jockey's become increasingly unhinged and is attacking all the constables, screaming at the officers. At least he doesn't discriminate. He's abusing everyone, Indian or English, Protestant or Catholic, Hindu or Muslim. It's really bad, the formal complaints are piling up."

"Keep your head down, Habi."

Le Fanu then telephoned Caldicott, ostensibly to check on progress and announce his own arrangements but, really, it was to ease his guilt.

"I appreciate the call, LF. The working environment's awful. Jepson's lost his mind, literally. He's irrational and unpredictable, the rages are fearsome and the prejudice appalling. Whitney's fielding complaints from all quarters. So's Jamieson, but he's just throwing them in the bin."

"When I get back I'll pass all this along to Whitney and Willingdon. They know already, but more information might help them get something done."

"It's dangerous. Policemen have died because of him, and there'll be more if this isn't stopped."

"I'll be back as soon as I can."

It was an easy promise to make but keeping it might be more difficult.

Wilson arrived back at five and Le Fanu conveyed the news from Madras.

"The man's a menace. And he's been a compromise choice in every appointment. Wish I could've done more to prevent that." Sir Maurice paused, surveyed the passing traffic. "I always thought I could stymie him but somehow never did. Right to the end. Now I'm still dealing with the bugger even though I'm up here."

"Sorry to bring it up."

"Don't be. It just makes me determined to destroy the man."

Le Fanu met Metcalfe back at the hospital. Wilson would be in contact later, and have the driver come back.

Metcalfe sat him down in the same conference room. "Chris, it will be tough for you seeing her looking terrible."

"She did the last time I saw her."

"This'll be worse. But remember, she's much better than a couple of days ago and improved even from this morning. The signs are good. Keep calm, and don't try to resolve everything today."

He was soon shown into a high-ceilinged, spacious upstairs room done out in light colours, a roof fan rotating slowly. The large windows were shaded but the room less darkened than the one at Trimulgherry. Her bed was pushed against the side wall so she might look out.

She was propped up with her face leaning left against a bank of pillows and arms outside a sheet drawn up to her chin. Her eyes were closed and cheeks hollow, but her hair was brushed. Le Fanu stood at the door for a minute, then crept to the chair by the bed and sat down.

It was five minutes before she realised he was there, given the drowsiness brought on by the deluge of drugs.

Her eyes were brighter than last time, and the smile less forced.

“Thank you for getting me in here, Chris. And for coming back up. That was lovely of you.” She reached out, he took the hand.

“Thank Sir Maurice. He took over at the other place, ordered people about and had you here within minutes.”

“I will, but I know you’ve helped, too. Your being here means a lot. There are few people I can call on now.” She looked away. His own earlier emotion returned.

“Ro, I know, and …”

“Your support is important to me. The doctors tell me I was almost gone and that you and Sir Maurice have probably …”

“Don’t upset yourself. That’s all done with. Now you must return to full health, and this is the best place for that.”

“I’m very grateful, but at some point I must leave …”

“Don’t bother about that yet. Maurice and I are working up some possibilities. You’ll have your own, of course, but there’s time enough. Concentrate on getting well.”

She squeezed his hand. “I’m sorry to cause these complications.”

“You’d do the same for me.”

“Yes, but you’ve got a new life to be getting on with.” There was no reproach in the comment but he felt it, anyway.

“Metcalfe says you’ll be here at least another week and likely longer, though you’re making great progress. Get on with that and don’t bother about anything else, or me for that matter.”

“I don’t want your work or your life to suffer because of me.”

“Neither will. I’m just here to make sure you recover fully.”

"Thank you, again."

Her eyes closed, she was exhausted.

He waited a few minutes until she was well asleep, let go her hand and left quietly, closing the door.

A few minutes later he updated Wilson by telephone, went back downstairs at the hotel for dinner, had a couple of whiskies, and spent the rest of the evening wondering why his life was always so byzantine.

Twenty-three

Habi called at seven the next morning, and Le Fanu was on the train to Bezwada by eight, having told Wilson he would return to Hyderabad as soon as possible. Wilson would advise Ro.

He settled into first class, preparing for the six- or seven-hour journey from the Deccan Plateau dryness down to the hotter, more humid Andhra country, where massive nineteenth-century irrigation projects had extended local landowners' trading patterns and wealth. Back to British India, then, in many ways a foreign country after Hyderabad.

As they rolled by the countless villages and small towns and down the slopes towards the coast, he watched the change in agriculture, and fortunes. Up here it was hard scrabble. Down there, heavier rainfall and plentiful water meant crops were better, bigger, more frequent. That produced a strong merchant class, better transport and higher incomes. But despite those improvements, British India still struggled to make its mark. Population growth was steep, improving services a problem given the endless battles between a government trying to levy taxes and farmers avoiding them. Much of the Congress's success here came from leading anti-tax campaigns.

A local police officer and a servant met him at the bustling Bezwada station. They set off immediately, the driver desperately navigating through the crowded streets and around those irrigation canals that were responsible for local wealth. India was always puzzling, he thought, as they crossed the Ryves Canal that commemorated a British engineer here in the Gandhian heartland.

Then they were out in the greener coastal lands en route to Guntur which, both as town and district, had dominated the Non-Cooperation campaign in the south. Thousands were arrested and jailed. Some died in police or army firings. The place remained fragile, and hostile in the eyes of his Madras superiors.

And there was a new factor. The Americans were here. British American Tobacco decided Guntur was an excellent source for its raw product so directly contracted a host of farmers. Most BAT officials were English, but its American component bothered the Raj because the press there championed Gandhi, stirred by an historical fondness for 'independence'. Add a large American missionary presence, and the mixture was volatile.

Tobacco and rice fields, along with the district's renowned chilli crops, yielded to a cluster of villages surrounding Guntur, and Le Fanu was soon in the sprawling town itself, at the imposing new tan-coloured stone courthouse complex near both the two-level, archwayed entrance to the town's police station and the Collector's office. These had been busy places over the past four or five years.

Habi was standing outside the District Superintendent's office, and Le Fanu assumed the two Indian policemen with him were the police college classmates.

"Good afternoon, sir." Habi introduced Le Fanu to the other two. They had been discussing, he said, the Muslim murder as well as the district's Hindu–Muslim affairs. The latter were strained.

“And, sir, before we go in, there’s been another Muslim murder here, reported just a few hours ago. Sorry for bringing more bad news.”

Another policeman emerged to announce that the District Super was ready for them.

“Well, Chris, it’s been a while.” A short, tubbyish man with a fierce moustache and open smile was waiting just inside the door. Le Fanu grabbed his extended hand and returned the smile.

“Lachlan! I’d forgotten you were here. Habi, this is Superintendent Heatherly. We’re very lucky he’s in charge. Lachlan, Assistant Superintendent Muhammad Habibullah of the Crime Unit.”

“Habi, delighted to meet you having admired the work from afar. Hope you can introduce some of that magic here.”

“You can relax, Habi,” Le Fanu cut in, “Lachlan’s among the few liberals left. That’s why he’s out here and not in Madras.”

“More nonsense being cranked up down there, too, according to my few remaining friends. The Jockey’s lost both his head and the horse’s, it would appear.”

Habi joined in the laughter, knowing he was in friendly territory.

“Lachie, what’s it like here in Guntur now?”

“I arrived about a year ago. The worst of Non-Cooperation had passed by then and we’ve started rebuilding public trust, but there’s a seriously long way to go. We won’t ever retrieve all our lost supporters. Thousands went to jail, thousands refused to pay tax, there were rebels in the forest lands. They all have bitter memories of what we did to them. Now we’ve got the socialists.”

“Really?”

"Watch a man called N G Ranga. He's still only mid-twenties, born in an agricultural village, but a bright boy who went to college here. Now he's in Oxford developing extreme socialist ideas that get fed back here to his many followers among the peasantry. There's some missionary support in there, too."

"Difficult combination, sir."

"It is, Habi, and the absence of sensible directives from headquarters does not help."

"I couldn't possibly say, sir."

"You've trained him well, Chris."

"Au contraire, I do all the learning. And because Habi's bothered by the Muslim developments, so am I."

"Which is why I've reviewed all our records on the murder and the general situation here. We've had a rising number of small incidents recently, and noticed an unusually high number of odd visitors. There's no real Hindu nationalist group here yet, but we're watching a couple of people who've taken in these strangers and staged a couple of meetings just before the murder."

"There's a link, sir?"

"I reckon so, Habi, but there's no conclusive evidence yet. More a series of obvious possible connections, nothing we could take to court."

"Lachie, what about the murder itself?"

"Thanks to Caldicott's connections, we now know a lot more. Ashraf Haider, the victim, spoke both Urdu and Telugu. I knew him, a merchant trader and a good man who looked after people, very active in the mosque. And he'd been a moderate member of Congress for some time. He was uncomfortable there once the Gandhi campaign started, being more interested in steady development than immediate independence. But having made a commitment, he stuck with the campaign."

"Not unusual amongst Muslims generally, sir. We've seen that across the country."

"Yes, and that's why Ashraf Haider left Congress earlier this year, it was going in a direction he did not like. Then he was killed, just three or four months later."

"Any progress?"

"Not as much as I'd like, LF. We've a few people under review, including the outsiders, but no real evidence. Again, your information provided a deeper background that my people are working with now. But we were worried there might be more killings and ..."

"Now there's been another one. Habi mentioned that. But we've already been talking longer than I'd planned, mainly because of finding you here, Lachie, so where's this new victim?"

"In a small trading quarter up in the northern section of town, just around from the neighbourhood mosque."

"You've been there already, Habi?"

"Yes, done the initial scene of crime sweep. Now we've got the place under guard. My college colleagues have put on some good men so the site won't be disturbed."

"What do your initial reports suggest, Lachie?"

"I'll tell you on the way."

They reached the scene in ten minutes. Heatherly withdrew his men while Le Fanu and Habi advanced slowly. The victim was lying hard up against the wall of a small shed in a courtyard off Guntur's main street. There was nothing else apart from a few broken boxes and a couple of fabric bales strewn around an area hemmed in by similarly small buildings with no windows. A small alley cut through the space.

"When was he found?"

"About half an hour before I called you this morning, sir."

Le Fanu had found nothing unusual around the body yet. "And what do we know so far?"

"My colleagues are trying to identify him, sir. There was probably more than one attacker. There are severe wounds and fractures all over the body, he might have been struck with hammers or heavy planks. And he was possibly attacked elsewhere because there are no signs of a struggle here, and little blood."

"He's been shifted?"

"We think so."

"Time of death?"

"The local IMS man should have been here long ago. The body's been there a while."

"Slack."

"Yes, sir."

"Right, let's go back."

They walked back slowly to the marked perimeter, checking for anything they might have missed. Nothing.

Heatherly and his contingent were waiting. "What do you think, Chris?"

"Most likely killed somewhere else then left here. If the medical examiner can estimate the time of death, we'll work out *when* the victim might have been shifted, and that might indicate how *far* he was transported. Habi tells me the examiner was summoned hours ago. Where is he?"

"No idea, but we've kept calling."

"Not good enough. What else can your men tell us?"

"No one in the immediate vicinity knows the man, which supports the idea he was killed elsewhere and dumped here. No one heard or saw anything. This area is mainly warehouses and storerooms, few people live here. Workers found the body when they opened up this morning."

"What time do they leave at night?"

"Most are gone by, say, seven, the odd straggler a little later. By nine the place is deserted. And as you see, there are no streetlights."

"So he could have been dumped anytime between nine last night and six this morning and no one would know. That's a hell of a window."

"That will remain open until we get a time of death," Habi sneaked in.

"We're losing time, that's certain."

"Chris," said Heatherly, "I'm told there's a guard who passes by a couple of times a night. They're trying to find him."

"That'll be helpful. Any papers on the victim, any markings?"

"None so far. This is looking like those other killings, unfortunately. It appears to be random but isn't, few clues to go on, little to identify killer or killers. It looks planned."

A disturbance broke out behind as an English voice berated the policemen guarding the perimeter. Le Fanu thought he recognised the voice, but that didn't seem possible. The man shouted more loudly as he came closer, complaining that his right of way was restricted.

"I'm the bloody medical examiner, you fools."

It was Lieutenant Colonel Statham, and he was ropeable.

"Oh, it's you, Le Fanu, that explains a lot, pompous ass."

"Chris, you know Statham?" Heatherly was surprised, so was Habi.

"We met in Secunderabad. He was treating my friend, Mrs McPhedren."

"Until you knew better than we medical men and took her to the Osmania. When did she die? A few hours later, as I told you she would?"

Heatherly was stunned by the bluntness. "Go easy, Statham …"

"I will not. This man questioned my expertise in public. Then he and his police pal up there dragged the woman away when she deserved to die in peace."

Habi looked puzzled.

"Happy to report," Le Fanu replied, "she looked a lot better when I spoke to her yesterday, and the Osmania *experts* are cautiously optimistic she'll recover fully."

"Sheer bloody luck."

"More the result of expert care, I think, care that you could not or *would* not provide, probably because she's Anglo-Indian."

Statham went quiet.

"So," Le Fanu continued, "I hope you're better at determining time of death than you are at predicting its likelihood."

Statham snarled something under his breath, then, "Where's the bloody body?"

Two constables steered him towards the victim, careful not to disturb the scene.

"You make friends so easily, Chris." Heatherly looked innocent.

"I know, one of my great skills. Many people like Statham admire me."

"The odd I-G and First Member included, I hear."

"Odd being the operative word."

"The reforms really have changed things. The local Collector's a good enough fellow, but his predecessors were hardliners, especially during the Gandhi campaign. Demanded police go in full bore when that was not the smartest strategy."

"You know Statham well?"

"No, he's here short term, and that seems to be a pattern on his record. Doesn't stay anywhere long, and there's usually a reason for that in my experience."

"We had to get my friend out of his hospital, and although the Osmania is more modern, his approach was a good part of the problem."

"Not surprised."

Statham was returning, still accompanied by the constables, to his obvious annoyance. By the time he reached them he was red faced and not from exertion.

"Well," said Heatherly, "what do you think?"

"You're all too precious about your bloody crime scene."

"Thanks for that professional observation," Le Fanu shot back, "but I'm only interested in your alleged expertise on advising possible time of death."

"Everything I've heard about you, Le Fanu, seems to be true. Be that as it may, my best estimate is your man died somewhere between midnight and two this morning."

"Can you guarantee that?" Le Fanu knew he couldn't.

"No, the body has changed too much over this amount of time."

As soon as he finished speaking, Statham knew he'd been hooked.

Le Fanu looked at his watch, then Statham, then Habi and Heatherly, and raised his eyebrows. Statham slunk off.

Twenty-four

Le Fanu and Habi spent the rest of the day sifting through the available evidence before discussing it with Heatherly and his senior officers. By early evening, they were no closer to identifying either victim or killers but certain of a connection to the earlier murders.

Heatherly took them to the local club where they were received coolly by Europeans who had friends in Madras so knew Le Fanu by reputation, or by someone's version of that reputation. There were sidelong glances throughout the evening, a clear separation of social and physical distance and audible, indignant conversation as soon as they left.

"Sorry, Chris, they're all gun-shy here after the Gandhi demonstrations. Anyone who was even vaguely sympathetic to Congress before all that has reverted to being the full reactionary, either because they believe it or because the peer pressure's so great."

"Not your fault, Lachlan."

"And I'm sorry my presence added to the tension." Habi was unusually subdued.

"It was an honour to have you there, Habi. You're better than most, if not all of them. They must listen to people like you, not shut you out, if we're to make any headway."

"Thank you, sir, but acceptance seems a long way off."

They walked across the wide, dusty compound to the car. Given the modest buildings planted in this large space behind high walls, Le Fanu thought of it as a constructed oasis, an escape from the reality beyond those walls. Guntur presaged the new India, but in here they clung hard to the old one.

Once in the car, Heatherly canvassed possible actions.

"I'd value your thoughts. I could arrest and question some or all of the newcomers tomorrow. Or we could wait in case more information might turn up."

Habi spoke first. "Sir, your situation here is different from the one in Madras. If those people we've just left are apprehensive, then the rest of town will be the same. So if we arrest a gaggle of strangers on suspicions alone, there'll be trouble. It'll be seen as more Raj bullying."

"Good point, Habi," said Le Fanu. "Lachie, you don't want more trouble than necessary."

"You match my thoughts, but sometimes I wonder if the soft option seems best simply because I don't want to choose the hard one. You don't think some limited arrests might put people on notice, help subdue the communal barbs?"

"We'd have to gauge possible benefits against the size of the risk, sir, and on that basis the potential returns look low to me."

"Chris, I see why you rely on this man. Pity that lot back in the club haven't heard this conversation."

"Agreed on both counts, Lachie."

"So we're agreed? We sit it out tomorrow and see what else we can dredge up?"

They pulled into the compound of the travellers' bungalow Heatherly had arranged. It would be comfortable. The extended touring and camping done traditionally by officials all over the country was dying out now as cars made for easier travel, but a myriad of these bungalows allowed the British a home away from home, no matter where they were.

Five servants dressed in white tunics appeared, already alerted that food was unnecessary but ready to provide drinks and sweets. They would be on duty until those guests left and, as usual these days, Le Fanu felt guilty at putting them to so much trouble.

Their rooms ready and bags already unpacked, Le Fanu asked for tea and for Habi to join him on the veranda. It was dark, pleasantly warm. Flickers of light flashed around the compound, the odd birdsong broke the silence, and fireflies sparkled beyond the low bungalow lights.

"This is what I've always enjoyed most about being in the *mofussil*, Habi." In the south, strong distinctions were made between Madras-based officials and those stationed out in the country. For the former, being in the *mofussil* was a curse to be applied to the latter.

"I agree, sir, but it's a false sense of security. Tomorrow we're back out there trying to prevent things happening to people who don't appreciate us."

That evening at the club had affected him.

"Pay them no attention, Habi. They're the past."

"I'm not so sure. These people talk to their friends in Madras, and it's clear what they think. And I doubt they're too bothered about a dead Muslim."

Le Fanu remembered that remark later, as he neared sleep, and told himself to look out for his friend in the coming days.

After breakfast they met again at Heatherly's office. There was no additional information and, as they had resolved to sit tight, Le Fanu wondered what he might do next.

"Sir, return to Hyderabad. I'll watch things here today and call you tonight. We'll just be doing normal investigations and you'd be wasted here when you have other things to do. Catch the train from Bezwada, in two hours you'll be there by late afternoon."

Habi was right, but Le Fanu wondered if going back put his personal needs above professional demands. And what about Habi's best interests?

"I agree, Chris," said Heatherly. "We've good people here to assist, and I'll go in the field as well."

A few minutes later he was in a car bound for Bezwada, then on to the train for Hyderabad. Habi had called ahead and Wilson was waiting. The time had passed surprisingly fast, and Le Fanu realised he'd mostly slept.

"Welcome back, Chris, hope it went well. The Osmania reports are even better now. I checked before coming here and you're allowed to visit later."

They returned to the hotel, Le Fanu cleaned up and they had a late tea.

"Any progress down there, Chris?"

"There are now two Guntur murders, and it looks increasingly like an organised affair. The emerging links between all these incidents are becoming even stronger. I'd better get upstairs and call Whitney. Give me ten minutes, and I'll be ready for the next move here."

He spoke to Whitney for more minutes than ten as the Chief Secretary asked searching questions and made several pertinent points concerning next steps.

"Chris, the pro-Hindu group here in the ICS ran that anti-Brahmin campaign very effectively, and the more misguided ones now think it would be smart to restrict Muslim entry to government services. It's completely mad and would weaken their own positions, but they don't see that. I'll get them sorted, but we can't afford more bad publicity."

"Understood, Charles, we'll do everything possible to avoid that, but we need solid evidence that allows us to act, the sooner the better."

"I'll keep pushing people here until your return. Any idea when that'll be?"

"I'm seeing Ro in a few minutes. She's apparently a lot better. Once I see how she is, I'll let you know about a return, but it should be within two or three days."

"That's fine. If we need you sooner, I'll contact you. Give my best to Mrs McPhedren."

Half an hour later, she certainly did look better. The drapes were back to allow in the late afternoon sun she was enjoying sitting up in bed, supported by pillows. The sunken cheeks had disappeared, and she looked healthier.

"Ro, you look so much better, and have an appetite by the look of it. How's the food?"

"It would not meet your high standards but is just what a sick woman needs. That's the second meal today and no bad effects yet. I hear you've been off travelling."

He told her about Guntur, and Habi.

"Poor Habi. He's such a good soul, and a clever one. This will be hard for him."

"It is. He doubts the government's commitment to solving the murders, and that goes against everything he believes in. It has hit his relationship with Caldicott, and perhaps even with me. He's pessimistic and that's so unlike him."

They talked for a while longer, avoiding anything personal. As he left, Le Fanu realised he had enjoyed the discussion. She was relaxed, they were comfortable with each other. On the way out he saw Metcalfe, who told him they were delighted with her progress and might declare her out of danger the following day.

"Of course, Chris, that again raises the question of how long she'll remain here and where she'll go when we let her out. Any thoughts?"

"The situation remains the same. I'd better get someone to check with the General, but she won't be able to work for a while, will she?"

"Several weeks at least."

"In which case her place there could be in doubt."

"See what you can find out and let me know. I might be able to help."

As the car carried him back to the hotel through the wide, unclogged Hyderabadi roads, he struggled to think where Ro could go if she had to leave her employer. She had no family left nearby and there was no obvious other place for her, Madras the possible exception.

Wilson had a formal dinner engagement that night, at the Falaknuma Palace where the Nizam was entertaining visiting dignitaries from Europe. So Le Fanu ate alone, sat outside for a while then went back up to his room.

A couple of minutes later, Caldicott called.

"Sorry it's late, Chris, but I thought you'd be up. How's Ro?"

"A lot better, thankfully."

"Glad to hear it, but you won't like this news. Well, then again you might. I've heard from my Delhi spy friends."

"Go ahead, I'm alone."

"MI5 and MI6 have been tracking the movements of Virendranath Chattopadhyaya, a Bengali who's been in England and Europe for years. At one time he edited a radical journal pushing Indian independence. More recently, he's been based in Germany, living with an American journalist, Agnes Smedley. The Americans arrested her a few years ago for being involved with the Ghadar movement. She was basically a front for the organisation."

"This is not sounding good."

"Well, 5 and 6 have linked the pair of them to some of our suspects. Nothing clear cut yet, but enough to suggest the activities here in Madras have an international dimension. Smedley's been in direct touch with them, ostensibly seeking interview materials, but 5 and 6 reckon she's sending coded signals from Chattopadhyaya."

"But why attack Muslims? That's likely to cause a rebound on Hindu communities in areas where the killings occur."

"Yes, and before I forget, there are already signs of that happening in the village that got hit. A few Hindus got roughed up there last night."

"There you are."

"Our London friends suggest the radicals think it worth the risk. The revolutionaries consider the Madras Government so weak that a serious Hindu–Muslim stoush might bring it down."

"Probably optimistic, and it would be at a hell of a cost."

"You and I might think so, but these are all offshoots from the American gangs that colluded with Germany to create trouble in India, and that had Curzon-Wyllie assassinated. Any damage incurred along the way is secondary to the goal."

"Does Whitney know about this?"

"I wanted to discuss it with you first. What do you think? How long will you be up there?"

"After this news, not long. But I'll confirm tomorrow. Let me call Whitney tonight."

"By the way, these intelligence reports also suggest possible radical activity in Hyderabad. Better alert Wilson, given the Muslim dimension there."

It felt like an entire barrage of problems was rolling towards him at once.

Twenty-five

He breakfasted with Wilson at the hotel and conveyed Caldicott's news.

"No surprise. Hyderabad's a target for all the groups wanting change in India. The Nizam's done good things but some of his citizens think he's a tightwad and that they're rack rented. I don't know if that's true but the impression's there. A few campaigners have arrived but we've immediately sent them back from whence they came."

"This might be different. We're starting to identify an international reach. Hard to see an American or European interest in some of our districts, I know, but right now it seems to be there. And this lot are armed and prepared to act."

"I'll get on it right away, thanks for the tip. What's your plan for the day?"

"Writing reports for Whitney and Willingdon, but I suspect The Jockey will come demanding at some point."

"There is that. The car's at your disposal, and I suppose you'll see Mrs McPhedren later?"

"We need to sort out where she goes when she leaves hospital."

"Is that your problem?"

"If she can't go back to the General's then, yes, it might be. She's got no one else."

Wilson just looked quizzical.

"Well, you know," Le Fanu managed, "I can't just leave her to fend for herself."

"Of course not." Wilson was expressionless, hard to read. "Right, I must get off. Let me know if you need anything, otherwise we'll meet later."

"Right you are."

For the next hour or so Le Fanu sat in the gardens reviewing case files and reports, and reaching the same conclusion: there was a connection between several activist cells focusing their attention on south India. And as yet, his side had no counter.

A servant announced a call from Madras. Le Fanu hurried up to his rooms. It was Whitney.

"Sorry to bother you, but please return to Madras as soon as possible."

"What's happening?"

"Three armed men tried to barge into the Amir Mahal an hour ago. Luckily the guards were on alert, and we also had some police units in training nearby."

The Amir Mahal was a small but significant Madras enclave, home to Nawab Sir Ghulam Mohammad Ali Khan, the Prince of Arcot and acknowledged leader of south India's Muslims. He was a national figure, too, having been President of the All India Muslim Association and active in the South India Islamic League that was now connected to the Muslim League. The British stripped real power from his family in the mid-nineteenth century but, recognising its spiritual significance, still paid out a handsome annual retainer.

"An assassination attempt?"

"We're assuming so until proven otherwise."

"And you have these men?"

"We do, awaiting your attention."

"Hindus?"

“Seems so. Not that it means much at this early stage, apart from ruling out any Muslim factional dimensions.”

“Anything else I need to know?”

“Well, you’re the official authority on matters Muslim so I’m reporting this to you. But we’re having trouble keeping Jepson away from it, what with you and Habi both out of the city.”

“I’ll call Habi, he can be back there quickly.”

“Good man.”

“And I’ll be there as fast as I can.”

Having telephoned Habi and sent him back to Madras, Le Fanu informed Wilson, packed, then visited Ro before going to the station.

She was even better now, and the chat again pleasant if general.

The train journey took forever, aggravated by his being mostly awake. Finally, they dragged through the outer northern suburbs, then into Madras Central and its frenetic activity. It was second nature for him again, he was relieved to note as he followed the police porters to the waiting car. Neither noise nor people bothered him. He was home, he thought, surprised.

He, Habi and Caldicott were to meet as soon as he arrived so the driver dropped him at the intelligence office where he climbed the narrow, drab stairway to the nondescript offices.

“LF, thanks for getting back so quickly.”

“I was having to stretch things out up there, so this excitement is welcome in some ways.”

“Mrs McPhedren is better, sir?”

“Much, Habi.” Le Fanu wondered about the real nature of the question. “So what’s the latest on the Prince of Arcot?”

A small van had arrived outside the Amir Mahal's guarded gates at eight-thirty that morning. As the two guards checked the driver's papers, three armed men burst from the back of the vehicle. But because the van lacked rear windows, they had not noticed three other guards sitting in a lean-to off the main gatehouse. Those reserve guards saw the three gunmen so grabbed their own weapons and deployed. At the same time, one of the police units under training passed the gate. Its commanding officer saw all the rifles, stopped his vehicle and put all his armed men into action. The invaders were outnumbered.

Initially, the Prince's advisors argued the armed men should be retained in the Amir Mahal until he determined their fates, but the police officer rang Caldicott rather than headquarters. Caldicott called Whitney who despatched a senior secretary who had the gunmen arrested.

Whitney then really antagonised Jepson, insisting Le Fanu run the case as part of his new responsibilities, given the prince was Muslim and the incident had occurred at a Muslim site. The Chief Secretary had the prisoners held in old Secretariat cells rather than at police headquarters. Jepson complained to Jamieson, who complained to Willingdon, who told them both to bugger off, according to Caldicott's information.

"Has anyone questioned the prisoners yet?"

"No, sir," replied Habi, "we're leaving that to you."

"What language do they speak?"

"Hindustani mainly, so far, but what else we don't know."

"Which means you sit in on the interviews, Habi. You're better at that language than me, by a very long way."

"Yes, sir."

"Jackson, any idea who they are?"

"No identifying papers, LF, but I've wired their photographs to Delhi in the hope someone might recognise them. And I sent their fingerprints as well."

"Either Delhi or the Calcutta Fingerprint Bureau should give us something. Ironic that Azizul Haque and Hem Chandra Bose who set up that new system in 1897 were Muslim and Hindu."

"Their boss did well, too," said Caldicott. "Sir Edward Henry had just retired as Commissioner of the London Met when I came here at the end of the war."

"Legendary. Began as a Lloyds clerk, studied at night, passed the ICS exam, then got posted to Bengal where those two geniuses worked for him."

"We Indians are always ready to help, sir," Habi muttered.

"Not all of you these days, Habi." Caldicott tried to sound light but failed.

Le Fanu jumped in. "Habi, any specific questions you want to ask these men?"

"I've a set of questions we can start with."

Cool to chilly.

"Let's get to the Secretariat and give those questions a run. Jackson, keep digging into their backgrounds, and let us know immediately you discover anything."

"Of course, LF."

A few minutes later the driver dropped them outside the Secretariat to be greeted by two armed constables.

"Superintendent," one said, "the prisoners are in those very old cells in the ramparts."

"Must be uncomfortable there, those cells might not have been used for a hundred years. Whitney's outdone himself. The prisoners won't be ready for your questions after being in there."

"No, sir," Habi replied.

The constable continued. "But the Chief Secretary has a room reserved for you inside, sir, so when you're ready I'll show you there and bring the prisoners in."

"Thank you, constable, but when we're organised bring them one at a time."

"Yes, sir."

The constable led them up the steps, along a corridor inside the main entrance, then into a medium-sized room with high windows and little other than a table bearing writing materials and surrounded by ill-matched chairs. The constable placed two chairs behind the table, one in front.

"Thank you, constable, bring over the first man. When you bring him in, remain on guard just inside the door. Will your colleague be comfortable guarding the other two?"

"Those old cells are better than the ones at headquarters, sir, they're six feet thick and the door's about three, with solid bars. My colleague will be fine."

Le Fanu and Habi made themselves comfortable, pored over Habi's questions and agreed he begin the interview with Le Fanu to follow up where necessary.

"Habi, thanks for being here."

"Happy to be working with you again, sir."

A knock at the door and the constable escorted in the first prisoner, an unusually tall man who was sinewy rather than muscular and with a craggy face, cropped beard, cheap Western clothes and defiant look.

"Who are you?" Habi asked in Hindustani.

"Go fuck yourself."

"Great start," said Le Fanu.

The man looked at him, surprised, and spat on the floor. The armed constable moved but Le Fanu motioned him back.

"If we want," Le Fanu continued in Hindustani, "we can leave you in those cells for days and forget you're there. They haven't been used for a while, a century or so. Who knows what else is lurking in there."

The man remained defiant.

"Or we can send you over to police headquarters. The cells are better but the reception hotter. Several policemen there had friends killed out at that village, and if they think you were involved you'll very quickly meet with an accident."

That registered. Le Fanu had no intention of relocating the prisoners, but it did not hurt for them to think he might, and that there would be consequences.

"So either you answer these questions, or really go fuck yourself over at headquarters."

"So," said Habi, "who are you?"

"Raghat Rai."

"From where?"

"Patna."

In the newish state of Bihar, hived off from Bengal in 1912 and prominent in Gandhi's campaigns.

"Why are you here?"

"Go …"

"Remembering we can truck you across town to new cells and angry guards."

"I'm here to see friends."

"Who are they and where do they live?"

The man became flustered.

"What are the names of the men you came to Madras with?"

"I don't know."

"None of them?"

"No."

"Constable," said Le Fanu, "get that vehicle ready because we'll need it soon. And tell your friends at headquarters that this fellow is on the way. Don't check him in officially. No one will know he's there and it might stay that way for several days. Plenty of time for those interested to pay him a visit."

"The people I travelled here with I did not know. My friends travelled with other groups."

"All to Madras?"

"Yes."

"Why?"

"We weren't told until we arrived."

"And you were told to kill the Prince of Arcot."

"No."

"So you went there with loaded rifles for no reason."

"No."

"You mean," said Le Fanu, "you had no reason to go there, or you had another reason?"

"You're confusing me."

"I'm not sure who's confusing whom here, Habi, are you?"

"No sir, I think this man went to kill the prince. That's intent to commit murder under the Indian Penal Code, a very serious charge."

"With a possible death sentence?"

"I should think so, sir."

The man looked worried.

"So," Habi continued, "why did you go there?"

"I don't know."

“Then,” Le Fanu interjected, “tell us which of your friends killed our police colleagues?”

“I don’t know where the other groups went. We all had different places in Madras.”

“How many groups?” Habi resumed.

“Don’t know, at least five.”

That was news, and not good.

“What were their targets?”

“Don’t know. We were only told what we had to do.”

“Who is your leader?”

“He is not with us, he gives orders from elsewhere.”

“In Madras?”

“I think so, a messenger comes every day.”

Could be located anywhere.

“And what were your orders?” Le Fanu asked.

“To wait.”

“For what?” Habi shot in.

“Instructions.”

“And what were your instructions?”

“To go to the Amir Mahal.”

“And kill the Prince of Arcot.”

“No.”

“Listen,” said Le Fanu, “we don’t want to retrace that circular path. Tell us now or I’ll charge you with intention to murder the Prince of Arcot and send you to immediate trial.”

“No.”

“No what?”

“We were not sent to kill the prince.”

“So why were you there?”

“To kidnap him.”

Twenty-six

The next morning, Le Fanu, Habi and Caldicott finally agreed they were facing a serious conspiracy with international dimensions rather than random, unrelated events. Jackson had reconsidered overnight and conceded, although he did not say so expressly Le Fanu noticed. That conspiracy challenge was made all the more serious by the difficulty in getting an agreed strategy across the whole of the force and the ICS.

"Sir, The Jockey claims this as the work of madmen so we should just send in armed constables to arrest them, or shoot if necessary."

"I know, Habi, and I share your frustration. Somehow we must persuade him otherwise."

"More precisely, LF, *you* must convince him otherwise." Caldicott elbowed Habi in the ribs.

At least they're agreed on that, Le Fanu thought, better than having them in combat mode.

"Thanks very much, Jackson. Remind me to offer you similar help sometime."

"I'll make a note in my diary."

"Do either of you have any useful idea how I might persuade the idiot to take this seriously?"

"Sir, the Chief Secretary will be more useful on that than we mere underlings." Habi returned the elbow jolt.

"I think I'll do that, it's the only way to make sensible progress, obviously."

"Good luck, LF."

Half an hour later, having telephoned ahead, Le Fanu was in Whitney's office.

"Your information's excellent as always, Chris, but worrying. Willingdon agrees."

"Jepson's attitude makes it worse. That worries me most. We don't need another Jallianwala Bagh, but he'll create one if he has his way."

"Willingdon's already telephoned him this morning to reinforce the fact you're in charge. I gather The Jockey's response was colourful."

"If it was anything like his club outburst then Willingdon would have been underwhelmed."

"He was, confirmed."

"So Jepson's contained for the moment?"

"Yes, ordered not to leave home or headquarters without clearance from the Governor."

"Has that ever happened before?"

"No, but there's a first time for everything. Given this situation and Jepson's propensities, there was no other choice. Now, what sort of approach are you considering?"

"We must be patient and that won't be popular among Jepson's supporters. But we don't yet have enough evidence to move decisively. Hopefully, we'll get better intelligence over the next thirty-six to forty-eight hours, and then we can move more confidently. Do you agree, and will Willingdon support us?"

"Yes on both counts."

"Good."

"And that will give us time to manoeuvre something else."

"Oh yes?"

"I'm definitely to be replaced, and Willingdon opposes Jamieson getting the post."

"There was surely no chance of that happening?"

"Not entirely out the window. He has supporters, you know, including Jepson."

"Surely that is not a problem given The Jockey's antics? Why the need for time?"

"Because Willingdon has lit upon a novel scheme to outrage the locals."

"Bar the one who gets the nod."

"*All* the locals."

"You mean he's going outside the Madras ICS?"

"That's the idea. Whisky?"

"Normally a bit early for me but given that news, why not? It's unprecedented."

Whitney fished a bottle of Highland Park from a cupboard, poured two measures and lit a cigar before Le Fanu could blink.

"As you've said before, Chris, unprecedented times, and Willingdon's so angered by the conservative response to reforms, he's decided no one here's up to the task. Cheers."

"Cheers. They'll hate him."

"We've discussed that. His thinks that because most of them do already and he's on the way out, he's free to wreak havoc." Smoke floated about the room.

"What about his successor?"

"Willingdon cleared it with Goschen, who happily agreed. He doesn't want to deal with the reactionaries either, even though he's not as liberal as Willingdon. So an outsider it will be."

"Whose name is?"

"HE has someone in mind but the arrangement is not yet confirmed so I can't say. Sorry, Chris. But you'll be happy. A politico out of the Rajput states up north."

"That will anger them even more. You know the sort of thing: 'not even a district man' and 'not one of us'. He'll have a hard time."

"As will those who cross him."

"Aha. Hard man. This just gets better."

"As I say, you'll like him, and he appreciates good police work."

"Which means he won't appreciate Jepson."

"He's been advised of The Jockey's skills or lack thereof."

"And does he know about Jamieson?"

"Yes. Willingdon's really thought this through. He's determined to leave a senior team his successor can work with and make progress. And that includes you, despite your protestations about wanting to be somewhere else."

"What do you mean?"

"Willingdon's told the new man you should be in charge of the police, substantive I-G."

"But you know I'm almost certain to leave."

"Perhaps so, but now you'll have a decision to make."

Between three posts in three different places, Le Fanu thought.

"Not sure how I feel about that."

"You don't have to make the decision right now. Give yourself at least thirty seconds."

"Ha. Thanks for that. Most generous."

"Cheers again. So what do I tell Willingdon?"

"About the I-G spot?"

"No, of course not. About what we're doing to beat this conspiracy."

"That we're still gathering information, consider the situation serious, and will advise him definitively within two days."

"I'd prefer to have more than that when I stand before him."

"Embroider it. Give him a few details, especially the international dimension."

"He'll probably call you in."

"Fine, let me know. When will your replacement be announced?"

"Perhaps on the same timeline you've just provided, so think hard about your decision."

As soon Le Fanu's driver exited Fort St George and turned left towards George Town, they encountered a demonstration, a League rather than Congress one that seemed to include every Muslim in town. Even the women had turned out, in a separate section. It was huge, well organised, peaceful and impenetrable. The driver looked anxious.

"Sit tight, Maran. Nothing you can do. It looks quiet enough so they'll pass eventually."

The procession was at least sixteen persons wide, covering the whole road and surrounding cars, bullock carts, hand barrows, wandering cows and cyclists. Some pedestrians squeezed up against walls or, if they could, escaped across to the beach. The marchers carried banners:

Freedom for Muslims.

Muslims Want Peaceful Change.

Muslims Are Indians, Too.

Congress Should Support Hindus *and* Muslims.

Fair Treatment For Muslims.

As the leaders passed the car, Le Fanu got out.

"I am Superintendent Le Fanu and I respect your right to march. So long as there's no trouble, you'll go unchallenged."

A tall, distinguished man dressed in *shalwar kameez* stopped. His hair had receded and silvered, but a luxuriant beard framed the fine-boned, etched face that probably originated in Persia.

"Thank you, Superintendent. I've heard of you. I am Shameel Musharaff and lead this march on behalf of Islam United. We're peaceful but want change, and want to work with the Hindus in Congress. Our goal is the same: to have India control more of its own affairs and the Raj to leave, eventually. No offence to you, whom I know to be a good man, but some of your colleagues are not, especially the Inspector-General who caused several deaths recently in addition to many earlier ones. There's no place for men like him in India."

The surrounding crowd murmured approval but there was no shouting, no surge, no threats.

"Shameel Musharaff, I'm honoured to meet you and wish you well. Stay peaceful and this march will go unhindered, but make the points you want then disperse."

"We will, and I hope you and I meet again soon."

"I welcome that."

The crowd eventually passed, and the traffic resumed its daily chaos as Le Fanu reached George Town and Caldicott's office.

At the bottom of the stairs an elderly, one-legged woman had a tiny stall selling carved wooden miniatures of the goddess Parvati and her flute. The mother of Ganesh, and a central Shaivite deity. Parvati had a better life than this woman.

"How much do you charge for the Parvati?" Le Fanu asked, in Tamil.

"Just fifty rupees, Sahib," she replied softly.

It was an outrageous sum, but she was a deserving cause. Proud but humble, if not above overcharging an overlord.

"You ask a lot but I like your skill, so I will give you thirty rupees," he said, handing over the money that she palmed in a blur, then a second later handed him a package. He wondered what it was, because he had not seen her wrap the carving.

He thrust it in his pocket and climbed the stairs before signing in with the constable stationed inside the door.

"Hello, LF, come through, Habi's here."

The office seemed even more crowded than before. Another constable was juggling a pile of documents that towered around him. Similar stacks dotted Caldicott's desk, and Habi was balancing several more while trying to read a file.

"Looks like the archives have been transferred from Egmore."

"For once, LF, Delhi has been helpful. This all arrived by special courier late last night. We have intelligence reports on most of the visitors, on some of the incidents that occurred up north, and copies of key reports from London, Europe and North America."

"Is it helping?"

"Sir, there's a long way to go, but we're already seeing more links between these visitors and the victims here. Our Muslim murders are politically motivated, inspired from overseas, and almost certainly committed by one or other of these northern suspects. They're assassins."

"Literally?"

"LF, the documentation identifies at least two of the visitors as hired killers."

That was bad news. "Sorry to hear that, even if it's no real surprise."

Habi flipped through some files. "And almost all the others belong to Hindu organisations that persecute Muslims. They're out to cause trouble."

"To the point of murder?"

"If these documents are correct, to the point of killing as many Muslims as possible."

"Clearly a conspiracy?"

"Yes."

"Do we know where these characters are now, apart from those already in prison?"

"We do, so when do we round them up?"

Habi looked dubious. "Sir, I want to catch these people as much as anyone else, but we should be careful. We don't know how many more people they've recruited here, or how far this organisation extends. If we move too quickly we could leave much of the gang intact and just store up more trouble for later. I don't want any more Muslims murdered, but if we go off too early, a lot more might die as a result."

"I hear you, Habi, and I have to guarantee the Chief Secretary and the Governor we'll get the whole organisation. Jackson, can we expect more intelligence like this?"

"Probably, but I can't guarantee when, or how helpful it might be."

"What about our own people on the ground here?"

"We have more than twenty officers hidden around the city, and they're reporting in regularly, but nothing major yet."

"So sometime in the next day or so we'll have to make a judgement call."

"Unless we have an unexpected breakthrough, yes."

Le Fanu thought about Chester Barnes's mysterious Muslim journalist and looked at his watch. "Right, I'll return to my office and get Whitney up to date. I'll call you later."

Back in Fort St George he telephoned Barnes.

"Thought you'd forgotten me, LF. Stood me up for dinner."

"Sorry, been in Hyderabad, twice, and Guntur. And when I'm here I've no time to spare at all. You'll have heard about Jepson and all that?"

"And the Muslim murders?"

"Of course. And I wondered if you might help me with that."

"How?"

"Your Muslim journalist."

"Yes?"

"Have you heard from her?"

"Not since yesterday but I can contact her."

"That would be good, I need all the information I can get."

"Pressure?"

"Of course. And this is a conspiracy. You can't print that yet but when I get it all, I'll let you know."

"Fair enough. Let me contact her. Then I'll telephone you tonight and we can meet."

"Thanks."

Twenty-seven

Le Fanu imagined he had only just fallen asleep when the telephone rang, and woke to find that he had. It was just one in the morning. He had stayed up late to take Barnes's call that came in at midnight. Yes, his secret journalist might have something useful. Le Fanu should call in to his office as soon as possible.

"Sir, sorry to call at this hour but I knew you'd want to know."

"Know what, Habi?" It had to be serious.

"The Jockey, sir. He's really done it now."

"Fuck. Tell me the worst."

"He ordered four truckloads of men to surround a building containing several of our suspects, northerners, and launched a raid."

"Under whose authority?"

"His own, ignored all the other instructions he'd been given. The station chief involved didn't even know his men had been ordered out."

"Which station?"

"Jepson went away out to Saidapet about ten last night, barged in, bullied the duty sergeant then commandeered the men and the trucks. We only heard an hour ago after the duty sergeant finally found his chief who phoned through to headquarters. I was in the building by chance and someone told me."

"Where's Jepson now?"

“You mean apart from up that creek of effluent and lacking a paddle?”

“Very good, Habi. Yes, apart from that expedition.”

“It’s not good. Several of the northerners were in an apartment building near Adyar. I suppose that’s why he chose Saidapet, it’s close by. So he ordered two truckloads of men to surround the building, and sent another two in to arrest the targets.”

“And that went wrong.”

“Very much so. Our suspects had posted armed guards. They were taking no chances after what happened at the village. As soon as our men tried to go in, the guards opened fire. That woke the rest of them who all rushed to other windows and started firing.”

“And our men were out in the open?”

“Sadly, yes.”

“Casualties?”

“Seven dead policemen and two innocent passers-by so far. Several policemen injured.”

“That fool doesn’t just have blood on his hands now, they’re permanently immersed in the stuff. For fuck’s sake. What was he thinking?”

“Probably very little.”

“He has to go. These deaths can’t go unpunished. He’s already responsible for too many and now this. Where is he?”

“Still out there.”

“Doing what?”

“That’s just it, sir. He told someone out there he has the northerners under siege. That person called me and said, if anything, it was the other way around. The Jockey and the surviving police are pinned down. The apartment block’s in a cul de sac where The Jockey insisted the trucks be parked. Our men can't move. If they do, they're shot at. But he seems to think he has the upper hand."

"Even by his standards, this is fucking unbelievable. What have we done so far?"

"I've organised another large police contingent that is on standby and will move only on your instruction. The military also have a couple of hundred soldiers on alert in case you need them. I'll call Assistant Superintendent Caldicott now, if you think that necessary."

"Excellent, Habi, and yes, call him. Tell the military we would like their assistance so they should move their men out there immediately. Send ours out there, too. Give me the location and I'll leave here right away."

"Sir, I have your driver on deck now, so I'll come with him, collect you and we can pick up Assistant Superintendent Caldicott on the way."

"Ahead of me as usual, Habi. I'll alert Whitney."

He took five minutes to settle. Jepson must surely have some mental problem to have acted so irresponsibly and caused the deaths of even more good men. Once again, the Raj would look as if it had no conscience, no care for the Indians in its employ. That handed moral advantage straight to Congress, and probably the Muslim League as well because there would be Muslims among the dead and wounded. And the innocent bystanders. All because of Jepson.

"Charles, seriously bad news, I'm sorry." He passed on the information.

"Fuck. What do we have to do to get rid of this moron? The only sliver of good news here is that Jepson can't possibly survive. He's more dangerous to us than the criminals he's supposed to catch. Who'd work with him or follow his orders now? You'd be signing your own death warrant. I'll get Willingdon up to speed then start proceedings against the idiot. What are you doing?"

Le Fanu outlined the plans.

"That sounds like the best we can do with this mess. Be careful, Chris. I don't usually say that because I know anyone working with you will be safe, but we can't afford any more fatalities."

"Understood."

As he ended the call, car lights slashed across the lawns and into his windows, so he collected his jacket and went out. Jackson was already aboard. Habi had somehow gained them a little more time. Le Fanu took the front seat beside the driver, who looked shocked. If anyone had to sit there, it would be Habi, normally. No European would.

"Sorry, Thiruma, don't want to invade your space but this is an emergency."

The man remained puzzled, and uneasy.

"Sir, my man at the scene telephoned again, from a nearby house. No change. The Jockey's ordering his men to mount another charge on the apartment block, but they're going slow. They're not disobeying, but all their rifles seem to have developed mysterious problems."

"Good on them."

"LF, any immediate ideas? We'll be there in fifteen minutes."

"We can't make firm plans until we assess the damage. If The Jockey is uncooperative, we'll have to improvise. Habi, I should have asked for an ambulance, and a strait jacket."

"On the way, sir. Some ambulances were there already but they're busy with the casualties so I thought another one might be helpful."

"Habi," said Caldicott, "you're extraordinary. I'd never have thought of that."

"You would have, had you been in my place."

Le Fanu perceived further thawing in the icy relationship. "What about the additional manpower, Habi?"

"We'll rendezvous with the army and our own units three blocks back from the siege, because that's what it is now. We just don't know who's besieging whom."

"That's life around Jepson," Caldicott observed.

"Amen that." Le Fanu contemplated all the imminent services for the dead.

"We're now a block away from the meeting point," Habi commented. They fell silent. No matter the level of caution, care or consideration, apprehension always set in at this point. The war had prepared Le Fanu for that.

They turned a corner to find the backup trucks in line, ready to proceed. Soldiers and policemen were in parade ranks, officers conducting arms and ammunition inspections.

Le Fanu gathered the officers and issued instructions. Everyone remounted their vehicles. Le Fanu's car led the convoy, slowly, through streets filling with spectators attracted by the commotion. Even more potential casualties, he thought.

"Jackson, I'll slow us down. Then I need you to get out and take control of one of our units. Seal off the entrance to this cul de sac, then back at least two streets. We don't need any more civilian casualties."

"Will do, LF."

"Then come forward and rejoin us."

The car slowed to a crawl, Jackson stepped out surely, athleticism on show. The driver picked up pace, turned them towards, then into, the danger area.

"Let's get everyone organised, Habi. I want remaining units to come in on both sides, but tell them not to move until you say so. We need to locate our units that are in trouble, and the crazy architect of all this. Then wait for Jackson, so the two of you can come up together. But be careful."

"And you, too, sir."

Habi slipped into the darkness while Le Fanu drew his old Webley Mk IV revolver, checked his ammunition then advanced, cautiously. He noticed the glow of lights peeping around a corner about one hundred yards ahead and heard noise, but less than expected. The street was narrow and unlit, the distracting glare ahead reducing his night vision. He felt vulnerable, hand tightening on the revolver. Cramped fingers made for poor shooting and that was bad in this sort of situation.

It was like being back in Mesopotamia, creeping through dark, unfamiliar streets and lanes in unfamiliar towns. The problem was that defenders always knew these places better than pursuers.

He imagined sounds, stopped at every one of them, eyes straining to distinguish between the imagined and the real. A headache was well on the way. Something scuttled out of a laneway, hopefully four rather than two legged. His heart rate was rising, breathing heavier. Looking up, he saw nothing, couldn't even make out where the roofs finished and the sky began. Blackness. Not much better looking straight ahead. The pressure was building and he was both sweating and shivering. He hated that sensation.

Reaching the corner he peered around, dazed again by more intense light. The police trucks were still running, presumably because their lights were on to illuminate the apartment block. Dumb. Jepson apparently thought light meant he could see what was happening. All that did was expose his own position. He was better off in darkness. His men were now immediate targets if they moved.

The glare meant Le Fanu could not see movement inside the building. Those truck lights had to be turned off. And he wondered if anyone knew what was at the back of the apartments. There would be doors, but did they lead to an escape or was that a dead end as well? He cursed. Should have asked Habi, who would know.

Le Fanu pulled back into the darkness, took a deep breath, then jumped when someone touched him on the arm.

"What the …"

"Sorry, sir. Thought you'd have heard us." Habi and Caldicott had appeared noiselessly and taken far less time than him to get there. "We saw you looking around the corner, sir."

Another black mark. He hadn't thought about anyone looking for or at him while he was looking ahead. He was well out of practice.

"Well done, you two. Where are our reinforcements?"

Caldicott waved behind. "Several in the doorways either side of this laneway, the rest around the last corner and on alert. We've an officer back there waiting for a torch signal that we'll flash if they're needed."

Caldicott and Habi were up to it. He told them what little he had seen up front.

"Those lights have to go out, sir."

"I agree, Habi."

"I'd go up but Jepson's not likely to listen to me." Caldicott looked glum.

"That's my job." Le Fanu hoped he sounded convincing, still shaking from the tap on the arm.

"I'll come with you, sir."

"Thanks, Habi, but no. We need you here to help Jackson coordinate the police and military. Watch me, at least until the lights go out. After that we'll deal with things as they come."

He looked around the corner again, shielding his eyes from the intensity to hopefully retain some vision. A rifle shot, stone chipping off a wall above him. Le Fanu ducked back.

"They know we're here, then," he said. "Bloody Jepson can't get anything right. I'll crawl along the base of the wall, then you two lay down fire as I move out. Three, two, one."

He dropped on his belly and slithered through the dust as fast as he could while Habi and Caldicott fired multiple rounds into the apartment. Something furry brushed past his face and he shuddered. Return fire razed the walls just above him, but it seemed the shooters' line of sight did not include him. Even so, the ricochets were scary. Habi and Caldicott kept firing.

Now he was in behind a truck and among cowering policemen. He shook one at the shoulder. "Where's your officer in charge?"

"Sir, Inspector Allen-Chalmers was shot during the first round of firing. He's dead."

Shit, a dead European. Because of the war and normal human feelings aside, Le Fanu rated Indians higher, but his superiors mostly did not. A European death here meant heads would roll, Jepson's the first, hopefully.

"Why are the lights on?"

"Inspector-General's orders, sir."

"Right, I'm in command now. I need the lights off and the truck stopped. Can you do that?"

"Yes, sir."

"Good man. The rest of you, fire at my command. Aim at that building but keep your heads down. Ready man?"

"Sir."

"GO and FIRE."

The man clambered into the cab as the others laid down heavy fire that drew a response. But in a second the truck engine was cut and the lights gone.

"Who the fuck did that? Turn those fucking lights back on," came an enraged voice from the darkness ahead.

Jepson.

"Ignore that, men. You're under my command now."

"Thank you, sir, much appreciated." The relief was obvious.

Habi materialised out of the dark. "Well done, sir. You need the rest of the men up here yet?"

"We need more lights doused first. You go across to that one, I'll go over there. Once you've done that, call the rest up. You others, ready to fire. Three, two, one."

With more rifles now deployed, the firing was intense and drew a weaker response as Habi and Le Fanu crabbed across to their destinations and extinguished two more sets of lights.

"I'll have you fucking mutineers fucking jailed." Jepson's voice grated during a lull in the firing.

"Rather that than be killed by your mad ideas," came a response from the ranks.

"Quiet!" roared Le Fanu. "The enemy is in that building and they love this, makes their job easier. Turn off the lights in those other trucks, now."

"Le Fanu, you bastard, I'll have you on a charge as well, you fucking …"

The lights died and the area went quiet. Le Fanu could make out details on the building. It was pockmarked with bullet damage, most of the windows shot out. Light glinted off weapons in several places. They had a fair force in front of them.

He went ahead to the other trucks and found Jepson hunched behind the wheel of one.

"Fucking Le Fanu, I'll …"

"Shut the fuck up. Sir. You've now killed a lot more of us and endangered the rest of these men. I'm relieving you of command as I'm in charge of this operation. You did this unauthorised, and I'll be reporting that way."

"They'll cut you down, you tarbrush shagger. You'll …"

"Enough." Le Fanu clipped handcuffs onto Jepson's wrists before the man realised what was happening.

"By the living Jesus, Le Fanu, I'll …"

At which Le Fanu took a large, wrapped bandana from his hip pocket and tied it over Jepson's mouth. A couple of nearby policemen began to clap.

"Quiet," Le Fanu shouted, "we still have to get out of here. You three, escort the Inspector-General to the rear. Keep low and drag him in the dirt if necessary."

The arrest party set out under sporadic fire, the guards protecting their prisoner by dragging him in the dirt, face down.

Caldicott appeared. "I've got the rest on standby, LF."

"We can either try to take the building, or get out of here. I propose the latter. Too many men have died already. And we've no intel on the building."

Now Habi arrived. "Sir, there are doors at the back but

the locals tell me there are no laneways or alleys off from there. Bad mistake by these people. They're sealed off."

"Excellent. We'll get our men to safety and the reinforcements can stand guard overnight. Then we can return to town, rework the strategy and regroup in the morning. Make sure that bloody Jepson's on the floor of the most uncomfortable truck."

A few minutes later, they restarted the trucks, reversed them unlit out of the tight space and came under no fire. Even those trapped in the apartment block had recognised the stalemate.

Twenty-eight

At Fort St George, Jepson was frogmarched upstairs by his willing guardians who went slowly, maximising their enjoyment, revenge and later storytelling potential.

"Come on, you fellows, don't make a meal of it," Le Fanu had to say, but didn't mean it. Like them, he was enjoying momentary victory over a man who had made many people's lives miserable and ended some far too early.

Jepson struggled all the way, unintelligible comments streaming out from behind the gag. Those were clearly not complimentary, and his face reddened with every step up the stairs. News had spread. There were far more people at work than normal at five in the morning, the Jepson parade a popular event. Le Fanu fancied, too, that he saw a senior policeman or three whose natural home was at the Marina rather than here.

The escort party pushed on to Whitney's office where the man himself was as meticulous as ever, but the several senior civil servants in attendance were trying surreptitiously to wave away the inevitable smoke.

"In all my years," the Chief Secretary said, stabbing the cigar towards Jepson to underscore the point, "I've never seen anything like this. Remarkable. Inspector-General Gagged. Not the Count of Monte Cristo, I grant you, but astonishing enough. Steer him into my office."

The three policemen surrounded their erstwhile boss, shunted him into the office and edged him into a wing-backed chair. Jepson more or less fell on it. The policemen then looked at a loss as to what they might do next, and Le Fanu ushered them to the door.

"See Assistant Superintendent Habibullah, he'll look after you. Well done."

"Thank you, sir, for everything." They smiled. Le Fanu tried not to, but failed.

As he walked back into Whitney's office he heard The Jockey in full voice. The gag was gone, then. He closed the outer door, then the one to the inner sanctum.

"You'll not hear the end of this, Le Fanu. Insubordination to the point of treason." Jepson was grubby from head to foot, the infamous riding boots scuffed beyond repair and the uniform torn in several places.

"Don't be bloody stupid, you fucking fool." The publicly winsome Whitney flashed into a wild one privately. "You've delivered several more good men to needless deaths. Eight at last count. Eight! You fucking fraud. You've bluffed your way into every one of your posts, but you'll not bluff your way out of this. With your record, you'll be lucky to escape a disciplinary hearing. If I have my way, you'll fuck off without a pension. You should face court but that'll never happen. London couldn't stomach the notoriety, nor Delhi."

He smashed the cigar butt into a tray, looking like he would rather have used Jepson's face.

"How dare you," countered Jepson. "You're as much a disgrace as this other snivelling mess. Le Fanu and Whitney, the pair that sold Madras out to the natives. Fucking weak, both of you. Too bloody soft by half. Bloody Hindu this, Muslim that. They need to be taught a lesson, by people like me. My friends will support me You're both finished and you know it."

He was breathless, wild eyed, dishevelled, and Le Fanu wondered if he was having a medical moment so offered him water. Jepson swept it aside onto the carpet.

"Any more of that, Jepson, and I'll have you in the cells down here. I hear they've seen better days, but you're scarcely dressed for the Connemara so that doesn't matter really, does it? Drink, Chris? It's been a long night."

Le Fanu wondered the wisdom of that but nodded anyway.

Whitney poured two generous measures into elegant crystal tumblers apparently reserved for very special occasions, because Le Fanu had never seen them before.

"*Sláinte*, Chris. Very well done."

"Well done, my arse. The man'll be charged and dismissed." Jepson was still handcuffed so, given his weight and shape, wedged into the chair and unable to lever himself out.

"Now listen to me, you dumb shit." This controlled, angry Whitney surfaced rarely. "I've already spoken with Willingdon about your latest exploits, and to say he's unimpressed would qualify as understatement of the year. He wants your balls, Jepson, preferably mounted in silver over the fireplace in his country house study. To put it mildly, you're fucked."

"I've never heard …"

"Do I look like someone who wants you to speak? Now here's the good news. Against my wishes, the Governor has some ideas for you because, according to him, Delhi wants this dealt with quietly. If I had my way it would be in the cell with you, key lost. For a very long time."

"I don't need any deals from you."

"Actually, you do, very much so. Willingdon's suggestion is that you 'retire' immediately on health grounds. I think that's shorthand for do so immediately, otherwise he'll have his boot buried up your substantial arse quick smart."

"I don't have to …"

"Yes, you do."

Le Fanu felt like he was at Wimbledon. Whitney served, Jepson tried to return, only to be smashed by an overhead.

"Because, you complete failure," Whitney continued, "you've been responsible for far too many deaths, you've embarrassed every official between here and Whitehall, and you are, as they say, on the nose." Whitney looked Jepson up and down. "Literally and figuratively."

"I'll not tolerate this level of abuse, I'll …"

"Do precisely nothing. Apart from resign. You'll be under guard at the D'Angelis for a day or so until we arrange passage for you, then you'll be off back home. The size of your pension, if any, is still under review, so if I were you, I'd behave. That might help you get some food, too, though by the look of you, that isn't urgent. No grog, though, HE heard about your bravura performance at the club. Not impressed."

"Fuck off."

"That would be you, not me or Le Fanu. You're getting what's been due for a long time, Jepson, the disciplinary equivalent of a damn good kicking. Your treatment of staff, the local population and everyone else you encounter has been abysmal, and this payback is totally inadequate but will have to do."

"I …"

"Enough, I think. It's time for you, as you so elegantly put it, to fuck off. Chris, would you be so good as to open my door, please?"

Le Fanu discovered four armed guards from the Military Police outside that door.

"Oh,"Whitney continued,"forgot to mention one thing. Change of plan. The Governor had the hotel in mind for you but left me discretion. I think you're far too uncivilised to be let loose on a reputable hotel. Too dangerous for all concerned. So you're having a week's holiday in one of the luxurious cells out at the St Thomas Mount barracks while we decide finally what to do with you."

He gestured to the MPs. "Gentlemen, come in, meet your newest guest."

The soldiers came in, two grabbed Jepson at each shoulder, pulled him up then, flanked by the other two, escorted him out. They heard him curse non-stop all the way down the stairs.

"Another drink, Chris?"

"In honour of that cameo? Oh yes, sir."

"Overly dramatic, perhaps, but understandable in the circumstances, I think."

"Completely."

The measures were again generous.

"Revenge is all very well, Chris, but we've just seen why we'll lose India, because we've now got more fools like that in the service than we had back in the nineteenth century. There's a vast difference between conservative and downright stupidly racist. That prick is clearly among the latter and has too many colleagues here, sadly."

"You really think so?"

"I wish I didn't, but yes. That's why we can't get support for the reforms, even though passing them'd actually guarantee us a longer stay in a much friendlier form. It's idiots like Jepson who scream for tough justice, more jailings for so-called political crimes and all the rest. It's why the fear of Indianisation is growing rather than declining."

"Gaines says his generation all expect a short career and are prepared for that. Pity, he's very good."

"His generation's not the problem, just the sad beneficiaries of ours. Jepson and his ilk think India owes them, when they should be thinking in the reverse, as you do. And me, to a lesser degree."

"The more I see of you, Charles, the more complex you become."

"Glad to hear it. Now, you know Jepson has been blackguarding you?"

"Well, yes, but why do you raise it now?"

"Because he's been spreading downright lies about your loyalty, your morality and anything else he can think of. And he's been actively aided and abetted by the egregious Jamieson."

"I know they dislike me …"

"Chris, they *fear* you because you represent everything that challenges their future."

"That's a bit dramatic, isn't it?"

"Afraid not. But nothing to worry about. Willingdon was fed some nonsense he didn't believe, but asked me and I put him straight. You're in good standing."

"For what?"

"Permanent I-G, for one."

Le Fanu suddenly felt tired. And perhaps looked it.

"Chris, go home, have breakfast and a rest. Be back here at, say, twelve and we'll begin to work out what happens next. Job well done, by the way."

By the time he reached Mylapore, Le Fanu was good only for a long, hot shower and falling immediately into a deep sleep as soon as he hit the pillow. He awoke around eleven, five hours later, showered again, ate a late breakfast and felt much better.

It also felt like the previous evening's events had been a dream rather than an event.

Habi set him right during their telephone discussion.

"Oh, yes, sir, it all did happen. Nine deaths now, but all the wounded now appear to be out of danger. Bad enough, though."

"I hope you got some rest."

"Assistant Superintendent Caldicott and I went to our homes and had some sleep before getting back here just now."

"What's the latest on the siege site?"

"Little movement in the building reported, and our troops are guarding all possible exits and the general area. They've also done a thorough search for tunnels. Nothing found so far, and the military are awaiting our instructions."

"I'll talk to Whitney to see what the powers that be think currently."

He passed on the news about Jepson.

"My military contact told me that The Jockey was badly behaved upon arrival at the Mount."

"It's like he's lost all reason."

"I agree, sir, and that cost several of our men their lives. He should be punished."

"The Chief Secretary's trying to achieve that but politics will intervene. The Raj has an image to protect, and that's not best served by putting Jepson through the trial he richly deserves."

"A pity, sir. But I'll let you know as soon as I hear anything more."

“Thanks, Habi, your work has helped us take back the initiative in all this.”

“My job, sir.”

Caldicott took the same line.

“Thank you, LF, but you did all the hard stuff, I was there as backup.”

“You did it well. Any more intelligence reports?”

“Delhi’s promising me something substantial but I’ve no idea what it is.”

“I’ve just remembered. Barnes wanted me to call him first thing about some possible new information. Last night’s adventure blocked that out, Let me contact him and I’ll get back to you.”

A quick call confirmed the editor was in his office so Le Fanu had the driver rush him there, but not before he called Whitney to reschedule that meeting.

“Sorry for the delay in getting back to you, Chester, but I can now give you an accurate account of last night’s affair.”

“That’s fair compensation so apology accepted.”

“What about your mystery journalist?”

“Not good news for you if she’s right.”

“Why?”

“Somehow, she’s tapped some really good intelligence channels inside the Muslim community that access the more radical Hindu groups here in India and overseas. The bits she is telling me about seem credible.”

“Is she in danger?”

“She says not, but given what she claims to know, she shouldn’t be so relaxed. Last night and the other day indicate these groups and their followers are determined and committed. Am I wrong?”

"No, and if she met me I'd tell her so, but I'm guessing she won't?"

"At this stage, no, so I'll pass your views on to hopefully strengthen mine."

"What's she telling you?"

"That there are definite links to the Ghadar movement among the suspects here, that there's a distinct revolutionary bent to their activities, and that Madras hasn't seen the worst yet."

"That's not good news."

"It gets worse. She believes armed revolutionary reinforcements are on the way here now, from around India and even from overseas."

The rest of the day was a maelstrom.

Twenty-nine

He expected Habi, Caldicott or Whitney when the telephone rang at seven the next morning. Having slept little and taken breakfast early, he was already tired at the start of what promised to be a long day.

"Good morning, Chris."

"Ro. Well, yes, of course, good morning. I hadn't …"

"… expected to hear from me. And here I was thinking you'd become articulate recently."

"You know, just a surprise to hear you. A good surprise, of course."

"I'm teasing you. Sir Maurice got me access to a telephone here in the Osmania and thought you should hear directly from me that I'm much better. Still in hospital and will be for a few more days, but improving rapidly, thanks to the pair of you."

"The least we could do. You're an …"

"… important person, I know. And I appreciate that. But I'm very grateful, because had I stayed at Trimulgherry I'd no longer be with you, I'm told."

"Statham and his team were lacking some vital resources."

"Including humanity, I hear."

He remembered her incisive mind.

"You've heard about Guntur, then?"

"Sir Maurice recounts all your adventures to me, or at least the ones he knows about."

"Very good of him."

"Oh Chris, it's lovely to bring you back to earth now and then, you're such a good person."

"I'm normally good, yes, just get busy, and bothered. You'll have heard about the latest blunder down here?"

"What will happen to Jepson?"

"He won't be around for much longer."

"And that gives you even more food for thought because they'll want you to replace him."

"There'll be several good candidates. It's no certainty that …"

"Don't be so self-effacing. I'll bet Whitney's already told you the job's yours, and you're losing sleep because you've got competing opportunities. Sir Maurice wants you here and there's a post for you back across the Bay of Bengal."

"How on earth …?"

"No one's told me anything but I can read the signs. You're restless and preoccupied. Given you love your work so much, and Madras, it's obvious you've other offers."

Was he that transparent?

"I'll admit there's some substance to your views."

"And that your new Penang friend adds further complication."

"Ro, I …"

"You don't have to say anything. Just know that I know. Now, I should go because Dr Metcalfe's glaring at me. I just wanted to let you know I'm on the mend."

"Have you thought any more about …"

"Where I might go? I've no definite plans until I hear back from one or two people. It won't be with the General, however, because I'm superfluous to requirements there."

"Please keep me informed, and I'll telephone you soon if I'm not back in Hyderabad. Delighted to hear you're much better."

"Bye, Chris."

He wondered what Maurice was up to. It was a relief that Ro was out of danger, but there were more straightforward ways of informing him. But he had enjoyed the conversation. That might simply have been a break from talking to policemen and fools like Jepson, but he knew there was more to it. He appreciated her accurate assessments, and her analysis made him wonder about Jenlin Koh. He'd heard nothing further about her travels.

A servant broke into his thinking to announce Habi's arrival. Had that been arranged? He couldn't remember anything.

"Good morning, Habi. Can I get you something? I've eaten but there's plenty available."

"Just coffee, sir. Sorry to barge in but I wanted to see you directly."

"Any time, Habi, you know that."

"Thank you. Sir, I was at a Muslim meeting last night."

"The League?"

"No, despite Assistant Superintendent Caldicott's fears, I haven't gone political, yet." An interesting comment. "It was a gathering of Muslims who have a wide range of political and social views, and are concerned about these murders and the wider implications."

"That's understandable …"

"You know it's hard to keep anything secret in this city, sir. The Muslim communities are bothered by the arrival of these revolutionary gangs. Many Muslims regard them as assassination squads, and you can see why."

"I can. Do we have any more news from Guntur?"

"Nothing helpful. And the Muslims know that. They're beginning to think we're doing nothing and that police don't care what happens to Muslims."

"You know that's not true, Habi."

"I do, but they don't, for certain, and that's bad for us. Some Muslim leaders are openly saying the government favours Hindus."

"That's completely wrong."

"Not entirely, sir. There are more Jepsons in the force and the civil service than anyone realises, and there is all that talk about excluding Muslims from some service posts."

"How can we reassure the Muslim communities?"

"They've elected a delegation of five to meet the Chief Secretary and the Governor."

"Would you like me to arrange this?"

"If you would, sir."

"Of course, if you think it absolutely necessary."

"I do. Yes, I'm Muslim, but you know I'm not totally devout. That English boarding school I attended saw to that."

Le Fanu detected regret, the first time he had heard that.

"But," Habi continued, "this isn't just about religion. If their suspicions turn to animosity, then Madras will face major communal clashes. Right now, that would be doubly bad. The Chief Secretary and the Governor are going, Jepson'll be replaced, but no one knows who the replacements will be. Will they be sympathetic, or law and order merchants with no concern for the cultures they're dealing with?"

"I understand. I'll arrange the meeting."

"And I appreciate that, but you might not be here much longer, either. If you replaced Jepson, the Muslims would be more relaxed because they trust you. But if it's not you, tension will rise."

First Ro, now Habi, not to mention Wilson, Whitney and lord knows who else. And it was still early in the day.

"Habi, I hear you. I'm not sure what's happening to Jepson, let alone his position, but let me fix this meeting for you. Where are you going now?"

"To my office. At least Jepson won't be there today so that makes it easier, even if technically we don't have a boss."

British India's reliance on institutional hierarchy was strangling, so Le Fanu understood Habi's pessimism. The chain of command was paramount, especially in the major cities. While a Collector had considerable district discretion, central officials had far less, so an absent boss caused problems in a workforce unused to having discretion over decisions. There would be confused people at headquarters and around Madras today who welcomed The Jockey's fall, but looked in vain for his replacement.

"I'll see if I can find out what's happening on that front."

"That'd be good."

"Come on, then, if you're ready, I'll drop you at your office."

While they talked along the way, Habi seemed distracted so Le Fanu again noticed little of the street life passing by outside their little bubble of Raj privilege. For perhaps the first time, Le Fanu felt uneasy in Habi's presence.

"How are you and Caldicott getting along, Habi?" Might as well take it on directly.

"Very well. There were difficult moments earlier but those have passed."

"I'd noticed that. Glad it's resolved."

"We still differ over the government's approach, but we're working well together, despite the frustratingly slow progress on these cases."

"I share that frustration. But if you and Jackson have resolved your differences, then forgive me for asking but why are you not your normal good self?"

"I'm concerned about this communal issue, sir, and the murders are central to that, so not solving them makes me nervous, and critical of our failures."

"Patience, Habi. We've had cases like this before."

"Not with such high stakes. If we don't solve these, we could face major riots in which hundreds if not thousands might die. And we've had too many unnecessary deaths already."

"Go easier on yourself, we'll get there." Le Fanu regretted the platitude. Habi was right. The stakes were high. "Sorry, Habi, I didn't mean to sound patronising."

"I didn't take it that way, sir. Besides, it's not my only worry. My wife is ill, has been for a while."

Le Fanu wanted to disappear right into the well-upholstered seats, realising instantly that since his return he'd not once asked Habi about his family. He had been too wrapped up in his own affairs. Yet Habi had constantly asked after Ro.

"Habi, I'm so sorry to hear that and I apologise profusely for not having been more of a friend. I've been far too self-centred. Is there anything I can do?"

"Thank you, sir, but no. The doctors can't work out what's wrong, and that's more worrying than the illness.

They can't treat her because they don't know what they're dealing with."

"Is she in hospital?"

"No, because they can't treat her. She's at home, unable to do much. I've got an extra servant in and that helps, but the kids are worried."

Now Le Fanu felt even worse. Habi worked long hours, went to Guntur without protest or avoidance. He had been taken for granted, as the British did routinely in India.

"I don't know what to say, Habi. I'm no friend at all, but please let me help if I can. And work fewer hours, stay at home."

"We're not solving anything now so if I work less that'll only get worse."

He watched Habi trudge up the stairs at headquarters. There went the very reason British India could survive, yet it ignored loyal Indians at every turn. And he was as guilty of that as all the reactionaries he criticised.

He went straight to Whitney's office, explained Habi's request, and the Chief Secretary volunteered to approach the Governor. If the Muslims could meet those two, Habi might feel progress was being made.

Le Fanu returned to his own office, telephoned the Osmania and asked for Rory Metcalfe.

"Good morning, Superintendent."

"Chris, please, Rory. I owe you so much for your excellent work with Ro, Mrs McPhedren."

"Thank you, and as you've heard for yourself, she's much brighter."

"Wonderful news. How much longer will she be with you?"

"No more than a week, I'd reckon. Has she made any arrangements yet?"

"No, but I'm working on that. I'll let you know."

"Fair enough."

"There's something else. Do you have any reason to come to Madras?"

"I'm open to any chance for a change of scenery. Why?"

"My Assistant Superintendent's wife has some sort of illness the Madras General people can't fathom. She's at home struggling and not improving."

"And you'd like me to have a look at her."

"Would you be open to that? She's a Hindu Christian and my man Habi's a quizzical Muslim."

"To me, she's a patient in need of help, nothing else. Of course I can come."

"Let me see what I can organise, and of course I'll pay the fares and put you up at a hotel."

"Happy to help."

Now he had to convince Habi this was a good idea, and that might not be easy.

Whitney called with an answer from Willingdon.

"Habi, good news. The Governor and Chief Secretary will meet the Muslim delegation this evening. It'll be at the Governor's office. You can arrange that with them? They won't be overwhelmed?"

"They should be fine."

"And you'll accompany them?"

"Perhaps not a good idea, sir. They might feel spied on, or that they're only there because we've engineered it. They must focus on the Chief Secretary and HE. But thanks for the thought, and for arranging this."

"You're right. This is an important moment, so I'm glad the meeting will happen. Do we have any more news on our revolutionaries?"

"Are we now calling them that officially, sir?"

"The evidence gives us cause, and the label might prompt more urgency among senior ranks. So, yes, let's do that."

"There's still a stalemate at the apartment block, so things must be grim in there. We should determine a course of action soon. And we're getting more intelligence about the new contingent's movements. Some are coming from Bombay, others up from Colombo. So far we've about fifty possible names."

"This is growing too rapidly, Habi, so we need a clear plan, I agree."

"Sir, I'll talk to my Muslim friends and confirm arrangements, and check further with Assistant Superintendent Caldicott."

"Thanks, Habi. Now, about your wife."

"Sir?"

"You know Dr Metcalfe from the Osmania basically saved Mrs McPhedren's life?"

"Yes."

"He will be in Madras for a visit soon. Would you let me arrange for him to see your wife?"

"Sir, I'm grateful, but …"

"There'll be no cost."

"I can't allow that, sir, I …"

"I'd say the same because that's what we do. But allow me to arrange this as an apology for taking you for granted. It won't make up for my thoughtless behaviour, I know. You've helped me on so many occasions and never once asked for anything. It would mean a lot to me if you agreed."

"Sir, I do. And thank you."

"No, Habi, thank *you*. And please understand, your support and friendship mean a lot to me."

"Then you'll stay as Inspector-General?"

Thirty

Later that morning Le Fanu trudged up to Caldicott's lair, still conflicted and distressed by his discussion with Habi. Was it all becoming too much? Could he not handle both the job and his life without ignoring people like Habi who supported him the most? And the lack of progress was a real concern.

"Jackson, I hope you've got some good news to cheer me up.?"

"The Jockey's gone?"

"Not news. Try again."

"Pass."

"No help, then. What should we do about these besieged revolutionaries?"

"The unit commander just asked me the same question. I told him it's not mine to answer. Can you get Whitney to make a ruling?"

"Better if we go with a suggestion. Dare we risk another raid? Do we know who else is in there? If there are civilians, they'll be getting desperate."

Another twinge. This had been going on for two days and he wasn't sure that civilian aspect had been investigated. He of all people should know.

"We're fortunate. The building had been emptied to make urgent improvements, so our visitors simply went in and camped. They're the only ones in there."

Why hadn't he known that?

He was letting things slide.

Meanwhile, Habi was handling the Muslim murders virtually alone.

"A raid, then?"

"Any more deaths will bring bad publicity, and even if we grab everyone inside, there's no guarantee it's all of them or that we'll get good information. We know they have significant reinforcements on the way. Would we do better letting this run a bit?"

"You're suggesting we let them loose?"

"Yes, and no. The trucks have already been pulled back, leaving the troops hidden in the alleyways. If those troops just withdraw quietly overnight, the apartment inmates wake up to much the same as they saw the night before. It might take them a while to realise they're on their own."

"And what do we do?"

"Our main risk lies with the quality of surveillance. Up to now we've practically failed with this lot. Lost them. If we adopt this strategy we can't repeat that, so we'll need all our very best undercover people."

"So we let the revolutionaries wander off, meet up with their pals, and we follow them."

"Slightly more complicated than that but, essentially, yes."

"And the anticipated result?"

"We find out exactly what these characters are planning, and catch every last one of them."

"It's risky, with huge potential for poor publicity."

"We've got bad publicity now, what with the bungling and deaths and speculation about The Jockey. Seen the *Mail*? A lurid but accurate account of his antics. How'd they get that?"

"It didn't come from me. Barnes has his own sources. Have you considered all the possibilities if we do this?"

"Losing contact is the big risk, because we'd lose control and there'd be a bigger band of baddies out there."

"That's not comforting."

"An immediate raid would be more dangerous. We'd only get a fraction of the gang, at best, then have to winkle the plans out of them, and we might lose even more of our own people. The reactionaries will revolt and the whole thing'll spiral out of control."

"Have you discussed this with anyone?"

"Only you here in Madras, but a few select others in Delhi, in India Intelligence."

"Do they have experience in this sort of thing?"

"Almost all of them were police either here or back Home before they became spies."

"D'you trust them?"

"Never entirely, but they've been helpful so far."

"What do they think of this plan?"

"A couple are concerned, but the rest think it's the best way forward."

Le Fanu leaned back and stared at the roof. No inspiration there. "This is my call, Jackson. Whitney and Willingdon will go with whatever I recommend, so we must be sure. Are you?"

"Of course not, but it's the least worst option."

"And your Delhi devils think the same?"

"Yes."

"Then let's take a deep breath and trust we're good enough to track these people because if we aren't, we'll all be very deep in manure. The risk of more deaths in a raid is the most compelling argument, but I see the wider merits. Very bold. There'll be a lot at stake for you, too."

"Delhi will be pleased."

"Is that important?"

"Well …"

"So they're lining you up for a job."

"I was going to mention it later. There's nothing definite. In fact, it's all extremely vague. But there have been suggestions."

"Not surprising, you're very good. But don't jump too soon, I need your help to prevent any major disasters here."

"I'm flattered, LF, but how long will you be here? The only reason I'm interested in Delhi is because of the changes here, including your probable departure."

"I …"

"LF. You're everyone's pick to replace Jepson, and we all hope you do. But Habi and I know you've a few considerations that complicate an automatic acceptance. If you refuse it, there's no other obvious choice. That means anything's possible, even another Jepson. I grant you no one could be that bad, but you know the point I'm making."

"And fair enough. I know my uncertainty makes life difficult for you."

"And Habi. He's wondering what'll happen to him so he's considering options, in Singapore."

"He's talked with you and said that?"

"Yes."

He really was losing touch, with everything.

"What's your current thinking, LF?"

"As usual, I don't know."

"Then may I say, in the kindest possible way, please decide tout de suite and make life much more straightforward for many people."

"Including you and Habi."

"Especially me and Habi."

This was now officially one of those times when he had no idea what to do for the best.

"First off, I'll suggest this strategy to Whitney and the Governor. They'll probably agree, so best get the military prepared. When do you want to start? Tonight?"

"Might as well. Apart from anything else, the new revolutionaries are imminent. An early move will get the current residents out making more contacts we can track."

"Update your Delhi friends, then. What are they dangling in front of you, anyway?"

"Head of Domestic Intelligence for the Princely States, to start with."

"They really do want you. And rightly so. Will you take it?"

"This is getting circular, LF. It'll be harder for me to accept if you stay, but if you go I'm there like a shot. You're Madras's last vestige of hope."

"It would be nice if things were more straightforward."

"With you, that's unlikely. Speaking of which, there's something else I must say, and you'll find it worrying."

"Now what?"

"That ship Jenlin Koh's on. My Singapore counterpart has told me it failed to make its most recent scheduled position call."

"Meaning what?"

"They don't know its precise position, or if it's still on the scheduled route."

"When was that call due?"

"Midnight just passed. There's no need for concern, yet. Apparently this happens quite often in the area the ship's now sailing through. Some atmospheric oddities cause radio failures. But I thought you should know."

"Thanks, Jackson. Tell me if you hear anything more, obviously."

As the driver spirited him away, Le Fanu puzzled again why these things always coincided. The news about Jenlin's ship did not worry him, overly, but added another distraction to what was already a host of them, and blurred his concentration further following the conversation with Ro sparked by Sir Maurice Wilson that Le Fanu had no idea how to read. Then, he also had to assess his job opportunities as much, if not more, by personal as professional considerations, and that bothered him. Not because he thought the professional more important, but because he did not trust his personal judgement, given its poor track record.

Needing more time to think, he asked the driver to go up Mount Road to Cathedral Road then head out to the coast and back to the Secretariat by way of police headquarters.

The confusion of George Town dissolved into the ordered stateliness of Mount Road with its major commercial buildings and outlets.

Controlling India had provided financial opportunities for Great Britain, hence the rise of the despised box wallahs, Britons who pursued Indian commercial careers in trading, insurance, law, industry and the professions. While they profited, Indians did not necessarily do so. Even Romesh Chunder Dutt, one of the first Indians allowed into the ICS, argued that. His economic history suggested the East India Company destroyed Indian industry and that British India prevented its resurrection. Dutt retired from the ICS to become a president of the Indian National Congress.

His argument retained its original power, Le Fanu thought. It underlay Mahatma Gandhi's case for returning India to traditional crafts and products. The homespun khadi cloth campaign was less about the craft than a symbolic rejection of British goods. British cloth was manufactured in Lancashire from Indian cotton then sold back to India, creating profit for Britain and loss for India. The British struggled to counter the Dutt–Gandhi argument because, essentially, it was true.

So here in Madras, the lawyers, bankers, insurance agents and all the rest plied their trades, gathered at the clubs, mixed with each other, kept India at bay and moaned about change, not realising local sentiment was now running strongly against them. Gandhi was unfathomable to them but not to his now millions of followers.

He stopped at the *Mail* building but Barnes was out, his secretary knew not where or was not saying, so he continued through the heartland of British Madras, past the Thousand Lights mosque then turned away towards the ocean past St George's Cathedral. Christianity just another part of the British campaign to turn India into something it was not. His last appearance there was for his marriage that turned into a disastrous failure.

Track record.

By the time he glimpsed the ocean he was downcast, with too many things to fix across too many fields. The white glitter of the headquarters building did not help. He could be top man there but had hated the position last time. Too much bureaucracy, too much dealing with people he disliked, too little contact with real police work. Solving crimes and helping people were what he did best, but he had done neither as Acting Inspector-General.

Could it be different this time? Who knew? As it was, he had a worried Habi, Caldicott ready to cut and run, Willingdon and Whitney about to disappear, his personal life in a mess.

By the time he climbed the Secretariat steps, he wished he had come straight there rather than take that reflection time. Time to think turned into time to brood, and he was world class at that. His ex-wife had said so, incessantly. So had Ro and, more recently, Jenlin.

He reached Whitney's office, resolved to convince him of Caldicott's plan, but would not mention that Delhi had approved. The Chief Secretary was headed there, but the place still did not impress him. It would be enough for Whitney to know Le Fanu thought it the best approach.

After several minutes of discussion, they went to Willingdon's office and gained assent. Le Fanu returned to his own office, telephoned Caldicott, then checked with Gaines on everything new that had come in. Not much. *Criminal Investigation* still sat on the desk, but he might as well not have read it, he thought, given the lack of progress. Perhaps Hans Gross had a volume on how criminal investigators might better conduct their lives? No, that was probably best left to his fellow Austrian, Freud.

Thirty-one

Later that night, the military quietly withdrew from the positions controlling the besieged revolutionaries. One by one, over decent intervals, soldiers arrived at the trucks parked a good distance away so their leaving would go unnoticed. Le Fanu, Caldicott and Habi had arrived earlier in the evening but Le Fanu was now alone, supervising, while the other two ran investigations and monitored intelligence updates back in town.

It was done, successfully he thought, by midnight and half an hour later he arrived at Mylapore to find his colleagues perched on the veranda drinking tea.

"Made yourselves at home, then."

"Yes, thank you, sir. Excellent service here, most of the other nearby restaurants are closed now."

"How did it finish up, LF?"

"Very well. Our sentries reported no movement within the building, so we might just have gotten away with it. Now to see what our friends do."

"That's why we're here, sir, apart from raiding your kitchen. Independently, we've both had information suggesting the second wave of visitors has arrived. And we think it's serious."

"This is no amateur thing, LF. A group of twenty or so got off a ship in Bombay that came indirectly from the United States, but it's unclear where they all boarded. Some in New York but others at European ports as the ship sailed towards the Suez. Once in Bombay they split up into twos and threes then moved independently towards Madras, but all the groups were in contact with each other constantly."

"Highly planned, then."

"Very much so. Some came across from Bombay into Hyderabad, others went to Delhi and Nagpur then set out for Madras, but stopped in places like Vizagapatam and Guntur. From there, they began arriving in Madras, about two hours ago."

"Explains why those strangers turned up in Guntur, then."

"Sir, we're not sure about them. They may have been in an earlier group, perhaps even the original one."

"How many are we looking at altogether?"

Habi and Caldicott exchanged glances. "Sir, perhaps as many as one hundred and fifty."

"What?"

"LF, we suggested it was serious. Habi, tell him about the ones you've been watching."

"Sir, my contacts tracked a group that gathered in London where many of them were living. They drifted across the channel to France and Germany where they met some others before boarding three different ships, all bound for Colombo. They broke up again there. Some then came here by train directly, others travelled to Mysore state and others again to Madura before boarding buses. This group has also started arriving in Madras."

"And you've been able to follow this?"

"It's been a big effort, LF. Intelligence connections in England, America and Europe have helped, along with MI5 and MI6 contacts in various places. Then, once the targets arrived in India, intelligence and undercover agents tracked the splinter groups."

"That's seriously good work. What now?"

"We need to discuss that. As you know, the original idea was to let the besieged lot out so they might lead us to the new ones. And thanks for making that happen. However, there are far more new players than we anticipated, and information on their whereabouts much better."

"You think there's more risk in waiting now?"

"Sir, we're not sure. From the police viewpoint, it's still a good plan. However, the political one could be different. Will the Governor and Chief Secretary be happy with possibly two hundred new problems roaming Madras, even if we're watching them?"

"Good question. Do we have any idea what these people are up to?"

"Not really, LF. They have a plan, clearly, but we've no information on what that might be."

"Which suggests there's value in letting them run."

"Again, sir, from our police perspective, yes."

"Let me sound out Whitney and Willingdon first thing. We can't do any more until then, so you two go home and rest. And see your kids in the morning, Habi."

Once they'd gone, Le Fanu read that day's *Mail*, culled the post and checked messages. There was a letter from his mother, predictably nothing from his brother, a subscription invoice from the Cosmopolitan Club golf section, three invitations to dinner that went straight in the bin, and bargain opportunities for him to buy world standard and much in demand local goods. They followed the dinner invitations.

It was two in the morning before he went to bed but at least he slept, if disturbed by dreams that involved armed hordes arriving in India by ship and travelling about by train.

By eight, he was with Whitney and Willingdon, drinking coffee amidst the fog.

Willingdon looked tired. "How bad is this, Chris?"

Le Fanu repeated the information from Habi and Caldicott.

"And the intelligence is sound?"

"I think we can rely on it. For once, several agencies collaborated to give us a good picture, although we still don't know what the revolutionaries are aiming to do where, or when."

"That's a longer list of exceptions than I'd like." The Governor looked out from under the hoods, lifted the patrician nose and clamped a hand to the back of his neck. "We've no idea what they're up to, but there's a lot of them. You think we should let them run?"

"Reluctantly, yes. My natural inclination is to hit them hard, and now. However, our big weakness is that we don't know their objectives, or if hidden local allies will react when we take them off the streets. And I'm also mindful of the publicity angle. We don't need more bad news. But neither can we risk leaving a major conspiracy intact."

"Charles?"

"LF's put it well. It's difficult, but my gut feeling is to let them run."

"So none of us are happy but see no alternative. Let them run it is."

"Very good, sir."

"LF," Willingdon continued, "I hear you've a few options available personally?"

How did he know or, precisely, what did he know? Had someone told him about Hyderabad? Le Fanu assumed

Willingdon knew about Penang. He looked at Whitney. An imperceptible shake of the head denied knowledge.

"Sir, I think you know about Penang. Is there anything else of interest?"

"Nice try. I hear they're enticing you into the Nizam's service. You could do much worse, I grant, but your many talents would be far better used here. My successor knows about you, too, in case you're wondering. After Jepson we need a sensible appointment, and that's you."

"Thanks for the vote of confidence, sir, but right now I'm concentrating fully on these revolutionaries."

"Well said, but we all know that's impossible with so much going on for you now professionally and personally. Any more news on that ship?"

Madras, gossip centre of the Empire.

"Not so far, sir."

"And Mrs McPhedren?"

What was this, a reminder of his tics?

"Well recovered, sir."

"Glad to hear it. You're a fine officer, LF, and a decent man. That's a rare combination in my experience. Try not to upset the balance. And good luck with this plan we've just agreed. We might need some. But there's at least some good news you can pass on to Habi especially."

"Sir?"

"Charles and I met with the Muslim leaders last night as arranged. It went well, I think. Charles, you agree?"

"As well as it could have done, yes."

"We reassured them we're doing everything possible to solve these murders and defuse communal tension. They're much happier with you being involved, Chris, and were acerbic about Jepson. I told them they could see me at any time and get a fair hearing. They left satisfied, though finding the murderers would help immeasurably. Please do convey the news to Habi."

"I will, sir. He'll be very pleased."

He returned to his own office where Gaines told him Sir Maurice Wilson had telephoned. It was at times like this Le Fanu hated Antonio Meucci or Alexander Graham Bell or whoever it really was that invented the thing.

"Thanks for getting back to me, Chris. Thought I'd update you on Mrs McPhedren."

This had to be a campaign.

"Thanks, Maurice, I have spoken with her, thanks to you."

"Didn't think you'd mind hearing from her directly. She's making an excellent recovery."

"That reminds me, I'm getting Metcalfe down here to look at Habi's wife who's unwell."

"Sorry to hear that."

"Anything in particular we need to discuss now, Maurice?"

"Time's drawing in, LF. Ro needs somewhere to go. Metcalfe says she can't work for at least three months and she's no family or friends anywhere near here from what I can gather."

"I did ask and she says she has some possibilities."

"Which means she doesn't. We all know you're a great policeman, but you're hopeless at reading women. If she starts to worry, it will undermine her recovery."

"Maurice, I'm resolved. If she has to come down and stay with me, that's what will happen."

"You have to know how that'll look."

"Even with my limited skills, yes, I do. I'd rather look

after her best interests than those of people who despise me anyway."

"Interesting logic."

"How much longer before we know the real timetable?"

"Metcalfe is very pleased. He thinks she could be released in the next week."

"That soon? It might work out well. He could accompany Ro here, then examine Habi's wife. I'll take care of things with Metcalfe directly. Maurice, thank you for the timely call."

"And what about you, Chris? What news of Miss Koh?"

"We've lost track of her. She set sail from Singapore to Colombo with a view to travelling on here, it seems, but Caldicott tells me the ship failed to make its last position call. It's in a communication vacuum, apparently."

"And when she does arrive, how will she deal with Mrs McPhedren?"

He hadn't thought of that.

"Oh, it'll be fine. Jenlin's a modern person."

"So you think. Be very careful. You know you'd be much safer and more comfortable here."

"Funny thing is, Willingdon has the opposite view."

"Nice to be in demand. Look after yourself, Chris."

Still not ten and he felt the weight of two days' work on him already. Things were becoming more complicated rather than less, and the thought of Ro and Jenlin in the same place at the same time was daunting, despite his bravado.

He contacted Metcalfe and made sure he was available should Ro be released within the week. Luckily, the Scot was keen to visit Madras and open to any possible arrangements. Le Fanu promised they would eat at Acharappan Street.

He had still to see Krishna Rao, so he called Barnes and arranged to meet there at seven.

Throughout the day, Gaines supplied additional material, priority going to reports from Habi and Caldicott. Contacts between the revolutionary splinter units were increasing noticeably, with clear evidence confirming that those who left the besieged apartment block were already contacting the newcomers. Habi's undercover officers were working with Caldicott's Special Branch team, both units stretched trying to track all the suspects now at large.

"Superintendent, what if one or other in this gang escapes our oversight? It's a big risk."

"Sometimes we must take a calculated risk. This is one of them."

"I see the argument but don't envy you the responsibility."

"Thank you."

"We also have additional reports from Guntur. They raise further the likelihood of the Guntur killings and the revolutionaries being connected. You might want to look at them."

"Well organised. Thought any more about joining the police? You're wasted in the ICS."

"Thanks for the compliment and, yes, I have become more interested. And the atmosphere is better here than at the Board. I hear the First Member's still campaigning to replace Sir Charles, although other rumours tell me that will not happen."

"All news to me."

"I suspect not, Superintendent, but I respect your discretion. The First Member's not the man for the job at this or any other point. He's far too self-centred for a position that demands the complete reverse."

"You really are wasted in the ICS."

"It'll do me well enough for now, but please keep asking, sir, I might change my mind. But here's the new Guntur information, especially on the new victim. You should have a look."

Lachlan Heatherly's team had done well. Badsir Shah, whose body was found in the alley, had come to Guntur specifically to work for Ashraf Haider. He had participated in the Gandhi demonstrations but spent most of his time dispensing the food his employer had supplied to Congress. And a few hours before his death, Badsir Shah had been seen with the northerners. That almost guaranteed links between those visitors and the two murders.

Le Fanu sent that immediately to Habi and Caldicott, knowing it would vindicate further the former's argument and hoping the latter's opposition might diminish.

By six-thirty he was up to date, professionally at least, and feeling more confident, so set out for Acharappan Street, looking forward to seeing his friend and eating good food. Krishna Rao was waiting at the door with a garland of flowers that he placed around Le Fanu's neck.

"Superintendent Le Fanu, we have been waiting for you ever since your return to Madras. Welcome back to our humble establishment. We have all the best dishes ready for you."

"My apologies, Krishna Rao, but life has been too hectic for even your excellent food. I'm very pleased to be here now, I can tell you."

Barnes was already there so they sat down to cold drinks. The other patrons looked puzzled when, as the first foods were placed on the plantain leaf, Le Fanu placed his palms together before his face and muttered "Govinda", the invocation to Lord Vishnu. Krishna Rao knew his best European client's tastes, so they did not follow the normal food sequence but ate their way through spiced rice; *ghasi*, a gravy of peas and coconut; sambar, that today had beans in the lentil and coconut curry; *masala dosa*, the stuffed pancake signature dish of south India; and several other delicacies before finishing with the vadas, Le Fanu's favourites.

By eight, he and Barnes had demolished the food, finished their cold drinks and headed to D'Angelis for a drink or two. As a waiter was showing them to a table, Le Fanu noticed three women walking towards them, the British business delegation members.

"Good evening, ladies. I thought you'd be at a formal dinner somewhere."

The lawyer responded. "And good evening to you, too, Superintendent. We managed to escape that dreariness and were recommended to come here. Might you introduce us to your friend?"

"Oh, of course, and please do sit down and join us."

He stumbled through the introductions to be further embarrassed by how easily Barnes slipped into conversation with them. Within five minutes it was a very chatty, friendly group.

"Superintendent," said the engineer, "you and Sir Charles made it possible for us to complete our appointments here. Our tour leader was hopeless, as you may have noticed. The people you sent with us were excellent, and we three at least have made some good business contacts here. Not so sure about the rest but they're mostly lightweights, anyway. So, thanks, and cheers." She lifted a champagne flute towards him, joined by the other two.

"And we're delighted to now meet Mr Barnes," said the fashion designer, with whom Chester had been in deep conversation. "Tell us about your lives out here. It all seems so exotic."

Barnes glanced briefly at his friend and immediately took charge. For the next two hours Le Fanu enjoyed the conversation without revealing any of his complications, despite close questioning on his personal status. Barnes was brilliant and took all three addresses as they parted.

Back home it had been, he thought, a good day, made better now by the full moon in a clear sky over the palm trees, accompanied by all the usual night noises. Some times in Madras were excellent.

Thirty-two

That sense disappeared quickly, even though the next morning started well enough as he reviewed the overnight cables.

Just after ten, Habi burst in.

"Sir, you must come with me. Now."

Le Fanu snatched his hat from a hook and set off to catch Habi who was already back out the door and halfway down the stairs.

"Habi, hold up, tell me what's happening."

"In the car, sir." The answer floated eerily back up the stairwell.

Le Fanu jumped down the stairs two and three at a time, hoping he would not trip. Even so, Habi was in the car drumming his fingers on the window by the time Le Fanu reached the kerb. The door was barely shut before Habi ordered the driver to go, fast.

"Where are we off to, Habi?" asked Le Fanu, catching breath and balance.

"Periamet, sir."

"Why are …?" That was a major Muslim centre. Perhaps he did not want to know.

"Yes, sir. There's a serious incident under way in the heart of the leather industry area."

Leather and skins were Muslim-run industries, given Hindu reverence for the cow.

"Habi, tell me it's not what I think it is."

"Can't, sir, because it is."

"What happened, and what are we up against?"

"As the main leather shops were opening for business, about eight truckloads of troublemakers arrived, armed with iron bars and other weapons, including guns, although there's been no firing so far. Maybe that's being held in reserve."

"And what do we know about these invaders?"

"Unfortunately from our strategy point of view, the ringleaders are from the revolutionary group, and they've recruited a large number of local supporters."

"Is this a straightforward Hindu versus Muslim affair?"

"Unfortunately, again, yes. And the Muslims have come off badly. No deaths so far but serious injuries, broken limbs and the like. And massive property damage."

"So far? You meant it's still going?"

With the driver at maximum speed and swerving to avoid obstacles in the crowded George Town streets, Le Fanu seized the door strap like it was a lifebuoy.

"Yes, sir. By the time the military arrived, several blocks were already in trouble because the protagonists had gathered support so quickly. It only started about forty minutes ago. Police were first there but had to withdraw. They're in reserve, and the military's the front line."

Now they were encountering huge crowds. The bonus for Le Fanu was the driver now going at snail's pace in the jammed streets, an old snail at that.

Le Fanu let go of the strap. "How far are we from the centre of it, Habi?"

"About three hundred yards, sir."

"Is the military contingent there?"

"A small one, last I saw before fetching you. The rest deployed to deal with pockets of violence."

A dull roar came up from the crowd and seeped into the car interior, even though the windows were closed. Le Fanu saw Hindu and Muslim groups circling each other warily. Some were armed with lathis, the wooden stave mainstays for beat policeman. Others carried pickets ripped off fences, lumps of timber liberated from mills or merchants' yards. One or two had iron bars. He even saw one man with boxing gloves. That had to be planned.

"Habi, we're jammed here. Let's push through on foot. Where's Jackson?"

"In his office getting the latest updates, but he is coming here."

"Let's go, then."

It was a struggle to open the doors. Crowds were packed solid around the car, and a couple of Muslims began rocking it, friends rushing to assist.

"Habi. Draw your pistol and hold it up." Le Fanu did likewise.

The rockers quietened, edging back, mainly because they saw Habi whom one of them identified. They began apologising and Habi hurried them on.

As the two men shoved ahead, yard by yard, sometimes pushed back before they could go forward, they heard breaking glass, sticks on tin walls and, occasionally, staves on flesh. All the while the noise, shouting, frequent screams and general hubbub hit a level Le Fanu had not experienced for a long time.

They had risked turning the revolutionaries loose. That gamble looked lost, with all the possible and likely consequences.

Reaching a small intersection, they turned right into an alleyway and confronted three injured Muslims squatting hard up against the wall, all with hair matted in blood. Le Fanu was too slow to turn away, detecting the physical reactions he hated so much. His stomach churned. He felt faint, and dizzy, his sight began to blur. A major attack.

Habi pushed up, offering a water flask and a small paper cone containing brownish powder. "Take this, sir. Ayurvedic medicine, better than anything Western. It'll fix you quickly."

Le Fanu tipped it into his mouth. Acidic, not unpleasant. Sloshed it down with water. Several deep breaths. Stretched up on his toes a couple of times. Felt better, vision clearing.

"Habi, you might have done the trick."

"Yes, sir. Can we now go and link up with the military and our men?"

The mass of people tightened even more the further they went, the levels of violence escalating with the noise. More injured. People trying to give medical aid. Not an ambulance in sight. Organised gangs of Hindus and Muslims. Lots of religion-baiting and abuse. Fistfights in doorways. Looking up, he saw kids arranging rocks to tip on unsuspecting heads. And water pots. And other pots whose contents were likely to be far less pleasant.

They were close to a standstill, and had to barge through to reach the military and police units that had done little but form a self-protective hollow square. A couple of junior officers looked stunned. All around them shops were being smashed, contents looted, owners, including women and children, assaulted. It was close to uncontrollable.

"Habi, get those officers over to me if you can." Le Fanu began speaking to some of the soldiers and policemen, reassuring them, trying to instil calm.

The two officers arrived looking apprehensive.

“Nothing to worry about, you two. You’ve done well so far.” Le Fanu reasoned that reassurance did not necessarily have to be accurate. “Names?”

They identified themselves.

“Good. Here’s what we’ll do. The immediate task is to get this area under control, so we’ll combine the police and army units. I want you to get back over there, form them up in two open lines, the one in front kneeling. Got it? You two stand at the opposite ends of the standing line. The back one. Clear?”

They nodded.

“Good. Get on with it.”

They raced away and did a good job. The lines formed immediately.

“Habi, I need you to make sure they’re armed and ready, so a quick rifle inspection, please.”

That took a couple of minutes.

Seeing this activity, the crowd shuffled back, people at the front urging those behind to retreat. The noise softened as the crowd sensed what was happening.

Le Fanu could now hear himself. “You two, well done. Back here.”

The officers scurried back, leaving two orderly lines of combined troops.

“Next, I want the standing line to about-face. When that’s done, the kneeling line should stand. When I give the order to move, the lines should move away from each other, slow time. That will start clearing this space. If we get lucky, people will move away, perhaps even leave entirely. Now, I want rifles at the shoulder, but aimed in the air. Most of all, I want fingers well away from triggers. That’s really important. Insist on that. We want to create an implied threat. If we fire, the illusion is broken. Understand?"

"Yes, sir."

"Good. Get in position, get the lines organised, rifles at the shoulder in the air. Then wait for my order."

Two minutes later that was done.

"Lines, advance!"

Slowly, surely, steadily the lines separated. People began leaving. As the distance narrowed between the lines of soldiers and the walls towards which they were advancing, that trickle of people grew larger. The troops were clearing the area, the noise began subsiding. They could still hear it in nearby lanes and open spaces, though.

Habi came up. "I've had a look nearby, sir. You could use the same tactic by walking the men double file through the lanes then running this same trick in the squares."

"Good thinking."

This area was now clear, the troops had reached the walls. The officers had the good sense to turn the lines inward.

Le Fanu signalled them over. "Excellent. Now apply the same principle to nearby areas that Assistant Superintendent Habibullah has reconnoitred. First, double file down the alleyways until you reach open spaces, then reapply what you've done here. Repeat as necessary. Clear?"

"Yes, sir."

"Well done. You'll have to do this one by yourselves, given the tight spaces. But you know now you can, so go ahead. We'll be back here gathering intelligence if you need us. Once you've cleared the area, rendezvous back here."

The two officers set off and got the procedures under way. Le Fanu heard more areas fall silent. With luck they might get out of here low key.

"Pity we couldn't arrest a few, Habi, but I'll settle for escaping without a major skirmish. The start looked as bad as anything I've seen for a while. Have you spoken with anyone yet?"

"A couple of merchants. As we feared, organised Hindu groups came in, threatened the Muslims, told them to leave, then started smashing up the shop and assaulting the inhabitants. Lots of anti-Muslim talk."

"Did those merchants have any idea who these people might be?"

"Interesting. The first Hindus in were clearly from the north, but after that more locals appeared and were as organised. This might have been in preparation for a while."

"Political angles?"

"The usual. The Muslims kill cows. They supported the Turks over Indians during the war. They want all of India to be Muslim. The Hindus are restricted. Political freedom will come only with a Hindu-led movement. Nothing new. Apart from the planning and organisation."

"That's the difference. Injuries?"

"We've been lucky. Lots of cuts and bruises, some broken limbs. Plenty of shock and discomfort. Importantly, though, still no deaths."

"That's a life raft to which we can cling when any consequences come along. This could have been a hell of a lot worse."

"Agreed."

The two officers reappeared, confident and successful. Their troops followed with a collective swagger.

"Success, sir," one of the officers said. "The whole area cleared. We've men checking the injured and going house to house to account for everyone. No shots fired, all troops safe."

"Very well done, you two. And tell your men the same. We've all learned something here today."

"Yes, sir. Thank you, sir, for your excellent leadership."

"Leaders are only as good as those they command. You and your men did the hard work here. Once you've completed your checks, do a rifle inspection then get the men back to barracks. The trucks are nearby, I take it?"

"Yes, sir."

"Good. Get things moving, then."

Habi disappeared into a shop to then emerge with a Muslim carrying a tray of fresh lime sodas.

"Perfect, Habi, please thank him."

"We've been very lucky, sir, but we'll take some criticism for letting these people loose."

"Some of that will be fair, most of it opportunistic, a chance taken to give us a kicking. It would help if we knew more about what really is developing here."

"I saw Assistant Superintendent Caldicott somewhere in all this a while ago. Haven't seen him since, but he was going shop to shop with his people, searching for information. Hopefully we'll hear from him before we see the Chief Secretary and the Governor."

"That'd be helpful. I'll try to see Chester Barnes before I do anything else, and make sure he gets an accurate report for the *Mail*. We'll be pilloried in *The Hindu*."

"We'll get a fair hearing in the Muslim papers, sir, so that'll show up in those 'Native Newspaper Reports' that Delhi places so much importance on."

"You almost sound cynical, not like you at all."

"Not sure about the value of those things."

"Just another part of the bureaucracy, eh?"

"We'll have plenty of that after this, multiple reports required for a disturbance this size."

"But as you say, Habi, no deaths. Imagine if The Jockey had been in charge."

"Not a good thought, sir. But those two young officers were right. You did a wonderful job today. Anything could have happened here."

"We're a good team, and if I look like having forgotten that lately, I apologise."

"You've a lot on your mind, sir."

"And you were especially important today, Habi. I'd have been a mess if you hadn't produced that Ayurvedic brew. It really sorted me out, I might have to use it regularly. What was it?"

"No idea, sir. Something my wife gave me. I don't believe in any of that nonsense. Glad it worked, though."

Thirty-three

It was late afternoon by the time Willingdon convened the review session. They were sitting in a circle, no desk or table. A good sign, Le Fanu thought. Sitting in control behind his desk would have suggested Willingdon had serious concerns.

"Gentlemen, thanks for coming. It's been a difficult day. First off, what's the sum total of damage?"

Caldicott spoke up. "Your Excellency …"

"Sir will do in here, Jackson."

"Thank you, sir. I've been asked to report on this. No deaths."

"Excellent result. All of you, well done."

"Forty-five injuries, none serious. Several broken arms – uncomfortable for the victims but they're still alive. Multiple bumps, bruises and abrasions, fewer than ten really serious cuts. No major head injuries. So on the personnel side, we've come out well. We estimate up to two thousand people having been involved."

Willingdon spread his arms, palms out. "One of the biggest outbreaks we've had here for some time. The Non-Cooperation crowds were bigger but less violent, so that small a number of casualties is a great achievement. LF, you'll hate this and say it was a team effort, which it was, but your work was outstanding."

"Thank you, sir." Le Fanu was uncomfortable, remembering his near collapse at the start and Habi's apparently magic brew.

"And on the material side?" Willingdon asked.

Caldicott glanced at his notes. "We're still working on that, sir, but initially at least forty shops had windows and/or doors damaged and associated stock loss. A small amount of looting, perhaps a couple of hundred pounds worth. No buildings destroyed, all currently being repaired. Some roads damaged, three army vehicles with broken windows and two with slashed tyres. Oddly enough, though, no fires. In these things if the intent is to inflict maximum damage, fires are always present."

"We're straying into motive here," Willingdon commented, "but before we do that, anything else on damage?"

"Just to say, sir," Habi added, "the Muslim community leaders you met have asked me to pass on their thanks for having handled this so well."

"Better pass them onto yourself and LF, Habi, you two ensured we escaped so lightly."

"Thank you, sir. The community's accounting matches that from Assistant Superintendent Caldicott: very little stock loss and all people safe, even if shocked."

"LF, am I wrong in thinking there's something odd here?"

"You've referred to motive, sir, and, yes, there is something different here that we've begun discussing amongst ourselves. Habi can start."

"Sir, the Muslim community had heard about a likely raid but expected a basic one: a lot of looting, plenty of destruction, more deadly attacks on people. None of it happened."

"Could that be down simply to your excellent work?"

"We're always happy to take credit, sir, and we are professional. But normally we'd have anticipated far more difficulty regaining control, far more deaths, injuries and damage."

"So what's going on?"

Caldicott again. "It's possible this attack was brought on earlier than planned. If so, that's probably more because of the village uproar than the confrontation at the apartments. Those two episodes weren't planned, and signalled the revolutionaries' presence earlier than they wanted."

"So they went off half-cocked here?" Willingdon was scribbling on a pad.

"Sir," Le Fanu came in, "that's our basic view, mainly because this happened almost as soon as the revolutionary reinforcements reached Madras. It's unlikely that was the plan. Habi commented during the riot that there were fewer new people and more locals than expected."

"LF, are you telling me you think this was a training run, that there's more to come?"

Le Fanu looked around at Habi, Caldicott and Whitney who'd been unusually silent. They nodded.

"There's potentially much more to come, simply because of the numbers now involved and the high levels of local recruitment. That last bit has surprised us. But perhaps not so much a training run. That tag implies planning. This was more reactive."

"Which is the point at which we might review our own actions." Whitney was without cigar, the first time in Le Fanu's memory. He'd either run out, forgotten his supply, been banned by Willingdon, or distracted by the moment. Whichever way, it was notable.

"Let me put on record here," Whitney continued, "that despite this riot, it was a sound decision to let the apartment dwellers roam. We'll be criticised by Congress and *The*

Hindu, but we've opened up more of this earlier than would otherwise have occurred. That makes us better prepared."

"Charles, I agree. My own sense is that we'd have faced a much more dangerous attack later had we not followed this course. Which brings us neatly to what we do next."

"We're not fully decided yet, sir," said Le Fanu. "We reckon more attacks are planned, so Habi and Jackson have our undercover people out there, working around the clock gathering further information. And they're working closely with the Muslim community that is also collecting information." He did not mention Barnes's secret journalist.

"Jackson," he continued, "is accessing all the Delhi and London intelligence sources, given the international dimension. Then, of course, we still have the Tanjore and Guntur murders as ongoing matters because they're intricately connected to this broader campaign."

"So, LF, more of the same?" Mischievous.

"If you say so, sir."

"Touché. Gentlemen, we should get back to work. I'd like this thing fixed rapidly so please redouble your efforts. We can't afford anything to go wrong from here."

As they all departed Whitney wordlessly steered Le Fanu into his office and shut the door. The Chief Secretary headed straight to the humidor, selected a cigar and lit up rapidly.

"Looks like you needed that, Charles."

"I do. Willingdon had me in there earlier and asked me not to smoke. Hell. Might be a good thing I'm going, too many non-smoking zealots about now, and who knows, the new Governor might be one of them." Smoke rings floated out like a string of lenticular clouds.

"Thanks for your support in there."

"Oh, Willingdon was always on side, I just wanted to make sure it was said."

"You were very quiet."

"Unlike my normal garrulous self, you mean? I had something else on my mind."

"Which is why I'm here?"

"My replacement has been determined. He'll arrive in the next two to three days. Then there'll be three days of handing over, then I'll be gone."

"So it's finally come. I'm extremely sad to see you leave, Charles, because you've given me enormous support for which I'm both thankful and grateful."

"Only what you deserve, but the new man is good."

"Can you tell now?"

"C W E Carbine. Sir Colin. Heard of him?"

"Of course, a really big Rajputana States name, a Foreign and Political Department legend. So we're getting an outsider. That'll really upset the locals, especially aspirants like Jamieson. But why would Carbine accept? He's been a long-serving Resident and an advisor to princes up there. He could have any post he wanted. Why the benighted south?"

"Are you saying this Chief Secretary's post is unworthy, when I've spent all this time getting it?" They both laughed.

"Of course not, Charles, but people like Carbine have wide choices and horizons. South for them stops at Hyderabad, if that far. So why's he coming?"

"He and the new Governor were best friends at Oxford. Goschen mentioned he needed an experienced and independent friend at hand, and Carbine said he'd enjoy a change of scenery. More importantly, their wives are great friends. It's a smart move on Goschen's part. Willingdon thinks Carbine will be good and is telling some local ICS pomposities that, including Jamieson."

"Sounds like HE's enjoying the opportunity."

"You could be forgiven for thinking that. Willingdon advised Goschen that the reactionary nature of the Madras ICS, especially near the top of the tree, made implementing change impossible. Bringing someone new in makes sense, even if it upsets people like Jamieson."

"It shouldn't be this difficult, should it?"

"Which brings us to the related point. We've just a few days to finalise things before I disappear, and I want to do so successfully. Among other things, that includes helping you make a sensible career move."

"Thanks, Charles, I know I haven't made it easy, and without you …"

"Oh, I've helped, but you've made it all work. Professionally, at least. Sorry, I'm hopeless at resisting temptation. But really, you're …"

"A mess in my private life. Agreed. Let's just get this professional stuff sorted out, at least. I'll talk to you soon, no doubt."

As he left, Le Fanu looked back at Whitney lounging in his chair, staring out the open terrace doors to the Bay of Bengal, perhaps reflecting on a Madras career and the one to come in Delhi. All the threatened change had finally arrived.

Unsettled to a degree that even his new office now seemed too small, Le Fanu set off to visit Habi at headquarters. After all, Jepson was no longer there. That knowledge allowed him to enjoy the surroundings for the first time in a while, a reminder that despite all the problems, he had enjoyed Madras.

It had a real history. They passed the Ice House founded by Swami Vivekananda, the mystic who mesmerised the West by his 1890s appearance at the World Congress of Religions in Chicago, then became a European star. India had given much to the West. The University of Madras, now on the right, had provided Ramanujan, one of the greatest ever mathematicians, and currently in Oxford.

With the possibility he might now be giving all this up, he had the driver detour yet again to the Kapileswarar Temple in Mylapore, a thousand years old with its gopurams hosting the myriad of Hindu gods and goddesses that bewildered most Westerners. Unlike some of the Mahatma's European followers, Le Fanu had never felt the need to convert to Hinduism, but he appreciated its reflection, comprehensive embrace of life and tolerance for variation that prevailed, despite this riot. He had found none of that in Protestantism.

That was the differential within the Raj, he supposed: between those who learned from India and those, like Jepson and Jamieson, who repelled it at every turn, trying to make it British.

Staying in Madras would mean dealing with much more of that, no matter how good Goschen and Carbine might be. He was exhausted by the thought of having to rebuild the quality relationships he'd had Willingdon and Whitney. And he still had to work out what to do with Ro. Wilson's Hyderabad offer was attractive, but Ro was a complication there and could be here in Madras as well. That left Penang. A great job and a new relationship, but another colonial setting beginning to experience change.

The more he thought about it, the bigger the imminent changes became. Perhaps that was now a constant in his life.

It was an odd feeling to pull up in the rear yards at headquarters. Since his return from Penang, he'd scarcely been here because of Jepson, yet it had previously been his whole life. And his motorbike was still here somewhere, he thought. Something else he had yet to see since being back.

As he climbed the stairs, people called cheery greetings or passed on congratulations for the handling of the riot. The atmosphere had transformed, underlining just how bad Jepson's regime had been for morale and performance. This was like the old days, Le Fanu thought. Perhaps the police could deal with change under the right leadership. But was he that leader? Several people here thought so, because they were now telling him that openly.

He walked around to Habi's office where a clerk said his boss had received a message before rushing out, saying he would return shortly. Le Fanu ordered coffee and set to checking and amending the case boards that were the hallmark of the Crime Unit's procedures. He had missed that work.

Habi raced in half an hour later, stopped when he saw Le Fanu and looked worried. "Sir, I've just been to the Secretariat looking for you."

"Sorry to put you to the bother, Habi, I should have called ahead. I needed to get out of there. But why were you looking for me?"

Habi looked stricken. "Sir, I've news. Perhaps you should sit down."

"Habi, I've never seen you like this. Is it your wife? Metcalfe's due here any day so …"

"No, sir, it's not my wife."

"Well, then …"

"Sir, I've had a message from our Singapore contact. It's about that ship Miss Koh is on."

"What about it?"

"Sir, the authorities haven't heard from it for several days so have declared it officially missing. I'm sorry."

Thirty-four

Le Fanu returned to his Secretariat office where Whitney, already briefed by Habi, ordered him home. Le Fanu protested he could still work, but the Chief Secretary insisted he needed time and space to think.

But that was what bothered him. When the worst news was there being none, like now, he handled time and space badly. The ship had been out of contact long enough to be declared missing, and no one knew anything more. No search had been mobilised, at least not from Singapore that he knew of, because the ship was theoretically closer to Ceylon where the agents reported nothing other than the scheduled arrival date being thirty-six hours away.

It must have been like this in no man's land during the war, he thought. At least there, people occasionally came looking.

At home, there was little to do but watch the clock because he couldn't concentrate. Whitney was right, in a way. At work Le Fanu might be hindrance rather than help. But handling a case was better diversion than reading some meaningless book, or gardening, or staring at a wall. Eating had no attraction and he didn't even want a drink, trying to remain clear-headed despite the anxiety.

He'd had his share of luck. Surviving the entire war, for a start. And his career had been good. The early postings went well, promotion came easily. The Crime Unit was a highlight. And all that happened in India where he wanted to be, rather than in some London civil service office. Whenever anything or anyone difficult loomed up, like a Jamieson or a Jepson, he had coped. Right now, he had excellent career options when many of his colleagues had none.

At least, he had until this news arrived.

Fate was a bitch, or a bastard. So was the irony of having this occur at precisely the point when his blighted personal life, the one blot in the landscape, was about to improve because of Jenlin Koh, who was now missing. Perhaps Buddhism would be more beneficial than Hinduism at this point, but either beat watching the clock. The less news arrived, the slower time passed, another odd equation.

The shipping agents still knew nothing. Nor did the weather people. Caldicott was fruitlessly draining his contacts. Habi's Special Branch people were even out in the city and the port listening for rumours. Chester Barnes was checking his Colombo and Singapore counterparts. Le Fanu telephoned his Straits Settlements friends who spoke with Jenlin's father, who put all his Peranakan trading networks on alert. The sum result of all this activity? Nothing.

It was if the *Marie Celeste* was now abroad in the Bay of Bengal.

And it was still just two in the afternoon, with a long night and longer days stretching ahead. He might go mad, his head producing wild imaginations: Jenlin in a lifeboat, or captured by pirates, or swimming alone, or who knows what. He cursed the day he ever read Freud.

Because with Jenlin, he believed his life had turned for the better, even though he had returned to Madras without any clear agreement on their future. There was a mutual if unexpressed assumption they would be together and, over time, resolve what that meant practically. He had not heard from her, because she set off just a short time after him. Had she written, the letters would still be en route. The notes he penned to her on the ship were sent off only after he reached Madras. She would not have seen them.

It was true that he had known her for just a short time and that the cultural gulf was wide, despite his love of Asia and her obvious comfort in the West. But he had anticipated no problems, even if her father was still uncomfortable with an *ang mo* hanging around his daughter. They had discussed living together in Madras, but the businesses she ran for her father and herself made that difficult. Le Fanu could more easily pitch up in Penang or Singapore. It would work out.

Now this. It consumed him. Resolve crumbling, purpose gone, alarm rising alongside despair. He must maintain hope but had no idea how to do so.

A car rolled in under the porticade at his front door. Whitney, Caldicott and Habi climbed out, then went to a following vehicle from which they hauled boxes of records, files and publications.

"LF," said Whitney, "I said you should be home, but given you're useless without work, we've brought the office and ourselves here to you. We'll work here and really go through all the materials on these revolutionaries. One or other of us will slip out from time to time, but this is now the office. Can your people bring coffee? We'll need it. And we'll probably eat you out of house and home."

For two hours they said little but reviewed everything, renewing the case boards Habi had brought. By early evening, they had covered everything on the Muslim murders, the three disturbances and the peripatetic revolutionaries. They knew who and where they were, to whom they were talking. The one piece still missing? What these people were planning.

"Gentlemen," said Whitney, "I haven't had this much fun in a long time. I should switch to the police."

Le Fanu wondered if they could ban cigar smoking.

"Better than going to Delhi, sir."

"I agree, Habi. However, we've a decision to make."

"Our next step?" Caldicott suggested.

Le Fanu was absorbed in a file. They looked at him, congratulating themselves silently for having distracted him so fully.

"Yes, our next step," Whitney confirmed. "LF, might you join us? LF?"

Le Fanu gradually realised what was happening and looked up.

"I was suggesting we've a decision to make."

"Quite right, Charles, this is all much clearer now."

"How long do we spend trying to guess their grand plan?"

"Sir Charles," said Caldicott, "perhaps a little longer. I'm expecting more from my contacts overnight."

"Habi?"

"I'm not so sure. The longer we go, the closer they are to finalising their plan, and that's surely a big event. They haven't come all this way for nothing. It'll disrupt Madras and endanger many citizens. I see Assistant Superintendent Caldicott's point, but we might better move on quickly now."

Le Fanu looked from one to the other, pleased the disagreement was professional and amicable. But it complicated his own thinking that he was not sure he could trust. A surprising amount of time had passed since he last looked, though.

"Chris?"

"I can see both sides …"

"Diplomatic corps for you, then."

"I wouldn't last long there. Sorry, Jackson, I'm leaning towards Habi's view. Periamet changed my thinking. It was my call there to wait and it blew up. Picking up at least some of them right away might help uncover their objectives. There are far more of them here now. And these papers confirm that many of the new arrivals have been involved in direct action. We've had little of that down here and don't want it to take root."

"What are you suggesting?" Whitney had fountain pen paused over notepad.

"Draw up a prime target list. No more than six names. Pick them up now, interview them separately but simultaneously."

"I agree," said Habi, "but we'll need two more interviewers if we bring in six."

"Gaines can be one. It'll be excellent experience for him."

"Good idea," said Whitney. "And the other?"

"Would Willingdon do it? He knows as much as anyone."

"He'll jump at it, I'll alert him."

"Just so you all know," Caldicott interceded, "I'm happy with this even though I suggested we wait. On balance, this is probably the right move."

"Let's get it planned, then." Whitney lit another cigar.

Over the next hour they identified the target list and how those on it would be caught. Six small action teams were created comprising known, trusted police and army personnel. Each group was to headed by a military officer, with a senior officer having overall command.

“Sorry, Chris,” said Whitney, “I can’t let you run things in the present circumstances. But operational headquarters will remain here. We’ll stay with you until these characters are captured in case we have to vary the plan.”

“It’s a very good plan, sir,” said Habi. “You really should be in the police.”

“Thanks, Habi. Once these targets are in custody, we’ll interview them at the Secretariat. I’ve made special arrangements so we can liaise as closely as possible during the questioning. And Willingdon’s on the spot there. Could you get some more food organised here, LF?”

“Le Fanu disappeared into the kitchen.

“Clever move, Sir Charles. Keep him occupied. This whole exercise has been worthwhile.”

“We owe him a lot, Habi. I had food ordered, but cancelled because he needs something to do. I’m very worried about him.”

“We all are.” Caldicott smashed a fist into his other palm. “He handles these personal things poorly, and this one is worse because he sees a future with Miss Koh.”

“Any more news?”

“No, and the more time passes, the more likely news will be bad rather than good.”t

Habi chipped in. “My Harbour Board friend thinks the same. We must keep hoping, but experience and history are not on our side.”

They heard Le Fanu returning so switched subjects.

“Fifteen minutes to food. Anyone for tea or coffee, or something stronger?”

Habi settled for orange juice but the others took a single malt as they waited for the exercise to begin.

The raids were set for ten. In the four hours until then,

Whitney diverted them with outrageous stories from his civil service past: who in the south fathered the most illegitimate children (it might have been a chap called Tottenham), the notorious drunks, who lost most money in the great 1906 bank crash, which governors had local mistresses, ICS men who gambled away careers, secret letter writers to the press, the worst Collectors of all time. Le Fanu knew some of the latter, but learned more about the Raj in the south tonight than on any other single occasion. The evening raced by, punctuated only by telephone calls from officials concerning minor details.

Progress reports began coming in at ten fifteen. Minor altercations occurred at just two locations. All those listed were under arrest and being transported to the Secretariat.

"Well, that was fun, gentlemen, time now to do our part at Fort St George. Remember the script. Good luck. Thanks for the hospitality, Chris." Whitney stilled looked immaculate.

Two cars carried them through the darkened streets. Le Fanu enjoyed travelling the city at night, it was a different being. By day it was a busy, almost tortured place but by night a giant village where all kept to themselves, except for members of the Raj on a mission.

At the Secretariat, clerks directed them to the separate interviewing rooms.

Alone for the first time in hours, Le Fanu reviewed his questions, wondered who he might encounter, and hoped Jenlin Koh was alive in the Bay of Bengal somewhere out to the south-west.

Thirty-five

His prisoner was seated at a table in a small anteroom on the Secretariat's upper level, a stenographer off at another table awaiting work. In his early thirties, the interrogee looked earnest and clean cut, with brushed-back black hair that complemented a tan-coloured face whose planes and edges cast interesting shadows, broken only by flashes from the dark green eyes. Might be an intellectual.

"Do you know why you're here?"

"Yes, I am imprisoned by the Raj that indecently tyrannises India."

Certainly an ideologue. "Name?"

"Bhaskar Ganguly."

Bengali. "You're a long way from home."

"India is my home, and my mission."

"Which mission would that be?"

"To free India and create a Hindu nation."

"And why have you come to Madras?"

"To help my brothers and sisters here achieve the mission I have just been mentioning."

That slight twist in India's otherwise impeccable use of English.

"How do you propose to do that?"

"By educating people in the south as to India's necessary goals and actions that will hound out you British."

"And that includes causing riots and attacking Muslims?"

"We Hindus must be in charge so we can be delivering the true India."

This looked like being a long night.

"Have you had food and drink?"

"I will be touching nothing from an impure foreign imperialist."

A very long night.

"Tell me, Bhaskar Ganguly, where are you from?"

"I am coming from Calcutta."

"Age."

"I am being twenty-four."

"Occupation."

"Studying the history of India at Presidency College within the University of Calcutta, so that I may better understand how to rid my country of you British."

Bright boy, then, the best went to Presidency, and the most difficult. Many Congress leaders had been there. So had Romesh Chunder Dutt, that economist and ex-ICS man whose work still bothered the Raj long after his death.

"So why are you here in Madras?"

"I have answered that question."

"Not to my satisfaction. How did you reach here?"

"I was coming by train."

"And you stopped in Guntur."

"I have some friends there."

"How does a Presidency College boy have friends in Guntur?"

Unexpectedly, that caused a hesitation.

"I, well, we, I mean I have some, some friends there."

"Friends from where?"

"They were, having been in the north. I met them there."

"At a training camp to harass Muslims. Two Muslims have been murdered in Guntur, you were a visitor there, and you say Hindus should control India. It doesn't look good for you."

"I went to Guntur to see friends."

"And to murder Muslims."

"No."

"You'll need to prove your whereabouts or I'll charge you with murder."

"Excuse me, but before arresting me you must prove with evidence that I was there."

Knows his rights, well schooled, well trained. "How many others are in your gang from Calcutta?"

"I am not being in any gang. We are a registered society dedicated to asserting Hindu rights."

"And terrorising Muslims, in Guntur and elsewhere."

"No, that is, well, I am telling you that is not right."

"All of it or just part of it?"

"I am not understanding."

"The terrorising Muslims bit, the murders in Guntur bit, or the murders elsewhere bit?"

"You are confusing me."

The stenographer looked confused, too.

"Have you terrorised Muslims?"

"No."

"Have you demonstrated against Muslims?"

Yes."

"Where?"

"Many places."

"Including Madras?"

"Yes."

Aha. "In the past two days?"

"Yes."

"Why?"

"To assert Hindu rights."

So we have him on the disturbances. "And you helped harass Muslims in Guntur."

"I paraded against Muslims there."

"And helped kill two of them."

"No."

"We'll break now, Mr Ganguly. Please reconsider your answers carefully. You've admitted to taking part in serious demonstrations here in Madras. You've admitted to being in Guntur and demonstrating against Muslims. Muslims were murdered there at that time, so we must identify where you were, and when, at the times of the killings. You'll be treated as a murder suspect if your answers are unsatisfactory. I'll return in fifteen minutes. Stenographer, you may take a break, too."

He posted a guard with Ganguly then went to the retreat room where they would meet to check facts, ideas and progress. It was a small library with comfortable chairs and good lighting. All the files were on three campaign tables stretched along the length of one wall, blocking the shelves. Caldicott was there already.

"Hello, Jackson, hope we don't need access to those shelves."

"Shouldn't be a problem, LF, that's the fiction section. Mind you, it could be the best place to check my chap's story. That's all fiction."

"Nice line. Mine has swallowed the 'we of the proletariat' hymnal, even though he's from Presidency College."

"In Calcutta? Home to Congress, socialists and troublemakers? Subash Chandra Bose went there, the chap who now runs the youth wings and the radical papers. More communist than socialist, I reckon. Your man might be a fellow traveller."

"I'll ask. You getting anywhere?"

"Slowly. They're well skilled in avoiding detail or answering anything directly."

"We'll need to coordinate carefully. But my man does admit to being in Guntur."

"Good luck."

Le Fanu gathered water and sweets, put them on a tray and went back into the room, placing the temptations in front of Bhaskar Ganguly, who seemed undecided. He wanted to take them, but had probably been instructed to refuse everything.

"Up to you, Mr Ganguly, but you'll be here all night apart from scheduled bathroom breaks, and the way you're going, we'll be here all tomorrow until this time tomorrow night, at least. So if you feel hungry or thirsty now, I suggest you take something."

Ganguly hesitated, took a glass of water and snatched a vada which he ate whole. No food for a while, then. Good. Made him edgy. He downed the water, then another. Good.

"The next bathroom break is in four hours." There was no set time, but all forms of anxiety helped soften anyone under questioning. Ganguly looked more nervous.

"Now then, Mr Ganguly. What is your connection to Mr Subash Chandra Bose?"

A startled look up, then to the left. Giveaway.

"I am not ..."

"You have come here at the express order of Mr Bose to harass Muslims."

"No, I ..."

"Answer the question properly. Did you come to harass Muslims?"

"Yes."

"As ordered by Mr Bose."

"No."

That seemed genuine. "Is Mr Bose aware of your presence here?"

"No, he would, well, he would not, that is, he would be unhappy I am here."

"Why?"

"Because I have disobeyed him. He wants me to concentrate on Congress work, but I have taken up the cause of the Hindus."

"On whose order?"

"The Society for the Advancement of Hindus. It is based in Patna but has many strong branches in Calcutta."

That group appeared nowhere in the files. Something to be checked later.

"And that group sent you south?"

"Yes, but it was not, um … it was different, not what I expected."

"You thought you would just be demonstrating, but the group wanted more direct action."

"Yes."

"Like attacking Muslims."

"Yes."

"In Guntur."

"Yes."

"And you saw that."

"Yes."

"And in other places besides Guntur."

"No, but I heard of actions elsewhere."

"What did you do while these attacks were happening?"

"I tried to keep out of the way, to hide. I did not want to attack anyone."

"Good man. But you did see who carried out the attacks in Guntur."

"I cannot, they will …"

"Mr Ganguly, if you tell the truth you'll get all possible assistance and protection so you can get back to your Calcutta life. If you don't take this chance, you'll have to hide forever."

"I am frightened."

"I know, we'll help you."

"Yes, I did see who led the attacks in Guntur."

"You saw the murders."

"Yes."

Le Fanu took a small writing pad and a pencil from his side of the table, pushed them across to Ganguly, a now trembling and reduced version of the brash student who appeared first. He was a mixture of relief, fear, anxiety and exhaustion.

"Mr Ganguly, please write down the names of those involved in the Guntur attacks. Once you do so, I will arrange another break for you. I will get you coffee and hot food, then you can rest in the cell for the night, undisturbed. Do you understand?"

"Yes."

"Thank you for helping me, and I hope our protection will help re-establish your life. Otherwise these criminals will own you."

Le Fanu returned to the library to write up his notes and revise the boards. It seemed he was the first to get a breakthrough because no other accounts had yet appeared. Luck, he thought. A well-meaning young man, in over his head, with no idea how to escape. He should have cracked him earlier, probably, but it gave them the Guntur killers and a lot more to investigate about the organisation and intentions of these gangs now in Madras. With more luck, that should help solve the Madras and Tanjore murders.

A clerk advised that Sir Maurice Wilson had telephoned and wished to speak with him. Le Fanu went off to his own room and placed the call.

"Thanks for calling me back, LF. I hear you're really busy down there."

Of course he knew. "You continue to be amazing, Maurice, and must have eyes in every room in every department here."

"Just old friends, LF. And that's the reason for the call. By the way, I've heard about the ship, and I do hope that gets clarified positively and quickly. It's a terrible position for you to be in."

"It is difficult. I'm fortunate there's so much to be going on with here. I've just opened up the Guntur murders and should have some culprit names by early tomorrow."

"Very well done, but I do hope you get good news. And I'm sorry to bring more complications. I spoke earlier to Metcalfe who tells me they'll release Mrs McPhedren three days from now. She's well enough, and they're in the middle of a serious influenza outbreak so need the space. When she comes out I'll put her up for a night in that hotel you stayed in, but we need a longer term solution."

"Of course, and I'm glad you've told me now. Having the extra time to think is helpful. I'll speak to her the first chance I get, but has she yet identified any real possibilities?"

"She's been trying to but, as we know, her own family is fairly remote and dispersed, and she's no friends here who could put her up. Metcalfe sees her return to work being at least four months away now, possibly six."

"Much as things stood a few days ago, then."

"In reality, there are few real options."

"In that case, she comes back down here and stays at my house."

Silence reigned at the other end.

"Chris, you mentioned that possibility on an earlier occasion, and I admire you for offering, but it can't happen."

"Why not?"

"Your reputation will be ruined."

"Maurice , my reputation disappeared a long time ago. Besides, when she was here last time, things went well."

"Only because you wanted to marry her. You were the talk of the town before that and remained in the gossip gun sights long afterwards. Given that the marriage fell through, the stories now will be even more colourful. Sorry about the choice of words, no offence intended."

"I know that, Maurice, and I appreciate your concern. But there's really no other choice."

"But there is. Come up here and work for me. Take a house. She can join you and we can make sure the Madras nonsense doesn't recur."

"That's a powerful argument."

"And I'm authorised to offer you an even bigger financial arrangement. You'll earn more than double what you do now. The work is better, and the house provided. Within five years, you'll be very well off, maybe even wealthy."

"God, you're making it difficult. But I can't just drop everything here and race up there. Even if I say yes, it'll take two to three months at least, and that returns us to Ro."

"At a pinch I could handle that."

"Which is your way of saying it would be really difficult, I know."

"Well read. Yes, it would be. Where does that leave us?"

"Somewhere in the middle ground, and can I say Ro would hate us trying to determine her future like this. Whatever we agree she'll have to confirm, and that's no certainty. She's very independent."

Le Fanu remembered moments from the past, warmly. That was a surprise.

"As I have discovered," Wilson responded.

"I suggest she stays in the hotel that one night. We get her on a train, I'll get the ticket, she moves into Mylapore for the time being. I work out what I'm going to do, and we develop things from there. Staying in Madras has challenges for me, and you'll know Whitney wants me to stay on so your offer is welcome, but I still also have the Penang one."

"And when Miss Koh's ship sails in and she finds Ro at your house?"

"Right now we don't know where Miss Koh's ship is, but when it does arrive, or she does, I'll deal with that then. I'll think of something."

"Very strategic, Micawber."

"Your doubts noted, along with your concern and literary superiority. Seriously, I do value your help, but this is the only possible action now. I must support Ro and would feel bad if I didn't. What other people think is up to them, as always."

"If anything, LF, attitudes down there are hardening. This won't go down well. But you always have the escape route here. Just tell me when you need it opened."

"Thanks again, Maurice. Call me when she's out and what train she'll be on."

Thirty-six

Very early next morning the Secretariat was a strange place, deserted apart from the frenetic investigation going on in a small corner of the building that represented British power in south India. Somehow, now, it seemed less permanent, less convincing.

The prisoners were back in their cells, the interrogators gathered to check on their collective progress. Everyone looked tired, apart from Habi who, typically, had gained energy.

"Sirs, my prisoner was most helpful." Of course he was, Le Fanu thought, Habi would have tied him in knots. "He's an Allahabad student who got caught up in a Hindu organisation but is quite tolerant of Muslims." And especially the one who was questioning him, Le Fanu had no doubt.

Le Fanu conducted a quick poll. Four of the six interviewees were students.

Willingdon elaborated on his. "She's a young woman, early twenties, and comes from a progressive Brahmin family in Ahmedabad. They allowed her to attend a woman's college there, and that's where she connected into a national network run out of Bengal."

"Was it the Society for the Advancement of Hindus?" asked Le Fanu.

"Yes, that's the one."

"Any other prisoner mention that?"

"Mine," Caldicott noted.

"Bhaskar Ganguly was my man, another student, from Calcutta. He reckons the society is strong there but based in Patna."

"Mine is from Patna, and confirms that the headquarters are there."

"On the evidence, then," Le Fanu continued, "we have a Hindu advocacy group based in Patna but stretching across northern India, and actively recruiting students. My guess is that society was taken over by some characters with very different ideas from the real founders. Mr Ganguly witnessed the Guntur murders and was very shaken. That was not what he had joined to do."

"I agree," said Whitney, riffling through his notes. "My candidate was another woman, mid-twenties, a law graduate looking for work. She offered up information immediately. Believing she had joined a debating society, she was most distressed when they made an unexpected stop in Vizag and ordered to harass Muslims."

"LF," said Caldicott, "Delhi suggests this group is fairly new and targeting women. Having them involved makes the travelling groups look less suspicious. Other reports match the experience Sir Charles has described."

"I really do think I'll transfer to the police," Whitney said.

A welcome light touch, because this long day was still far from over.

"I agree with Charles," Willingdon intoned, "but did anyone else get a reference to Savarkar? Mine said it was prescribed reading for her group, but she did not name the society. Are we assuming all the cells belong to that one organisation?"

Le Fanu saw unanimous nods. "Do we have anything more specific on that organisation, Jackson?"

"Not much more than we've heard already. Delhi hasn't taken it seriously so far but will now, I can guarantee. But, LF, back to your earlier comment suggesting the group might have been taken over by another set of people. I raise that because the three murders and all the other rioting and so on does not fit the profile we're getting here. Your Mr Ganguly was scared, the two women as well. That's half of our witnesses reporting the occurrence of ugly incidents a long way out of line with their expectations."

"Jackson," Whitney looked in desperate need of a puff, "let me ask this just to get it out of the way. Is it possible these suspects were trained to give these answers that make them look like ingénues?"

"It is possible, Sir Charles, but these students were genuinely shocked by what they saw. They're frightened. Has anyone heard any references so far to leaders who sound more like criminals than crusaders?"

"Sir," Gaines looked hesitant in this company, "my suspect mentioned a menacing man from Nagpur. I got a name for and ran a check on him. He's listed in the Delhi reports, and has a long criminal record that includes prison terms for violence."

Willingdon and Habi had heard similar references to such a man.

Le Fanu looked around the group. "Right, let's investigate him further. Jackson, get copies of whatever you have on him and any regular associates to us. Then check with Delhi. At this point, he's the key to unravelling our murder cases. And we need to know where he is.

Tomorrow's priority will be to get descriptions from those of our prisoners who saw him."

"I'll have all that for you early tomorrow, well, later this morning, LF."

"Anything else? We're now much closer to identifying the killers in the Muslim murder cases. That's a hate campaign we must stop quickly. So great work, everyone. Get some rest."

The group broke up slowly, mainly because of exhaustion, and Habi held back until he and Le Fanu were alone.

"Sir, the Muslim community is extremely grateful for all you've done, and when we get the murderers they'll be even more pleased."

"Habi," said Le Fanu, "you represented their best interests when that was unpopular, they should be thanking you."

"It's just another time we've been a good team, sir, and I hope that will remain the case."

"I know what you're asking but, right now, I don't know what I'll do."

"Do you have any more news on the ship?"

"I haven't been able to check for the past few hours, of course, and there probably won't be anything now until after daylight. What is it now?"

"Three, sir."

"Long time since I was working at this hour, Habi."

"A good reminder for us that police work never stops, sir. But I hope you get good news."

"Thanks, my friend."

"And, sir, I would appreciate it if Dr Metcalfe could examine my wife when he comes to Madras. There's no sign of improvement, and my children are very worried. I can deal with it but they can't, and my wife is now extremely anxious herself."

"Consider it done, Habi, I'll contact Metcalfe at a decent hour later. Now go home and rest."

Hunched in the back of the car going home, Le Fanu felt cold, even though the temperature still matched that of a decent Scottish summer day. It was strange how the British could adapt to some things and not others, he thought. Learn to handle India's weather, but neither its people nor its ways. Just assume Britain's 'superior' way of life should be imitated by Indians, then get upset when it was not. He was reminded of Lord Harris's infamous later nineteenth century comment: 'India will be incapable of governing itself until it learns to play cricket.' Even first class cricketer Caldicott recognised that as nonsense, another sign of British cultural deafness.

He realised, too, that discontent with such British hubris shaped his own restlessness and his presently indecisive approach to everything but police work. The way British India was now, he was not sure he wanted to stay, and had a shrewd idea that was warping his personal relationships.

The Jepson/Jamieson irritants were symptomatic of British India's struggle to transform. They and many of their colleagues wanted to hang onto the past and deny Indians a future. He wanted India to progress steadily rather than gain immediate independence, but even that moderate view put him into a distinctly small minority. Could he remain part of that?

This ghost hour trip home was one of few times he had seen nothing whatsoever stirring in Madras. That was deceptive, and the British deceived. He and the others were now dealing with an invasion by new people and ideas of which the government had been ignorant, despite the panoply of new intelligence services and information systems at work. They could not hold back change.

Exhausted, he slept for just three hours before the accumulated professional and private turmoil awoke him. Thinking there was nothing else to do, he set off for the office, via Mount Road and the *Mail* office.

Fortunately, Chester Barnes was also an early riser that day. "Well don't you just look dreadful," he said as Le Fanu straggled in from the stairs.

"And the same to you, although you might look slightly better."

"Now that the friendly greetings are over, would you like coffee?"

"At this time of the day? Probably better than whisky, though I'm tempted."

"It must be bad. Any news about the ship?"

"Chester, I got in at three, had almost no sleep, and came hoping you might have something."

"Sorry, mate. I came in early to check with Singapore and Colombo but there's nothing new. This is awful for you."

"I'm beginning to understand what families went through when they lost track of their boys at the Western front. The nothingness just eats away. It's hard to fix on anything. All the wondering, the vivid imagining of what might be happening. Or not."

"Sure you don't need a whisky?"

"I'd love one but it wouldn't be a good idea."

"I'll keep doing my best to find anything helpful."

"I know, but the helplessness is hard to take."

"But you weren't helpless last night. As usual, someone helpfully told us there was a lot of activity at the Secretariat."

Le Fanu described events in detail and plans in general.

"Not to be printed until I say so, but it shouldn't be long."

"Can I follow a related line? Whitney's almost gone, Jepson has gone, effectively, Willingdon's on the way out. How vulnerable is Madras?"

"You know there's a Whitney replacement? No?"

He passed on the Carbine story.

"So," he continued, "thought is being given to continuity but it's a fair question. From the outside everything looks normal, but from the inside it does not. The ICS lacks a united view, more than ever. The police are challenged. Only a few top commercial people see that. Is that fragility? Yes. Danger? Not immediately, but yes, if we let things like this conspiracy get away."

"Have we?"

"We're playing catch-up and that's never good. Ideally we'd be ahead of these revolutionaries, but we're not. Resistance and alternatives to British rule are growing and we respond with repression, and that won't succeed in the long run."

"So where does that leave you?"

"Stranded in Madras with the chance of taking a job I hated last time and might hate again, while the woman I care about is somewhere on a missing ship."

"That's all?"

"There's a possible job in another colonial setting that also depends on the currently unfindable lady."

"You know a publisher would never accept this in a novel?"

"There's also the former lover who has been at death's door, and is about to return to my house because she has nowhere else to go."

"Beats Dickens. But is that really happening, Chris? Ro's coming back?"

"On a train from Hyderabad tomorrow, probably. The Osmania can't afford the space."

"What happens if the missing Jenlin turns up?"

"Jenlin's a modern woman. They both are. It'll work out."

"For some reason, I'm reminded of an ostrich."

"It has to work out."

"The ICS wives will have a field day."

"While their husbands allow India to drift off into the unknown."

"Have you read that new novel, *A Passage to India*?"

"I have bought but not yet read it."

"It angers people who think India should be tamed and not developed. And it suggests interracial relationships are impossible. You should be a star character, you've all the experience."

"Well, thank you. Time for me to go to work, but I needed that chat, Chester."

"Take care."

Thirty-seven

The car took him straight down Mount Road, over the Cooum River with the Gymkhana Club and its golf course away to the right, past the Sir Thomas Munro statue. A governor from East India Company days, Munro created the land revenue tax systems that Jamieson's Board of Revenue still imposed. No wonder there were frequent calls for the statue's removal. Then came the boundaries of Fort St George, a turn along Flagstaff Road and into the heart of the Presidency's administration.

Jackson Caldicott was at Le Fanu's office, discussing the previous night's work with Gaines.

"Good morning. We'll have you in the police yet, Gaines."

"Sir, Assistant Superintendent Caldicott is claiming me for the intelligence services."

"I'm sure he is. Jackson, come on through. Gaines, perhaps some coffee?"

Caldicott looked strained. Le Fanu felt the same. Yesterday had been hard, and aggravated by too little sleep since.

"Anything new?"

"A couple of things, LF. We have more information on our Nagpur man, one Nitish Rambal. He created that society Ganguly mentioned, and has a Central Provinces police record for assault and robbery. Most of his victims have been Muslim. The police there think he's more thug than zealot, all the assaults were connected with robberies. So it's a little different from what we had imagined. Rather than latch onto a group, he latched onto the *idea* of these Hindu identity movements as an opportunity to exploit Muslims."

"He has followers, though."

"The CP police think that his gang members provide the bulk of the membership, with more outsiders drifting in recently, especially in Nagpur where Savarkar is well known. Our students here are just gullible, not knowing what they were getting into."

"One thing bothers me, Jackson. If he's just a bash and grab merchant, why all the planning, expense and organisation here in Madras? That's a huge and expensive exercise for a petty thug."

"There's no easy or obvious answer. The available evidence suggests he convinced his followers that the targets here were all wealthy Muslims, so pickings would be large. I know that's boring compared to the alternatives, so might not be convincing."

"And he was prepared to murder to get those rewards, in a planned way? Has he been responsible for any deaths up there in CP?"

"Not that the records show."

"So this looks out of character?"

"I'd have to agree."

"Well, at least we have a name and a theory but we need a better explanation, I think."

"I'll get on it. But there is something else, LF."

"Yes?"

"I'm getting really concerned about what might happen here."

"These cases?"

"No, with my position."

"I can understand why."

"I'm not sure you do. We've no idea what you'll do, but your attitude has been odd as well. Habi and I have patched it up, but you didn't help. You just sided with him and ignored me."

"If I gave you that impression, I certainly didn't mean to. I would never knowingly reject any of your ideas without thought."

"I accept that, but you'll understand my nervousness. Jepson bastardised me and Habi and there are no guarantees it won't happen again. The madman's off the scene now, but he's done the Lazarus act before."

"He won't be back this time, and I'm sorry he took it all out on you."

"You'll understand that sounds a bit self-centred? Habi and I suffered in our own rights, not as your proxies. It was our work and our units in the firing line. You were off in the Straits Settlements. And when you did come back, you seemed oblivious to what was happening."

"Time was against me."

"It was, but so was attitude. We were run ragged, you concentrated on your own problems, not wanting to be here. Will you accept the I-G offer when it comes along? Because it will, if it hasn't already. There's no one else, and you're really good at it, despite what you think. But you've got a missing girlfriend, a former one ill in Hyderabad, and job offers in all directions. Your decision has consequences for Habi and me, yet you've not once come and discussed it with us."

This was a low point. Le Fanu felt like going home, shutting the door and sleeping for weeks. But he couldn't.

"Jackson, you're right. The worst thing about this is that I consider you and Habi friends more than colleagues. So you having to say all this makes me feel pretty small."

"That's not the intention. Habi and I have to make decisions too. He's had an offer from Singapore he really wants to discuss with you. But you haven't been available."

"Well …"

"And so do I, because I'm getting an offer from Delhi. Should I accept? I don't know. You brought me in here and I was delighted, being a bored box wallah was not my idea of a future. You've encouraged me, got me to where I am, and I want to stay working with you. But if you go, no one has any idea what this place will be like, apart from in trouble. Delhi looks a better option. To repeat: whatever you decide has an impact. So you need to talk to me, and talk to Habi."

He left soon after, Le Fanu chastened by knowing the criticism was warranted. He had a lot to think about, and do, if he was to be both good friend and good colleague.

The telephone rang. Wilson. "She'll be on the train that arrives in Madras five pm day after tomorrow. I wanted to give you ample warning. Are you still thinking about our possible arrangement?"

"I am, Maurice, along with many other things."

"No ship news yet?"

"No." His voice faltered.

"Very difficult. Stay strong. Any changes this end I'll let you know."

No sooner had he gone than there was another call. Willingdon.

"Sorry, but we need to resolve these cases quickly, and the matter of our revolutionaries. In their infinite wisdom, our Delhi masters have decided this is now nationally significant and that we must fix it so they don't look bad. The story appeared in the *Times of India*, so naturally assumes gigantic proportions. Any ideas?"

"Sir, I'll come round. If Habi's available, I'll get him, and Caldicott, and Gaines. We'll do more interviews and expedite any other arrests. Jackson's identified a likely ringleader so we'll grab him. We'll fashion something for Delhi."

Habi and Jackson were soon on their way while Gaines cleared his diary and arranged more interview sessions. Once they'd gathered, Le Fanu outlined the approach, concentrating on Nitish Rambal's arrest and getting a better idea of the man's objectives. They all then went off to the interview rooms.

Le Fanu was back in the library with Bhaskar Ganguly, who looked far better than he had a few hours earlier.

"Mr Ganguly, I hope you've remembered some additional information for me."

"There's nothing else. I just want to get out of here and go home."

"I'll arrange that as soon as you provide the information I think you still have."

"There's nothing else."

"What about Nitish Rambal?"

The forced calm evaporated.

"How? Well, I. No, I …"

"You'll know him as leader of the Society for the Advancement of Hindus."

"Yes, sorry, no. I mean, I know …"

"Let me tell you something. The Central Provinces police consider him a petty, vicious thief who bashes people before they have a chance to cooperate. It's a sport for him.

He terrorises Muslims who only want to get on with their lives and not bother anyone else."

"No, he is …"

"A fraud, so far as protecting your interests are concerned. He and his thug friends created this society as an excuse to persecute Muslims, to bash and rob them. Is that what you wanted to do – *did* do?"

"No, I had no idea. It was all a horrible surprise."

"Especially when you witnessed the murders."

"Yes."

"What really happened?"

"The plan was to confront Muslims and tell them to be keeping away from Hindus. But when we met the Muslims in Guntur, Mr Rambal's people went mad, kicking and hitting them. It was vicious, then some of those mad people were producing clubs and beating Muslims and robbing them. That was how the deaths happened."

"And what did you do?"

"I tried to stop them but they were hitting me as well. So I approached Mr Rambal and he was telling that if I said anything to anybody, I would be killed. He's being a very dangerous man. I don't want him to know where I am or that I have spoken to you. He threatened to kill my family."

"Tell me, why did he come to the south and bring all those people? Why did he not just stay in Nagpur?"

"When we were being all together, he explained the trip as part of the society's national programme. We were coming from all over the country, he said, so we could create a large national movement and complement the Mahatma's work. The south was an important starting place, he said, because so many sacred Hindu sites here must be protected."

"Did you believe him?"

"At the time, but later he was saying something very different. In a smaller group he said there were many very wealthy Muslims here and that they were all being soft. He and his men would be stealing a lot of money from them, then escape to Ceylon and catch a ship to Singapore."

"It was that simple? That there were lots of Muslim targets here?"

"Yes."

"Then why murder them? And why in places like Guntur and Tanjore?"

"Two reasons. The first was being to scare the rest of us and threaten us. If we told anyone, we would be getting the same treatment. That worked, we were all scared. The second reason was to scare the Muslims. Rambal was thinking that if Muslims saw examples of how far he and his men would go, then news would spread. Muslims would not resist and would be handing everything over immediately. That did not work well because your village raid came before he was ready. But I am still frightened."

"We'll protect you and your family but you must help me. Where is he now?"

"Just before you arrested me I heard he was still in Madras, but he may have been moving by now."

"Where was he then?

"Staying with a distant relative from Nagpur. In Perambur, the railway worker centre. You are knowing there are railway factories in Nagpur? Rambal worked there and so did his relative who was then coming here for work a few years ago. Rambal recruited Nagpur railway workers by telling them they could be good Hindus by robbing Muslims and making much money. All his direct assistants come from Nagpur."

"Do you have the Perambur address?"

Ganguly nodded.

"Write it down."

When they all compared notes later, it was evident the prisoners had decided to cooperate. The interrogators now had deeper insights, more detailed facts, closer understanding of the networks involved, and a clearer picture of criminal exploitation going under the guise of advancing Hindu interests. And the prisoners had provided precise addresses for the ringleaders, if they were still here.

Le Fanu immediately sent several army and police units to make arrests.

An hour later the commanders returned with every person on the list apprehended.

Willingdon was delighted when informed him by telephone.

When Le Fanu went around to the Chief Secretary's office, Whitney promptly produced yet another bottle of champagne.

"I can leave happily now, Chris, thanks to you, as always."

Le Fanu remembered the dressing down from Caldicott. This success came with a price attached, and he could not predict the consequences of that.

"Just the job, sir. It's what we do."

"And just what I'd expect you to say. Any news from Colombo?" Le Fanu shook his head. "Don't give up hope."

Le Fanu said nothing, because he was losing hope.

Thirty-eight

"You missed the cue about me being able to leave happily, Chris, not like you."

"Sorry, Charles, I have a lot more on my mind than normal. Besides, I thought you were speaking rhetorically."

"Teach you a lot of word chopping at Edinburgh, did they? But you're not up to repartee, are you?"

"No."

"Well I'm afraid the moment has arrived. I'm off day after tomorrow and really don't know what to think, now that it's happening. Madras has been home for a long time, and I know it all here."

"Know it all, indeed."

"Your brain is not entirely absent, then. Good. You know what I mean. There is the thought that a change of job will be good, then when you get it you realise there are new things to deal with, and in this case a new place. New Delhi. Good God."

"The place is really still under construction, isn't it?"

"Yes, there are a few more years to go yet before it will be finished. However, the Secretariat's completed, so I'll have an office. More importantly, my wife has seen the new Lutyens bungalow we'll be occupying and is very pleased. That makes things easier."

"Forget God, Lutyens and Baker must be making a fortune."

"Even if the Government of India coffers are rattling

empty. This show of grand permanence comes too late in the piece, I fear. The 1919 reforms gave Congress a sniff of self-rule, so now it wants the whole bag of tricks."

"That'll take years, won't it? Home Rule, or whatever version there might be of that?"

"You didn't hear me say this, but I'm not so sure. Think how much the world has changed since 1914. The Ottoman Empire had been around for, what, four hundred years? Now it's gone, and we're the beneficiaries in the 'Middle East', as that *Times* journalist Valentine Chirol calls it. I met him, you know, when he was out writing his commentaries on India. He's not convinced about our permanence, either, in private at least."

"Are the problems here that serious?"

"Yes, because we're handling them badly. Take this thing we've been dealing with. That sort of large scale communal strife is new down here, and it confirms how much change is going on. Our people don't know what to do and won't listen to expertise. Keep an eye on that, because careers here will be shorter than they have been. Remember the Ottomans."

"Very cheerful."

"Feigned excitement ahead of being relocated among the dinosaurs. Have you seen the Viceroy's Council membership? Completely moribund. Anyway, there's someone here in the building you must meet."

Whitney muttered into the telephone and poured three whiskies. As he finished arranging them on the side table, there was a knock at the door.

It opened to a taller, older man than Le Fanu. He was slim, loped like a thoroughbred across the distance between them. The full head of hair was fair on top but greying elsewhere, as was the flowing moustache cut well above the top lip. Strong chin, well shaped face. Lightweight Savile Row suit, impressive shoes. Quite the professional.

"Colin, there you are. Come and meet LF. Sir Colin Carbine, Superintendent Chris Le Fanu, chief problem solver for the Government of Madras."

"Chris. May I call you that straight off? Against protocol and form, I know, but you're an important person. Please call me Colin."

This was unlike anything Le Fanu had encountered in India previously.

"Thank you very much, er, Colin. Welcome to Madras. We're fortunate to have you here."

"Do I take that to mean you're staying?"

"You're well briefed, I see, and from the same school of diplomacy as Charles."

"*Sláinte*," was Whitney's response.

"Charles did outline your situation and I know it's a difficult time for you. But I need you here. Madras has resisted the reforms more fiercely than anywhere else, constantly rejected suggestions from Delhi, and mad I-Gs don't instil confidence."

Whitney sat them at his side table near the French doors, and they spent two hours discussing Madras, exchanging information on careers, thoughts about the future, present and likely future challenges, and sizing each other up.

Le Fanu liked the man, but would still miss the outgoing Chief Secretary's strange mix. Back at their first meeting, Le Fanu had wondered how he could ever deal with what appeared to be a genuine nineteenth-century conservative. Over the years, however, Whitney somehow became Le Fanu's strongest and most persistent supporter.

He would get on well with Carbine, though, if he stayed.

"And what chance you deciding to do that, Chris?"

It was a straight, open question.

"Right now, Colin, I don't know. We'd get on, and your friendship with the new Governor will streamline things. That's all fine, even if the government's finances and politics are not. I know Madras and like it, though some Europeans will tell you I'm far too liberal. But I still don't know what best to do and, as you now know, there's a personal complication."

"Understood, Chris, but just know there's a very senior post waiting for you, now or later."

"That's good to know. Now I'd better get on with snaring our troublemakers from the north. There's quite a few of them about today, it seems."

"We'll get along fine. Just make sure you stay."

As he walked away, Le Fanu knew he could work with Whitney's successor. That had been an unknown until now, so if he stayed, the work would be satisfying. But would it make being Inspector-General any easier than last time?

Gaines awaited. "Glad you're back, sir. There are several things I need to catch you up on. But the Assistant Superintendents are in your office."

Habi and Caldicott were comfortable in each other's presence when he walked in. Perhaps he was now the common irritant.

"Sorry to keep you. Whitney introduced me to his replacement and that turned into a long discussion. You'll like him, and he'll be a good Chief Secretary. Well disposed towards the police and anxious to support us."

"That's good news, sir. Sir Charles has helped us survive."

"And I'm confident Sir Colin will, too. You heard anything, Jackson?"

"All those who work for him up north have nothing but praise, and you know that's rare. So it sounds like he'll be good. Does that encourage you to stay, LF?"

"Don't you start. This is about me being indecisive, for which I apologise, again. Now, Gaines mentioned there were things I need to know?"

"Habi will explain."

"Sir, we've retraced Nitish Rambal's movements since he left Nagpur. He took the most convoluted route of anyone, changing trains several times and also used buses. Then, he doubled back through several cities and went to ground often. But he contacted his section leaders regularly throughout the journey, and we have proof of that."

"So he had a clear plan?"

"Yes, and it was followed to the letter by all of them. And we think we can prove he had intent to kill."

"In Guntur?"

"As well as in Madras and Tanjore. Because, sir, we can place Rambal in all those places on or before the day the killings occurred."

"You mean wherever he's been in the Presidency, Muslims were killed?"

"Without a doubt."

"Brilliant. Will the evidence stick?"

"I've asked the District Superintendents and the Commissioner to have their people gather more details, but it looks stronger and stronger. Bhaskar Ganguly places him at the murder scene in Guntur, so that's an excellent start.

We're identifying other group members who might give witness for the other murders. Twenty-four hours and we should have him."

"That really is magnificent, Habi."

"Well done, Habi." Caldicott clapped him on the shoulder.

"My team has done very good work, sir."

"I know, Habi, but they have an outstanding leader."

"LF, the background checking corroborates this. All Rambal's previous patterns are replicated here. The only variation, sadly, is that so far as we can tell, this is the first time he set out to kill. CP authorities suspect he was involved in a couple of suspicious deaths earlier but couldn't prove it. So the serious intent here does continue something of his pattern."

"And that will stand up well in court when we get there. What's our thinking now?"

"That we go and get him. He's still in Perambur with four gorilla guards. It could be dangerous. Habi and I think it is a military task. If you agree, he and I will go as advisors, but a couple of army platoons will deter the goons from turning ugly. We'll close off six blocks around his location. We don't want any more bloodshed."

"Sounds like a good plan. Get that under way immediately."

On their way out, Habi and Caldicott passed Gaines who came in with a telegram from Sir Maurice Wilson. Everything was on schedule in Hyderabad. Dr Metcalfe would accompany Ro to Madras and, once there, examine Habi's wife. Le Fanu telephoned D'Angelis and confirmed a reservation for Metcalfe. Then he telephoned home to get preparations started there. And he made a diary note.

It would not do to miss them off that train. Despite his bravado, deep down he knew Maurice and Chester were right. This could go badly.

He wrote up reports, revised the case boards for the next hour, glanced at the telephone frequently, willing it to ring. How was the operation going? The clock must have stopped. No, it was still ticking. Eating food passed some time, as did drinking many cups of coffee. Gaines tried to distract him, but failed.

Finally, towards ten, Habi telephoned. "Sir, I'm at the Perambur Police Station. Things haven't quite gone to plan so I wanted to let you know what's happening."

"No one hurt, I hope?"

"No, we're all fine but there's another standoff. Rambal's completely shut off, but decided to tough it out, so he and the gorillas are inside the building with our military units outside. Neither camp is moving. No shots fired so far."

"Should I come over, Habi?"

"If you've nothing better to do, sir, you're always welcome."

"I'd rather be there than here."

Traffic was minimal now, so the driver went straight out of the Secretariat onto the coast road, left towards George Town and past the High Court grounds then along First Line Beach. A few lights illuminated upper levels of the big trading houses, but otherwise all was quiet as they moved into the northern suburbs and Perambur. They soon encountered the first roadblock where Le Fanu got out and started to walk in.

A uniformed soldier let him through the barrier. "Up one block then turn left, sir. From there, two blocks on. No gunshots so far, sir, but go carefully."

He walked slowly. Being this close to the railway workshops, the area had many warehouses and artisanal workshops, as well as several small food outlets. Just a couple of those remained open, probably because the soldiers were around. The streets were poorly lit. This section of the city attracted minimal support from the Corporation housed in the opulent Ripon Building near the railway station.

Having taken that first turn left, he saw movement ahead at the two block mark. The soldier's instructions were perfect.

Now Le Fanu slowed even more, adjusting to the light and trying to blend in. Staying close to the walls and in the shadows, he was again back in Shaiba and checking doorways. Steady. Passing the first block, he was soon close to the next barricade, but before reaching it he met Habi and Caldicott who spoke softly.

"Welcome aboard, LF. Nothing so far."

"Good evening, Habi. Excellent directions."

"The military are planning the next move, sir. It has been quiet, but we know Rambal and the gang are in there. We've coffee if you'd like some."

"No thanks, Habi, I've had a gallon already."

An army officer arrived. "Oh, hello sir, glad you're here. We've decided to go in. There's a blind spot in the building where we can ram a door, throw in a light explosive to create confusion, and rush the place. It should be straightforward enough."

"Be careful, Lieutenant, this man has gone from thief to killer, and we don't know what frame of mind he's in."

"Thanks, sir, we'll go steadily. Stand by."

He slipped back around the corner and they heard muffled instructions, people moving, the odd rifle rattle, leather gear being adjusted, objects placed on the ground. Then it went silent.

Standing in the dark, Le Fanu had vivid memories of nights like this during the war – the waiting, tension, apprehension, and fear. A senior officer back then told him that if he ever lost the fear he should be very, very cautious, because he'd probably become overly confident. He hoped this lieutenant still felt the fear.

Then came the sound of a door being smashed, followed immediately by a muffled explosion. Shafts of light bounced off the walls up ahead. Then came shouting in English, Tamil and Hindi. And the gunfire began.

Thirty-nine

Le Fanu looked over at Habi and Caldicott. Instinctively, they moved towards the corner, revolvers drawn. The gunfire continued but none came their way. Caldicott dropped into a crouch, looked cautiously around the bottom of the wall then pulled back.

"They're all in the building, bar a couple of men left guarding the door."

"Good sign." Le Fanu was still worried. "We'll give them a couple of minutes."

That turned into five as the firing subsided then petered out. Silence. They were left standing a little back from the corner, with Habi on lookout. Le Fanu hated this time.

"Sir, activity."

Le Fanu looked around the corner, then led the other two out while putting away his revolver.

The lieutenant and his team were flanking three men handcuffed together, all Indians but dressed in standard Western clothes. One had blood coming through an arm bandage, the other two looked dazed.

"Superintendent Le Fanu." The lieutenant looked pleased with himself. "Allow me to introduce you to Mr Nitish Rambal."

It was the bandaged one, a slim, wiry, haggard man whose black hair stranded over his right eye, almost meeting the straggly moustache that stretched along thin lips and under a sharp nose.

"Are you sure?"

"Helpfully, he was carrying identification, and he matches the descriptions in your intelligence reports. The other two we're still trying to identify. But we have a collection of papers you'll want to look at." He handed over two bundles of documents. "As we found them."

"That was a lot of noise to get three people."

"There were more, sir. A couple of them opened up, the others joined in."

"Casualties?"

"Seven dead, I'm afraid."

"Any of your men?"

"No, sir. No injuries at all."

"I'm thankful for that. What's next?"

"We'll get the dead out, debrief, then return to barracks. You'll have my report in the morning. And I thought we could transfer these three to you now so you can get on with your inquiries."

"Good idea. Lend us a couple of your men for guard duty while we return to the Secretariat. I'll arrange transport for them back to barracks."

Within an hour, the three of them were sitting across from Rambal at a table back in the Secretariat library room where Le Fanu had interviewed Ganguly. The other two prisoners were in cells, officers checking their identities.

"Well, Mr Rambal," Caldicott began, "you've had quite a journey."

A couple of Hindi obscenities came back, something to do with Caldicott enjoying the attentions of a donkey.

"Excellent start; this'll go well."

More obscenities followed.

Le Fanu had never seen Habi so angry, a reminder of

what Rambal and his gang had done to Muslims, and of the terror they inflicted on Ganguly and the others tricked into their organisation. He nudged Habi, and nodded for him to proceed.

"Nitish Rambal, I'm charging you with the murder of Ashraf Haider in Guntur. We expect to also charge you with the murders of Muslims here in Madras, in Tanjore and another in Guntur."

The man turned away, refusing to look at Habi. The guard moved towards him, but Le Fanu waved the man back.

"Do you hear me, Mr Rambal?" Habi continued.

Rambal spat on the floor.

Habi looked exasperated.

Caldicott took over. "Rambal, think very carefully about your actions. We have you for one murder, for sure, three others almost certainly. You'll probably hang, but a judge might be lenient. Not if you keep up this behaviour, however."

"You're an imperialist pig, and he's a corrupt Muslim. Good combination." Another spit.

"He speaks!" Habi cried. "Rambal, you've also directly or indirectly caused the deaths of several other innocent people by inciting violence among your gang. The rope will stretch your neck for sure, no matter what my colleague says, so say what you like about me."

"India will prevail by beating the British and the Muslims. Hindus will prevail."

Le Fanu had heard enough. "You're a disgrace to Hindus. This nonsense just helped you rob Muslims of everything they'd earned by hard work. You're not a Hindu, you're a parasite."

Rambal looked at them balefully. "You'll all be cut down, if not by me then by those who follow."

"Guard, take him away."

The guard leapt forward, pulled Rambal to his feet and shoved him out the door.

"No point prolonging that," Le Fanu said. "We've got the necessary evidence and should have even more soon. All we'll get from him is that rubbish. His lawyer will put up all sorts of excuses but we can handle that. Habi, are you still angry?"

"This is one of the few times, sir, perhaps the only one, where I've really hated a fellow countryman, Hindu or Muslim. That thug used a bogus religious ideology to rob and kill people. If that's what we have become, then this country will need a greater god than any of those we have now if it is to survive. And that will be so whether Indians rule or you British. There are so many Muslims here, we must be able to live together with Hindus."

"I know, Habi, I agree," Caldicott put in. "Most Hindus and Muslims see good in each other and resist all the opportunities for hate, and we have to promote that. More miscreants like Rambal will come along, unfortunately, that's inevitable. But we must resist them."

"And all that intelligence you've gathered is part of that resistance, Jackson. Well done, both of you, and I'm sorry if I've been in the way."

"Sir, it's too late at night or early in the morning, or whatever it is, to discuss this sensibly any more. I think I'll go home." Habi looked drained.

"Of course, Habi. Metcalfe will be here later and get around to you as soon as he arrives."

"Thank you, sir." He got up and shuffled out.

"LF, this has really hit Habi. It has affronted all his belief in India and Indians. He's starting to see a real Hindu–Muslim divide opening up."

"That's understandable. The Muslim League and Mr Jinnah have the right political ambitions, to protect the interests of Muslims, but automatically make the Congress look like a partisan group. Any moves towards independence must be united."

"Time you went home, too. Jamieson and co. will have you in irons if they hear that heresy."

"You're right. This is one of those occasions where we solve the case but the problem remains. We keep cleaning up the mess politicians can't solve. Not my favourite part of the job."

"Do you think it'll become more like this?"

"I hope not, Jackson, but I'm pessimistic. Our future challenges will be different and bigger, and I'm not sure we can handle that."

"Happy prospect."

"And lots to think about. Delhi?"

"Nothing's changed. Depends a lot on you, but this case has changed my views on several things. I can see this intelligence work becoming really critical as well as interesting."

"So you must think hard about this opportunity."

"And I assume you're taking your own advice?"

"I'm probably the last person you should listen to. Go home."

He reached Mylapore near four in the morning. Life was becoming nocturnal. The streets were quiet again, peaceful, belying reality. A shower helped him relax, and he fell asleep immediately to be awoken by the birds three hours later. Another big day looming, and he remembered Whitney's personal invitation to attend his farewell lunch hosted by Willingdon. Le Fanu groaned – all his least favourite people gathered in one place to farewell the one person who had given him any help, apart from Willingdon.

And that helped him remember he had hated the social side of being Inspector-General.

It was nine when he reached the office to discover Rambal's two associates were also now identified and charged with the same offences. Legal opinion declared the cases sound and predicted smooth process. Le Fanu wondered if the lawyers might rule similarly on his present situation.

Finalising the paperwork took another couple of hours but the real pressure was off now. He hoped Caldicott and Habi felt the same. It came time for the lunch, and as the car drew into the Banqueting House precinct he felt the pressure return, in different form.

He joined a long line of the high and mighty being greeted by Willingdon and the guest of honour whose presence, of course, was signified by a cloud of smoke. The line moved slowly. He was tempted to leave, but stayed because he owed the Chief Secretary a great deal. Finally, he reached the entrance.

"LF, thanks so much for coming, I know you love these things."

"This one is special, Charles. I'm very sad to see you go."

"I can put in a word for you in Delhi."

"Just what I need, another option. I'll let you know."

Willingdon was talking to someone else but heard that. "You should take that offer, Chris, and I can do the same up there. Though having me vouch for you might make the

Delhi mavens suspicious."

"I'm sure it would be of great assistance, Your Excellency."

"Enjoy the lunch, LF. As best you can." Whitney shook his hand again and winked.

Somehow he dragged through the next two and a half hours, watching several people who had loathed Whitney now fawning over him. Few of them, if any, had a hope in hell of getting to Delhi.

Jamieson delivered a cloying speech full of unsubtle allusions to his own abilities. That suggested he'd somehow missed the fact Colin Carbine was already appointed, even if not present today, having returned north to finalise his exit there. Willingdon seemed bemused by this and also looked as if he wished he was somewhere else, perhaps in his cricket nets at the Governor's mansion. Jamieson was followed by a couple of his Masonic mates, a public display of the private networks that underlay European Madras. There weren't that many Europeans in the city, but they created considerable cabals.

The English food was terrible and his table companions affable enough, though it transpired none of them had ever actually met Whitney. There were a couple of senior military men, a Presbyterian minister, some commerce types and a lawyer. No women, of course, something else Le Fanu felt sure must change soon.

Willingdon's oration was pitch perfect and got all the Whitney hues. Le Fanu was pleased that Willingdon also considered the Chief Secretary a complex, even contradictory person who was sometimes the opposite of what he seemed or even claimed to be. The Governor suggested slyly that such complexity would be vital in dealing with the future

India, the implication being he doubted anyone here had it. That was why Carbine had been appointed, but Le Fanu was surprised to hear it articulated, even if so subtly that many present missed it.

In reply, Whitney was brilliant. It was funny, self-deprecating, insightful, provocative, learned and occasionally wistful. They were watching the end of a generation. Whitney had arrived during the later nineteenth century at the height of the Empire, arguably, and was now contemplating both its later forms and its fate. It was sobering, and made Le Fanu reflect further on his own position, choices and possibilities.

There came a touch at the elbow from a table mate, and Le Fanu realised Whitney was referring to him.

"Superintendent Le Fanu has this morning, while most of you were still abed, disbanded a most dangerous communal threat that endangered the good state of Hindu–Muslim relations in this Presidency. He will say, correctly, it was a team effort, but it is right we recognise here the leadership he has provided our police force over these recent years, sometimes in spite of great opposition. This is just the latest good service he has done us, and while I am not pleased to leave here, I do so in the knowledge that he is my friend. I wish him all *bon chance* in what is to come."

At that, Willingdon rose and began clapping in Le Fanu's direction. Those around him stood, as did most of the hall, although he noticed Jamieson and a few others did not. He felt embarrassed, did not know what to do, half rose and bowed, then sat.

On the way out several people congratulated him but he made for Whitney, who cut him off quickly.

"Meant every word of it, Chris. You're important here. I've always valued your work and ideas; you'll always be my friend."

That rang in his ears as he directed the driver to the railway station which he reached in good time. He collected a police porter and divined at which platform the train would arrive. He had a few minutes to spare so bought a chai off a wandering seller and a paper at the news stand. Predictably, *The Hindu* had a different view of affairs from the one Barnes posted in the *Mail.* One or two Europeans looked at him oddly.

Just on four, the train from Hyderabad steamed in lowly to halt in a squeal of brakes, as porters and waiting greeters streamed forward. He had bought first class tickets so walked towards the front carriages as doors opened and people stepped down. It was a couple of minutes before he saw Metcalfe alight, turn at the bottom of the steps and extend his hand back up.

Ro handed Metcalfe her two suitcases then took his hand and descended slowly. From this distance she looked slighter than ever but dressed smartly in a long, dark-blue skirt paired with a cream blouse and blue cardigan, set off by a broad-brimmed blue panama hat. She reached the platform, the porter took the bags and pointed back. She saw Le Fanu, waved, smiled and walked towards him on Metcalfe's arm.

"Chris, thank you for arranging all this and for meeting me, well, both of us really."

"The least I might do."

"Chris, nice to see you again," said Metcalfe, "and I'm assuming you want me to go to work straight away."

"D'Angelis first, Rory, freshen up, then work. We'll drop you there, take Ro to Mylapore, then my driver will return at five to take you to Habi's, if that's acceptable."

"Absolutely fine."

Forty

Metcalfe kept up a lively chat until they reached the hotel. For the first few minutes after that, though, as the driver made for Mylapore, neither of them knew quite how to start.

Eventually, she looked across at him. “Chris, I know how difficult this is for you, on several levels, so thank you, and I’ll keep out of your way as much as possible, I promise.”

“No need, Ro. You come and go as you please, and stay as long as you need. It’s wonderful to see you looking much better. You had us really worried.”

From there it was easier. They talked about her trip down, the passing sights, what it was like for her being back in Madras, what he had been doing, the political situation, his prospects. It was a while since he’d enjoyed such a normal conversation.

As they turned into the driveway, Le Fanu looked across and saw she was smiling. “Welcome back, I hope it helps you to a full recovery.”

“It’s lovely to be back, and I’m sure it will. This is so much better than the General’s. That was dark and formal, quite unlike here where I always felt relaxed.”

He wondered if his memories matched hers at that moment. Reading history was much easier than being a part of it, he thought. “Well, I hope you’ll feel relaxed this time as well. That will help get you back to your best form.”

As they drew up at the door, all the servants who had worked for Ro rushed out in welcome. She was delighted, and Le Fanu noticed several glancing at him furtively, checking his reaction. Shared history, indeed.

"Ro, you know where everything is and your room awaits. Make yourself at home, again. I have things to sort out back at the office, finalising the reports on these Muslim murders I was telling you about."

"What a cheerful job you have."

"It's not always like this, you know that. I'll be back in a couple of hours and we can have dinner together. I'm sure the cook has prepared something special in honour of your return. There are some new books over there somewhere, if you need them. I haven't had much time to read myself. Anyway, see you in a bit."

He did not need so much to return to the office as find time to think, and adjust. The offer to have her stay had been an unquestioned necessity of doing the right thing. What he had not counted on was feeling quite so … well … emotional at her return. It was obvious now that Ro being in the house would reprise their past. The servants' reactions confirmed that. She probably felt the same, revisiting what might have been. Had things gone according to plan, she would have been the lady of the house for some time now.

So he reached the office and began formalising trial papers, making lists of evidence to be tendered, consolidating witness rosters, and constructing the full bureaucratic litany. None of it made him think more logically about this new situation, but did prompt consideration of its full impact on his life. After all, it could remain that way for at least three months, during which all aspects of his life might change dramatically.

After about an hour Lord Willingdon entered unexpectedly, bearing a bottle of Talisker and two fine crystal tumblers. "I heard you were here, Chris, so wanted to thank you informally for this great result. And for including me in the case. I haven't had that much fun in ages."

"Oh, sir, I …"

"Now listen, I'm off soon anyway and we can't sit here with you calling me sir all night. We know each other well enough. Freeman from now on in private. Agreed?"

"An honour, Freeman."

"Not so sure about that, but I will tell you, jobs like mine would be a hell of a lot easier if there were more people like you involved. Drink? I don't suppose I can tempt you to transfer into the ICS? I think I could fix that."

He certainly knew how to pour a good whisky, and there was no assumption of water. "Your good health, Chris; thank for the great work, and here's to a bright future. Cheers."

They settled in their chairs, savouring the peat and oil sensations drifting up from the glasses.

"I can really smell this now, you know, without Charles's damn cigars clogging the atmosphere."

They laughed. "I'm going to miss him, sir … Freeman. He supported me strongly when most others didn't, and you've done the same."

"Carbine will be good. We couldn't put anyone in from here and expect progress, especially not that bloody Jamieson. He can't hold the same course for more than a second."

"Carbine'll need help."

"And especially from the police. So now I'm asking the obvious question. Will you take the I-G's position?"

There it was.

"What Charles said today was entirely correct," Willingdon continued, "and most people in that room knew so even if they didn't like it. Madras will do well, if you take over and restore the force to where it was before Jepson buggered it up."

Le Fanu sipped at the malt, swirled it around, let it trickle down his throat to feel the burn. "Freeman, I'm not sure how much you know about my situation."

"You mean with offers from Penang and Hyderabad, Mrs McPhedren living at your house, and Miss Koh's whereabouts presently undetermined? Anything I've missed? Charles has kept me up to date, and I'm not entirely blind."

"I didn't mean to … yes, somehow I get myself into these complicated positions. Solving murder cases always seems so much easier."

"You're not alone. You know my wife's predilection for mad projects and the colour mauve, of course? Everyone does. She's an accomplished woman who has helped me at every turn, but every time a new venture looms into sight, I always find office matters to deal with. Which is why we're here now, both of us. Tell me, do you have any idea what you really want in life?"

"I've never really asked myself that."

"It's a useful exercise. Did it myself several years ago and discovered an enthusiasm for public service, and here I am. We've made sacrifices for that, and there've been disappointments, but mostly I've done what I really want to do, that makes life pleasant and satisfying."

Over the next hour they discussed their careers, the highs and lows, and Le Fanu did start thinking about what he really wanted. The job had always come first, but that had been the same for Willingdon who made it work, apparently without complications. Was there a personality trait that made the difference?

Then there was the contrast between past and future. Willingdon was optimistic about Britain's future in India and the Empire, more so than Whitney. But Willingdon had to be, probably, being a principal figure. It might be different for Le Fanu. No matter where he pitched up, he would always be in the police, at the sharp end of the imperial project where high flown policies and visions met local attitudes and aspirations. He had seen a lot of change already, and doubted the wisdom of at least some recent Raj decisions. Could he maintain his enthusiasm in the face of that rising doubt?

"I'd better be off, have to inspect a new mauve room back at the house. Hope this chat helps, Chris, and I look forward to hearing your positive response to my I-G question."

"Freeman, thank you, and not just for the Talisker. It has been enlightening. I'll let you know soon."

"No rush. 'Night."

Willingdon had already refreshed the glass, so Le Fanu sat sipping, and thinking that it might all be starting to turn out well.

The telephone rang.

Metcalfe. "Chris, my apologies for interrupting. I telephoned the house and they told me where you were."

"I'm very pleased to hear from you. You've seen Habi's wife?"

"Yes, and I've called Habi already, but you've been very kind here so I thought I'd let you know, too. She'll be fine. It turns out she's had severe stomach problems. Having questioned her, it's almost certainly a simple reaction to particular foods. Careful food selection will remove most of the problem, but I've given her a couple of drugs to help. I'll see her before I go back, just to be sure."

"That's a real relief, Rory. I'm very grateful you've come down."

"It's a great excuse to get here, and I'm pleased it's nothing serious. Habi's relieved, I know. Hope to see you before I go back."

He was shaking, and had not realised the full extent of his concern. Habi had seen him through many difficult moments, and he had taken that for granted. The solution to this medical problem would help Habi immeasurably, but might also help Le Fanu rebuild the friendship and the professional bond that meant so much. There was another strong Madras connection to consider.

Remaining a while longer, to enjoy the last of the whisky in the glass, he thought – at the end of a period in which he had slept something like four hours out of forty-eight – that the horizon might, indeed, be clearing. The murders were settled, communal tension halted, Habi's situation improved, Ro was well, and here. Curiously, that last point occurred to him as a settlement rather than a problem. He really was tired. That was reinforced when he stood to order his desk and pack for home. It was an effort to move.

It was also the moment Habi and Caldicott arrived.

"I'm about to go home, Willingdon's been here. But it's great to see you both. Metcalfe called me, Habi. Very good news about your wife."

"It is, sir, and thank you again for arranging …"

"I'm just so happy that all is well. Willingdon asked me to thank you both, too."

"Sir …"

"We have the cases finalised, I'm just doing the last papers now and we can finish them off tomorrow and …"

"LF. Sit down, please."

"If you don't mind, Jackson, I'm …"

"Sir, please, will you sit down. It's important."

"Oh …" He sat, finished the whisky.

"LF, there's no easy way to tell you this."

"What?"

"Sir, Jackson and I …"

Jackson? Since when did Habi use first names?

"Habi, this …"

"Chris, we've had telegrams from both Singapore and Colombo to say that Jenlin's boat sank, probably a couple of days ago, but they're trying to confirm that."

"Sank? How …"

"We've got no solid details yet, but another ship found a lot of wreckage that seems to be from the *Asiatic.*"

"And they found lifeboats?"

"Just one so far, with about a dozen people in it."

Silence.

"Jenlin?"

"Sir, she was not on that lifeboat, unfortunately. Nor among another dozen or so other people pulled out of the sea so far."

Caldicott lifted another whisky bottle from his bag and half filled the glass that Le Fanu lifted to his mouth automatically. "But they must …"

"Yes, Chris, they're still searching, but Jenlin's among the people listed officially as missing."

"Sir, we're so sorry, this is dreadful news."

"Come on, Chris, we're getting you home."

All the way down the stairs, supported by the other two, he could think only of Jenlin alone in the ocean, alone, struggling. She had to be alive. Ships like that did not sink these days.

When they reached Mylapore, his friends supported him out of the car, up the steps and inside where Ro was waiting, having been telephoned earlier by Habi. They sat silently, Habi drinking tea, the others something stronger.

"Habi, Jackson. This has been a hard thing for you to do, and I thank you. You're wonderful friends I haven't deserved lately, if ever. I'll just go up and try to sleep now, I think. Please come back in the morning, I'd appreciate that."

He shook hands with them both and stumbled up the stairs.

"Ro, it's a really good thing that you've turned up today. Just let me know if you need anything, anything at all, and we'll be back in the morning to work out what we might do next."

"Thank you, Jackson. I'm sorry my return has brought such bad news."

"It's good news for him you're here, Mrs McPhedren. Hindus and Muslims alike believe that God knows our fate, but we can also help determine our own destiny. Please ask me immediately if I can help in any way."

"Habi, he relies on you so much."

The two men hesitated, said goodbye, looked up the stairs and went out to the car.

Le Fanu undressed, found in his pocket the forgotten Parvati bought from the old woman at the foot of the stairs to Caldicott's city office. Looking closely, he found a small inscription on the back: 'Go Home British'. Did she know the true nature of that office's work, and was she an agent of the Congress or even the revolutionaries? India really was changing.

He stood under the shower for several minutes, clear-headed despite the whisky, then dried off, got into bed and drifted.

Half an hour later there was a remembered click of the door. He was dreaming. Then came the familiar susurrus of silk leaving skin and a slight depression on the other side of the bed, her arms enveloping him. Warmth.

Thank you for reading
A Greater God.
I hope you enjoyed it.

It would be most appreciated if you could write a
CUSTOMER REVIEW of the book on Amazon.
Word-of-mouth is essential for any author to succeed.

This has been the fourth Superintendent Le Fanu Mystery
series, all set in 1920s Madras.
All the books are also available as ebooks.

* * * * *

Please visit my website and blog
brianstoddartwriter.com
and find my books on Amazon
See the following pages

* * * * *

About the Author

A writer, academic, blogger and commentator with forty years' experience of Asia, Brian Stoddart grew up in New Zealand, completed a PhD in Australia in the history of modern India, became a senior university executive in Australia and has lived and worked in India, Malaysia, Cambodia, Lao PDR, China, Indonesia to name but a few countries. He is also an acknowledged international authority on sport and culture, being a frequent keynote speaker at international conferences on issues such as governance and politics of Asian and other sport. In addition to working on aid and development projects dealing with higher education reform, he also lectures – on passenger cruise ships. He has written or co-authored sixteen non-fiction works. His *A House in Damascus: Before the Fall* won gold and silver recognition at the 2012 eBook Lit Awards.

Dividing his time between Australia, New Zealand and elsewhere, Brian reads crime fiction avidly, watches international affairs and sport, and collects Asian antiques.

A Greater God is the fourth book in the Superintendent Le Fanu Mystery series.

A Madras Miasma

The first Superintendent Le Fanu Mystery

The British are slowly losing the grip on the subcontinent. The end of the colonial enterprise is in sight, and the city on India's east coast is teeming with intrigue. A grisly murder takes place against the backdrop of political tension and Superintendent Le Fanu, a man of impeccable investigative methods, is called in to find out who killed a respectable young British girl and dumped her in a canal, her veins clogged with morphine.

Le Fanu, a man forced to keep his own personal relationship a secret for fear of scandal in the face of British moral standards, begins to investigate, but he quickly slips into a quagmire of Raj politics, rebellion and nefarious criminal activities that threaten to bury not only his case but the fearless detective himself.

A Madras Miasma tells a classic tale of murder, corruption and intrigue with a sharp eye on British colonial politics and race relations. It is a story which, like its main protagonist, has its heart firmly in the right place.

The Pallampur Predicament

The second Superintendent Le Fanu Mystery

The Pallampur Predicament sees our intrepid British policeman on the trail of the murderers of an Indian Rajah. Under pressure from his superiors, pining for his lost love and allergic to the sight of blood, Le Fanu must navigate through a political minefield of colonial intrigue.

As the British tighten their grip on the subcontinent, Gandhi's peace movement, British secret agents and armed pro-independence rebels complicate Le Fanu's investigations further, and he soon finds himself in a predicament of violent, opposing forces that are unwilling to compromise.

A Straits Settlement

The third Superintendent Le Fanu Mystery

The indomitable superintendent is promoted to Inspector-General of Police, which proves more boring than he had envisaged. Instead of pushing papers across his desk, Le Fanu focuses on the disappearance of a senior Indian civil service officer and an apparently unrelated murder. As the two incidents intertwine, the world-weary detective is drawn into spheres of indentured labour recruitment and antiquities theft.

But as bureaucratic politics make his position vulnerable, his superiors send him across the Bay of Bengal to pursue the cases in the Straits Settlements. Le Fanu immediately becomes embroiled in the activities of secret societies and the British colonial intelligence services. The appearance of a mysterious Chinese woman renders his professional life uncertain as he wonders anew about the British imperial future.

Acknowledgements

My first thanks go to all those readers who kept asking when this book would appear! There is no greater incentive (or pressure) for a writer, so that has spurred me on.

The novel's running theme – of rising social and political anxiety among 1920s Muslims in south India – was inspired by the work of my great friend Dr Kenneth McPherson. Sadly, Ken died in 2010 but, as a devotee of historical fiction, he would have loved Le Fanu, given all our discussions on how to write up our findings creatively. His last book was *'How Best Do We Survive?' A Modern Political History of the Tamil Muslims*. I like to think he would have drawn enormous pleasure from knowing not only that it is recognised as a marvellous and important book, but that it also inspired a crime novel. Assistant Superintendent Habibullah is a direct descendant of Ken's writings.

Ken might also have drawn parallels between his work, as invoked here, and the contemporary atmosphere in Narendra Modi's India, where the world's second largest Muslim population feels pressured by the more extreme exponents of *Hindutva* that emanates from the writings of V D Savarkar who appears in these pages.

Some other academics might be surprised to learn they have had a part in the Le Fanu stories. My contemporaries Chris Baker and David Washbrook wrote significant works on the history of modern south India that help provide context for these stories. David is now at Trinity College Cambridge. In 2017, Chris and his wife Pasuk Phongpaichit won the Grand Fukuoka Prize for their wonderful writings on the history and culture of Thailand. Le Fanu is a long way from that. Not so far, though, from David Arnold's work on the history of the Madras Presidency police. There is no one model for Arthur Jepson, "The Jockey", but David's account provides many ideas.

Robin Jeffrey is a long-standing friend, a great writer (as befits a former journalist) and a Le Fanu supporter, as is Kama Maclean, one of his students who now teaches at the University of New South Wales and writes on revolutionary politics. She might see the odd influence here.

S Muthiah, Sriram V and Nikhil Raghavan continue to provide me with ideas through their blogs and other writings on Madras heritage and history. Much of the work appears in *The Hindu* (which features throughout these books), so reading that paper becomes mandatory, and that, in turn, keeps me thinking about south India during the periods when I cannot be there. So, for example, watching the Chennai Super Kings win the 2018 Indian Premier League cricket tournament and following from afar their Chepauk home matches was really research. After all, Assistant Superintendent Caldicott played there. Research also includes following the byzantine politics of the south and all the connections into business and society.

Many writer friends around the world continue to provide encouragement, like Jeff Siger and the 'Murder Is Everywhere' blog group; and Liam McIlvanney, academic and Ngaio Marsh award-winning crime writer based at the University of Otago in New Zealand.

This time, I am especially grateful to Adrian McKinty, the hugely talented and erudite winner of the Ned Kelly and Edgar Awards. He is a wonderful example of how even the great names in crime writing support their fellow conspirators, and his praise for Le Fanu is yet another source of encouragement.

Adrienne Charlton is a brilliant editor, so many thanks to New Zealand writer Vicki Adin for making the introduction. Like all writers, I think I'm pretty good, and it takes someone like Adrienne to impose that extra discipline to make the finished work even better. Inevitably, we disagreed on a few things ('not enough hyphens, Brian'; 'too many semicolons, Adrienne'), but her work has been outstanding with all errors, infelicities and illogicalities remaining mine. And additionally, her book and cover designs have been equally important. Please do not retire too soon, Adrienne. You are much appreciated.

Gail and Paul Kordic, in-laws, had a hand in getting this book finished. They provided a writing retreat at their Manjimup farm in the south of Western Australia, along with a supply of wine from their vineyard. Perhaps surprisingly, in view of the latter contribution, that sanctuary allowed me to write a huge number of words and finish the substantive draft, for which I am very grateful.

As always, my greatest thanks go to Sandi, and to our girls Kirsten and Laura. They put up with the madness the writing of these novels brings on, amidst all the other projects and activities that thankfully crowd my life. None of this would happen without their support and encouragement, and for that I love them dearly. So does Le Fanu.

Brian Stoddart
Queenstown, Manjimup and Sydney

CPSIA information can be obtained
at www.ICGtesting.com
Printed in the USA
BVHW070728281118
534064BV00026B/119/P

9 780648 393801